PANDEMONIUM

Lost Souls

First published 2012 by Jurassic London
SW8 1XN, Great Britain

www.pandemonium-fiction.com

978-0-9570392-8-5 (Limited Edition)
978-0957646209 (Paperback)
978-0-9570392-9-2 (eBook)

Illustrated by Vincent Sammy
karbonk.deviantart.com

eBook conversion by handebooks.co.uk

PANDEMONIUM

LOST SOULS

Stories of Loss and Redemption

Edited and introduced by Anne C. Perry and Jared Shurin
Illustrated by Vincent Sammy

For Robert W. Chambers and Richard Owen

CONTENTS

INTRODUCTION

ANNE C. PERRY & JARED SHURIN

Thieves, liars and ministers; artists, soldiers and fugitives. The authors in *Lost Souls* are no less interesting than their stories – and in many cases, the two are so well intertwined as to be inseparable.

The collection begins, appropriately enough, with the truly lost. Stephen Crane examines New York's homeless population in "An Experiment in Misery". John Galsworthy's "Quality" depicts the end of an era: the disappearance of the traditional artist. Mary Wilkins Freeman and Calista Patchin both focus on personal losses. Their stories feature characters that live unheralded lives, or fail to meet their potential.

Benjamin Disraeli's Ixion is a literally lost soul, as is the nameless king in Mary Coleridge's "The King is Dead, Long Live the King". But both show that power alone is no path to redemption. Charles Bayly's "P'r'aps" and Richard Garnett's "The Demon Pope" portray the relationship between those who rule and those who serve, albeit in very different contexts.

Getting lost in a good book is a common phrase, but only scratches the surface of the deep relationship between readers, writers and fiction. The outcasts of Bret Harte's "Poker Flat" are trapped in defined roles, but find an escape in stories. Accordingly, William Cheney's "Miranda Higgins" reflects on Harte's own literary legacy. George Gissing and Sir Arthur Conan Doyle present two different looks at an unhealthy obsession with books – as objects and as symbols. May Wentworth's "Emperor Norton" serves an example of how a fictional (or non-fictional) character can change over time.

No survey of this particular era's lost souls would be complete without addressing World War I. Robert Chambers' "Marooned" is a different sort of war story – a study of inaction and insanity, souls not lost but abandoned. Stories by Latrobe Carroll and Anne Douglas Sedgewick take place far from the battlefield. They examine how grief destroys families and ends relationships; how the war did not cause just the death of young men, but the death of a generation. John Reynolds' contribution, a work of non-fiction, details another sort of war, when it describes the lost souls serving time in a nineteenth century prison.

All is not lost – and the final stories in this collection are tales of the found. David Bryher contributes a clever fairytale, inspired by Basque folklore, of beating the Devil at his own game. Amelia B. Edward's bureaucratic ghost gets its revenge in "The Four-Fifteen Express" and Mary Wilkins Freeman's "The Parrot" has a woman finding a kindred spirit in the unlikeliest of forms. O. Henry's "A Double-Dyed Deceiver" concludes *Lost Souls* with tale of redemption, pure and simple – one with parallels to the author's own life.

The lost of *Lost Souls* are not purely contained within the stories. Many of these tales have not been reprinted for over a century, and many of the authors have become forgotten themselves. Narrowing the hundreds of candidates down to twenty-one stories was a difficult task, but we hope that this selection – varied though it may be – brings a few abandoned tales and unfamiliar names back to readers.

We are extraordinarily grateful to the talented Vincent Sammy. Any tale connected with illustrations this stunning will never be forgotten.

Anne C. Perry & Jared Shurin
London
August 2012

❧LOST❧

Stephen Crane (1871 - 1900) began writing as a child and was published in his early teens. By the age of 20, he dropped out of college to become a full-time writer. Within a year, he was regularly published in the Tribune and other newspapers. Crane reached national attention when he finished The Red Badge of Courage.

The young Crane was a celebrity, but one quickly dogged by scandal. At the age of 24, Crane was embroiled in a court case involving a New York City prostitute, harming his reputation in the process. Over the course of his brief life, Crane was caught up in one adventure after another – trapped in an open boat at sea, witness to the Spanish-American and Greco-Turkish Wars, romantically involved with a prominent madam. He also also became friends with Henry James, H.G. Wells and many others. Always sickly, Crane died at the age of 28. He spent the final months of his life at a spa in Germany, dictating his last novel to his friends.

Crane wrote "An Experiment in Misery" in 1894. At the time, he was impoverished from the cost of publishing his first book, A Girl of the Streets, himself. In order to gain material for his work, Crane immersed himself in the lives of the New York City's homeless (a population greatly swollen by the the depression of that year). Dressing as one of the city's unfortunates, he even went so far as to spend the night in one of the city's many flophouses.

The introductory and concluding parts of "An Experiment in Misery", which help establish Crane's own relationship to (and within) the story, only appeared in its original publication in The New York Press. They were later removed when the story was collected into a book in 1896.

AN EXPERIMENT IN MISERY

STEPHEN CRANE

I

Two men stood regarding a tramp.

"I wonder how he feels," said one, reflectively. "I suppose he is homeless, friendless, and has, at the most, only a few cents in his pocket. And if this is so, I wonder how he feels."

The other being the elder, spoke with an air of authoritative wisdom. "You can tell nothing of it unless you are in that condition yourself. It is idle to speculate about it from this distance."

"I suppose so," said the younger man, and then he added as from an inspiration: "I think I'll try it. Rags and tatters, you know, a couple of dimes, and hungry, too, if possible. Perhaps I could discover his point of view or something near it."

"Well, you might," said the other, and from those words begins this veracious narrative of an experiment in misery.

The youth went to the studio of an artist friend, who, from his store, rigged him out in an aged suit and a brown derby hat that had been made long years before. And then the youth went forth to try to eat as the tramp may eat, and sleep as the wanderers sleep.

New York Press. April, 1894.

II

It was late at night, and a fine rain was wirling softly down, causing the pavements to glisten with hue of steel and blue and yellow in the rays of the innumerable lights. A youth was trudging slowly, without enthusiasm, with his hands buried deep in his trousers' pockets, towards the down-town places where beds can be hired for coppers. He was clothed in an aged and tattered suit, and his derby was a marvel of dust-covered crown and torn rim. He was going forth to eat as the wanderer may eat, and sleep as the homeless sleep. By the time he had reached City Hall Park he was so completely plastered with yells of "bum" and "hobo," and with various unholy epithets that small boys had applied to him at intervals, that he was in a state of the most profound dejection. The sifting rain saturated the old velvet collar of his overcoat, and as the wet cloth pressed against his neck, he felt that there no longer could be pleasure in life. He looked about him searching for an outcast of highest degree that they too might share miseries, but the lights threw a quivering glare over rows and circles of deserted benches that glistened damply, showing patches of wet sod behind them. It seemed that their usual freights had fled on this night to better things. There were only squads of well-dressed Brooklyn people who swarmed towards the bridge.

The young man loitered about for a time and then went shuffling off down Park Row. In the sudden descent in style of the dress of the crowd he felt relief, and as if he were at last in his own country. He began to see tatters that matched his tatters. In Chatham Square there were aimless men strewn in front of saloons and lodging-houses, standing sadly, patiently, reminding one vaguely of the attitudes of chickens in a storm. He aligned himself with these men, and turned slowly to occupy himself with the flowing life of the great street.

Through the mists of the cold and storming night, the cable cars went in silent procession, great affairs shining with red and brass, moving with formidable power, calm and irresistible, dangerful and gloomy, breaking silence only by the loud fierce cry of the gong. Two rivers of people swarmed along the sidewalks, spattered with black mud, which made each shoe leave a scar-like impression. Overhead elevated trains with a shrill grinding of the wheels stopped at the station, which upon its leg-like pillars seemed to resemble some monstrous kind of crab squatting over the street. The quick fat puffings of the engines could be heard. Down an alley there were sombre curtains of purple and black, on which street lamps dully glittered like embroidered flowers.

A saloon stood with a voracious air on a corner. A sign leaning against the front of the door-post announced "Free hot soup to-night!" The swing doors, snapping to and fro like ravenous lips, made gratified smacks as the saloon gorged itself with plump men, eating with astounding and endless appetite, smiling in some indescribable manner as the men came from all directions like sacrifices to a heathenish superstition.

Caught by the delectable sign the young man allowed himself to be swallowed. A bar-tender placed a schooner of dark and portentous beer on the bar. Its monumental form up-reared until the froth a-top was above the crown of the young man's brown derby.

"Soup over there, gents," said the bar-tender affably. A little yellow man in rags and the youth grasped their schooners and went with speed toward the lunch counter, where a man with oily but imposing whiskers ladled genially from a kettle until he had furnished his two mendicants with a soup that was steaming hot, and in which there were little floating suggestions of chicken. The young man, sipping his broth, felt the cordiality expressed by the warmth of the mixture, and he beamed at the man with oily but imposing whiskers, who was presiding like a priest behind an altar. "Have some more, gents?" he inquired of the two sorry figures before him. The little yellow man accepted with a swift gesture, but the youth shook his head and went out, following a man whose wondrous seediness promised that he would have a knowledge of cheap lodging-houses.

On the sidewalk he accosted the seedy man. "Say, do you know a cheap place to sleep?"

The other hesitated for a time gazing sideways. Finally he nodded in the direction of the street, "I sleep up there," he said, "when I've got the price."

"How much?"

"Ten cents."

The young man shook his head dolefully. "That's too rich for me."

At that moment there approached the two a reeling man in strange garments. His head was a fuddle of bushy hair and whiskers, from which his eyes peered with a guilty slant. In a close scrutiny it was possible to distinguish the cruel lines of a mouth which looked as if its lips had just closed with satisfaction over some tender and piteous morsel. He appeared like an assassin steeped in crimes performed awkwardly.

But at this time his voice was tuned to the coaxing key of an affectionate puppy. He looked at the men with wheedling eyes, and began to sing a little melody for charity.

"Say, gents, can't yeh give a poor feller a couple of cents t' git a bed. I got five, and I gits anudder two I gits me a bed. Now, on th' square, gents, can't yeh jest gimme two cents t' git a bed? Now, yeh know how a respecter'ble gentlem'n feels when he's down on his luck, an' I –"

The seedy man, staring with imperturbable countenance at a train which clattered overhead, interrupted in an expressionless voice "Ah, go t' h!"

But the youth spoke to the prayerful assassin in tones of astonishment and inquiry. "Say, you must be crazy! Why don't yeh strike somebody that looks as if they had money?"

The assassin, tottering about on his uncertain legs, and at intervals brushing imaginary obstacles from before his nose, entered into a long explanation of the psychology of the situation. It was so profound that it was unintelligible.

When he had exhausted the subject, the young man said to him, "Let's see th' five cents."

The assassin wore an expression of drunken woe at this sentence, filled with suspicion of him. With a deeply pained air he began to fumble in his clothing, his red hands trembling. Presently he announced in a voice of bitter grief, as if he had been betrayed, "There's on'y four."

"Four," said the young man thoughtfully. "Well, look-a-here, I'm a stranger here, an' if ye'll steer me to your cheap joint I'll find the other three."

The assassin's countenance became instantly radiant with joy. His whiskers quivered with the wealth of his alleged emotions. He seized the young man's hand in a transport of delight and friendliness.

"B' Gawd," he cried, "if ye'll do that, b' Gawd, I'd say yeh was a damned good fellow, I would, an' I'd remember yeh all m' life, I would, b' Gawd, an' if I ever got a chance I'd return the compliment," he spoke with drunken dignity, "b' Gawd, I'd treat yeh white, I would, an' I'd allus remember yeh."

The young man drew back, looking at the assassin coldly. "Oh, that's all right," he said. "You show me th' joint that's all you've got t' do."

The assassin, gesticulating gratitude, led the young man along a dark street Finally he stopped before a little dusty door. He raised his hand impressively. "Look-a-here," he said, and there was a thrill of deep and ancient wisdom upon his face, "I've brought yeh here, an' that's my part, ain't it? If th' place don't suit yeh, yeh needn't git mad at me, need yeh? There won't be no bad feelin', will there?"

"No," said the young man.

The assassin waved his arm tragically, and led the march up the steep stairway. On the way the young man furnished the assassin with three pennies. At the top a man with benevolent spectacles looked at them through a hole in a board. He collected their money, wrote some names on a register, and speedily was leading the two men along a gloom-shrouded corridor.

Shortly after the beginning of this journey the young man felt his liver turn white, for from the dark and secret places of the building there suddenly came to his nostrils strange and unspeakable odours, that assailed him like malignant diseases with wings. They seemed to be from human bodies closely packed in dens; the exhalations from a hundred pairs of reeking lips; the fumes from a thousand bygone debauches; the expression of a thousand present miseries.

A man, naked save for a little snuff-coloured undershirt, was parading sleepily along the corridor. He rubbed his eyes, and, giving vent to a prodigious yawn, demanded to be told the time.

"Half-past one."

The man yawned again. He opened a door, and for a moment his form was outlined against a black, opaque interior. To this door came the three men, and as it was again opened the unholy odours rushed out like fiends, so that the young man was obliged to struggle as against an overpowering wind.

It was some time before the youth's eyes were good in the intense gloom within, but the man with benevolent spectacles led him skilfully, pausing but a moment to deposit the limp assassin upon a cot. He took the youth to a cot that lay tranquilly by the window, and showing him a tall locker for clothes that stood near the head with the ominous air of a tombstone, left him.

The youth sat on his cot and peered about him. There was a gas-jet in a distant part of the room, that burned a small flickering orange-hued flame. It caused vast masses of tumbled shadows in all parts of the place, save where, immediately about it, there was a little grey haze. As the young man's eyes became used to the darkness, he could see upon the cots that thickly littered the floor the forms of men sprawled out, lying in death-like silence, or heaving and snoring with tremendous effort, like stabbed fish.

The youth locked his derby and his shoes in the mummy case near him, and then lay down with an old and familiar coat around his shoulders. A blanket he handled gingerly, drawing it over part of the coat. The cot was covered with leather, and as cold as melting snow. The youth was obliged to shiver for some time on this affair, which was like a slab. Presently, however, his chill gave him peace, and during this period of leisure from it he turned his head to stare at his friend the assassin, whom he could dimly discern where he lay sprawled on a cot in the abandon of a man filled with drink. He was snoring with incredible vigour. His wet hair and beard dimly glistened, and his inflamed nose shone with subdued lustre like a red light in a fog.

Within reach of the youth's hand was one who lay with yellow breast and shoulders bare to the cold drafts. One arm hung over the side of the cot, and the fingers lay full length upon the wet cement floor of the room. Beneath the inky brows could be seen the eyes of the man exposed by the partly opened lids. To the youth it seemed that he and this corpse-like being were exchanging a prolonged stare, and that the other threatened with his eyes. He drew back watching his neighbour from the shadows of his blanket edge. The man did not move once through the night, but lay in this stillness as of death like a body stretched out expectant of the surgeon's knife.

And all through the room could be seen the tawny hues of naked flesh, limbs thrust into the darkness, projecting beyond the cots; upreared knees, arms hanging long and thin over the cot edges. For the most part they were statuesque, carven, dead. With the curious lockers standing all about like tombstones, there was a strange effect of a graveyard where bodies were merely flung.

Yet occasionally could be seen limbs wildly tossing in fantastic nightmare gestures, accompanied by guttural cries, grunts, oaths. And there was one fellow off in a gloomy corner, who in his dreams was oppressed by some frightful calamity, for of a sudden he began to utter long wails that went almost like yells from a hound, echoing wailfully and weird through this chill place of tombstones where men lay like the dead.

The sound in its high piercing beginnings, that dwindled to final melancholy moans, expressed a red and grim tragedy of the unfathomable possibilities of the man's dreams. But to the youth these were not merely the shrieks of a vision-pierced man: they were an utterance of the meaning of the room and its occupants. It was to him the protest of the wretch who feels the touch of the imperturbable granite wheels, and who then cries with an impersonal eloquence, with a strength not from him, giving voice to the wail of a whole section, a class, a people. This, weaving into the young man's brain, and mingling with his views of the vast and sombre shadows that, like mighty black fingers, curled around the naked bodies, made the young man so that he did not sleep, but lay carving the biographies for these men from his meagre experience. At times the fellow in the corner howled in a writhing agony of his imaginations.

Finally a long lance-point of grey light shot through the dusty panes of the window. Without, the young man could see roofs drearily white in the dawning. The point of light yellowed and grew brighter, until the golden rays of the morning sun came in bravely and strong. They touched with radiant colour the form of a small fat man, who snored in stuttering fashion. His round and shiny bald head glowed suddenly with the valour of a decoration. He sat up, blinked at the sun, swore fretfully, and pulled his blanket over the ornamental splendours of his head.

The youth contentedly watched this rout of the shadows before the bright spears of the sun, and presently he slumbered. When he awoke he heard the voice of the assassin raised in valiant curses. Putting up his head, he perceived his comrade seated on the side of the cot engaged in scratching his neck with long finger-nails that rasped like files.

"Hully Jee, dis is a new breed. They've got can-openers on their feet." He continued in a violent tirade.

The young man hastily unlocked his closet and took out his shoes and hat. As he sat on the side of the cot lacing his shoes, he glanced about and saw that daylight had made the room comparatively commonplace and uninteresting. The men, whose faces seemed stolid, serene or absent, were engaged in dressing, while a great crackle of bantering conversation arose.

A few were parading in unconcerned nakedness. Here and there were men of brawn, whose skins shone clear and ruddy. They took splendid poses, standing massively like chiefs. When they had dressed in their ungainly garments there was an extraordinary change. They then showed bumps and deficiencies of all kinds.

There were others who exhibited many deformities. Shoulders were slanting, humped, pulled this way and pulled that way. And notable among these latter men was the little fat man, who had refused to allow his head to be glorified. His pudgy form, builded like a pear, bustled to and fro, while he swore in fishwife fashion. It appeared that some article of his apparel had vanished.

The young man attired speedily, and went to his friend the assassin. At first the latter looked dazed at the sight of the youth. This face seemed to be appealing to him through the cloud wastes of his memory. He scratched his neck and reflected. At last he grinned, a broad smile gradually spreading until his countenance was a round illumination. "Hello, Willie," he cried cheerily.

"Hello," said the young man. "Are yeh ready t' fly?"

"Sure." The assassin tied his shoe carefully with some twine and came ambling.

When he reached the street the young man experienced no sudden relief from unholy atmospheres. He had forgotten all about them, and had been breathing naturally, and with no sensation of discomfort or distress.

He was thinking of these things as he walked along the street, when he was suddenly startled by feeling the assassin's hand, trembling with excitement, clutching his arm, and when the assassin spoke, his voice went into quavers from a supreme agitation.

"I'll be hully, bloomin' blowed if there wasn't a feller with a nightshirt on up there in that joint."

The youth was bewildered for a moment, but presently he turned to smile indulgently at the assassin's humour.

"Oh, you're a d d liar," he merely said.

Whereupon the assassin began to gesture extravagantly, and take oath by strange gods. He frantically placed himself at the mercy of remarkable fates if his tale were not true.

"Yes, he did! I cross m'heart thousan' times!" he protested, and at the moment his eyes were large with amazement, his mouth wrinkled in unnatural glee.

"Yessir! A nightshirt! A hully white night shirt!"

"You lie!"

"No, sir! I hope ter die b'fore I kin git anudder ball if there wasn't a jay wid a hully, bloomin' white nightshirt!"

His face was filled with the infinite wonder of it. "A hully white nightshirt," he continually repeated.

The young man saw the dark entrance to a basement restaurant. There was a sign which read "No mystery about our hash!" and there were other age-stained and world-battered legends which told him that the place was within his means. He stopped before it and spoke to the assassin. "I guess I'll git somethin' t' eat."

At this the assassin, for some reason, appeared to be quite embarrassed. He gazed at the seductive front of the eating place for a moment. Then he started slowly up the street. "Well, good-bye, Willie," he said bravely.

For an instant the youth studied the departing figure. Then he called out, "Hol' on a minnet." As they came together he spoke in a certain fierce way, as if he feared that the other would think him to be charitable. "Look-a-here, if yeh wanta git some breakfas' I'll lend yeh three cents t' do it with. But say, look-a-here, you've gota git out an' hustle. I ain't goin' t' support yeh, or I'll go broke b'fore night. I ain't no millionaire."

"I take me oath, Willie," said the assassin earnestly, "th' on'y thing I really needs is a ball. Me t'roat feels like a fryin'-pan. But as I can't get a ball, why, th' next bes' thing is breakfast, an' if yeh do that for me, b' Gawd, I say yeh was th' whitest lad I ever see."

They spent a few moments in dexterous exchanges of phrases, in which they each protested that the other was, as the assassin had originally said, "a respecter'ble gentlem'n." And they concluded with mutual assurances that they were the souls of intelligence and virtue. Then they went into the restaurant.

There was a long counter, dimly lighted from hidden sources. Two or three men in soiled white aprons rushed here and there.

The youth bought a bowl of coffee for two cents and a roll for one cent. The assassin purchased the same. The bowls were webbed with brown seams, and the tin spoons wore an air of having emerged from the first pyramid. Upon them were black moss-like encrustations of age, and they were bent and scarred from the attacks of long-forgotten teeth. But over their repast the wanderers waxed warm and mellow. The assassin grew affable as the hot mixture went soothingly down his parched throat, and the young man felt courage flow in his veins.

Memories began to throng in on the assassin, and he brought forth long tales, intricate, incoherent, delivered with a chattering swiftness as from an old woman.

"Great job out'n Orange. Boss keep yeh hustlin' though all time. I was there three days, and then I went an' ask Jim t' lend me a dollar. ' G-g-go ter the devil,' he ses, an' I lose me job."

"South no good. Damn n' work for twenty-five an' thirty cents a day. Run white man out. Good grub though. Easy livin'."

"Yas; useter work little in Toledo, raftin' logs. Make two or three dollars er day in the spring. Lived high. Cold as ice though in the winter."

"I was raised in northern N'York. O-o-oh, yeh jest oughto live there. No beer ner whisky though, way off in the woods. But all th' good hot grub yeh can eat. B' Gawd, I hung around there long as I could till th' ol' man fired me. ' Git t' hell outa here, yeh wuthless skunk, git t' hell outa here, an' go die,' he ses. ;You're a hell of a father,' I ses, 'you are,' an' I quit 'im."

As they were passing from the dim eating place, they encountered an old man who was trying to steal forth with a tiny package of food, but a tall man with an indomitable moustache stood dragon fashion, bar ring the way of escape. They heard the old man raise a plaintive protest. "Ah, you always want to know what I take out, and you never see that I usually bring a package in here from my place of business."

As the wanderers trudged slowly along Park Row, the assassin began to expand and grow blithe. "B' Gawd, we'e been livin' like kings," he said, smacking appreciative lips.

"Look out, or we'll have t' pay fer it t'night," said the youth with gloomy warning.

But the assassin refused to turn his gaze toward the future. He went with a limping step, into which he injected a suggestion of lamblike gambols. His mouth was wreathed in a red grin.

In the City Hall Park the two wanderers sat down in the little circle of benches sanctified by traditions of their class. They huddled in their old garments, slumbrously conscious of the march of the hours which for them had no meaning.

The people of the street hurrying hither and thither made a blend of black figures changing yet frieze-like. They walked in their good clothes as upon important missions, giving no gaze to the two wanderers seated upon the benches. They expressed to the young man his infinite distance from all that he valued. Social position, comfort, the pleasures of living, were unconquerable kingdoms. He felt a sudden awe.

And in the background a multitude of buildings, of pitiless hues and sternly high, were to him emblematic of a nation forcing its regal head into the clouds, throwing no downward glances; in the sublimity of its aspirations ignoring the wretches who may flounder at its feet. The roar of the city in his ear was to him the confusion of strange tongues, babbling heedlessly; it was the clink of coin, the voice of the city's hopes which were to him no hopes.

He confessed himself an outcast, and his eyes from under the lowered rim of his hat began to glance guiltily, wearing the criminal expression that comes with certain convictions.

III

"Well," said the friend, "did you discover his point of view?"

"I don't know that I did," replied the young man; "but at any rate I think mine own has undergone a considerable alteration."

"The comments of the American press on the death of Stephen Crane and the estimates of his position in native literature are in striking contrast to the comments of the same press five years ago. When The Red Badge of Courage and The Black Riders were put upon the market their author was the most thoroughly abused writing man between the Atlantic and the Pacific. The slim little volume of verse was the target of nearly every critic, joker and parodist in the country.

It is only justice to add, however, that the very writers who were the severest in their satires and criticisms of Stephen Crane when he was alive were the first to pay honest and unembittered tributes to his memory"
– The New York Times (14 July 1900)

"Quality" was first published in 1912. In it, John Galsworthy (1867 - 1933) succinctly captures the end of an era. The story's young narrator is nostalgic for the artisanal craftsmanship of yore — yet also confesses that he purchases the impersonal, mass produced products of the new industrial age. The tragedy comes not from the death of the artist, but from the recognition that his passing was inevitable.

Galsworthy is best remembered for his Foryste Saga, a trilogy of novels that explored social mores amongst the upper middle classes in the Edwardian Era. Although he refused a knighthood, Galworthy was awarded the Nobel Prize for Literature shortly before his death, in 1932. Galsworthy was the first president of International PEN (now PEN International).

QUALITY

JOHN GALSWORTHY

I knew him from the days of my extreme youth, because he made my father's boots; inhabiting with his elder brother two little shops let into one, in a small by-street now no more, but then most fashionably placed in the West End. That tenement had a certain quiet distinction; there was no sign upon its face that he made for any of the Royal Family merely his own German name of Gessler Brothers; and in the window a few pairs of boots. I remember that it always troubled me to account for those unvarying boots in the window, for he made only what was ordered, reaching nothing down, and it seemed so inconceivable that what he made could ever have failed to fit. Had he bought them to put there? That, too, seemed inconceivable. He would never have tolerated in his house leather on which he had not worked himself. Besides, they were too beautiful the pair of pumps, so inexpressibly slim, the patent leathers with cloth tops, making water come into one's mouth, the tall brown riding boots with marvellous sooty glow, as if, though new, they had been worn a hundred years. Those pairs could only have been made by one who saw before him the Soul of Boot so truly were they prototypes incarnating the very spirit of all foot-gear. These thoughts, of course, came to me later, though even when I was promoted to him, at the age of perhaps fourteen, some inkling haunted me of the dignity of himself and brother. For to make boots such boots as he made seemed to me then, and still seems to me, mysterious and wonderful.

I remember well my shy remark, one day, while stretching out to him my youthful foot:

"Isn't it awfully hard to do, Mr. Gessler?"

The Inn of Tranquility: Studies and Essays. London: William Heinemann, 1912.

And his answer, given with a sudden smile from out of the sardonic redness of his beard: "Id is an Ardt!" Himself, he was a little as if made from leather, with his yellow crinkly face, and crinkly reddish hair and beard, and neat folds slanting down his cheeks to the corners of his mouth, and his guttural and one-toned voice; for leather is a sardonic substance, and stiff and slow of purpose. And that was the character of his face, save that his eyes, which were grey-blue, had in them the simple gravity of one secretly possessed by the Ideal. His elder brother was so very like him though watery, paler in every way, with a great industry that sometimes in early days I was not quite sure of him until the interview was over. Then I knew that it was he, if the words, "I will ask my brudder," had not been spoken; and that, if they had, it was his elder brother.

When one grew old and wild and ran up bills, one somehow never ran them up with Gessler Brothers. It would not have seemed becoming to go in there and stretch out one's foot to that blue iron-spectacled glance, owing him for more than say two pairs, just the comfortable reassurance that one was still his client.

For it was not possible to go to him very often his boots lasted terribly, having something beyond the temporary some, as it were, essence of boot stitched into them.

One went in, not as into most shops, in the mood of: "Please serve me, and let me go!" but restfully, as one enters a church; and, sitting on the single wooden chair, waited for there was never anybody there. Soon, over the top edge of that sort of well rather dark, and smelling soothingly of leather which formed the shop, there would be seen his face, or that of his elder brother, peering down. A guttural sound, and the tip-tap of bast slippers beating the narrow wooden stairs, and he would stand before one without coat, a little bent, in leather apron, with sleeves turned back, blinking as if awakened from some dream of boots, or like an owl surprised in daylight and annoyed at this interruption.

And I would say: "How do you do, Mr. Gessler? Could you make me a pair of Russia leather boots?"

Without a word he would leave me, retiring whence he came, or into the other portion of the shop, and I would continue to rest in the wooden chair, inhaling the incense of his trade. Soon he would come back, holding in his thin, veined hand a piece of gold-brown leather. With eyes fixed on it, he would remark: "What a beaudiful biece!"

When I, too, had admired it, he would speak again. "When do you wand dem?"

And I would answer: "Oh! As soon as you conveniently can."

And he would say: "To-morrow fordnighd?" Or if he were his elder brother: "I will ask my brudder!"

Then I would murmur: "Thank you! Good-morning, Mr. Gessler."

"Goot-morning!" he would reply, still looking at the leather in his hand. And as I moved to the door, I would hear the tip-tap of his bast slippers restoring him, up the stairs, to his dream of boots. But if it were some new kind of foot-gear that he had not yet made me, then indeed he would observe ceremony divesting me of my boot and holding it long in his hand, looking at it with eyes at once critical and loving, as if recalling the glow with which he had created it, and rebuking the way in which one had disorganized this masterpiece. Then, placing my foot on a piece of paper, he would two or three times tickle the outer edges with a pencil and pass his nervous fingers over my toes, feeling himself into the heart of my requirements.

I cannot forget that day on which I had occasion to say to him: "Mr. Gessler, that last pair of town walking-boots creaked, you know."

He looked at me for a time without replying, as if expecting me to withdraw or qualify the statement, then said:

"Id shouldn'd 'ave greaked."

"It did, I'm afraid."

"You goddem wed before dey found demselves?"

"I don't think so."

At that he lowered his eyes, as if hunting for memory of those boots, and I felt sorry I had mentioned this grave thing.

"Zend dem back!" he said; "I will look at dem."

A feeling of compassion for my creaking boots surged up in me, so well could I imagine the sorrowful long curiosity of regard which he would bend on them.

"Zome boods," he said slowly, "are bad from birdt. If I can do noding wid dem, I dake dem off your bill."

Once (once only) I went absent-mindedly into his shop in a pair of boots bought in an emergency at some other firm's. He took my order without showing me any leather, and I could feel his eyes penetrating the inferior integument of my foot. At last he said: "Dose are nod my boods."

The tone was not one of anger, nor of sorrow, not even of contempt, but there was in it something quiet that froze the blood. He put his hand down and pressed a finger on the place where the left boot, endeavouring to be fashionable, was not quite comfortable.

"Id 'urds you dere," he said. "Dose big virms 'ave no self-respect. Drash!" And then, as if something had given way within him, he spoke long and bitterly. It was the only time I ever heard him discuss the conditions and hardships of his trade. "Dey get id all," he said, "dey get id by adverdisement, nod by work. Dey dake it away from us, who lofe our boods. Id gomes to this bresently I haf no work. Every year id gets less you will see." And looking at his lined face I saw things I had never noticed before, bitter things and bitter struggle and what a lot of grey hairs there seemed suddenly in his red beard!

As best I could, I explained the circumstances of the purchase of those ill-omened boots. But his face and voice made so deep impression that during the next few minutes I ordered many pairs. Nemesis fell! They lasted more terribly than ever. And I was not able conscientiously to go to him for nearly two years.

When at last I went I was surprised to find that outside one of the two little windows of his shop another name was painted, also that of a boot-maker making, of course, for the Royal Family. The old familiar boots, no longer in dignified isolation, were huddled in the single window. Inside, the now contracted well of the one little shop was more scented and darker than ever. And it was longer than usual, too, before a face peered down, and the tip-tap of the bast slippers began. At last he stood before me, and, gazing through those rusty iron spectacles, said:

"Mr.___, isn'd it?"

"Ah! Mr. Gessler," I stammered, "but your boots are really too good, you know! See, these are quite decent still!" And I stretched out to him my foot. He looked at it.

"Yes," he said, "beople do nod wand good boods, id seems."

To get away from his reproachful eyes and voice I hastily remarked: "What have you done to your shop?"

He answered quietly: "Id was too exbensif. Do you wand some boods?"

I ordered three pairs, though I had only wanted two, and quickly left. I had, I do not know quite what feeling of being part, in his mind, of a conspiracy against him; or not perhaps so much against him as against his idea of boot. One does not,

I suppose, care to feel like that; for it was again many months before my next visit to his shop, paid, I remember, with the feeling: "Oh! well, I can't leave the old boy so here goes! Perhaps it'll be his elder brother!"

For his elder brother, I knew, had not character enough to reproach me, even dumbly.

And, to my relief, in the shop there did appear to be his elder brother, handling a piece of leather.

"Well, Mr. Gessler," I said, "how are you?"

He came close, and peered at me.

"I am breddy well," he said slowly "but my elder brudder is dead."

And I saw that it was indeed himself but how aged and wan! And never before had I heard him mention his brother. Much shocked, I murmured: "Oh! I am sorry!"

"Yes," he answered, "he was a good man, he made a good bood; but he is dead." And he touched the top of his head, where the hair had suddenly gone as thin as it had been on that of his poor brother, to indicate, I suppose, the cause of death. "He could nod ged over losing de oder shop. Do you wand any boods?" And he held up the leather in his hand: "Id's a beaudiful biece."

I ordered several pairs. It was very long before they came but they were better than ever. One simply could not wear them out. And soon after that I went abroad.

It was over a year before I was again in London. And the first shop I went to was my old friend's. I had left a man of sixty, I came back to one of seventy-five, pinched and worn and tremulous, who genuinely, this time, did not at first know me.

"Oh! Mr. Gessler," I said, sick at heart; "how splendid your boots are! See, I've been wearing this pair nearly all the time I've been abroad; and they're not half worn out, are they?"

He looked long at my boots a pair of Russia leather, and his face seemed to regain steadiness. Putting his hand on my instep, he said:

"Do dey vid you here? I 'ad drouble wid dat bair, I remember."

I assured him that they had fitted beautifully.

"Do you wand any boods?" he said. "I can make dem quickly; id is a slack dime."

I answered: "Please, please! I want boots all round every kind!"

"I will make a vresh model. Your food must be bigger." And with utter slowness, he traced round my foot, and felt my toes, only once looking up to say: "Did I dell you my brudder was dead?"

To watch him was painful, so feeble had he grown; I was glad to get away.

I had given those boots up, when one evening they came. Opening the parcel, I set the four pairs out in a row. Then one by one I tried them on. There was no doubt about it. In shape and fit, in finish and quality of leather, they were the best he had ever made me. And in the mouth of one of the Town walking-boots I found his bill.

The amount was the same as usual, but it gave me quite a shock. He had never before sent it in till quarter day. I flew down-stairs, and wrote a cheque, and posted it at once with my own hand.

A week later, passing the little street, I thought I would go in and tell him how splendidly the new boots fitted. But when I came to where his shop had been, his name was gone. Still there, in the window, were the slim pumps, the patent leathers with cloth tops, the sooty riding boots.

I went in, very much disturbed. In the two little shops again made into one was a young man with an English face.

"Mr. Gesslerin?" I said.   He gave me a strange, ingratiating look.

"No, sir," he said, "no. But we can attend to anything with pleasure. We've taken the shop over. You've seen our name, no doubt, next door. We make for some very good people."

"Yes, yes," I said; "but Mr. Gessler?"

"Oh!" he answered; "dead."

"Dead! But I only received these boots from him last Wednesday week."

"Ah!" he said, "A shockin' go. Poor old man starved 'imself."

"Good God!"

"Slow starvation, the doctor called it! You see he went to work in such a way! Would keep the shop on; wouldn't have a soul touch his boots except himself. When he got an order, it took him such a time. People won't wait. He lost everybody. And there he'd sit, goin' on and on I will say that for him not a man in London made a better boot! But look at the competition! He never advertised! Would 'ave the best leather, too, and do it all 'imself. Well, there it is. What could you expect with his ideas?"

"But starvation!"

"That may be a bit flowery, as the sayin' is but I know myself he was sittin' over his boots day and night, to the very last. You see I used to watch him. Never gave 'imself tune to eat; never had a penny in the house. All went in rent and leather. How he lived so long I don't know. He regular let his fire go out. He was a character. But he made good boots."

"Yes," I said, "he made good boots."

And I turned and went out quickly, for I did not want that youth to know that I could hardly see.

"The genuine reformer is never content with pointing out the evils of a system, he has an improving plan. Galsworthy only shows us the shadows, with the lights that lie beside them, not those lights which shall scatter them at last. He is an artist, and the artist's vision is not of the future, but of today."
— Sheila Kay-Smith, "John Galsworthy" (1916)

As a young woman, Mary Wilkins (1852 - 1930) studied for one year at Mount Holyoke before leaving to return to her parents' home in Vermont. There she tried, unsuccessfully, to publish children's verse. Her family's worsening financial situation forced them to seek employment as servants to a local family, the Tylers. The experience particularly embarrassed Freeman, due to her (one-sided) romantic attachment to the Tylers' oldest son.

Following the death of her father in 1883, Wilkins left Vermont and moved back to her birthplace of Randolph, Massachusetts. That same year, she won a short story contest (and $50) from the Boston Sunday Budget for her first adult short story. Elated, Wilkins threw herself into writing for adults, and soon became one of the most popular authors of her era.

Wilkins was strongly attached to her local community, which provided the inspiration for volumes of short stories and novels about New England life – with an emphasis on sincerity rather than twee romanticism. "Amanda Todd", from People of Our Neighborhood (1898) is one such example. Although the "crazy cat lady" is a familiar trope, rarely is the archetype treated with the sympathy and courtesy that it is here.

Mary Wilkins married Dr. Charles Freeman in 1902. The marriage was a complete failure. She found New Jersey less creatively satisfying than New England ("I have not a blessed thing to write about", she said of her new home). The jovial Freeman was an alcoholic, and used his wife's income to support his addiction. He was institutionalised a number of times and the two finally legally separated in 1922. Charles Freeman died a year later, leaving his estranged wife a bequest of one dollar.

In 1926 she received the William Dean Howells Medal for distinction in fiction. Later, Freeman joined Edith Wharton and two others as the first women inducted into the National Institute of Arts and Letters. In A Thousand of the Best Novels (1919), compiled by an association of American librarians, Mary Wilkins Freeman is given four entries (Wharton has three).

AMANDA TODD: THE FRIEND OF CATS

MARY WILKINS FREEMAN

Amanda Todd's orbit of existence is restricted of a necessity, since she was born, brought up and will die in this village, but there is no doubt that it is eccentric. She moves apart on her own little course quite separate from the rest of us.

Had Amanda's lines of life been cast elsewhere where circumstances had pushed her, instead of hemming her in, she might have become the feminine apostle of a new creed, have founded a sect, or instituted a new system of female dress. As it is she does not go to meeting, she never wears a bonnet, and she keeps cats.

Amanda Todd is rising sixty, and she never was married. Had she been, the close friction with another nature might have worn away some of the peculiarities of hers. She might have gone to meeting, she might have worn a bonnet, she might even have eschewed cats, but it is not probable. When peculiarities are in the grain of a person's nature, as they probably are in hers, such friction only brings them out more plainly and it is the other person who suffers.

The village men are not, as a rule, very subtle, but they have seemed to feel this instinctively. Amanda was, they say, a very pretty girl in her youth, but no young man ever dared make love to her and marry her. She had always the reputation of being "an odd stick", even in the district school. She always kept by herself at recess, she never seemed to have anything in common with the other girls, and she always went home alone from singing-school. Probably never in her whole life has Amanda Todd known what it is to be protected by some devoted person of the other sex through the nightly perils of our village street.

The People of Our Neighborhood. New York: Melville Publishing, 1903.

There is a tradition in the village that once in her life, when she was about twenty-five years old, Amanda Todd had a beautiful bonnet and went to meeting.

Old Mrs. Nathan Morse vouches for the reliability of it, and, moreover, she hints at a reason. "When Mandy, she was 'bout twenty-five years old," she says, "George Henry French, he come to town, and taught the district school, and he see Mandy, an' told Almira Benton that he thought she was about the prettiest girl he ever laid eyes on, and Almiry, she told Mandy. That was all there ever was to it, he never waited on her, never spoke to her, fur's I know, but right after that, Mandy, she had a bunnit, and she went reg'lar to meetin'. 'Fore that her mother could scarcely get her to keep a thing on her head out-of-doors – allers carried her sunbunnit a-danglin' by the strings, wonder she wa'n't sunstruck a million times – and as for goin' to meetin', her mother, she talked and talked, but it didn't do a mite of good. I s'pose her father kind of upheld her in it. He was 'most as odd as Mandy. He wouldn't go to meetin' unless he was driv, and he wa'n't a member. 'Nough sight ruther go out prowlin' round in the woods like a wild animal, Sabbath days, than go to meetin'. Once he ketched a wildcat, an' tried to tame it, but he couldn't. It bit and clawed so he had to let it go. I guess Mandy gets her likin' for cats from him fast enough. Well, Mandy, she had that handsome bunnit, and she went to meetin' reg'lar 'most a year, and she looked as pretty as a picture sittin' in the pew. The bunnit was trimmed with green gauze ribbon and had a wreath of fine pink flowers inside. Her mother was real tickled, thought Mandy had met with a change. But land, it didn't last no time. George Henry French, he quit town the next year and went to Somerset to teach, and pretty soon we heard he hed married a girl over there. Then Mandy, she didn't come to meetin' any more. I dunno what she did with the bunnit – stamped on it, most likely, she always had consider'ble temper – anyway I never see her wear it arterwards."

Thus old Mrs. Nathan Morse tells the story, and somehow to a reflective mind the picture of Amanda Todd in her youth decked in her pink-wreathed bonnet, selfishly but innocently attending in the sanctuary of Divine Love in order to lay hands on her own little share of earthly affection, is inseparable from her, as she goes now, old and bare-headed, defiantly past the meeting-house, when the Sabbath bells are ringing.

Weak in faith though she may be, she is, perchance, as strong in love as the best of us.

However, if Amanda Todd had elected to go bare-headed through the village street from feminine vanity, rather than eccentricity, it would have been no wonder. Not a young girl in the village has such a head of hair as Amanda. It is of a beautiful chestnut color, and there is not a gray thread in it. It is full of wonderful natural ripples too – not one of the village girls can equal them with her papers and crimping-pins — and Amanda arranges it in two superb braids wound twice around her head. Seen from behind Amanda's head is that of a young beauty; when she turns a little, and her harsh old profile becomes visible, there is a shock to a stranger.

Amanda's father had a great shock of chestnut hair, which was seldom cut, and she inherits this adornment from him. He lived to be an old man, but that ruddy crown of his never turned gray.

Amanda's mother died long ago; then her father. Ever since she has lived alone in her shingled cottage with her cats. There were not so many cats at first; they say she started with one fine tabby, who became the mother, grandmother and great-grandmother to armies of kittens.

Amanda must destroy some when she can find no homes for them, otherwise she herself would be driven afield, but still the impression is of a legion.

A cat is so covert, it slinks so secretly from one abiding place to another, and seems to duplicate itself with its sudden appearances, that it may account in a measure for this impression. Still there are a great many. Nobody knows just the number – the estimate runs anywhere from fifteen to fifty. Counting, or trying to count, Amanda Todd's cats is a favorite amusement of the village children. "Here's another," they shout, when a pair of green eyes gleams at them from a post. But is it another or only the same cat who has moved? Cats sit in Amanda's windows; they stare out wisely at the passers-by, from behind the panes, or they fold their paws on the ledge outside in the sunshine. Cats walk Amanda's ridge-pole and her fence, they perch on her posts and fly to her cherry trees with bristling fur at the sight of a dog. Amanda has as deadly a hatred of dogs as have her cats. Every one which comes within stone throw of her she sends off yelping, for she is a good shot. Kittens tumble about Amanda's yard, and crawl out between her fence-pickets under people's feet. Amanda will never give away a kitten except to a responsible person, and is as particular as if the kitten were a human orphan, and she the manager of an asylum.

She will never, for any consideration, bestow one of her kittens upon a family who keeps a dog, or where there are many small children. Once she made a condition that the dog should be killed, and she may be at times inwardly disposed to banish the children.

Amanda Todd is extremely persistent when she has selected a home which is perfectly satisfactory to her for a kitten. Once one was found tied into a little basket like a baby on the doorstep of a childless and humane couple who kept no dog, and there is a story that Deacon Nehemiah Stockwell found one in his overcoat pocket and never knew how it came there. It is probable that Amanda resorts to these extreme measures to save herself from either destroying her kittens or being driven out of house and home by them.

However, once, when the case was reversed, Amanda herself was found wanting. When she began to grow old, and the care of her pets told upon her, it occurred to her that she might adopt a little girl. Amanda has a comfortable little income, and would have been able to provide a good living for a child, as far as that goes.

But the managers of the institution to whom Amanda applied made inquiries, and the result did not satisfy them. Amanda stated frankly her reason for wishing to take the child, and her intentions with regard to her. She wished the little girl to tend her cats and assist her in caring for them. She was willing that she should attend school four hours per day, going after the cats had their breakfast, and returning an hour earlier to give them their supper. She was willing that she should go to meeting in the afternoon only, and she could have no other children come to visit her for fear they would maltreat the kittens. She furthermore announced her intention to make her will, giving to the girl, whom she should adopt, her entire property in trust for the cats, to include her own maintenance on condition that she devote her life to them as she had done.

The trustees declared that they could not conscientiously commit a child to her keeping for such purposes, and the poor little girl orphan, who had the chance of devoting her life to the care of pussy cats and kittens to the exclusion of all childish followers, remained in her asylum.

So Amanda to this day lives alone, and manages as best she can. Nobody in the village can be induced to live with her; one forlorn old soul preferred the almshouse.

"I'd 'nough sight ruther go on the town than live with all them cats," she said.

It is rather unfortunate that Amanda's shingled cottage is next the meeting-house, for that, somehow, seems to render her non-church-going more glaringly conspicuous, and then, too, there is a liability of indecorous proceedings on the part of the cats.

They evidently do not share their mistress' dislike of the sanctuary, and find its soft pew cushions very inviting. They watch their chances to slink in when the sexton opens the meeting-house; he is an old man and dim-eyed, and they are often successful. It is wise for anybody before taking a seat in a pew to make sure that one of Amanda's cats has not forestalled him; and often a cat flees down one flight of the pulpit stairs as the minister ascends the other.

We all wonder what will become of Amanda's cats when she dies. There is a report that she has made her will and left her property in trust for the cats to somebody, but to whom? Nobody in this village is anxious for such a bequest, and whoever it may be will probably strive to repudiate it. Some day the cats will undoubtedly go by the board; young Henry Wilson, who has a gun, will shoot some, the rest will become aliens and wanderers, but we all hope Amanda Todd will never know it.

In the meantime she is undoubtedly carrying on among us an eccentric, but none the less genuine mission. A home missionary is Amanda Todd, and we should recognize her as such in spite of her non-church-going proclivities. Weak in faith though she may be, she is, perchance, as strong in love as the best of us. At least I do not doubt that her poor little four-footed dependents would so give evidence if they could speak.

Calista Halsey Patchin (1847 - 1920) was born in Ohio and graduated from the State University of New York. In 1879, she became the first female reporter hired by the Washington Post. Her book, Two of Us (1879) is considered an early feminist work, exploring as it does the subject of women with careers in the Arts.

In 1880, she married Dr. Robert Patchin and moved to Iowa, where she was an active proponent of the local literary scene.

"The Professor" is a snapshot of a man's legacy, capturing how he became part of, and somehow diminished by, the small town in which he lived. Although let down by the ultimate twist – which is as random as it is regrettable – "The Professor" is an insightful look at grief, hypocrisy and loss.

THE PROFESSOR

CALISTA HALSEY PATCHIN

The professor had been dead two months. He had left the world very quietly, at that precise hour of the early evening when he was accustomed to say that his "spirit friends" came to him. The hospital nurse had noticed that there was always a time at twilight when the patient had a good hour; when pain and restlessness seemed to be charmed away, and he did not mind being left alone, and did not care whether or not there was a light in the room. Then it was that those who had gone came back to him with quiet, friendly ways and loving touch. He said nothing of this to the nurse. It was an old friend who told me that this had been his belief and solace for years.

When the professor had first come to town he had spoken of the wife who would follow him shortly, from the East. He did not display her picture, he did not talk about her enough so that the town, though it made an honest effort, ever really visualized her. She would come – without a doubt she would come – but not just yet. It was only that the East still held her. Gradually, he spoke of her less and less often, with a dignified reserve that brooked no inquiry, and finally not at all.

The town forgot. It was only when his illness became so serious that all felt someone should be written to, that it was discovered there was no one. The professor, when he was appealed to, said so. Then also, the hospital nurse noticed that at the twilight hour, when he talked quietly to his unseen friends, there was always one who stayed longer than the rest.

But he had been dead two months now, and the undertaker was pressing his bill, and there were other expenses which had been cheerfully borne by friends at the time, and indeed if there had been no other reason, it remains that something must become of the personal possessions of a man who leaves neither will nor known

Prairie Gold: By Iowa Authors and Artists. Chicago: Reilly & Britton, 1917.

heirs. So the professor's effects were appraised, and a brief local appeared in the daily paper until it had made a dent in the memory of the public, apprising them that his personal property would be offered at public auction at two p.m. of a Thursday, in his rooms on the third floor of the Eureka Block.

It was the merest thread of curiosity that drew me to this sale. I did not want to buy anything. It was a sort of posthumous curiosity, and it concerned itself solely with the individuality of the dead man.

Not having had the opportunity of knowing him well in life, and never having known until I read his obituary what I had missed, I took this last chance of trying to evolve the man from his belongings. All I did know was that he was a teacher of music of the past generation in a Western town which grew so fast that it made a man seem older than he was. More than this, he was a composer, a music master, who took crude young voices, shrill with the tension of the Western winds and the electric air, and tamed and trained them till they fell in love with harmony. When he heard a voice he knew it. One of his contraltos is singing now in grand opera across the sea. A tenor that he discovered has charmed the world with an "upper note".

All the same, the professor had grown old – a new generation had arisen which knew not Joseph; he failed to advertise, and every young girl who "gave lessons" crowded him closer to the wall. Now and then there would appear in the daily paper – not the next morning, but a few days after the presentation of some opera – a column of musical criticism, keen, delicate, reminiscent – fragrant with the rosemary that is for remembrance. When "Elijah" was given by home talent with soloists imported from Chicago, it was the professor who kindly wrote, beforehand this time, luminous articles full of sympathetic interpretation of the great masters. And at rare intervals there would appear a communication from him on the beauty of the woods and the fields, the suburbs of the town and the country, as though he were some simple prophet of nature who stood by the wayside. And this was no affectation. Long, solitary walks were his recreation.

It was a good deal of a rookery, up the flights of narrow, dirty stairs to the third floor of the Eureka Block. And here the professor had lived and taught. Two rooms were made from one by the sort of partition which does not reach to the ceiling – a ceiling which for some inexplicable reason was higher in some places than in others.

The voice of the auctioneer came down that winding way in professional cadences. There were in the room about as many people as might come to a funeral where only friends of the family are invited. It was very still. The auctioneer took an easy conversational tone. There was a silent, forlorn sort of dignity about the five pianos standing in a row that put professional banter and cheap little jokes out of the question. The pianos went without much trouble – a big one of the best make, an old-fashioned cottage piano, a piano with an iron frame. One of the appraisers, himself a musician, became an assistant auctioneer, and kindly played a little – judiciously very little – on each instrument in turn.

Then came the bric-a-brac of personal effects – all the flotsam and jetsam that had floated into these rooms for years. The walls were pockmarked with pictures, big and little. There was no attempt at high art; the professor had bought a picture as a child might buy one – because he thought it was pretty. It was a curious showing of how one artistic faculty may be dormant while another is cultivated to its highest point. But no matter how cheap the picture, it was always conscientiously framed. And this was a great help to the auctioneer. Indeed, it was difficult to see how he could have cried the pictures at all without the frames.

By this time the rooms were fuller of people. There were ladies who had come in quietly, just to get some little thing for a remembrance of their old friend and teacher. These mostly went directly over to the corner where the music lay and began looking for something of "his". If it were manuscript music so much the better. But there was little of this. It appeared that with the professor, as with most of us, early and middle manhood had been his most productive time, and that was long enough ago for everything to have been duly published in sheet and book form – long enough, indeed, for the books themselves to have gone out of date.

There they were – long, green notebooks, bearing the familiar names of well known publishers, and with such a hydra-head of title as *The Celestina, or New Sacred Minstrel; a Repository of Music adapted to every variety of taste and grade of capacity, from the million to the amateur or professor.*

There were four or five of these. There was sheet music by the pile. There was an opera, "Joseph", the production of which had been a musical event.

Presently the auctioneer came that way. He had just sold a large oleograph, framed, one of those gorgeous historical pictures which are an apotheosis of good clothes. He approached an engraving of an old-fashioned lady in voluminous muslin draperies, with her hair looped away from her face in a *Book of Beauty* style.

"He liked that," murmured a lady.

"What do I hear!" cries the auctioneer, softly.

"Oh, such a little bid as that – I can't see it at all in this dark corner. Suppose we throw these peaches in – awfully pretty thing for dining room – and this flower piece – shall we group these three? – now, how much for all? Ah, there they go!"

"Here, ladies and gentlemen, is a gold-headed cane which was presented to the deceased by his admiring friends. It is pure gold – you know they would not give him anything else. How much for this? How much? No – his name is not engraved on it – so much the better – what do I hear?"

"Look at this telescope, gentlemen – a good one – you know the professor was quite an astronomer in his way – and this telescope is all right – sound and in good condition" – the auctioneer had officiated at a stock sale the day before. "You can look right into futurity through this tube. Five dollars' worth of futurity? Five – five and a half? Case and all complete."

There was a pocketful of odds and ends; gold pens, lead pencils, some odd pocket knives; these inconsiderable trifles brought more in proportion than articles of greater intrinsic value. Evidently this was an auction of memories, of emotion, of sentiment.

There was a bit of the beam of the bam that was burned down when the cow kicked over the historic lamp that inaugurated the Chicago fire – no less than three persons were ready to testify to their belief in the genuineness of the relic, had anyone been disposed to question it. But no one was. Nearly all the people in the room were the dead music teacher's personal friends; they had heard the story of all these things; they knew who had sent him the stuffed brown prairie chicken that perched like a raven above the door – the little old-fashioned decanter and wine glasses of gilded glass – the artificial begonias – that clever imitation that goes far toward making one forswear begonias forevermore. There were lamps of various shapes and sizes, there was a kit of burglarious looking tools for piano tuning, there was a little globe – "Who wants the earth?" said the auctioneer. "You all want it."

There was a metronome, which, set to go, began to count time in a metallic whisper for some invisible pupil. Over in the corner just beyond the music were the professor's books. Now we shall find him out, for what a man reads he is, or wishes to be. There was a good deal of spiritualistic literature of the better sort. There was a *History of Christianity and Paganism by the Roman Emperor Julian*, a copy of *She*, a long shelf full of *North American Reviews*, a dozen or so of almanacs, a copy of *Bluebeard*. There were none of the "popular" magazines, and if there had been newspapers – those vagrants of literature – they had gone their way. There was a manuscript play for parlor presentation, with each part written out in legible script, entitled, "The Winning Card".

All these and many more things which only the patient appraisers can fully know were sold or set aside as unsalable, until all was done. And then those who had known and loved him and those who had not known or cared for him came down the stairs together.

Fate stood on the landing. As always, Fate ran true to form. She was a woman; a little tired, as a woman might well be who had come a thousand miles; a little out of breath from the two flights of stairs. Her old-fashioned draperies clung about her; her hair was looped away from her face in a *Book of Beauty* style. The man who stood aside to let her pass was talking. "Of course," he was saying, "he was a side-tracked man. But I believe he stands the biggest chance of being remembered of any man in Iowa."

Swift protest at his first words clouded her face; sheer gratitude for his last words illumined it. She bent forward a little and went on up the stairs alone.

She faltered in the doorway, her hand fumbling at her throat. One of the men who had been talking below hastened to her side.

"It's all over," he said, then added, at the dumb misery that grayed her face, "– the auction."

"I – I – didn't come for that," the apathy in her voice holding it steady. "I – I am his wife. His last letter – he sent for me." A sob broke her speech. "It came last week – two months too late."

POWER

Mary Elizabeth Coleridge (1861 - 1907) was the great-grandniece of Samuel Taylor Coleridge. "I have no fairy god-mother," she once wrote, "but lay claim to a fairy great-great-uncle, which is perhaps the reason that I am condemned to wander restlessly around the Gates of Fairyland."

Coleridge was a talented writer in her own right. Her poetry was discovered by Robert Bridges, who upon reading one of her manuscripts at a relative's house insisted that the author be published. By the time she died of complications stemming from appendicitis, over two hundred of her poems had seen print, as well as several of her novels. In a memoir of Coleridge's life, Edith Sichel writes that "her novels were the novels of a poet, and this was her weakness and her strength".

"The King is Dead, Long Live the King" is a ghost story, but told from the ghost's perspective. A king, recently deceased, is forced to confront the legacy of his own reign. Despite the ethereal prose – the writing of a poet – this is a dark tale that takes several unexpected turns.

THE KING IS DEAD, LONG LIVE THE KING

MARY COLERIDGE

It was not very quiet in the room where the king lay dying. People were coming and going, rustling in and out with hushed footsteps, whispering eagerly to each other; and where a great many people are all busy making as little noise as possible, the result is apt to be a kind of bustle, that weakened nerves can scarcely endure.

But what did that matter? The doctors said he could hear nothing now. He gave no sign that he could. Surely the sobs of his beautiful young wife, as she knelt by the bedside, must else have moved him.

For days the light had been carefully shaded. Now, in the hurry, confusion, and distress, no one remembered to draw the curtains close, so that the dim eyes might not be dazzled. But what did that matter? The doctors said he could see nothing now.

For days no one but his attendants had been allowed to come near him. Now the room was free for all who chose to enter. What did it matter? The doctors said he knew no one.

So he lay for a long time, one hand flung out upon the counterpane, as if in search of something. The queen took it softly in hers, but there was no answering pressure. At length the eyes and mouth closed, and the heart ceased to beat.

"How beautiful he looks," they whispered one to another.

When the king came to himself it was all very still – wonderfully and delightfully still, as he thought, wonderfully and delightfully dark. It was a strange unspeakable relief to him – he lay as if in heaven. The room was full of the scent of flowers, and

Gathered Leaves from the Prose of Mary E. Coleridge. Sichel, Edith, ed. London: Constable and Company, 1910.

the cool night air came pleasantly through an open window. A row of wax tapers burned with soft radiance at the foot of the bed on which he was lying, covered with a velvet pall, only his head and face exposed. Four or five men were keeping guard around him, but they had fallen fast asleep.

So deep was the feeling of content which he experienced that he was loth to stir. Not till the great clock of the palace struck eleven, did he so much as move. Then he sat up with a light laugh.

He remembered how, when his mind was failing him, and he had rallied all his powers in one last passionate appeal against the injustice which was taking him away from the world just when the world most needed him, he had heard a voice saying: "I will give thee yet one hour after death. If, in that time, thou canst find three that desire thy life, live!"

This was his hour, his hour that he had snatched away from death. How much of it had he lost already? He had been a good king; he had worked night and day for his subjects; he had nothing to fear, and he knew that it was very pleasant to live, how pleasant, he had never known before, for, to do him justice, he was not selfish; it was his unfinished work that he grieved about when the decree went forth against him. Yet, as he passed out of the room where the watchers sat heavily sleeping, things were changed to him somehow. The burning sense of injustice was gone. Now that he came to think of it, he had done very little. True that it was his utmost, but there were many better men in the world, and the world was large, very large it seemed to him now. Everything had grown larger. He loved his country and his home as well as ever, but in the night it had seemed as if they must perish with him, and now he knew that they were still unchanged.

Outside the door he paused a moment, hesitating whither to go first. Not to the queen. The very thought of her grief unnerved him. He would not see her till he could once more clasp her in his arms, and bid her weep tears of joy only because he was come again. After all, he had but an hour to wait. Before the castle clock struck twelve, he would be back again in life, remembering these things only as a dream. He sighed a little to think of it.

"All that to do over again some day," he said, as he recalled his last moments.

Almost he turned again to the couch he had so lately left.

"But I have never yet done anything through fear," said the king.

And he smiled as he thought of the terms of the compact. His city lay before him in the moonlight.

"I could find three thousand as easily as three," he said. "Are they not all my friends?"

As he passed out of the gate, he saw a child sitting on the steps, crying bitterly.

"What is the matter, little one?" said the sentinel on guard, stopping a moment.

"Father and mother have gone to the castle, because the king's dead," sobbed the child, "and they've never come back again; and I'm so tired and so hungry! And I've had no supper, and my doll's broken. Oh! I do wish the king were alive again!"

And she burst into a fresh storm of weeping. It amused the king not a little.

"So this is the first of my subjects that wants me back!" he said.

He had no child of his own. He would have liked to try and comfort the little maiden, but there were other calls upon him just then. He was on his way to the house of his great friend, the man whom he loved more than all others. A kind of malicious delight possessed him, as he pictured to himself the deep dejection he should find him in.

"Poor Amyas!" he said. "I know what I should be feeling in his place. I am glad he was not taken, I could not have borne his loss."

As be entered the courtyard of his friend's house, lights were being carried to and fro, horses were being saddled, an air of bustle and excitement pervaded the place. Look where he might, he could not see the face he knew so well. He entered at the open door. His friend was not in the hall. Room after room he vainly traversed – they were all empty. A sudden horror took him. Surely Amyas was not dead of grief?

He came at length to a small private apartment, in which they had spent many a happy, busy hour together; but his friend was not here either, though, to judge by appearances, he could only just have left it. Books and papers were tumbled all about in strange confusion, and bits of broken glass strewed the floor,

A little picture was lying on the ground. The king picked it up, and recognized a miniature of himself, the frame of which had been broken in the fall. He let it drop again, as if it had burnt him. The fire was blazing brightly, and the fragments of a half-destroyed letter lay, unconsumed as yet, in the fender. It was in his own writing. He snatched it up, and saw it was the last he had written, containing the details of an elaborate scheme which he had much at heart. He had only just thrown it back into the flames when two people entered the room, talking together, one a lady, the other a man, booted and spurred as though he came from a long distance.

"Where is Amyas?" he asked.

"Gone to proffer his services to the new king, of course," said the lady. "We are, as you may think, in great anxiety. He has none of the ridiculous notions of his predecessor, who, indeed, hated him cordially. The very favour Amyas has hitherto enjoyed will stand in his way at the new court. I only hope he may be in time to make his peace. He can, with truth, say that he utterly disapproved of the foolish reforms which his late master was bent on making. Of course, he was fond of him in a way; but we must think of ourselves, you know. People in our position have no time for sentiment. He started almost immediately after the king's death. I am sending his retinue after him."

"Quite right," said the gentleman, whom the king now knew as one of his ambassadors. "I shall follow him at once. Between you and me, it is no bad thing for the country. That poor boy had no notion of statesmanship. He forced me to conclude a peace which would have been disastrous to all our best interests. Happily, we shall have war directly now. Promotions in the army would have been at a standstill if he had had his way."

The king did not stay to hear more.

"I will go to my people," he said. "They at least have no interest to make peace with my successor. He will but take from them what I gave."

He heard the clock strike the first quarter as he went. He was, indeed, a very remarkable king, for he knew his way to the poorest part of his dominions. He had been there before, often and often, unknown to any one; and the misery which he had there beheld had stirred and steeled him to attempt what had never before been attempted.

No one about the palace knew where he had caught the malignant fever which carried him off. He had a shrewd suspicion himself, and he went straight to that quarter.

"Fevers won't hurt me now," he said laughing. The houses were as wretched, the people looked as sickly and squalid as ever. They were standing about in knots in the streets, late though it was, talking together about him. His name was in every mouth. The details of his illness, and the probable day of his funeral, seemed to interest them more than anything else.

Five or six men were sitting drinking round a table in a disreputable-looking public-house, and he stopped to overhear their conversation.

"And a good riddance, too!" said one of them, whom he knew well. "What's the use of a king as never spends a farthing more than he can help? It gives no impetus to trade, it don't. The new fellow's a very different sort. We shall have fine doings soon."

"Aye!" struck in another, "a meddlesome, priggish sort of chap, he was, always aworritting us about clean houses, and such like. What right's he got to interfere, I'd like to know?"

"Down with all kings, says I," put in a third; "but if we're to have 'em, let 'em behave as sich. I like a young fellow as isn't afraid of his missus, and knows port wine from sherry."

"Wanted to abolish capital punishment, he did!" cried a fourth. "Thought he'd get more work out of the poor fellows in prison, I suppose? Depend on it, there's some reason like that at the bottom of it. We ain't so very perticular about the lives of our subjects for nothing, we ain't;" an expression of opinion in which all the rest heartily concurred.

The clock struck again as the king turned away; he felt as if a storm of abuse from some one he had always hated would be a precious balm just then. He entered the state prison, and made for the condemned cell. Capital punishment was not abolished yet, and in this particular instance he had certainly felt glad of it.

The cell was tenanted only by a little haggard-looking man, who was writing busily on his knee. The king had only seen him once before, and he looked at him curiously.

Presently the gaoler entered, and with him the first councillor, a man whom his late master had greatly loved and esteemed. The convict looked up quickly.

"It was not to be till to-morrow," he said. Then, as if afraid he had betrayed some cowardice, "but I am ready at any moment. May I ask you to give this paper to my wife?"

"The king is dead," said the first councillor gravely. "You are reprieved. His present majesty has other views. You will, in all probability, be set at large tomorrow."

"Dead?" said the man with a stunned look.

"Dead!" said the first councillor, with the impressiveness of a whole board.

The man stood up, passing his hand across his brow.

"Sir," he said earnestly, "I respected him. For all he was a king, he treated me like a gentleman. He, too, had a young wife. Poor fellow, I wish he were alive, again!"

There were tears in the man's eyes as he spoke.

The third quarter struck as the king left the prison. He felt unutterably humiliated. The pity of his foe was harder to bear than the scorn of his friends. He would rather have died a thousand deaths than owe his life to such a man. And yet, because he was himself noble, he could not but rejoice to find nobility in another. He said to himself sternly that it was not worth what he had gone through. He reviewed his position in no very self-complacent mood. The affection he had so confidently relied upon was but a dream. The people he was fain to work for were not ripe for their own improvement. A foolish little child, a generous enemy, these were his only friends. After all, was it worthwhile to live? Had he not better get back quietly and submit, making no further effort? He had learnt his lesson; he could "lie down in peace, and sleep, and take his rest". The eternal powers had justified themselves. What matter though every man had proved a liar? The bitterness had passed away, and he seemed to see clearly.

Thick clouds had gathered over the moon, and the cold struck through him. All at once a sense of loneliness that cannot be described rushed over him, and his heart sank. Was there really no one who cared – no one ? He would have given anything at that moment for a look, a single word of real sympathy. He longed with sick longing for the assurance of love.

There were yet a few moments left. How had he borne to wait so long? This, at least, he was sure of, and this was all the world to him. He began to find comfort and consolation in the thought; he forgave – indeed he almost forgot – the rest. Yet he had fallen very low, for, as he stood at the door of his wife's room, he hesitated whether to go in. What if this, too, were an illusion? Had he not best go back before he knew?

"But I have never yet done anything through fear," said the king.

His wife was sitting by the fire alone, her face hidden, her long hair falling round her like a veil. At the first sight of her, a pang of self-reproach shot through him. How could he ever have doubted?

She was wearing a ring that he had given her – a ring she wore always, and the light sparkled and flashed from the jewel. Except for this, there was nothing bright in the room.

He ardently desired to comfort her. He wondered why all her ladies had left her. Surely one might have stayed with her on this first night of her bereavement? She seemed to be lost in thought. If she would only speak, or call his name! But she was quite silent.

A slight noise made the king start, A secret door in the wall opened, the existence of which he had thought was known only to himself and his queen, and a man stood before her.

She put her finger to her lips, as though to counsel silence, and then threw herself into his arms.

"You have come," she said – "Oh, I am so glad! I had to hold his hand when he was dying. I was frightened sitting here by myself. I thought his ghost would come back, but he will never come back any more. We may be happy always now," and drawing the ring from her finger, she kissed it, weeping, and gave it to him.

When midnight struck, the watchers wakened with a start, to find the king lying stark and stiff, as before, but a great change had come over his countenance.

"We must not let the queen see him again," they said.

"Lives like [Mary Coleridge's] are not so unimportant as their slight impress on the huge bulk of the world might lead one to imagine. Like the gossamer seeds borne on chance winds to a desert spot to germinate and die, and to be followed in good time by sturdier plants capable of sustaining life, so these tenuous personalities attain new regions of the spirit, where until then bodily presences had not trod, and become the frail forerunners of more robust descendants, creating a foothold by their disappearance, broadening the foundation on which man rears his house of life."

    – The New York Times (27 August 1910)

Charles E. Bayly, Jr. (1897 - 1954) was born in Colorado and studied at Princeton. Bayly went overseas as a volunteer with the American Field Service and subsequently became a sous-lieutenant in the French artillery.

Bayly was a great patron of the arts, and later was made president of the Denver Art Museum. Over the course of his life, he translated a biography of Chopin and an anthology of contemporary short fiction.

Bayly was the son of Charles E. Bayly, president of the Bayly-Underhill Manufacturing Company, which manufactured overalls. "P'r'aps" is also set in a clothing factory, and was written while Bayly was a student at Princeton. The story is notable for its twinned depictions of powerlessness: the factory employee, trying to earn enough to get ahead of medical bills, and the narrator, held back by an feudal code of social conduct.

P'R'APS

CHARLES BAYLY JR.

Above the dim incessant purr of the machines on the floor above, rose the sharper clack of the typewriters and the steady tap of the adding machines. The foreman, standing behind me, was talking in an even monotone to one of the clerks, but the noise was so regular and blending that it seemed like the drowsy hum of bees over a clover field. The hot afternoon sun was streaming in the windows and seemed to mock the silent fans above us. I was checking up the day's orders and had been so long undisturbed that my task had grown perfectly mechanical. My subconscious mind directed my pencil but I was really asleep, my mind was vacant. Suddenly into this dead emptiness, life sprang. The sharp jangle of the telephone bell brought back all our wandering wits. Guiltily, as if caught in some misdeed, I pushed in the plug and answered.

"Hello."

"Hello, is Harry Meyers there?"

"Just a minute – I'll see." My fingers sought the index at the side of my desk, "Hello. Yes, he works here. If you'll give me your message. I'll send it up to him. We aren't allowed to call –"

"Tell him to come to St. Luke's Hospital at once."

"Nothing else?"

But the voice at the other end of the wire made no reply. The connection had been broken. I wrote the message down and rang hastily for a boy. Two days before, I had sent a message up to one of the women that her son had been injured in an automobile accident and her face as she came through the office was still in my mind.

The Best College Short Stories. Henry T. Schnittkind, ed. Boston: Stratford Company, 1919.

I turned to Mr. Swanson, the foreman, and asked him if he didn't think I should take the man to the hospital in my father's machine, which was waiting outside.

"No," he said. "Harry has a wheel and it is only a few blocks. He will get there just as quick."

An accident or hint of trouble spreads quickly in any gathering. As I gave the message to the boy to take upstairs, the men at their desks followed him with their eyes as he passed through the swinging door. But one by one they brought their minds back to their tasks and they, as I, forgot Harry Meyers and settled down into routine of the late afternoon.

That night at dinner, I suddenly remembered the incident and asked my father about it.

"Dad," I said. "Who is Harry Meyers?"

"I never heard of him," he answered.

"He works at the factory."

"Oh," he exclaimed, enlightened. "He's one of the two men there who run sewing machines. And he beats any two girls in the place. Why?"

"I just wondered," I replied. "He was called to St. Luke's this afternoon."

"Is that so? That's too bad. I think his wife's been sick for a long time. He's had a lot of trouble. They didn't say anything about her, did they?"

"No, they just said for him to come at once."

Then Mother broke in and asked if many men applied for work sewing and so the conversation drifted into other channels.

The next day was Saturday and, in the rush to get my work cleared up before noon, I forgot to inquire about Harry Meyers. He was only one among many, but for some reason he kept coming back into my mind and I thought of him as I was driving home that afternoon and determined to ask about him on Monday. Then, my chance did not come until noon. I had finished taking in the cash at the cafeteria and had got a tray for myself and come over near the windows to eat my lunch. Mr. Swanson brought his tray over and sat down beside me. I was looking down the long men's table and his glance followed mine.

"Which is Harry Meyers?" I asked.

"Harry doesn't eat here," he answered. "He always brings his own lunch and prefers to eat alone upstairs."

"You mean he doesn't even leave his machine at lunch hour?" I asked.

"No," Mr. Swanson replied. "He eats up there. He thinks he saves time. I think that if he didn't realize that without food he couldn't work at all, he wouldn't even stop for lunch. You know, he works on piece work and earns more money than any of the girls, but he is always after more."

"Well," I said, flippantly, "he certainly is ambitious."

Mr. Swanson turned around quickly.

"Oh, it isn't that. He's got to have the money. He's supporting a wife and mother. His wife's been sick for a long time and all the money he'd saved is gone. I lent him a little, not much – about fifty dollars. It's all I could afford. You know, I often do that for the people here in the factory. But now, I'm afraid he's up against it. He's been trying to get help from the Associated Jewish Charities. They keep putting him off."

"What about his wife?" I asked.

"Well, she was at the hospital for about two weeks. Friday, they decided to take her home, so they sent for him."

"Oh, that's good," I said. "What was the matter with her?"

"She was going to have a baby. They got a poor doctor and the child was still-born and she's never been well since. That's the trouble. People like that have to economize – and you see the result."

"Well, they took her home from the hospital. Is she going to get well?"

Mr. Swanson raised his hands. "I don't know," he said.

I asked him where they lived. I thought I might induce Mother to go to see her. Later, I decided not to mention the subject. The bell rang just then and we pushed our trays over the counter and went down to the office. That afternoon, a man came in with some things for the Labor Day parade. Mr. Swanson gave them to me to take upstairs.

"If you want to see Harry Meyers," he said, "Take these up to Margaret Jarman. He has the machine just across the aisle from her."

I knew Margaret. She served soup next to the cashier's window in the cafeteria and, as I knew that she had charge of the girls in the parade, I used to talk to her about it in moments when there would be a break in the line. So I took the bundles up to her and got a look at Harry Meyers. I had never seen him before, though I had been working in the factory all summer and I knew that he had worked there ever since I, as a youngster, had played hide-and-go-seek among the great dark piles of denim in the basement. He was working now as if his life depended upon it. His face was bent close over the machine, a thin, dark, Russian-Jewish face, lined with care and worry. He was younger than I had supposed – not more than twenty-six, I think – and his bright eyes and clean-cut Semitic face must have been very attractive before the trouble came. I went over to him.

"You're Harry Meyers, aren't you?" I shouted over the whirr and roar of the machines.

He looked up quickly. There was no expression whatever in his eyes and his face had that curious dead color that black hair and eyes seem to impart to a pale skin.

"What?" he asked.

"I wanted to inquire about your wife." I answered, rather puzzled by this blankness.

"Who sent you? What do you want?" The questions came with startling clearness, even though I could see no movement of the lips.

"Why?" I answered, vaguely embarrassed, "I just wanted to inquire. Nobody sent me. I was in the office Friday when they sent for you and I'm glad Mrs. Meyers is better."

"Who do you come from? What about my wife?"

"You don't understand. No one sent me." Suddenly there flashed over me the idea of what he feared. He thought that some word had come from his wife and that I was trying to break the news to him by degrees.

"I'm sorry if I startled you. I'm Samuel Morton. Mr. Morton is my father. I just wanted to ask you –"

"The boss, your fadder? I think you come – from her." He, too, was obviously relieved. "You see, they bring her Friday from the hospital."

"Yes, I know. I'm glad she's better."

"She was better. Last night she get worse – I send to the doctor. He say when I pay bill he come. I telephone again – I beg – I say Netta get worse - she die if he not come. He say he very busy. He come if he get time. When I go to work, he not yet there. When you come, I think –"

"I see," I replied. "And I'm sorry." The fire that had come into his eyes for a second had died down and he looked nervously at his machine. I took the hint.

"I'm sure it will be all right," I said. "Don't worry. She will be better when you go back."

His long hands, blue-stained with much handling of the cloth, had already taken up a piece of denim from the stack at his side. His feet were on the pedal, his face down to the machine, but I heard his answer and saw the weary shrug of his shoulders.

"P'r'aps."

Harry Meyers' wife died that night. The next day and the next his machine was vacant. On the third day, he was there again. There was no change, the nervous hands flew from one pile of goods to the machine and from there to the other pile; his face was the same ashen color, his eyes as expressionless. I put my hand on his arm. He looked up at me gravely.

"Of course," I said, "I can't even try to console you, but I wanted to tell you that I was sorry, we are all awfully sorry – I wish there were something – something we could do – or that there was something we could have done. But there wasn't really anything. We would have done anything we could. You realize that, don't you?"

My voice trailed off into silence before the look in his eyes. The lips moved – the word struggled out – his eyes sank to the machine.

"P'r'aps."

Benjamin Disraeli, The Earl of Beaconsfield (1804 - 1881) is modernly better known for his work in a different arena than writing. The most gifted politican of his era, Disraeli led the formation of the modern Conservative Party and twice served as Prime Minister. Disraeli was notably the first (and only) Prime Minister from a Jewish family – a heritage that he defended repeatedly to his peers and the public at large.

After Disraeli served in the House of Commons for almost forty years, Queen Victoria, long his admirer and friend, elevated him to the House of Lords in 1876.

Disraeli's legacy will forever be defined by his legendary rivalry with William Gladstone. The stark difference between the two figures is well represented in their literary output. The dour and stoic Gladstone spent his free hours translating the odes of Horace while the charismatic Disraeli reinterpreted Greek Myths as contemporary social satire.

"Ixion in Heaven" is undoubtedly charming – a witty comedy of manners that touches on politics, high society and the fleeting nature of popularity. The deposed King of Thessaly is, quite literally, a lost soul – whisked from Earth to Heaven after catching Jove's eye. Ixion proves that good manners and a sharp wit always carry the day, and soon finds his feet in his new, immortal home.

IXION IN HEAVEN

BENJAMIN DISRAELI,
EARL OF BEACONSFIELD

Part I

I

The thunder groaned, the wind howled, the rain fell in hissing torrents, impenetrable darkness covered the earth.

A blue and forky flash darted a momentary light over the landscape. A Doric temple rose in the centre of a small and verdant plain, surrounded on all sides by green and hanging woods.

"Jove is my only friend," exclaimed a wanderer, as he muffled himself up in his mantle, "and were it not for the porch of his temple, this night, methinks, would complete the work of my loving wife and my dutiful subjects."

The thunder died away, the wind sank into silence, the rain ceased, and the parting clouds exhibited the glittering crescent of the young moon. A sonorous and majestic voice sounded from the skies:

"Who art thou that hast no other friend but Jove?"

"One whom all mankind unite in calling a wretch."

"Art thou a philosopher?"

"If philosophy be endurance. But for the rest, I was sometime a king, and am now a scatterling."

"How do they call thee?"

"Ixion of Thessaly."

Alroy, Ixion in Heaven, The Infernal Marriage, Popanilla. London: Longmans, Green and Company, 1853.

"Ixion of Thessaly! I thought he was a happy man. I heard that he was just married."

"Father of Gods and men! For I deem thee such, Thessaly is not Olympus. Conjugal felicity is only the portion of the Immortals!"

"Hem! What! Was Dia jealous, which is common; or false, which is commoner; or both, which is commonest?"

"It may be neither. We quarreled about nothing. Where there is little sympathy, or too much, the splitting of a straw is plot enough for a domestic tragedy. I was careless, her friends stigmatized me as callous; she cold, her friends styled her magnanimous. Public opinion was all on her side, merely because I did not choose that the world should interfere between me and my wife. Dia took the world's advice upon every point, and the world decided that she always acted rightly. However, life is life, either in a palace or a cave. I am glad you ordered it to leave off thundering."

"A cool dog this. — And Dia left thee?"

"No; I left her."

"What, craven!"

"Not exactly. The truth is 'tis a long story. I was over head and ears in debt."

"Ah! That accounts for everything. Nothing is so harassing as a want of money! But what lucky fellows you Mortals are with your post-obits! We Immortals are deprived of this resource. I was obliged to get up a rebellion against my father, because he kept me so short, and could not die."

"You could have married for money. I did."

"I had no opportunity, there was so little female society in those days. When I came out, there were no heiresses except the Parcae, confirmed old maids; and no very rich dowager, except my grandmother, old Terra."

"Just the thing; the older the better. However, I married Dia, the daughter of Deioneus, with a prodigious portion; but after the ceremony, the old gentleman would not fulfil his part of the contract without my giving up my stud. Can you conceive anything more unreasonable? I smothered my resentment at the time; for the truth is, my tradesmen all renewed my credit on the strength of the match, and so we went on very well for a year; but at last they began to smell a rat, and grew importunate. I entreated Dia to interfere; but she was a paragon of daughters, and always took the side of her father. If she had only been dutiful to her husband, she would have been a perfect woman. At last I invited Deioneus to the Larissa races, with the intention of conciliating him. The unprincipled old man bought the horse that I had backed, and by which I intended to have redeemed my fortunes, and withdrew it. My book was ruined. I dissembled my rage. I dug a pit in our garden, and filled it with burning coals. As my father-in-law and myself were taking a stroll after dinner, the worthy Deioneus fell in, merely by accident. Dia proclaimed me as the murderer of her father, and, as a satisfaction to her wounded feelings, earnestly requested her subjects to decapitate her husband. She certainly was the best of daughters. There was no withstanding public opinion, an infuriated rabble, and a magnanimous wife at the same time. They surrounded my palace: I cut my way through the greasy-capped multitude, sword in hand, and gained a neighbouring Court, where I solicited my brother princes to purify me from the supposed murder. If I had only murdered a subject, they would have supported me against the people; but Deioneus being a crowned head, like themselves, they declared they would not countenance so immoral a being as his son-in-law. And so, at length, after much wandering, and shunned by all my species, I am here, Jove, in much higher society than I ever expected to mingle."

"Well, thou art a frank dog, and in a sufficiently severe scrape. The Gods must have pity on those for whom men have none. It is evident that Earth is too hot for thee at present, so I think thou hadst better come and stay a few weeks with us in Heaven."

"Take my thanks for hecatombs, great Jove. Thou art, indeed, a God."

"I hardly know whether our life will suit you. We dine at sunset; for Apollo is so much engaged that he cannot join us sooner, and no dinner goes off well without him. In the morning you are your own master, and must find amusement where you can. Diana will show you some tolerable sport. Do you shoot?"

"No arrow surer. Fear not for me, Aegiochus: I am always at home. But how am I to get to you?"

"I will send Mercury; he is the best travelling companion in the world. What ho! My Eagle!"

The clouds joined, and darkness again fell over the earth.

II

"So! Tread softly. Don't be nervous. Are you sick?"

"A little nausea; 'tis nothing."

"The novelty of the motion. The best thing is a beef-steak. We will stop at Taurus and take one."

"You have been a great traveller, Mercury?"

"I have seen the world."

"Ah! A wondrous spectacle. I long to travel."

"The same thing over and over again. Little novelty and much change. I am wearied with exertion, and if I could get a pension would retire."

"And yet travel brings wisdom."

"It cures us of care. Seeing much we feel little, and learn how very petty are all those great affairs which cost us such anxiety."

"I feel that already myself. Floating in this blue ether, what the devil is my wife to me, and her dirty earth! My persecuting enemies seem so many pismires; and as for my debts, which have occasioned me so many brooding moments, honour and infamy, credit and beggary, seem to me alike ridiculous."

"Your mind is opening, Ixion. You will soon be a man of the world. To the left, and keep clear of that star."

"Who lives there?"

"The Fates know, not I. Some low people who are trying to shine into notice. 'Tis a parvenu planet, and only sprung into space within this century. We don't visit them."

"Poor devils! I feel hungry."

"All right. We shall get into Heaven by the first dinner bolt. You cannot arrive at a strange house at a better moment. We shall just have time to dress. I would not spoil my appetite by luncheon. Jupiter keeps a capital cook."

"I have heard of nectar and ambrosia."

"Poh! Nobody touches them. They are regular old-fashioned celestial food, and merely put upon the side-table. Nothing goes down in Heaven now but infernal cookery. We took our chef from Proserpine."

"Were you ever in Hell?"

"Several times. 'Tis the fashion now among the Olympians to pass the winter there."

"Is this the season in Heaven?"

"Yes; you are lucky. Olympus is quite full."

"It was very kind of Jupiter to invite me."

"Aye! He has his good points. And, no doubt, he has taken a liking to you, which is all very well. But be upon your guard. He has no heart, and is as capricious as he is tyrannical."

"Gods cannot be more unkind to me than men have been."

"All those who have suffered think they have seen the worst. A great mistake. However, you are now in the high road to preferment, so we will not be dull. There are some good fellows enough amongst us. You will like old Neptune."

"Is he there now?"

"Yes, he generally passes his summer with us. There is little stirring in the ocean at that season."

"I am anxious to see Mars."

"Oh! A brute, more a bully than a hero. Not at all in the best set. These mustachioed gentry are by no means the rage at present in Olympus. The women are all literary now, and Minerva has quite eclipsed Venus. Apollo is our hero. You must read his last work."

"I hate reading."

"So do I. I have no time, and seldom do anything in that way but glance at a newspaper. Study and action will not combine."

"I suppose I shall find the Goddesses very proud?"

"You will find them as you find women below, of different dispositions with the same object. Venus is a flirt; Minerva a prude, who fancies she has a correct taste and a strong mind; and Juno a politician. As for the rest, faint heart never won fair lady, take a friendly hint, and don't be alarmed."

"I fear nothing. My mind mounts with my fortunes. We are above the clouds. They form beneath us a vast and snowy region, dim and irregular, as I have sometimes seen them clustering upon the horizon's ridge at sunset, like a raging sea stilled by some sudden super-natural frost and frozen into form! How bright the air above us, and how delicate its fragrant breath!

I scarcely breathe, and yet my pulses beat like my first youth. I hardly feel my being. A splendour falls upon your presence. You seem indeed a God! Am I so glorious? This, this is Heaven!"

III

The travellers landed on a vast flight of sparkling steps of lapis-lazuli. Ascending, they entered beautiful gardens; winding walks that yielded to the feet, and accelerated your passage by their rebounding pressure; fragrant shrubs covered with dazzling flowers, the fleeting tints of which changed every moment; groups of tall trees, with strange birds of brilliant and variegated plumage, singing and reposing in their sheeny foliage, and fountains of perfumes.

Before them rose an illimitable and golden palace, with high spreading domes of pearl, and long windows of crystal. Around the huge portal of ruby was ranged a company of winged genii, who smiled on Mercury as he passed them with his charge.

"The father of Gods and men is dressing," said the son of Maia. "I shall attend his toilet and inform him of your arrival. These are your rooms. Dinner will be ready in half an hour. I will call for you as I go down. You can be formally presented in the evening. At that time, inspired by liqueurs and his matchless band of wind instruments, you will agree with the world that Aegiochus is the most finished God in existence."

IV

"Now, Ixion, are you ready?"

"Even so. What says Jove?"

"He smiled, but said nothing. He was trying on a new robe. By this time he is seated. Hark! The thunder. Come on!"

They entered a cupolaed hall. Seats of ivory and gold were ranged round a circular table of cedar, inlaid with the campaigns against the Titans, in silver exquisitely worked, a nuptial present of Vulcan. The service of gold plate threw all the ideas of the King of Thessaly as to royal magnificence into the darkest shade. The enormous plateau represented the constellations. Ixion viewed the father of Gods and men with great interest, who, however, did not notice him. He acknowledged the majesty of that countenance whose nod shook Olympus. Majestically robust and luxuriantly lusty, his tapering waist was evidently immortal, for it defied Time, and his splendid auburn curls, parted on his forehead with celestial precision, descended over cheeks glowing with the purple radiancy of perpetual manhood.

The haughty Juno was seated on his left hand and Ceres on his right. For the rest of the company, there was Neptune, Latona, Minerva, and Apollo, and when Mercury and Ixion had taken their places, one seat was still vacant.

"Where is Diana?" inquired Jupiter, with a frown.

"My sister is hunting," said Apollo.

"She is always too late for dinner," said Jupiter.

"No habit is less Goddess-like."

"Godlike pursuits cannot be expected to induce

Goddess-like manners," said Juno, with a sneer.

"I have no doubt Diana will be here directly," said Latona, mildly.

Jupiter seemed pacified, and at that instant the absent guest returned.

"Good sport, Di?" inquired Neptune.

"Very fair, uncle. Mamma," continued the sister of

Apollo, addressing herself to Juno, whom she ever thus styled when she wished to conciliate her, "I have brought you a new peacock."

Juno was fond of pets, and was conciliated by the present.

"Bacchus made a great noise about this wine, Mercury," said Jupiter, "but I think with little cause. What think you?"

"It pleases me, but I am fatigued, and then all wine is agreeable."

"You have had a long journey," replied the Thunderer.

"Ixion, I am glad to see you in Heaven."

"Your Majesty arrived to-day?" inquired Minerva, to whom the King of Thessaly sat next.

"Within this hour."

"You must leave off talking of Time now," said Minerva, with a severe smile. "Pray is there anything new in Greece?"

"I have not been at all in society lately."

"No new edition of Homer? I admire him exceedingly."

"All about Greece interests me," said Apollo, who, although handsome, was a somewhat melancholy lack-a-daisical looking personage, with his shirt collar thrown open, and his long curls very theatrically arranged.

"All about Greece interests me. I always consider Greece my peculiar property. My best poems were written at Delphi. I travelled in Greece when I was very young. I envy mankind."

"Indeed!" said Ixion.

"Yes: they at least can look forward to a termination of the ennui of existence, but for us Celestials there is no prospect. Say what they like, Immortality is a bore."

"You eat nothing, Apollo," said Ceres.

"Nor drink," said Neptune.

"To eat, to drink, what is it but to live; and what is life but death, if death be that which all men deem it, a thing insufferable, and to be shunned. I refresh myself now only with soda-water and biscuits. Ganymede, give me some."

Now, although the cuisine of Olympus was considered perfect, the forlorn poet had unfortunately fixed upon the only two articles which were not comprised in its cellar or larder. In Heaven, there was neither soda-water nor biscuits. A great confusion consequently ensued; but at length the bard, whose love of fame was only equalled by his horror of getting fat, consoled himself with a swan stuffed with truffles, and a bottle of strong Tenedos wine.

"What do you think of Homer?" inquired Minerva of Apollo. "Is he not delightful?"

"If you think so."

"Nay, I am desirous of your opinion."

"Then you should not have given me yours, for your taste is too fine for me to dare to differ with it."

"I have suspected, for some time, that you are rather a heretic."

"Why, the truth is," replied Apollo, playing with his rings, "I do not think much of Homer. Homer was not esteemed in his own age, and our contemporaries are generally our best judges. The fact is, there are very few people who are qualified to decide upon matters of taste. A certain set, for certain reasons, resolve to cry up a certain writer, and the great mass soon join in. All is cant. And the present admiration of Homer not less so. They say I have borrowed a great deal from him. The truth is, I never read Homer since I was a child, and I thought of him then what I think of him now, a writer of some wild irregular power, totally deficient in taste. Depend upon it, our contemporaries are our best judges, and his contemporaries decided that Homer was nothing. A great poet cannot be kept down. Look at my case. Marsyas said of my first volume that it was pretty good poetry for a God, and in answer I wrote a satire, and flayed Marsyas alive. But what is poetry, and what is criticism, and what is life ? Air. And what is Air? Do you know? I don't. All is mystery, and all is gloom, and ever and anon from out the clouds a star breaks forth, and glitters, and that star is Poetry."

"Splendid!" exclaimed Minerva.

"I do not exactly understand you," said Neptune.

"Have you heard from Proserpine, lately?" inquired Jupiter of Ceres.

"Yesterday," said the domestic mother. "They talk of soon joining us. But Pluto is at present so busy, owing to the amazing quantity of wars going on now, that I am almost afraid he will scarcely be able to accompany her."

Juno exchanged a telegraphic nod with Ceres. The Goddesses rose, and retired.

"Come, old boy," said Jupiter to Ixion, instantly throwing off all his chivalric majesty, "I drink your welcome in a magnum of Maraschino. Damn your poetry, Apollo; and. Mercury, give us one of your good stories."

V

"Well! what do you think of him?" asked Juno.

"He appears to have a very fine mind," said Minerva.

"Poh! He has very fine eyes," said Juno.

"He seems a very nice, quiet young gentleman," said Ceres.

"I have no doubt he is very amiable," said Latona.

"He must have felt very strange," said Diana.

VI

Hercules arrived with his bride Hebe; soon after the Graces dropped in, the most delightful personages in the world for a soiree, so useful and ready for anything. Afterwards came a few of the Muses, Thalia, Melpomene, and Terpsichore, famous for a charade or a proverb. Jupiter liked to be amused in the evening.

Bacchus also came, but finding that the Gods had not yet left their wine, retired to pay them a previous visit.

VII

Ganymede announced coffee in the saloon of Juno. Jupiter was in superb good humour. He was amused by his mortal guest. He had condescended to tell one of his best stories in his best style, about Leda, not too scandalous, but gay.

"Those were bright days," said Neptune.

"We can remember," said the Thunderer, with a twinkling eye. "These youths have fallen upon duller times. There are no fine women now. Ixion, I drink to the health of your wife."

"With all my heart, and may we never be nearer than we are at present."

"Good! I'faith; Apollo, your arm. Now for the ladies. La, la, la, la! La, la, la, la!"

VIII

The Thunderer entered the saloon of Juno with that bow which no God could rival; all rose, and the King of Heaven seated himself between Ceres and Latona. The melancholy Apollo stood apart, and was soon carried off by Minerva to an assembly at the house of Mnemosyne. Mercury chatted with the Graces, and Bacchus with Diana. The three Muses favoured the company with singing, and the Queen of Heaven approached Ixion.

"Does your Majesty dance?" she haughtily inquired.

"On earth; I have few accomplishments even there, and none in Heaven."

"You have led a strange life! I have heard of your adventures."

"A king who has lost his crown may generally gain at least experience."

"Your courage is firm."

"I have felt too much to care for much. Yesterday I was a vagabond exposed to every pitiless storm, and now I am the guest of Jove. While there is life there is hope, and he who laughs at Destiny wall gain Fortune. I would go through the past again to enjoy the present, and feel that, after all, I am my wife's debtor, since, through her conduct, I can gaze upon you."

"No great spectacle. If that be all, I wish you better fortune."

"I desire no greater."

"You are moderate."

"I am perhaps more unreasonable than you imagine."

"Indeed!"

Their eyes met; the dark orbs of the Thessalian did not quail before the flashing vision of the Goddess. Juno grew pale. Juno turned away.

Part II

"Others say it was only a cloud."

I

Mercury and Ganymede were each lolling on an opposite couch in the antechamber of Olympus.

"It is wonderful," said the son of Maia, yawning.

"It is incredible," rejoined the cup-bearer of Jove, stretching his legs.

"A miserable mortal!" exclaimed the God, elevating his eyebrows.

"A vile Thessalian!" said the beautiful Phrygian, shrugging his shoulders.

"Not three days back an outcast among his own wretched species!"

"And now commanding everybody in Heaven."

"He shall not command me, though," said Mercury.

"Will he not?" replied Ganymede. "Why, what do you think? Only last night — hark! Here he comes."

The companions jumped up from their couches; a light laugh was heard. The cedar portal was flung open, and Ixion lounged in, habited in a loose morning robe, and kicking before him one of his slippers.

"Ah!" exclaimed the King of Thessaly, "the very fellows I wanted to see! Ganymede, bring me some nectar; and, Mercury, run and tell Jove that I shall not dine at home to-day."

The messenger and the page exchanged looks of indignant consternation.

"Well! what are you waiting for?" continued Ixion, looking round from the mirror in which he was arranging his locks. The messenger and the page disappeared.

"So, this is Heaven," exclaimed the husband of Dia, flinging himself upon one of the couches, "and a very pleasant place too. These worthy Immortals required their minds to be opened, and I trust I have effectually performed the necessary operation. They wanted to keep me down with their dull old-fashioned celestial airs, but I fancy I have given them change for their talent. To make your way in Heaven you must command. These exclusives sink under the audacious invention of an aspiring mind. Jove himself is really a fine old fellow, with some notions too. I am a prime favourite, and no one is greater authority with Aegiochus on all subjects, from the character of the fair sex or the pedigree of a courser, down to the cut of a robe or the flavour of a dish. Thanks, Ganymede," continued the Thessalian, as he took the goblet from his returning attendant.

"I drink to your *bonnes* fortunes. Splendid! This nectar makes me feel quite immortal. By the by, I hear sweet sounds. Who is in the Hall of Music?"

"The Goddesses, royal sir, practise a new air of Euterpe, the words by Apollo. 'Tis pretty, and will doubtless be very popular, for it is all about moonlight and the misery of existence."

"I warrant it."

"You have a taste for poetry yourself?" inquired Ganymede.

"Not the least," replied Ixion.

"Apollo," continued the heavenly page, "is a great genius, though Marsyas said that he never would be a poet because he was a god, and had no heart. But do you think, sir, that a poet does indeed need a heart?"

"I really cannot say. I know my wife always said I had a bad heart and worse head; but what she meant, upon my honour I never could understand."

"Minerva will ask you to write in her album."

"Will she indeed! I am sorry to hear it, for I can scarcely scrawl my own signature. I should think that Jove himself cared little for all this nonsense."

"Jove loves an epigram. He does not esteem Apollo's works at all. Jove is of the classical school, and admires satire, provided there be no allusions to gods and kings."

"Of course; I quite agree with him. I remember we had a confounded poet at Larissa who proved my family lived before the deluge, and asked me for a pension. I refused him, and then he wrote an epigram asserting that I sprang from the veritable stones thrown by Deucalion and Pyrrha at the re-peopling of the earth, and retained all the properties of my ancestors."

"Ha, ha! Hark! There's a thunderbolt. I must run to Jove."

"And I will look in on the musicians. This way, I think?"

"Up the ruby staircase, turn to your right, down the amethyst gallery. Farewell!"

"Good-bye; a lively lad that!"

II

The King of Thessaly entered the Hall of Music with its golden walls and crystal dome. The Queen of Heaven was reclining in an easy-chair, cutting out peacocks in small sheets of note-paper. Minerva was making a pencil observation on a manuscript copy of the song: Apollo listened with deference to her laudatory criticisms. Another divine dame, standing by the side of Euterpe, who was seated by the harp, looked up as Ixion entered. The wild liquid glance of her soft but radiant countenance denoted the famed Goddess of Beauty.

Juno just acknowledged the entrance of Ixion by a slight and very haughty inclination of the head, and then resumed her employment. Minerva asked him his opinion of her amendment, of which he greatly approved, Apollo greeted him with a melancholy smile, and congratulated him on being mortal. Venus complimented him on his visit to Olympus, and expressed the pleasure that she experienced in making his acquaintance.

"What do you think of Heaven?" inquired Venus, in a soft still voice, and with a smile like summer lightning.

"I never found it so enchanting as at this moment," replied Ixion.

"A little dull? For myself, I pass my time chiefly at Cnidos: you must come and visit me there. 'Tis the most charming place in the world. 'Tis said, you know, that our onions are like other people's roses. We will take care of you, if your wife come."

"No fear of that. She always remains at home and prides herself on her domestic virtues, which means pickling, and quarrelling with her husband."

"Ah! I see you are a droll. Very good indeed. Well, for my part, I like a watering-place existence. Cnidos, Paphos, Cythera — you will usually find me at one of these places. I like the easy distraction of a career without any visible result. At these fascinating spots your gloomy race, to whom, by the by, I am exceedingly partial, appear emancipated from the wearing fetters of their regular, dull, orderly, methodical, moral, political, toiling existence. I pride myself upon being the Goddess of Watering-places. You really must pay me a visit at Cnidos."

"Such an invitation requires no repetition. And Cnidos is your favourite spot?"

"Why, it was so; but of late it has become so inundated with invalid Asiatics and valetudinarian Persians, that the simultaneous influx of the handsome heroes who swarm in from the islands to look after their daughters, scarcely compensates for the annoying presence of their yellow faces and shaking limbs. No, I think, on the whole, Paphos is my favourite."

"I have heard of its magnificent luxury."

"Oh! 'Tis lovely! Quite my idea of country life. Not a single tree! When Cyprus is very hot, you run to Paphos for a sea-breeze, and are sure to meet every one whose presence is in the least desirable. All the bores remain behind, as if by instinct."

"I remember when we married, we talked of passing the honeymoon at Cythera, but Dia would have her waiting-maid and a bandbox stuffed between us in the chariot, so I got sulky after the first stage, and returned by myself."

"You were quite right. I hate bandboxes: they are always in the way. You would have liked Cythera if you had been in the least in love. High rocks and green knolls, bowery woods, winding walks, and delicious sunsets. I have not been there much of late," continued the Goddess, looking somewhat sad and serious, "since — but I will not talk sentiment to Ixion."

"Do you think, then, I am insensible?"

"Yes."

"Perhaps you are right. We mortals grow callous."

"So I have heard. How very odd!" So saying, the Goddess glided away and saluted Mars, who at that moment entered the hall. Ixion was presented to the military hero, who looked fierce and bowed stiffly. The King of Thessaly turned upon his heel. Minerva opened her album, and invited him to inscribe a stanza.

"Goddess of Wisdom," replied the King, "unless you inspire me, the virgin page must remain pure as thyself. I can scarcely sign a decree."

"Is it Ixion of Thessaly who says this? One who has seen so much, and, if I am not mistaken, has felt and thought so much. I can easily conceive why such a mind may desire to veil its movements from the common herd, but pray concede to Minerva the gratifying compliment of assuring her that she is the exception for whom this rule has been established."

"I seem to listen to the inspired music of an oracle. Give me a pen."

"Here is one, plucked from a sacred owl."

"So! I write — there! Will it do?"

Minerva read the inscription:

I have seen the world, and more than the world: I have studied the heart of man, and now I consort with immortals. The fruit of my tree of knowledge is plucked, and it is this: "Adventures are to the adventurous." — Written in the Album of Minerva, by Ixion in Heaven

"'Tis brief," said the Goddess, with a musing air, "but full of meaning. You have a daring soul and pregnant mind."

"I have dared much: what I may produce we have yet to see."

"I must to Jove," said Minerva, "to council. We shall meet again. Farewell, Ixion."

"Farewell, Glaucopis."

The King of Thessaly stood away from the remaining guests, and leant with folded arms and pensive brow against a wreathed column. Mars listened to Venus with an air of deep devotion. Euterpe played an inspiring accompaniment to their conversation. The Queen of Heaven seemed engrossed in the creation of her paper peacocks.

Ixion advanced and seated himself on a couch near Juno. His manner was divested of that reckless bearing and careless coolness by which it was in general distinguished. He was, perhaps, even a little embarrassed. His ready tongue deserted him. At length he spoke.

"Has your Majesty ever heard of the peacock of the Queen of Mesopotamia?"

"No," replied Juno, with stately reserve; and then she added with an air of indifferent curiosity, "Is it in any way remarkable?"

"Its breast is of silver, its wings of gold, its eyes of carbuncle, its claws of amethyst."

"And its tail?" eagerly inquired Juno.

"That is a secret," replied Ixion. "The tail is the most wonderful part of all."

"Oh! Tell me, pray tell me!"

"I forget."

"No, no, no; it is impossible!" exclaimed the animated Juno. "Provoking mortal!" continued the Goddess. "Let me entreat you; tell me immediately."

"There is a reason which prevents me."

"What can it be? How very odd! What reason can it possibly be? Now tell me; as a particular, a personal favour, I request you tell me."

"What! The tail or the reason? The tail is wonderful, but the reason is much more so. I can only tell one. Now choose."

"What provoking things these human beings are! The tail is wonderful, but the reason is much more so. Well then, the reason — no, the tail. Stop, now, as a particular favour, pray tell me both. What can the tail be made of, and what can the reason be? I am literally dying of curiosity."

"Your Majesty has cut out that peacock wrong," coolly remarked Ixion. "It is more like one of Minerva's owls."

"Who cares about paper peacocks, when the Queen of Mesopotamia has got such a miracle!" exclaimed Juno; and she tore the labours of the morning to pieces, and threw away the fragments with vexation. "Now tell me instantly; if you have the slightest regard for me, tell me instantly. What was the tail made of?"

"And you do not wish to hear the reason?"

"That afterwards. Now! I am all ears." At this moment Ganymede entered, and whispered the Goddess, who rose in evident vexation, and retired to the presence of Jove.

III

The King of Thessaly quitted the Hall of Music. Moody, yet not uninfluenced by a degree of wild excitement, he wandered forth into the gardens of Olympus. He came to a beautiful green retreat surrounded by enormous cedars, so vast that it seemed they must have been coeval with the creation; so fresh and brilliant, you would have deemed them wet with the dew of their first spring. The turf, softer than down, and exhaling, as you pressed it, an exquisite perfume, invited him to recline himself upon this natural couch. He threw himself upon the aromatic herbage, and leaning on his arm, fell into a deep reverie.

Hours flew away; the sunshiny glades that opened in the distance had softened into shade.

"Ixion, how do you do?" inquired a voice, wild, sweet, and thrilling as a bird. The King of Thessaly started and looked up with the distracted air of a man roused from a dream, or from complacent meditation over some strange, sweet secret. His cheek was flushed, his dark eyes flashed fire; his brow trembled, his disheveled hair played in the fitful breeze.

The King of Thessaly looked up, and beheld a most beautiful youth.

Apparently, he had attained about the age of puberty. His stature, however, was rather tall for his age, but exquisitely moulded and proportioned. Very fair, his somewhat round cheeks were tinted with a rich but delicate glow, like the rose of twilight, and lighted by dimples that twinkled like stars. His largo and deep-blue eyes sparkled with exultation, and an air of ill-suppressed mockery quivered round his pouting lips. His light auburn hair, braided on his white forehead, clustered in massy curls on each side of his face, and fell in sunny torrents down his neck. And from the back of the beautiful youth there fluttered forth two wings, the tremulous plumage of which seemed to have been bathed in a sunset: so various, so radiant, and so novel were its shifting and wondrous tints; purple, and crimson, and gold; streaks of azure, dashes of orange and glossy black; now a single feather, whiter than light, and sparkling like the frost, stars of emerald and carbuncle, and then the prismatic blaze of an enormous brilliant! A quiver hung at the side of the beautiful youth, and he leant upon a bow.

"Oh god! For god thou must be!" at length exclaimed Ixion. "Do I behold the bright divinity of Love?"

"I am indeed Cupid," replied the youth, "and am curious to know what Ixion is thinking about."

"Thought is often bolder than speech."

"Oracular, though a mortal! You need not be afraid to trust me. My aid I am sure you must need. Who ever was found in a reverie on the green turf, under the shade of spreading trees, without requiring the assistance of Cupid? Come! Be frank, who is the heroine? Some love-sick nymph deserted on the far earth; or worse, some treacherous mistress, whose frailty is more easily forgotten than her charms? 'Tis a miserable situation, no doubt. It cannot be your wife?"

"Assuredly not," replied Ixion, with great energy.

"Another man's?"

"No."

"What! An obdurate maiden?"

Ixion shook his head.

"It must be a widow, then," continued Cupid. "Who ever heard before of such a piece of work about a widow!"

"Have pity upon me, dread Cupid!" exclaimed the King of Thessaly, rising suddenly from the ground, and falling on his knee before the God. "Thou art the universal friend of man, and all nations alike throw their incense on thy altars. Thy divine discrimination has not deceived thee. I am in love; desperately, madly, fatally enamoured. The object of my passion is neither my own wife nor another man's. In spite of all they have said and sworn, I am a moral member of society. She is neither a maid nor a widow. She is..."

"What? What?" exclaimed the impatient deity.

"A Goddess!" replied the King.

"Wheugh!" whistled Cupid. "What! Has my mischievous mother been indulging you with an innocent flirtation?"

"Yes; but it produced no effect upon me."

"You have a stout heart, then. Perhaps you have been reading poetry with Minerva, and are caught in one of her Platonic man-traps."

"She set one, but I broke away."

"You have a stout leg, then. But where are you, where are you? Is it Hebe? It can hardly be Diana, she is so very cold. Is it a Muse, or is it one of the Graces?"

Ixion again shook his head.

"Come, my dear fellow," said Cupid, quite in a confidential tone, "you have told enough to make further reserve mere affectation. Ease your heart at once, and if I can assist you, depend upon my exertions."

"Beneficent God!" exclaimed Ixion, "if I ever return to Larissa, the brightest temple in Greece shall hail thee for its inspiring deity. I address thee with all the confiding frankness of a devoted votary. Know, then, the heroine of my reverie was no less a personage than the Queen of Heaven herself!"

"Juno! By all that is sacred!" shouted Cupid.

"I am here," responded a voice of majestic melody.

The stately form of the Queen of Heaven advanced from a neighbouring bower. Ixion stood with his eyes fixed upon the ground, with a throbbing heart and burning cheeks. Juno stood motionless, pale, and astounded. The God of Love burst into excessive laughter.

"A pretty pair," he exclaimed, fluttering between both, and laughing in their faces. "Truly a pretty pair. Well! I see I am in your way. Good-bye!" And so saying, the God pulled a couple of arrows from his quiver, and with the rapidity of lightning shot one in the respective breasts of the Queen of Heaven and the King of Thessaly.

IV

The amethystine twilight of Olympus died away. The stars blazed with tints of every hue. Ixion and Juno returned to the palace. She leant upon his arm; her eyes were fixed upon the ground; they were in sight of the gorgeous pile, and yet she had not spoken. Ixion, too, was silent, and gazed with abstraction upon the glowing sky.

Suddenly, when within a hundred yards of the portal, Juno stopped, and looking up into the face of Ixion with an irresistible smile, she said, "I am sure you cannot now refuse to tell me what the Queen of Mesopotamia's peacock's tail was made of?"

"It is impossible now," said Ixion. "Know, then, beautiful Goddess, that the tail of the Queen of Mesopotamia's peacock was made of some plumage she had stolen from the wings of Cupid."

"And what was the reason that prevented you from telling me before?"

"Because, beautiful Juno, I am the most discreet of men, and respect the secret of a lady, however trifling."

"I am glad to hear that," replied Juno, and they re-entered the palace.

V

Mercury met Juno and Ixion in the gallery leading to the grand banqueting hall.

"I was looking for you," said the God, shaking his head. "Jove is in a sublime rage. Dinner has been ready this hour."

The King of Thessaly and the Queen of Heaven exchanged a glance and entered the saloon. Jove looked up with a brow of thunder, but did not condescend to send forth a single flash of anger. Jove looked up and Jove looked down. All Olympus trembled as the father of Gods and men resumed his soup. The rest of the guests seemed nervous and reserved, except Cupid, who said immediately to Juno, "Your Majesty has been detained?"

"I fell asleep in a bower reading Apollo's last poem," replied Juno. "I am lucky, however, in finding a companion in my negligence. Ixion, where have you been?"

"Take a glass of nectar, Juno," said Cupid, with eyes twinkling with mischief; "and perhaps Ixion will join us."

This was the most solemn banquet ever celebrated in Olympus. Every one seemed out of humour or out of spirits. Jupiter spoke only in monosyllables of suppressed rage, that sounded like distant thunder.

Apollo whispered to Minerva. Mercury never opened his lips, but occasionally exchanged significant glances with Ganymede. Mars compensated, by his attentions to Venus, for his want of conversation. Cupid employed himself in asking disagreeable questions. At length the Goddesses retired. Mercury exerted himself to amuse Jove, but the Thunderer scarcely deigned to smile at his best stories. Mars picked his teeth, Apollo played with his rings, Ixion was buried in a profound reverie.

It was a great relief to all when Ganymede summoned them to the presence of their late companions.

"I have written a comment upon your inscription," said Minerva to Ixion, "and am anxious for your opinion of it."

"I am a wretched critic," said the King, breaking away from her. Juno smiled upon him in the distance.

*Ixion," said Venus, as he passed by, "come and talk to me."

The bold Thessalian blushed, he stammered out an unmeaning excuse, he quitted the astonished but good-natured Goddess, and seated himself by Juno, and as he seated himself his moody brow seemed suddenly illumined with brilliant light.

"Is it so?" said Venus.

"Hem!" said Minerva.

"Ha, ha!" said Cupid.

Jupiter played piquette with Mercury.

"Everything goes wrong to-day," said the King of Heaven, "cards wretched, and kept waiting for dinner, and by a mortal!"

"Your Majesty must not be surprised," said the good-natured Mercury, with whom Ixion was no favourite.

"Your Majesty must not be very much surprised at the conduct of this creature. Considering what he is, and where he is, I am only astonished that his head is not more turned than it appears to be. A man, a thing made of mud, and in Heaven! Only think, sire! Is it not enough to inflame the brain of any child of clay? To be sure, keeping your Majesty from dinner is little short of celestial high treason. I hardly expected that, indeed. To order me about, to treat Ganymede as his own lackey, and, in short, to command the whole household; all this might be expected from such a person in such a situation, but I confess I did think he had some little respect left for your Majesty."

"And he does order you about, eh?" inquired Jove.

"I have the spades."

"Oh! 'Tis quite ludicrous," responded the son of Maia. "Your Majesty would not expect from me the offices that this absurd upstart daily requires."

"Eternal destiny! Is it possible? That is my trick. And Ganymede, too?"

"Oh, quite shocking, I assure you, sire," said the beautiful cupbearer, leaning over the chair of Jove with all the easy insolence of a privileged favourite. "Really, sire, if Ixion is to go on in the way he does, either he or I must quit."

"Is it possible?" exclaimed Jupiter. "But I can believe anything of a man who keeps me waiting for dinner. Two and three make five."

"It is Juno that encourages him so," said Ganymede.

"Does she encourage him?" inquired Jove.

"Everybody notices it," protested Ganymede.

"It is indeed a little noticed," observed Mercury.

"What business has such a fellow to speak to Juno?" exclaimed Jove. "A mere mortal, a mere miserable mortal! You have the point. How I have been deceived in this fellow! Who ever could have supposed that, after all my generosity to him, he would ever have kept me waiting for dinner?"

"He was walking with Juno," said Ganymede. "It was all a sham about their having met by accident. Cupid saw them."

"Ha!" said Jupiter, turning pale. "You don't say so! Repiqued, as I am a God. That is mine. Where is the Queen?"

"Talking to Ixion, sire," said Mercury. "Oh, I beg your pardon, sire; I did not know you meant the queen of diamonds."

"Never mind. I am repiqued, and I have been kept waiting for dinner. Accursed be this day! Is Ixion really talking to Juno? We will not endure this."

VII

"Where is Juno?" demanded Jupiter.

"I am sure I cannot say," said Venus, with a smile.

"I am sure I do not know," said Minerva, with a sneer.

"Where is Ixion?" said Cupid, laughing outright.

"Mercury, Ganymede, find the Queen of Heaven instantly," thundered the father of Gods and men.

The celestial messenger and the heavenly page flew away out of different doors. There was a terrible, an immortal silence. Sublime rage lowered on the brow of Jove like a storm upon the mountain-top. Minerva seated herself at the card- table and played at Patience. Venus and Cupid tittered in the background. Shortly returned the envoys, Mercury looking very solemn, Ganymede very malignant.

"Well?" inquired Jove; and all Olympus trembled at the monosyllable.

Mercury shook his head.

"Her Majesty has been walking on the terrace with the King of Thessaly," replied Ganymede.

"Where is she now, sir?" demanded Jupiter.

Mercury shrugged his shoulders.

"Her Majesty is resting herself in the pavilion of Cupid, with the King of Thessaly," replied Ganymede.

"Confusion!" exclaimed the father of Gods and men; and he rose and seized a candle from the table, scattering the cards in all directions. Every one present, Minerva, and Venus, and Mars, and Apollo, and Mercury, and Ganymede, and the Muses, and the Graces, and all the winged Genii – each seized a candle; rifling the chandeliers, each followed Jove.

"This way," said Mercury.

"This way." said Ganymede.

"This way, this way!" echoed the celestial crowd.

"Mischief!" cried Cupid; "I must save my victims."

They were all upon the terrace. The father of Gods and men, though both in a passion and a hurry, moved with dignity. It was, as customary in Heaven, a clear and starry night ; but this eve Diana was indisposed, or otherwise engaged, and there was no moonlight. They were in sight of the pavilion.

"What are you?" inquired Cupid of one of the Genii, who accidentally extinguished his candle.

"I am a Cloud," answered the winged Genius,

"A Cloud! Just the thing. Now do me a shrewd turn, and Cupid is ever your debtor. Fly, fly, pretty Cloud, and encompass yon pavilion with your form. Away! Ask no questions; swift as my word."

"I declare there is a fog," said Venus.

"An evening mist in Heaven!" said Minerva.

"Where is Nox?" said Jove. "Everything goes wrong. Who ever heard of a mist in Heaven?"

"My candle is out," said Apollo.

"And mine, too," said Mars.

*And mine, – and mine, – and mine," said Mercury, and Ganymede, and the Muses, and the Graces.

"All the candles are out!" said Cupid; "a regular fog. I cannot even see the pavilion: it must be hereabouts, though," said the God to himself. "So, so; I should be at home in my own pavilion, and am tolerably accustomed to stealing about in the dark. There is a step; and here, surely here is the lock. The door opens, but the Cloud enters before me. Juno, Juno," whispered the God of Love, "we are all here. Be contented to escape, like many other innocent dames, with your reputation only under a cloud: it will soon disperse; and lo! The heaven is clearing."

"It must have been the heat of our flambeaux," said Venus; "for see, the mist is vanished; here is the pavilion."

Ganymede ran forward, and dashed open the door, Ixion was alone.

"Seize him!" said Jove.

"Juno is not here," said Mercury, with an air of blended congratulation and disappointment.

"Never mind," said Jove. "Seize him! He kept me waiting for dinner."

"Is this your hospitality, Aegiochus?" exclaimed Ixion, in a tone of bullying innocence. "I shall defend myself."

"Seize him, seize him!" exclaimed Jupiter. "What, do you all falter? Are you afraid of a mortal?"

"And a Thessalian?" added Ganymede.

No one advanced.

"Send for Hercules," said Jove.

"I will fetch him in an instant," said Ganymede.

"I protest," said the King of Thessaly, "against this violation of the most sacred rights."

"The marriage tie?" said Mercury.

"The dinner-hour?" said Jove.

"It is no use talking sentiment to Ixion," said Venus; "all mortals are callous."

"Adventures are to the adventurous," said Minerva.

"Here is Hercules! Here is Hercules!"

"Seize him!" said Jove. "Seize that man."

In vain the mortal struggled with the irresistible demigod.

"Shall I fetch your thunderbolt, Jove?" inquired Ganymede.

"Anything short of eternal punishment is unworthy of a God," answered Jupiter, with great dignity. "Apollo, bring me a wheel of your chariot."

"What shall I do to-morrow morning?" inquired the God of Light.

"Order an eclipse," replied Jove. "Bind the insolent Wretch to the wheel; hurl him to Hades; its motion shall be perpetual."

"What am I to bind him with?" inquired Hercules.

"The girdle of Venus," replied the Thunderer.

"What is all this?" inquired Juno, advancing, pale and agitated.

"Come along; you shall see," answered Jupiter.

"Follow me, follow me."

They all followed the leader, – all the Gods, all the Genii; in the midst, the brawny husband of Hebe bearing Ixion aloft, bound to the fatal wheel. They reached the terrace; they descended the sparkling steps of lapis-lazuli. Hercules held his burden on high, ready, at a nod, to plunge the hapless but presumptuous mortal through space into Hades. The heavenly group surrounded him, and peeped over the starry abyss. It was a fine moral, and demonstrated the usual infelicity that attends unequal connexions.

"Celestial despot!" said Ixion.

In a moment all sounds were hushed, as they listened to the last words of the unrivalled victim. Juno, in despair, leant upon the respective arms of Venus and Minerva.

"Celestial despot!" said Ixion, "I defy the immortal ingenuity of thy cruelty. My memory must be as eternal as thy torture; that will support me."

"The Demon Pope" is a comedic reversal of the traditional Faustian bargain. In this case, an ambitious young man makes a deal with the Devil, but it is the latter who suffers when the letter of the law is enforced. Satan winds up a figure of sympathy as he becomes engulfed in the poisonous politics surrounding the Papal seat.

Richard Garnett (1835 - 1906) was the keeper of Printed Books at the British Museum, but his contributions to literature extended well beyond curation. Garnett wrote fantasies, biographies, poetry, histories, bibliographies and drama. He had a personal interest in astrology, about which he wrote under the pen name of A. G. Trent, but died before he could publish his work on the subject.

THE DEMON POPE

RICHARD GARNETT

Truth fails not, but her outward forms that bear
The longest date do melt like frosty rime.

"So you won't sell me your soul?" said the devil.

"Thank you," replied the student, "I had rather keep it myself, if it's all the same to you."

"But it's not all the same to me. I want it very particularly. Come, I'll be liberal. I said twenty years. You can have thirty."

The student shook his head.

"Forty!"

Another shake.

"Fifty!"

As before.

"Now," said the devil, "I know I'm going to do a foolish thing, but I cannot bear to see a clever, spirited young man throw himself away. I'll make you another kind of offer. We won't have any bargain at present, but I will push you on in the world for the next forty years. This day forty years I come back and ask you for a boon; not your soul, mind, or anything not perfectly in your power to grant. If you give it, we are quits; if not, I fly away with you. What say you to this?"

The student reflected for some minutes. "Agreed," he said at last.

Scarcely had the devil disappeared, which he did instantaneously, ere a messenger reined in his smoking steed at the gate of the University of Cordova (the judicious reader will already have remarked that Lucifer could never have been allowed inside

The Twilight of the Gods. London: T. Fisher Unwin, 1888.

a Christian seat of learning), and, inquiring for the student Gerbert, presented him with the Emperor Otho's nomination to the Abbacy of Bobbio, in consideration, said the document, of his virtue and learning, well-nigh miraculous in one so young. Such messengers were frequent visitors during Gerbert's prosperous career. Abbot, bishop, archbishop, cardinal, he was ultimately enthroned Pope on April 2, 999, and assumed the appellation of Silvester the Second. It was then a general belief that the world would come to an end in the following year, a catastrophe which to many seemed the more imminent from the election of a chief pastor whose celebrity as a theologian, though not inconsiderable, by no means equalled his reputation as a necromancer.

The world, notwithstanding, revolved scatheless through the dreaded twelvemonth, and early in the first year of the eleventh century Gerbert was sitting peacefully in his study, perusing a book of magic. Volumes of algebra, astrology, alchemy, Aristotelian philosophy, and other such light reading filled his bookcase; and on a table stood an improved clock of his invention, next to his introduction of the Arabic numerals his chief legacy to posterity. Suddenly a sound of wings was heard, and Lucifer stood by his side.

"It is a long time," said the fiend, "since I have had the pleasure of seeing you. I have now called to remind you of our little contract, concluded this day forty years."

"You remember," said Silvester, "that you are not to ask anything exceeding my power to perform."

"I have no such intention," said Lucifer. "On the contrary, I am about to solicit a favour which can be bestowed by you alone. You are Pope, I desire that you would make me a Cardinal."

"In the expectation, I presume," returned Gerbert, "of becoming Pope on the next vacancy."

"An expectation," replied Lucifer, "which I may most reasonably entertain, considering my enormous wealth, my proficiency in intrigue, and the present condition of the Sacred College."

"You would doubtless," said Gerbert, "endeavour to subvert the foundations of the Faith, and, by a course of profligacy and licentiousness, render the Holy See odious and contemptible."

"On the contrary," said the fiend, "I would extirpate heresy, and all learning and knowledge as inevitably tending thereunto. I would suffer no man to read but the priest, and confine his reading to his breviary. I would burn your books together with your bones on the first convenient opportunity. I would observe an austere propriety of conduct, and be especially careful not to loosen one rivet in the tremendous yoke I was forging for the minds and consciences of mankind."

"If it be so," said Gerbert, "let's be off!"

"What!" exclaimed Lucifer, "you are willing to accompany me to the infernal regions!"

"Assuredly, rather than be accessory to the burning of Plato and Aristotle, and give place to the darkness against which I have been contending all my life."

"Gerbert," replied the demon, "this is arrant trifling. Know you not that no good man can enter my dominions? That, were such a thing possible, my empire would become intolerable to me, and I should be compelled to abdicate?"

"I do know it," said Gerbert, "and hence I have been able to receive your visit with composure."

"Gerbert," said the devil, with tears in his eyes, "I put it to you – is this fair, is this honest? I undertake to promote your interests in the world; I fulfil my promise abundantly. You obtain through my instrumentality a position to which you could never otherwise have aspired. Often have I had a hand in the election of a Pope, but never before have I contributed to confer the tiara on one eminent for virtue and learning. You profit by my assistance to the full, and now take advantage of an adventitious circumstance to deprive me of my reasonable guerdon. It is my constant experience that the good people are much more slippery than the sinners, and drive much harder bargains."

"Lucifer," answered Gerbert, "I have always sought to treat you as a gentleman, hoping that you would approve yourself such in return. I will not inquire whether it was entirely in harmony with this character to seek to intimidate me into compliance with your demand by threatening me with a penalty which you well knew could not be enforced. I will overlook this little irregularity, and concede even more than you have requested. You have asked to be a Cardinal. I will make you Pope…"

"Ha!" exclaimed Lucifer, and an internal glow suffused his sooty hide, as the light of a fading ember is revived by breathing upon it.

"For twelve hours," continued Gerbert. "At the expiration of that time we will consider the matter further; if, as I anticipate, you are more anxious to divest yourself of the Papal dignity than you were to assume it, I promise to bestow upon you any boon you may ask within my power to grant, and not plainly inconsistent with religion or morals."

"Done!" cried the demon. Gerbert uttered some cabalistic words, and in a moment the apartment held two Pope Silvesters, entirely indistinguishable save by their attire, and the fact that one limped slightly with the left foot.

"You will find the Pontifical apparel in this cupboard," said Gerbert, and, taking his book of magic with him, he retreated through a masked door to a secret chamber. As the door closed behind him he chuckled, and muttered to himself, "Poor old Lucifer! Sold again!"

If Lucifer was sold he did not seem to know it. He approached a large slab of silver which did duty as a mirror, and contemplated his personal appearance with some dissatisfaction.

"I certainly don't look half so well without my horns," he soliloquised, "and I am sure I shall miss my tail most grievously."

A tiara and a train, however, made fair amends for the deficient appendages, and Lucifer now looked every inch a Pope. He was about to call the master of the ceremonies, and summon a consistory, when the door was burst open, and seven cardinals, brandishing poniards, rushed into the room.

"Down with the sorcerer!" they cried, as they seized and gagged him.

"Death to the Saracen!"

"Practises algebra, and other devilish arts!"

"Knows Greek!"

"Talks Arabic!"

"Reads Hebrew!"

"Burn him!"

"Smother him!"

"Let him be deposed by a general council," said a young and inexperienced Cardinal.

"Heaven forbid!" said an old and wary one, *sotto voce*.

Lucifer struggled frantically, but the feeble frame he was doomed to inhabit for the next eleven hours was speedily exhausted. Bound and helpless, he swooned away.

"Brethren," said one of the senior cardinals, "it hath been delivered by the exorcists that a sorcerer or other individual in league with the demon doth usually bear upon his person some visible token of his infernal compact. I propose that we forthwith institute a search for this stigma, the discovery of which may contribute to justify our proceedings in the eyes of the world."

"I heartily approve of our brother Anno's proposition," said another, "rather as we cannot possibly fail to discover such a mark, if, indeed, we desire to find it."

The search was accordingly instituted, and had not proceeded far ere a simultaneous yell from all the seven cardinals indicated that their investigation had brought more to light than they had ventured to expect.

The Holy Father had a cloven foot!

For the next five minutes the Cardinals remained utterly stunned, silent, and stupefied with amazement. As they gradually recovered their faculties it would have become manifest to a nice observer that the Pope had risen very considerably in their good opinion.

"This is an affair requiring very mature deliberation," said one.

"I always feared that we might be proceeding too precipitately," said another.

"It is written, 'the devils believe,'" said a third: "the Holy Father, therefore, is not a heretic at any rate."

"Brethren," said Anno, "this affair, as our brother Benno well remarks, doth indeed call for mature deliberation. I therefore propose that, instead of smothering his Holiness with cushions, as originally contemplated, we immure him for the present in the dungeon adjoining hereunto, and, after spending the night in meditation and prayer, resume the consideration of the business tomorrow morning."

"Informing the officials of the palace," said Benno, "that his Holiness has retired for his devotions, and desires on no account to be disturbed."

"A pious fraud," said Anno, "which not one of the Fathers would for a moment have scrupled to commit."

The Cardinals accordingly lifted the still insensible Lucifer, and bore him carefully, almost tenderly, to the apartment appointed for his detention. Each would fain have lingered in hopes of his recovery, but each felt that the eyes of his six brethren were upon him: and all, therefore, retired simultaneously, each taking a key of the cell.

Lucifer regained consciousness almost immediately afterwards. He had the most confused idea of the circumstances which had involved him in his present scrape, and could only say to himself that if they were the usual concomitants of the Papal dignity, these were by no means to his taste, and he wished he had been made acquainted with them sooner. The dungeon was not only perfectly dark, but horribly cold, and the poor devil in his present form had no latent store of infernal heat to draw upon. His teeth chattered, he shivered in every limb, and felt devoured with hunger and thirst. There is much probability in the assertion of some of his biographers that it was on this occasion that he invented ardent spirits; but, even if he did, the mere conception of a glass of brandy could only increase his sufferings. So the long January night wore wearily on, and Lucifer seemed likely to expire from inanition, when a key turned in the lock, and Cardinal Anno cautiously glided in, bearing a lamp, a loaf, half a cold roast kid, and a bottle of wine.

"I trust," he said, bowing courteously, "that I may be excused any slight breach of etiquette of which I may render myself culpable from the difficulty under which I labour of determining whether, under present circumstances, 'Your Holiness', or 'Your Infernal Majesty' be the form of address most befitting me to employ."

"*Bub-ub-bub-boo*," went Lucifer, who still had the gag in his mouth.

"Heavens!" exclaimed the Cardinal, "I crave your Infernal Holiness's forgiveness. What a lamentable oversight!"

And, relieving Lucifer from his gag and bonds, he set out the refection, upon which the demon fell voraciously.

"Why the devil, if I may so express myself," pursued Anno, "did not your Holiness inform us that you *were* the devil? Not a hand would then have been raised against you. I have myself been seeking all my life for the audience now happily vouchsafed me. Whence this mistrust of your faithful Anno, who has served you so loyally and zealously these many years?"

Lucifer pointed significantly to the gag and fetters.

"I shall never forgive myself," protested the Cardinal, "for the part I have borne in this unfortunate transaction. Next to ministering to your Majesty's bodily necessities, there is nothing I have so much at heart as to express my penitence.

But I entreat your Majesty to remember that I believed myself to be acting in your Majesty's interest by overthrowing a magician who was accustomed to send your Majesty upon errands, and who might at any time enclose you in a box, and cast you into the sea. It is deplorable that your Majesty's most devoted servants should have been thus misled."

"Reasons of State," suggested Lucifer.

"I trust that they no longer operate," said the Cardinal. "However, the Sacred College is now fully possessed of the whole matter: it is therefore unnecessary to pursue this department of the subject further. I would now humbly crave leave to confer with your Majesty, or rather, perhaps, your Holiness, since I am about to speak of spiritual things, on the important and delicate point of your Holiness's successor. I am ignorant how long your Holiness proposes to occupy the Apostolic chair; but of course you are aware that public opinion will not suffer you to hold it for a term exceeding that of the pontificate of Peter. A vacancy, therefore, must one day occur; and I am humbly to represent that the office could not be filled by one more congenial than myself to the present incumbent, or on whom he could more fully rely to carry out in every respect his views and intentions."

And the Cardinal proceeded to detail various circumstances of his past life, which certainly seemed to corroborate his assertion. He had not, however, proceeded far ere he was disturbed by the grating of another key in the lock, and had just time to whisper impressively, "Beware of Benno," ere he dived under a table.

Benno was also provided with a lamp, wine, and cold viands. Warned by the other lamp and the remains of Lucifer's repast that some colleague had been beforehand with him, and not knowing how many more might be in the field, he came briefly to the point as regarded the Papacy, and preferred his claim in much the same manner as Anno. While he was earnestly cautioning Lucifer against this Cardinal as one who could and would cheat the very Devil himself, another key turned in the lock, and Benno escaped under the table, where Anno immediately inserted his finger into his right eye. The little squeal consequent upon this occurrence Lucifer successfully smothered by a fit of coughing.

Cardinal No. 3, a Frenchman, bore a Bayonne ham, and exhibited the same disgust as Benno on seeing himself forestalled. So far as his requests transpired they were moderate, but no one knows where he would have stopped if he had not been scared by the advent of Cardinal No. 4. Up to this time he had only asked for an inexhaustible purse, power to call up the Devil ad libitum, and a ring of invisibility to allow him free access to his mistress, who was unfortunately a married woman.

Cardinal No. 4 chiefly wanted to be put into the way of poisoning Cardinal No. 5; Cardinal No. 5 preferred the same petition as respected Cardinal No. 4.

Cardinal No. 6, an Englishman, demanded the reversion of the Archbishoprics of Canterbury and York, with the faculty of holding them together, and of unlimited non-residence. In the course of his harangue he made use of the phrase non obstantibus, of which Lucifer immediately took a note.

What the seventh Cardinal would have solicited is not known, for he had hardly opened his mouth when the twelfth hour expired, and Lucifer, regaining his vigour with his shape, sent the Prince of the Church spinning to the other end of the room, and split the marble table with a single stroke of his tail. The six crouched and huddling Cardinals cowered revealed to one another, and at the same time enjoyed the spectacle of his Holiness darting through the stone ceiling, which yielded like a film to his passage, and closed up afterwards as if nothing had happened. After the first shock of dismay they unanimously rushed to the door, but found it bolted on the outside. There was no other exit, and no means of giving an alarm. In this emergency the demeanour of the Italian Cardinals set a bright example to their ultramontane colleagues. "*Bisogna pazienzia*," they said, as they shrugged their shoulders. Nothing could exceed the mutual politeness of Cardinals Anno and Benno, unless that of the two who had sought to poison each other. The Frenchman was held to have gravely derogated from good manners by alluding to this circumstance, which had reached his ears while he was under the table: and the Englishman swore so outrageously at the plight in which he found himself that the Italians then and there silently registered a vow that none of his nation should ever be Pope, a maxim which, with one exception, has been observed to this day.

Lucifer, meanwhile, had repaired to Silvester, whom he found arrayed in all the insignia of his dignity; of which, as he remarked, he thought his visitor had probably had enough.

"I should think so indeed," replied Lucifer. "But at the same time I feel myself fully repaid for all I have undergone by the assurance of the loyalty of my friends and admirers, and the conviction that it is needless for me to devote any considerable amount of personal attention to ecclesiastical affairs. I now claim the promised boon, which it will be in no way inconsistent with thy functions to grant, seeing that it is a work of mercy. I demand that the Cardinals be released, and that their conspiracy against thee, by which I alone suffered, be buried in oblivion."

"I hoped you would carry them all off," said Gerbert, with an expression of disappointment.

"Thank you," said the Devil. "It is more to my interest to leave them where they are."

So the dungeon-door was unbolted, and the Cardinals came forth, sheepish and crestfallen. If, after all, they did less mischief than Lucifer had expected from them, the cause was their entire bewilderment by what had passed, and their utter inability to penetrate the policy of Gerbert, who henceforth devoted himself even with ostentation to good works. They could never quite satisfy themselves whether they were speaking to the Pope or to the Devil, and when under the latter impression habitually emitted propositions which Gerbert justly stigmatised as rash, temerarious, and scandalous. They plagued him with allusions to certain matters mentioned in their interviews with Lucifer, with which they naturally but erroneously supposed him to be conversant, and worried him by continual nods and titterings as they glanced at his nether extremities. To abolish this nuisance, and at the same time silence sundry unpleasant rumours which had somehow got abroad, Gerbert devised the ceremony of kissing the Pope's feet, which, in a grievously mutilated form, endures to this day. The stupefaction of the Cardinals on discovering that the Holy Father had lost his hoof surpasses all description, and they went to their graves without having obtained the least insight into the mystery.

❧STORIES❧

Francis Bret Harte (1836 - 1902) was born in Albany, New York and died in Camberley, England, but will forever be synonymous with California.

Although Harte only lived in California between 1853 and 1870, those years informed his writing for the rest of his life. "I do not pretend to say that many of my characters existed exactly as they are described," he wrote, "but I believe there is not one of them that did not have a real human being as a suggestion and a starting-point."

Harte's popularity peaked in 1870s. As his fortunes fell, he moved overseas and found that he was treated more kindly by British critics, who were less judgemental about the veracity (and repetitiveness) of his Western scenes.

Harte remains one of the defining writers of the American "local-color" movement. As one biographer wrote, Harte "made himself a historical literary figure by the utilization of only half his talents".

"Outcasts" contains stories within stories. The characters begin the tale as stereotypes, but as they travel, Harte makes it increasingly clear that they are each more complex than their initial characterisations would suggest.

The small lives and unheroic travels of the little band of outcasts stands in stark contrast to the epic journey in their reading material, Pope's Iliad. The final line of the story links the gambler, John Oakhurst, "the strongest and the weakest" of the outcasts, to Achilles, the character who most fascinates him. Oakhurst emulates the Greek hero and defies the gods by taking his fate into his own hands.

THE OUTCASTS OF POKER FLAT

BRET HARTE

As Mr. John Oakhurst, gambler, stepped into the main street of Poker Flat on the morning of the twenty-third of November, 1850, he was conscious of a change in its moral atmosphere since the preceding night. Two or three men, conversing earnestly together, ceased as he approached, and exchanged significant glances. There was a Sabbath lull in the air which, in a settlement unused to Sabbath influences, looked ominous.

Mr. Oakhurst's calm, handsome face betrayed small concern in these indications. Whether he was conscious of any predisposing cause was another question. "I reckon they're after somebody," he reflected; "likely it's me." He returned to his pocket the handkerchief with which he had been whipping away the red dust of Poker Flat from his neat boots, and quietly discharged his mind of any further conjecture.

In point of fact, Poker Flat was "after somebody". It had lately suffered the loss of several thousand dollars, two valuable horses, and a prominent citizen. It was experiencing a spasm of virtuous reaction, quite as lawless and ungovernable as any of the acts that had provoked it. A secret committee had determined to rid the town of all improper persons. This was done permanently in regard of two men who were then hanging from the boughs of a sycamore in the gulch, and temporarily in the banishment of certain other objectionable characters. I regret to say that some of these were ladies. It is but due to the sex, however, to state that their impropriety was professional, and it was only in such easily established standards of evil that Poker Flat ventured to sit in judgment.

Overland Monthly. January 1869.

Mr. Oakhurst was right in supposing that he was included in this category. A few of the committee had urged hanging him as a possible example, and a sure method of reimbursing themselves from his pockets of the sums he had won from them. "It's agin justice," said Jim Wheeler, "to let this yer young man from Roaring Camp – an entire stranger – carry away our money." But a crude sentiment of equity residing in the breasts of those who had been fortunate enough to win from Mr. Oakhurst overruled this narrower local prejudice.

Mr. Oakhurst received his sentence with philosophic calmness, none the less coolly that he was aware of the hesitation of his judges. He was too much of a gambler not to accept Fate. With him life was at best an uncertain game, and he recognized the usual percentage in favor of the dealer.

A body of armed men accompanied the deported wickedness of Poker Flat to the outskirts of the settlement. Besides Mr. Oakhurst, who was known to be a coolly desperate man, and for whose intimidation the armed escort was intended, the expatriated party consisted of a young woman familiarly known as the "Duchess"; another, who had won the title of "Mother Shipton"; and "Uncle Billy", a suspected sluice-robber and confirmed drunkard. The cavalcade provoked no comments from the spectators, nor was any word uttered by the escort. Only, when the gulch which marked the uttermost limit of Poker Flat was reached, the leader spoke briefly and to the point. The exiles were forbidden to return at the peril of their lives.

As the escort disappeared, their pent-up feelings found vent in a few hysterical tears from the Duchess, some bad language from Mother Shipton, and a Parthian volley of expletives from Uncle Billy. The philosophic Oakhurst alone remained silent. He listened calmly to Mother Shipton's desire to cut somebody's heart out, to the repeated statements of the Duchess that she would die in the road, and to the alarming oaths that seemed to be bumped out of Uncle Billy as he rode forward. With the easy good humor characteristic of his class, he insisted upon exchanging his own riding horse, "Five Spot", for the sorry mule which the Duchess rode. But even this act did not draw the party into any closer sympathy. The young woman readjusted her somewhat draggled plumes with a feeble, faded coquetry; Mother Shipton eyed the possessor of "Five Spot" with malevolence, and Uncle Billy included the whole party in one sweeping anathema.

The road to Sandy Bar – a camp that, not having as yet experienced the regenerating influences of Poker Flat, consequently seemed to offer some invitation to the emigrants – lay over a steep mountain range. It was distant a day's severe travel. In that advanced season, the party soon passed out of the moist, temperate regions of the foothills into the dry, cold, bracing air of the Sierras. The trail was narrow and difficult. At noon the Duchess, rolling out of her saddle upon the ground, declared her intention of going no farther, and the party halted.

The spot was singularly wild and impressive. A wooded amphitheater, surrounded on three sides by precipitous cliffs of naked granite, sloped gently toward the crest of another precipice that overlooked the valley. It was, undoubtedly, the most suitable spot for a camp, had camping been advisable. But Mr. Oakhurst knew that scarcely half the journey to Sandy Bar was accomplished, and the party were not equipped or provisioned for delay. This fact he pointed out to his companions curtly, with a philosophic commentary on the folly of "throwing up their hand before the game was played out". But they were furnished with liquor, which in this emergency stood them in place of food, fuel, rest, and prescience. In spite of his remonstrances, it was not long before they were more or less under its influence. Uncle Billy passed rapidly from a bellicose state into one of stupor, the Duchess became maudlin, and Mother Shipton snored. Mr. Oakhurst alone remained erect, leaning against a rock, calmly surveying them.

Mr. Oakhurst did not drink. It interfered with a profession which required coolness, impassiveness, and presence of mind, and, in his own language, he "couldn't afford it". As he gazed at his recumbent fellow exiles, the loneliness begotten of his pariah trade, his habits of life, his very vices, for the first time seriously oppressed him. He bestirred himself in dusting his black clothes, washing his hands and face, and other acts characteristic of his studiously neat habits, and for a moment forgot his annoyance. The thought of deserting his weaker and more pitiable companions never perhaps occurred to him. Yet he could not help feeling the want of that excitement which, singularly enough, was most conducive to that calm equanimity for which he was notorious. He looked at the gloomy walls that rose a thousand feet sheer above the circling pines around him; at the sky, ominously clouded; at the valley below, already deepening into shadow. And, doing so, suddenly he heard his own name called.

A horseman slowly ascended the trail. In the fresh, open face of the newcomer Mr. Oakhurst recognized Tom Simson, otherwise known as the "Innocent" of Sandy Bar. He had met him some months before over a "little game", and had, with perfect equanimity, won the entire fortune – amounting to some forty dollars – of that guileless youth. After the game was finished, Mr. Oakhurst drew the youthful speculator behind the door and thus addressed him: "Tommy, you're a good little man, but you can't gamble worth a cent. Don't try it over again." He then handed him his money back, pushed him gently from the room, and so made a devoted slave of Tom Simson.

There was a remembrance of this in his boyish and enthusiastic greeting of Mr. Oakhurst. He had started, he said, to go to Poker Flat to seek his fortune. "Alone?" No, not exactly alone; in fact (a giggle), he had run away with Piney Woods. Didn't Mr. Oakhurst remember Piney? She that used to wait on the table at the Temperance House? They had been engaged a long time, but old Jake Woods had objected, and so they had run away, and were going to Poker Flat to be married, and here they were. And they were tired out, and how lucky it was they had found a place to camp and company. All this the Innocent delivered rapidly, while Piney, a stout, comely damsel of fifteen, emerged from behind the pine tree, where she had been blushing unseen, and rode to the side of her lover.

Mr. Oakhurst seldom troubled himself with sentiment, still less with propriety; but he had a vague idea that the situation was not fortunate. He retained, however, his presence of mind sufficiently to kick Uncle Billy, who was about to say something, and Uncle Billy was sober enough to recognize in Mr. Oakhurst's kick a superior power that would not bear trifling. He then endeavored to dissuade Tom Simson from delaying further, but in vain. He even pointed out the fact that there was no provision, nor means of making a camp. But, unluckily, the Innocent met this objection by assuring the party that he was provided with an extra mule loaded with provisions and by the discovery of a rude attempt at a log house near the trail. "Piney can stay with Mrs. Oakhurst," said the Innocent, pointing to the Duchess, "and I can shift for myself."

Nothing but Mr. Oakhurst's admonishing foot saved Uncle Billy from bursting into a roar of laughter. As it was, he felt compelled to retire up the canyon until he could recover his gravity. There he confided the joke to the tall pine trees, with

*You could scarcely have told from the equal peace that
dwelt upon them which was she that had sinned*

many slaps of his leg, contortions of his face, and the usual profanity. But when he returned to the party, he found them seated by a fire – for the air had grown strangely chill and the sky overcast – in apparently amicable conversation. Piney was actually talking in an impulsive, girlish fashion to the Duchess, who was listening with an interest and animation she had not shown for many days. The Innocent was holding forth, apparently with equal effect, to Mr. Oakhurst and Mother Shipton, who was actually relaxing into amiability. "Is this yer a damned picnic?" said Uncle Billy with inward scorn as he surveyed the sylvan group, the glancing firelight, and the tethered animals in the foreground. Suddenly an idea mingled with the alcoholic fumes that disturbed his brain. It was apparently of a jocular nature, for he felt impelled to slap his leg again and cram his fist into his mouth.

As the shadows crept slowly up the mountain, a slight breeze rocked the tops of the pine trees, and moaned through their long and gloomy aisles. The ruined cabin, patched and covered with pine boughs, was set apart for the ladies. As the lovers parted, they unaffectedly exchanged a kiss, so honest and sincere that it might have been heard above the swaying pines. The frail Duchess and the malevolent Mother Shipton were probably too stunned to remark upon this last evidence of simplicity, and so turned without a word to the hut. The fire was replenished, the men lay down before the door, and in a few minutes were asleep.

Mr. Oakhurst was a light sleeper. Toward morning he awoke benumbed and cold. As he stirred the dying fire, the wind, which was now blowing strongly, brought to his cheek that which caused the blood to leave it – snow!

He started to his feet with the intention of awakening the sleepers, for there was no time to lose. But turning to where Uncle Billy had been lying, he found him gone. A suspicion leaped to his brain and a curse to his lips. He ran to the spot where the mules had been tethered; they were no longer there. The tracks were already rapidly disappearing in the snow.

The momentary excitement brought Mr. Oakhurst back to the fire with his usual calm. He did not waken the sleepers. The Innocent slumbered peacefully, with a smile on his good-humored, freckled face; the virgin Piney slept beside her frailer sisters as sweetly as though attended by celestial guardians; and Mr. Oakhurst, drawing his blanket over his shoulders, stroked his mustaches and waited for the dawn. It came slowly in a whirling mist of snowflakes that dazzled and confused the eye. What could be seen of the landscape appeared magically changed. He looked over the valley, and summed up the present and future in two words – "snowed in!"

A careful inventory of the provisions, which, fortunately for the party, had been stored within the hut and so escaped the felonious fingers of Uncle Billy, disclosed the fact that with care and prudence they might last ten days longer. "That is," said Mr. Oakhurst, sotto voce to the Innocent, "if you're willing to board us. If you ain't – and perhaps you'd better not – you can wait till Uncle Billy gets back with provisions." For some occult reason, Mr. Oakhurst could not bring himself to disclose Uncle Billy's rascality, and so offered the hypothesis that he had wandered from the camp and had accidentally stampeded the animals. He dropped a warning to the Duchess and Mother Shipton, who of course knew the facts of their associate's defection. "They'll find out the truth about us all when they find out anything," he added, significantly, "and there's no good frightening them now."

Tom Simson not only put all his worldly store at the disposal of Mr. Oakhurst, but seemed to enjoy the prospect of their enforced seclusion. "We'll have a good camp for a week, and then the snow'll melt, and we'll all go back together." The cheerful gaiety of the young man, and Mr. Oakhurst's calm, infected the others. The Innocent with the aid of pine boughs extemporized a thatch for the roofless cabin, and the Duchess directed Piney in the rearrangement of the interior with a taste and tact that opened the blue eyes of that provincial maiden to their fullest extent. "I reckon now you're used to fine things at Poker Flat," said Piney. The Duchess turned away sharply to conceal something that reddened her cheeks through its professional tint, and Mother Shipton requested Piney not to "chatter". But when Mr. Oakhurst returned from a weary search for the trail, he heard the sound of happy laughter echoed from the rocks. He stopped in some alarm, and his thoughts first naturally reverted to the whisky, which he had prudently cached. "And yet it don't somehow sound like whisky," said the gambler. It was not until he caught sight of the blazing fire through the still-blinding storm and the group around it that he settled to the conviction that it was "square fun".

Whether Mr. Oakhurst had cached his cards with the whisky as something debarred the free access of the community, I cannot say. It was certain that, in Mother Shipton's words, he "didn't say cards once" during that evening. Haply the time was beguiled by an accordion, produced somewhat ostentatiously by Tom Simson from his pack. Notwithstanding some difficulties attending the manipulation of this instrument, Piney Woods managed to pluck several reluctant melodies from its keys, to an accompaniment by the Innocent on a pair of bone castanets. But the crowning festivity of the evening was reached in a rude camp-meeting hymn, which the lovers, joining hands, sang with great earnestness and vociferation. I fear that a certain defiant tone and Covenanter's swing to its chorus, rather than any devotional quality, caused it speedily to infect the others, who at last joined in the refrain:

> *"I'm proud to live in the service of the Lord,*
> *And I'm bound to die in His army."*

The pines rocked, the storm eddied and whirled above the miserable group, and the flames of their altar leaped heavenward as if in token of the vow.

At midnight the storm abated, the rolling clouds parted, and the stars glittered keenly above the sleeping camp. Mr. Oakhurst, whose professional habits had enabled him to live on the smallest possible amount of sleep, in dividing the watch with Tom Simson somehow managed to take upon himself the greater part of that duty. He excused himself to the Innocent by saying that he had "often been a week without sleep". "Doing what?" asked Tom. "Poker!" replied Oakhurst, sententiously; "when a man gets a streak of luck, – n' luck – he don't get tired. The luck gives in first. Luck," continued the gambler, reflectively, "is a mighty queer thing. All you know about it for certain is that it's bound to change. And it's finding out when it's going to change that makes you. We've had a streak of bad luck since we left Poker Flat – you come along, and slap you get into it, too. If you can hold your cards right along you're all right. For," added the gambler, with cheerful irrelevance,

> *"'I'm proud to live in the service of the Lord,*
> *And I'm bound to die in His army.'"*

The third day came, and the sun, looking through the white-curtained valley, saw the outcasts divide their slowly decreasing store of provisions for the morning meal. It was one of the peculiarities of that mountain climate that its rays diffused a kindly warmth over the wintry landscape, as if in regretful commiseration of the past. But it revealed drift on drift of snow piled high around the hut – a hopeless, uncharted, trackless sea of white lying below the rocky shores to which the castaways still clung. Through the marvelously clear air the smoke of the pastoral village of Poker Flat rose miles away. Mother Shipton saw it, and from a remote pinnacle of her rocky fastness hurled in that direction a final malediction. It was her last vituperative attempt, and perhaps for that reason was invested with a certain degree of sublimity. It did her good, she privately informed the Duchess. "Just you go out there and cuss, and see." She then set herself to the task of amusing "the child", as she and the Duchess were pleased to call Piney. Piney was no chicken, but it was a soothing and original theory of the pair thus to account for the fact that she didn't swear and wasn't improper.

When night crept up again through the gorges, the reedy notes of the accordion rose and fell in fitful spasms and long-drawn gasps by the flickering campfire. But music failed to fill entirely the aching void left by insufficient food, and a new diversion was proposed by Piney – storytelling. Neither Mr. Oakhurst nor his female companions caring to relate their personal experiences, this plan would have failed too but for the Innocent. Some months before he had chanced upon a stray copy of Mr. Pope's ingenious translation of the Iliad. He now proposed to narrate the principal incidents of that poem – having thoroughly mastered the argument and fairly forgotten the words – in the current vernacular of Sandy Bar. And so for the rest of that night the Homeric demigods again walked the earth. Trojan bully and wily Greek wrestled in the winds, and the great pines in the canyon seemed to bow to the wrath of the son of Peleus. Mr. Oakhurst listened with quiet satisfaction. Most especially was he interested in the fate of "Ash-heels", as the Innocent persisted in denominating the "swift-footed Achilles".

So with small food and much of Homer and the accordion, a week passed over the heads of the outcasts. The sun again forsook them, and again from leaden skies the snowflakes were sifted over the land. Day by day closer around them drew the snowy circle, until at last they looked from their prison over drifted walls of dazzling white that towered twenty feet above their heads. It became more and more difficult to replenish their fires, even from the fallen trees beside them, now half-hidden in the drifts. And yet no one complained. The lovers turned from the dreary prospect and looked into each other's eyes, and were happy. Mr. Oakhurst settled himself coolly to the losing game before him. The Duchess, more cheerful than she had been, assumed the care of Piney. Only Mother Shipton – once the strongest of the party – seemed to sicken and fade. At midnight on the tenth day she called Oakhurst to her side.

"I'm going," she said, in a voice of querulous weakness, "but don't say anything about it. Don't waken the kids. Take the bundle from under my head and open it." Mr. Oakhurst did so. It contained Mother Shipton's rations for the last week, untouched. "Give 'em to the child," she said, pointing to the sleeping Piney.

"You've starved yourself," said the gambler.

"That's what they call it," said the woman, querulously, as she lay down again and, turning her face to the wall, passed quietly away.

The accordion and the bones were put aside that day, and Homer was forgotten. When the body of Mother Shipton had been committed to the snow, Mr. Oakhurst took the Innocent aside, and showed him a pair of snowshoes, which he had fashioned from the old pack saddle. "There's one chance in a hundred to save her yet," he said, pointing to Piney; "but it's there," he added, pointing toward Poker Flat. "If you can reach there in two days she's safe."

"And you?" asked Tom Simson.

"I'll stay here," was the curt reply.

The lovers parted with a long embrace. "You are not going, too?" said the Duchess as she saw Mr. Oakhurst apparently waiting to accompany him. "As far as the canyon," he replied. He turned suddenly, and kissed the Duchess, leaving her pallid face aflame and her trembling limbs rigid with amazement.

Night came, but not Mr. Oakhurst. It brought the storm again and the whirling snow. Then the Duchess, feeding the fire, found that someone had quietly piled beside the hut enough fuel to last a few days longer. The tears rose to her eyes, but she hid them from Piney.

The women slept but little. In the morning, looking into each other's faces, they read their fate. Neither spoke; but Piney, accepting the position of the stronger, drew near and placed her arm around the Duchess's waist. They kept this attitude for the rest of the day. That night the storm reached its greatest fury, and, rending asunder the protecting pines, invaded the very hut.

Toward morning they found themselves unable to feed the fire, which gradually died away. As the embers slowly blackened, the Duchess crept closer to Piney, and broke the silence of many hours: "Piney, can you pray?"

"No, dear," said Piney, simply. The Duchess, without knowing exactly why, felt relieved, and, putting her head upon Piney's shoulder, spoke no more. And so reclining, the younger and purer pillowing the head of her soiled sister upon her virgin breast, they fell asleep.

The wind lulled as if it feared to waken them. Feathery drifts of snow, shaken from the long pine boughs, flew like white-winged birds, and settled about them as they slept. The moon through the rifted clouds looked down upon what had been the camp. But all human stain, all trace of earthly travail, was hidden beneath the spotless mantle mercifully flung from above.

They slept all that day and the next, nor did they waken when voices and footsteps broke the silence of the camp. And when pitying fingers brushed the snow from their wan faces, you could scarcely have told from the equal peace that dwelt upon them which was she that had sinned. Even the law of Poker Flat recognized this, and turned away, leaving them still locked in each other's arms.

But at the head of the gulch, on one of the largest pine trees, they found the deuce of clubs pinned to the bark with a bowie knife. It bore the following, written in pencil, in a firm hand:

Beneath this tree
lies the body
of John Oakhurst,
who struck a streak of bad luck
on the 23rd of November, 1850
and
handed in his checks
on the 7th December, 1850

And pulseless and cold, with a Derringer by his side and a bullet in his heart, though still calm as in life, beneath the snow lay he who was at once the strongest and yet the weakest of the outcasts of Poker Flat.

Born in Massachusetts, William Cheney (1848 - 1925) made his first trip to California in 1867. He returned in 1875 never to leave again. Cheney served his new state well – first as an elected judge, then as a member of the State Senate. In 1884, he was elected to the Superior Court of Los Angeles County, where he oversaw all his jursidiction's criminal cases for six years.

Cheney believed that "to be a successful counselor to others, a man must know everything about some things and something about every thing." As well as law and literature, he also tried his hand at science, sculpture, painting and music (Cheney had a pipe organ installed in his own home). A Fellow of the Academy of Sciences, he published Can We Be Sure of Mortality? (1910), a rebuttal to the German naturalist Ernst Haeckel's The Riddle of the Universe (1901).

In this humorous story, Cheney tips his hat to the romantic image of California painted by Bret Harte. By 1885, when this story was first published, Bret Harte had been gone from California for more than fifteen years. As noted previously, however, Harte had continued to set the bulk of his literary work there until his death. Cheney's tale serves as a warning (albeit a friendly one) to those who would take any story too seriously.

MIRANDA HIGGINS

WILLIAM ATWELL CHENEY

He was a drummer; a moon-faced, big-eyed, round-cheeked, innocent drummer. He had been in California but a short time, and had been forwarded by his firm to secure the trade of the then booming town of Josie.

He drove a span of greys attached to a light spring wagon, loaded down with samples of dress goods, dry goods and small wares. He was innocent, I say, because this was his first experiment in that line of business, and his saucer eyes had not yet become contracted and steeled by unflinchingly gazing in the clear depths of honest purchasers; his peach-blow cheeks were not yet browned by the sun and conscientious resistance to insinuating bargain-drivers.

He sat back on his seat, permitting the lines to lie loosely on his knees, while he read a volume of Bret Harte's stories of California life. "Well, here I am at last," he said to himself, "among the very scenes he pictures; breathing the very mountain air once inhaled by Tennessee's partner; rattling over the very road that may have been trodden by Jim and Kentuck. How strange it all seems! To think that I, Samuel Kingston, am here among the genuine Californians, where I can see M'liss, and the rest of his heroines and heroes. Nobody ever opened up the pure, untainted streams of human life as did Bret Harte. Simplicity, honesty, honor and classic ignorance combined with rugged beauty and unadorned sweetness must be, as he represents them, found in their purest forms among the denizens of the grand forests, and the

Short Stories by California Authors. San Francisco: Golden Era, 1885.

ah – ah – grand canyons. I am wearied of the stilted formalities of city life; I am tired of the assuming beauty of civilized females. Sam, my boy – you have struck it! If you can find one of the simple, pure children of nature, with a generous heart, a self-sacrificing nature, and, of course, of the female sex, marry her, and be happy. I'll do it! I will search for one of the untamed savages, and she shall share my lot as certainly as my name is Samuel Kingston. How we will astonish the natives at Sacramento! Bret Harte was right. Here is the place to find the feminine soul untainted and pure as the leaping waters of the mountains. Get up, you lazy brutes!"

Sam jogged along, leaving first the fig and nectarine, then the oak trees behind him as he climbed higher and higher toward the divide which overlooked Bobtail Canyon. His horses squirmed up the dusty, stony grade, puffing and blowing, as they worked from side to side of the ever-ascending gimlet. Sam, deeply engaged in following the equally winding careers of Bret Harte's characters, looked up only now and then and bent searching glances to the roadside. His whole being was on the alert for the appearance of some of these peculiar individuals.

Bret Harte's work was his guide-book; it was his Murray. He was fond of Dickens, and had he visited London, he would have taken Pickwick as his model of an English gentleman, Sam's notions of Californians, simon-pure Californians, were not derived from California or Montgomery street, or from the business men of Sacramento. They were but hangers-on, but excrescences. Genuine Californians, according to his views, as derived from his constant perusal of Bret Harte, were to be found only among the everlasting mountains, in the gulches, canyons, and among the sluice boxes of the mines.

Sam reached the top of the divide, and, as his greys spread themselves loosely in the harness, swished their tails and tossed their beads, delightedly at the prospect of the downward trot, his eyes caught a glimpse of the gulch below.

There they are, just as his imagination had pictured them! Rambling, straggling streets tumbled up, jumbled up, rickety houses. Windows of glass and wood and potato sacks. (Chimneys of stone, mud-plastered wood, kerosene cans and fire-proof, but rusty and contradictory, stove pipe. "Bobtail Canyon" said Sam to himself, "Harte never wrote about it that I remember, but how unique it looks, how breezy, how picturesquely suggestive, the name! What legends must cling around such a distinctively characteristic California name as that."

The team of greys drove downward and around until, after rattling over a decidedly nervous bridge which crossed the creek, they trotted gaily in among the houses of Bobtail Canyon. A sign attracted Sam's attention. "Miners' Roost," it said in big black letters on a sign-board which wearily rested one end upon the ground and hung convulsively with the other to a rusty hook on the equally wearied porch which leaned against the bosom of a disgusted looking tavern that stared at Sam with wide open doors and windows. Not a soul was to be seen, the place was as silent as a grave-yard at full moon. Sam, somewhat dazed, got out of his wagon and pounded vigorously upon the front door, which stood invitingly open, with the butt of his whip.

"Hello! Hello the house!" he bawled. A cloud of dust floated through the corral rapidly, and a figure vaulted with a handspring over the fence.

"Hello y'eelf an whart's the matter?" said the figure as it came right end uppermost in front of Sam in the shape of a girl about eighteen years old. She was tow-headed, freckled-faced, pug-nosed and blue-eyed. Her feet were bare as well as a lengthy portion of limb visible above them, bare that is of artificial covering, though plentifully frescoed with dust. She wore a grimy calico dress and was otherwise unadorned.

"M'liss?" said Sam slowly but insinuatingly, looking at the lady in amazement.

"Say it agin an' say it louder, stranger," said the girl placing her hands on her hips.

"How artistically simple!" muttered Sam. "Isn't your name M'liss?"

"No 'tain't! my name's Randy, whart's your'n?"

"Mine?" answered Sam. "O mine is Sam Kingston. But tell me, isn't this a hotel?"

"Twar onct, but tain't now."

"Can't I put up here to-night?" asked Sam; "I have come a long way to-day."

"Reckon so. Whare yer doin' up hyer anyhow? Say you, Long Jim an you Snakey Jake c'm yer an' see te ther horses. Recken ye'll hevter put up't our cabin if yer stay hyer all night. C'm long."

She led the way around the remains of the old tavern to a cabin, rather more substantial in the rear, and introduced Sana to the interior without further ado. The furnishings were rough but neat and clean" enough and Sam was soon in the wakeful dreams of "Hartey" romance. Here was everything as described. He rambled around through the little straggling streets and made mental note. Here was a bar room, the bar indented with a multitude of arcs of circles where whisky Bill and Snorting Jerry had slammed their glasses down in emphatic argument, and there in the ceiling were bullet holes where some Black Daisy or One-Eyed Tom had applauded the emphasis. Kingston was in ecstasy. It seemed to him that he had but to touch a hidden spring somewhere, and the slouch hats, long boots, revolver belts, clinking glasses and historic dog fights and human conflicts, would all put in an appearance and begin their operations. It was a group in marble, it needed but life to make it a romantic feast. "Anyhow," said Sam, "I have found the girl. She is a thorough-bred. Such eyes, such freedom from conventionality, I never saw. What a heroine she would make for Harte. I'll capture her if I can."

He labored hard for the three days he stayed, during which his firm suffered from his negligence, and the siege he laid to her heart was something tremendous. He opened treasured samples of Smith, Brown & Co., and gave her a choice of knickknacks. It was a heavenly joy to him to hear her little screams of delight as she tried on the buttoned boots and displayed one trim booted ankle in contrast to its begrimmed comrade. "Keep them, Miranda," he said with the air of a prince.

"Shore yer ain't jokin', stranger?" she whispered sliding up to his side.

"Now could I joke with such a creature of nature as you are?" said Sam. "But you must call me Sammie."

"Call yer Sammie? Course I'll call yer anything for them boots. Yer a snakin' good feller," she whispered again as she threw her brown arms around Sam's neck and implanted a resounding kiss on his cheek, much like in sound to the pull of a horse's hoof from an adobe road. A quiver of delighted conquest went all over Sam. He drew her frowsy head to his manly bosom and said, "Oh Randy, did you ever love?"

"No," whispered she.

"Don't you love me just a little?" plaintively whined Sam.

"Yer bet," she replied anchoring her head on his shoulder.

"Will you be mine?" asked Sam trembling with apprehension.

"Your'n? Yer mean will I tie to you?"

"Yes," said Sam, "marry me."

"Ya-a-as," answered Mirande dropping her plump form into Sam's arms.

"Your father will not object, will he?" inquired Sam.

"My ole man? Wal now yer whispering. Te! he! He'll be something doggoned new ef he does. Count me in as your'n, Sammie."

Samuel Kingston, Esq, drummer, drove off the next morning to hasten through the business of his firm at Josie, which he accomplished in three or four days and returned to Bobtail Canyon.

Agreeably to the arrangements privately and previously made, he took Miranda Higgins and drove to the nearest Justice of the Peace at the county seat and was duly made a happy man in the possession of the untamed savage. He persisted in insanely calling her M'liss, much to the disgust of Miranda Kingston.

Sam was on the constant outlook for the outburst, which he expected, of some remarkable self-sacrificing deed on Miranda's part, and even meditated deliberately upon getting himself into some serious physical danger just for the sake of arousing the mountain spunk of his heroine, so that he might relate the wonderful prowess of this piece of unpolished nature to his friends at Sacramento.

The opportunity came, but not exactly as laid down in Sam's programme. They had started on the grade to the valley. Miranda was profusely decorated in brilliant calico and gay streaming ribbons, and perched her buttoned shoes upon the dash of the wagon, where they were ever present for her constant admiration. Sam complacently smiled and delighted in the happiness of having given this unsophisticated lady an opportunity to breathe the first breath of worldly fashion.

They were winding around up the grade when suddenly the sound of clattering hoofs and rattling wheels was borne on the breeze down the mountain to them. Sam looked up quickly, and up the grade two turns of the road from him he caught a momentary glimpse of a span of wild eyed horses and a buggy tearing down in a cloud of dust. In a minute they would be at the next turn and be upon him. The grade was wide enough for one wagon only. On one side a deep and precipitous wall fell away for two hundred feet; on the other a sheer precipice rose fifty more. There was but one crevice in the upper wall where a foothold could be had.

Miranda clinched her teeth, turned pale, and screaming, "a runaway!" climbed down from the wagon.

"Ah!" thought Sam, in the flash of a moment. "She is a heroine; she goes to throw herself upon the brutes and stay their course."

Miranda did nothing of the sort. She made 2:15 time for that crevice in the upper wall, and perching herself safely there, shouted as the cloud of dust drew nearer: "Shoot! Yer blamed fool, why don't yer shoot?"

"Sure enough," thought Sam, and as the wild team came round the bend he blazed away with his revolver. One horse fell, and in the twinkling of an eye a $400 span and a buggy were crashing down the precipice below. Miranda climbed down.

"Nothing like such presence of mind, M'liss, Miranda, I mean," he remarked, as she seated herself in the wagon once more.

"Ain't nothin' like cold lead an' heaven' a man with yer at sich times," replied Miranda, with a grin.

They reached Sacramento, and Sam, to give his wife an eye-opener on the wide, bad world, away from the pure atmosphere of the mountains, gave a reception to his friends at the Golden Eagle. They came in claw hammers and white kids. Drummers every one of them.

"Miranda is stunning," thought Sam. She wore a blue silk, and twined orange blossoms ornamented her head. The wild, sweet picturesqueness of bare and frescoed feet and ankles was gone; the untamed expression of the wide-open eyes was lost under the banged, flaming hair; the freckles, fashionable as they were, glared angrily in—contrast to the blue dress. Sam swept her regally into the center of the room and introduced her: "This is my mountain heroine, boys. She is a specimen of pure and undefiled nature. She's a mountain gem."

"Kingston," whispered a brazen-faced drummer to him on the sly, "you've done it now, you know."

"I know it," answered Sam, "I always intended to get one of her stamp. I am sick of cultured loveliness, and I found her, a wild rose, blossoming amid the rubbish of one of the most romantic mining camps you ever saw."

That night, when the guests had all retired, and while Miranda was unbuttoning her boots, she glanced up at Sara and said: "Say, ain't it about time to let up on this hyer mountain gem business?"

"Why, what do you mean, Randy" asked Sam, aghast. I am proud of your mountain origin; you are like a fresh breeze on the sandy desert."

"I'm glad yer think so," muttered Bandy, with a mouthful of pins, "only 'taint quite the kerrect 'thing."

"Oh, that's all right," replied Kingston.

"The people here appreciate that sort of a thing. You'll be quite a heroine."

"'S'nice fer yer to say so, Sammie, 'cause yer see I'm among strangers like. Dad'n I only kem out from Missouri, from the old Massysip, three weeks ago."

"We are what *we are because of* where *we are."*
  – William Atwell Cheney, Can We Be Sure of Mortality? (1910)

George Gissing (1857 - 1903) was born in Yorkshire. A promising student, his academic career came to an abrupt finish when he fell in love with a young prostitute, Marianne Helen Harrison (known as "Nell" — an unfortunate coincidence, given his life-long love for the works of Charles Dickens).

Gissing began stealing from other students, hoping to keep Nell off the streets, but he was caught and expelled. After spending a year abroad in Chicago, Gissing returned to Britain and found work as a teacher and a writer.

His first novel, Workers of the Dawn (1882) was self-published and drew heavily from his own relationship with Nell, now his wife. For the next twenty years, Gissing was a whirlwind of activity: travelling, writing and engaging in scandalous affairs of the heart. His literary output included a body of short stories, almost two dozen novels (more than one for each year as a professional writer) and several critical appreciations of Dickens.

The titular character of "Christopherson", an elderly bibliophile of faded glory, carries himself with a distinctly Dickensian air. The narrator, who is conveniently prying (and surprisingly judgemental), is at first amused, then horrified by the extent of Christopherson's obsession with books. Eventually, Christopherson is asked to sacrifice the passion that defines him. In the reader, Gissing evokes the sympathy that his narrator lacks.

Morley Roberts' The Private Life of Henry Maitland (1912) was a thinly-veiled biography of Gissing. A friend of Gissing's, Roberts concludes his work with a suitably valedictory note on the author's life and career: "Neither before his death nor after did he attain the artist's true and great reward of recognition in the full sense that would have satisfied him even if he had remained poor. Nevertheless there were some who knew. There are perhaps a few more who know now that he is gone and cannot hear them."

CHRISTOPHERSON

GEORGE GISSING

It was twenty years ago, and on an evening in May. All day long there had been sunshine. Owing, doubtless, to the incident I am about to relate, the light and warmth of that long-vanished day live with me still; I can see the great white clouds that moved across the strip of sky before my window, and feel again the spring langour which troubled my solitary work in the heart of London.

Only at sunset did I leave the house. There was an unwonted sweetness in the air; the long vistas of newly lit lamps made a golden glow under the dusking flush of the sky. With no purpose but to rest and breathe, I wandered for half an hour, and found myself at length where Great Portland Street opens into Marylebone Road. Over the way, in the shadow of Trinity Church, was an old bookshop, well known to me: the gas-jet shining upon the stall with its rows of volumes drew me across. I began turning over pages, and – invariable consequence – fingering what money I had in my pocket. A certain book overcame me; I stepped into the little shop to pay for it.

While standing at the stall, I had been vaguely aware of some one beside me, a man who was also looking over the books; as I came out again with my purchase, this stranger gazed at me intently, with a half-smile of peculiar interest. He seemed about to say something. I walked slowly away; the man moved in the same direction. Just in front of the church he made a quick movement to my side, and spoke.

"Pray excuse me, sir – don't misunderstand me – I only wished to ask whether you have noticed the name written on the flyleaf of the book you have just bought?"

The respectful nervousness of his voice naturally made me suppose at first that the man was going to beg; but he seemed no ordinary mendicant. I judged him to be

The House of Cobwebs and Other Stories. London: Constable and Company, 1906.

about sixty years of age; his long, thin hair and straggling beard were grizzled, and a somewhat rheumy eye looked out from his bloodless, hollowed countenance; he was very shabbily clad, yet as a fallen gentleman, and indeed his accent made it clear to what class he originally belonged. The expression with which he regarded me had so much intelligence, so much good nature, and at the same time, such a pathetic diffidence, that I could not but answer him in the friendliest way. I had not seen the name on the flyleaf, but at once I opened the book, and by the light of a gas-lamp read, inscribed in a very fine hand, "W. R. Christopherson, 1849".

"It is my name," said the stranger, in a subdued and uncertain voice.

"Indeed? The book used to belong to you?"

"It belonged to me." He laughed oddly, a tremulous little crow of a laugh, at the same time stroking his head, as if to deprecate disbelief. "You never heard of the sale of the Christopherson library? To be sure, you were too young; it was in 1860. I have often come across books with my name in them on the stalls – often. I had happened to notice this just before you came up, and when I saw you look at it, I was curious to see whether you would buy it. Pray excuse the freedom I am taking. Lovers of books – don't you think?"

The broken question was completed by his look, and when I said that I quite understood and agreed with him he crowed his little laugh.

"Have you a large library?" he inquired, eyeing me wistfully.

"Oh dear, no. Only a few hundred volumes. Too many for one who has no house of his own." He smiled good-naturedly, bent his head, and murmured just audibly:

"My catalogue numbered 24,718."

I was growing curious and interested. Venturing no more direct questions, I asked whether, at the time he spoke of, he lived in London.

"If you have five minutes to spare," was the timid reply, "I will show you my house. I mean –" again the little crowing laugh "– the house which was mine."

Willingly I walked on with him. He led me a short distance up the road skirting Regent's Park, and paused at length before a house in an imposing terrace.

"There," he whispered, "I used to live. The window to the right of the door – that was my library. Ah!"

And he heaved a deep sigh.

"A misfortune befell you," I said, also in a subdued voice.

"The result of my own folly. I had enough for my needs, but thought I needed more. I let myself be drawn into business – I, who knew nothing of such things – and there came the black day – the black day."

We turned to retrace our steps, and walking slowly, with heads bent, came in silence again to the church.

"I wonder whether you have bought any other of my books?" asked Christopherson, with his gentle smile, when we had paused as if for leave-taking.

I replied that I did not remember to have come across his name before; then, on an impulse, asked whether he would care to have the book I carried in my hand; if so, with pleasure I would give it him. No sooner were the words spoken than I saw the delight they caused the hearer. He hesitated, murmured reluctance, but soon gratefully accepted my offer, and flushed with joy as he took the volume.

"I still have a few books," he said, under his breath, as if he spoke of something he was ashamed to make known. "But it is very rarely indeed that I can add to them. I feel I have not thanked you half enough." We shook, hands and parted.

My lodging at that time was in Camden Town.

On afternoon, perhaps a fortnight later, I had walked for an hour or two, and on my way back I stopped at a bookstall in the High Street. Some one came up to my side; I looked, and recognized Christopherson. Our greeting was like that of old friends.

"I have seen you several times lately," said the broken gentleman, who looked shabbier than before in the broad daylight, "but I – didn't like to speak. I live not far from here."

"Why, so do I," and I added, without much thinking what I said, "do you live alone?"

"Alone? Oh no. With my wife."

There was a curious embarrassment in his tone. His eyes were cast down and his head moved uneasily.

We began to talk of the books on the stall, and turning away together continued our conversation. Christopherson was not only a well-bred but a very intelligent and even learned man. On his giving some proof of erudition (with the excessive modesty which characterized him), I asked whether he wrote. No, he had never written anything – never; he was only a bookworm, he said. Thereupon he crowed faintly and took his leave.

It was not long before we again met by chance. We came face to face at a street corner in my neighbourhood, and I was struck by a change in him. He looked older; a profound melancholy darkened his countenance; the hand he gave me was limp, and his pleasure at our meeting found only a faint expression.

"I am going away," he said in reply to my inquiring look. "I am leaving London."

"For good?"

"I fear so, and just –" he made an obvious effort "– I am glad of it. My wife's health has not been very good lately. She has need of country air. Yes, I am glad we have decided to go away – very glad – very glad indeed!"

He spoke with an automatic sort of emphasis, his eyes wandering, and his hands twitching nervously. I was on the point of asking what part of the country he had chosen for his retreat, when he abruptly added: "I live just over there. Will you let me show you my books?"

Of course I gladly accepted the invitation, and a couple of minutes' walk brought us to a house in a decent street where most of the ground-floor windows showed a card announcing lodgings. As we paused at the door, my companion seemed to hesitate, to regret having invited me.

"I'm really afraid it isn't worth your while," he said timidly. "The fact is, I haven't space to show my books properly."

I put aside the objection, and we entered. With anxious courtesy Christopherson led me up the narrow staircase to the second-floor landing, and threw open a door. On the threshold I stood astonished. The room was a small one, and would in any case have only just sufficed for homely comfort, used as it evidently was for all daytime purposes; but certainly a third of the entire space was occupied by a solid mass of books, volumes stacked several rows deep against two of the walls and almost up to the ceiling. A round table and two or three chairs were the only furniture – there was no room, indeed, for more. The window being shut, and the sunshine glowing upon it, an intolerable stuffiness oppressed the air. Never had I been made so uncomfortable by the odor of printed paper and bindings.

"But," I exclaimed, "you said you had only a few books! There must be five times as many here as I have."

"I forget the exact number," murmured Christopherson, in great agitation. "You see, I can't arrange them properly. I have a few more in – in the other room."

He led me across the landing, opened another door, and showed me a little bedroom. Here the encumberment was less remarkable, but one wall had completely disappeared behind volumes, and the bookishness of the air made it a disgusting thought that two persona occupied this chamber every night.

We returned to the sitting-room, Christopherson began picking out books from the solid mass to show me. Talking nervously, brokenly, with now and then a deep sigh or a crow of laughter, he gave me a little light on his history. I learnt that ho had occupied these lodgings for the last eight years; that he had been twice married; that the only child he had had, a daughter by his first wife, had died long ago in childhood; and lastly – this came in a burst of confidence, with a very pleasant smile – that his second wife had been his daughter's governess. I listened with keen interest, and hoped to learn still more of the circumstances of this singular household.

"In the country," I remarked, "you will no doubt have shelf room?"

At once his countenance fell; he turned upon me a woebegone eye. Just as I was about to speak again sounds from within the house caught my attention; there was a heavy foot on the stairs, and a loud voice, which seemed familiar to me.

"Ah," exclaimed Christopherson with a start, "here comes some one who is going to help me in the removal of the books. Come in, Mr. Pomfret, come in!"

The door opened, and there appeared a tall, wiry fellow, whose sandy hair, light blue eyes, jutting jaw-bones, and large mouth made a picture suggestive of small refinement but of vigorous and wholesome manhood. No wonder I had seemed to recognize his voice. Though we only saw each other by chance at long intervals, Pomfret and I were old acquaintances.

"Hullo!" he roared out, "I didn't know you know Mr. Christopherson."

"I'm just as much surprised to find that you know him!" was my reply.

The old book-lover gazed at us in nervous astonishment, then shook hands with the newcomer, who greeted him bluffly, yet respectfully. Pomfret spoke with a strong Yorkshire accent, and had all the angularity of demeanour which marks the typical Yorkshireman. He came to announce that everything had been settled for the packing and transporting of Mr. Christopherson's library; it remained only to decide the day.

"There's no hurry," exclaimed Christopherson. "There 's really no hurry. I'm greatly obliged to you, Mr. Pomfret, for all the trouble you are taking. We'll settle the date in a day or two – a day or two."

With a good-humoured nod Pomfret moved to take his leave. Our eyes met; we left the house together. Out in the street again I took a deep breath of the summer air, which seemed sweet as in a meadow after that stifling room. My companion evidently had a like sensation, for he looked up to the sky and broadened out his shoulders.

"Eh, but it's a grand day! I'd give something for a walk on Ilkley Moors."

As the best substitute within our reach we agreed to walk across Regent's Park together. Pomfret's business took him in that direction, and I was glad of a talk about Christopherson. I learnt that the old book-lover's landlady was Pomfret's aunt. Christopherson's story of affluence and ruin was quite true. Ruin complete, for at the age of forty he had been obliged to earn his living as a clerk or something of the kind. About five years later came his second marriage.

"You know Mrs. Christopherson?" asked Pomfret.

"No! I wish I did. Why?"

"Because she's the sort of woman it does you good to know, that's all. She's a lady – my idea of a lady. Christopherson's a gentleman too, there 's no denying it; if he wasn't, I think I should have punched his head before now. Oh, I know 'em well! Why, I lived in the house with 'em for several years. She's a lady to the end of her little finger, and how her husband can 'a borne to see her living the life she has, it's more than I can understand. By! I'd have turned burglar, if I could 'a found no other way of keeping her in comfort."

"She works for her living, then?"

"Aye, and for his too. No, not teaching; she's in a shop in Tottenham Court Road; has what they call a good place, and earns thirty shillings a week. It's all they have, but Christopherson buys books out of it."

"But has he never done anything since their marriage?"

"He did for the first few years, I believe, but he had an illness, and that was the end of it. Since then he's only loafed. He goes to all the book-sales, and spends the rest of his time sniffing about the second-hand shops. She? Oh, she'd never say a word! Wait till you've seen her."

"Well, but," I asked, "what has happened? How is it they're leaving London?"

"Aye, I'll tell you; I was coming to that. Mrs. Christopherson has relatives well off – a fat and selfish lot, as far as I can make out – never lifted a finger to help her until now. One of them 's a Mrs. Keeting, the widow of some City porpoise, I'm told. Well, this woman has a home down in Norfolk. She never lives there, but a son of hers goes there to fish and shoot now and then. Well, this is what Mrs. Christopherson tells my aunt, Mrs. Keeting has offered to let her and her husband live down yonder, rent free, and their food provided. She's to be housekeeper, in fact, and keep the place ready for any one who goes down."

"Christopherson, I can see, would rather stay where he is."

"Why, of course, he doesn't know how he'll live without the bookshops. But he's glad for all that, on his wife's account. And it's none too soon, I can tell you. The poor woman couldn't go on much longer; my aunt says she's just about ready to drop, and sometimes, I know, she looks terribly bad. Of course, she won't own it, not she; she isn't one of the complaining sort. But she talks now and then about the country – the places where she used to live. I've heard her, and it gives me a notion of what she's gone through all these years. I saw her a week ago, just when she had Mrs. Keeting's offer, and I tell you I scarcely knew who it was! You never saw such a change in any one in your life! Her face was like that of a girl of seventeen. And her laugh – you should have heard her laugh!"

"Is she much younger than her husband?" I asked.

"Twenty years at least. She's about forty, I think." I mused for a few moments.

"After all, it isn't an unhappy marriage?"

"Unhappy?" cried Pomfret. "Why, there 's never been a disagreeable word between them, that I'll warrant. Once Christopherson gets over the change, they'll have nothing more in the world to ask for. He'll potter over his books."

"You mean to tell me," I interrupted, "that those books have all been bought out of his wife's thirty shillings a week?"

"No, no. To begin with, he kept a few out of his old library. Then, when he was earning his own living, he bought a great many. He told me once that he's often lived on sixpence a day to have money for books. A rum old owl; but for all that he's a gentleman, and you can't help liking him. I shall be sorry when he's out of reach."

For my own part, I wished nothing better than to hear of Christopherson's departure. The story I had heard made me uncomfortable. It was good to think of that poor woman rescued at last from her life of toil, and in these days of midsummer free to enjoy the country she loved. A touch of envy mingled, I confess, with my thought of Christopherson, who henceforth had not a care in the world, and without reproach might delight in his hoarded volumes. One could not imagine that he would suffer seriously by the removal of his old haunts. I promised myself to call on him in a day or two. By choosing Sunday, I might perhaps be lucky enough to see his wife.

And on Sunday afternoon I was on the point of setting forth to pay this visit, when in came Pomfret. He wore a surly look, and kicked clumsily against the furniture as he crossed the room. His appearance was a surprise, for, though I had given him my address, I did not in the least expect that he would come to see me; a certain pride, I suppose, characteristic of his rugged strain, having always made him shy of such intimacy.

"Did you ever hear the like of that!" he shouted, half angrily. "It's all over. They're not going. And all because of those blamed books!"

And spluttering and growling, he made known what he had just learnt at his aunt's home. On the previous afternoon the Christophersons had been surprised by a visit from their relatives and would-be benefactress, Mrs. Keeting. Never before had that lady called upon them; she came, no doubt (this could only be conjectured), to speak with them of their approaching removal. The close of the conversation (a very brief one) was overheard by the landlady, for Mrs. Keeting spoke loudly as she descended the stairs. "Impossible! Quite impossible! I couldn't think of it! How could you dream for a moment that I would let you till my house with musty old books? Most unhealthy! I never knew anything so extraordinary in my life, never!" And so she went out to her carriage, and was driven away. And the landlady, presently having occasion to go upstairs, was aware of a dead silence in the room where the Christophersons were sitting. She knocked – prepared with some excuse – and found the couple side by side, smiling sadly. At once they told her the truth. Mrs. Keeting had come because of a letter in which Mrs. Christophorson had mentioned the fact that her husband had a good many books, and hoped he might be permitted to remove them to the house in Norfolk. She came to see the library — with the result already heard. They had the choice between sacrificing the books and losing what their relative offered.

"Christopherson refused?" I let fall.

"I suppose his wife saw that it was too much for him. At all events, they'd agreed to keep the books and lose the house. And there's an end of it. I haven't been so riled about anything for a long time!"

Meantime I had been reflecting. It was easy for me to understand Christopherson's state of mind, and without knowing Mrs. Keeting, I saw that she must be a person whose benefactions would be a good deal of a burden. After all, was Mrs. Christopherson so very unhappy? Was she not the kind of woman who lived by sacrifice – one who had far rather lead a life disagreeable to herself than change it at the cost of discomfort to her husband? This view of the matter irritated Pomfret, and he broke into objurgations, directed partly against Mrs. Keeting, partly against Christopherson. It was an "infernal shame", that was all he could say. And after all, I rather inclined to his opinion.

When two or three days had passed, curiosity drew me towards the Christophersons' dwelling. Walking along the opposite side of the street, I looked up at their window, and there was the face of the old bibliophile. Evidently he was standing at the window in idleness, perhaps in trouble. At once he beckoned to me; but before I could knock at the house-door he had descended, and came out.

"May I walk a little way with you?" he asked.

There was worry on his features. For some moments we went on in silence.

"So you have changed your mind about leaving London?" I said, as if carelessly.

"You have heard from Mr. Pomfret? Well – yes, yes – I think we shall stay where we are – for the present."

Never have I seen a man more painfully embarrassed. He walked with head bent, shoulders stooping; and shuffled, indeed, rather than walked. Even so might a man bear himself who felt guilty of some peculiar meanness.

Presently words broke from him.

"To tell you the truth, there's a difficulty about the books." He glanced furtively at me, and I saw he was trembling in all his nerves. "As you see, my circumstances are not brilliant." He half-choked himself with a crow. "The fact is we were offered a house in the country, on certain conditions, by a relative of Mrs. Christopherson; and, unfortunately, it turned out that my library is regarded as an objection – a fatal objection. We have quite reconciled ourselves to staying where we are."

I could not help asking, without emphasis, whether Mrs. Christopherson would have cared for life in the country. But no sooner were the words out of my mouth than I regretted them; so evidently did they hit my companion in a tender place.

"I think she would have liked it," he answered, with a strangely pathetic look at me, as if he entreated my forbearance.

"But," I suggested, "couldn't you make some arrangements about the books? Couldn't you take a room for them in another house, for instance?"

Christopherson's face was sufficient answer; it reminded me of his pennilessness. "We think no more about it," he said. "The matter is settled – quite settled."

There was no pursuing the subject. At the next parting of the ways we took leave of each other.

I think it was not more than a week later when I received a postcard from Pomfret. He wrote: "Just as I expected. Mrs. C. seriously ill." That was all.

Mrs. C. could, of course, only mean Mrs. Christopherson. I mused over the message – it took hold of my imagination, wrought upon my feelings; and that afternoon I again walked along the interesting street.

There was no face at the window. After a little hesitation I decided to call at the house and speak with Pomfret's aunt. It was she who opened the door to me.

We had never seen each other, but when I mentioned my name and said I was anxious to hear news of Mrs. Christopherson, she led me into a sitting-room, and began to talk confidentially.

She was a good-natured Yorkshirewoman, very unlike the common London landlady. Yes, Mrs. Christopherson had been taken ill two days ago. It began with a long fainting fit. She had a feverish, sleepless night; the doctor was sent for; and he had her removed out of the stuffy, book-cumbered bedroom into another chamber, which luckily happened to be vacant. There she lay utterly weak and worn, all but voiceless, able only to smile at her husband, who never moved from the bedside day or night. "He, too," said the landlady, "would soon break down." He looked like a ghost, and seemed "half-crazed".'

"What," I asked, "could be the cause of this illness?"

The good woman gave me an odd look, shook her head, and murmured that the reason was not far to seek.

"Did she think," I asked, "that disappointment might have something to do with it?"

Why, of course she did. For a long time the poor lady had been all but at the end of her strength, and this came as a blow beneath which she sank.

"Your nephew and I have talked about it," I said.

"He thinks that Mr. Christopherson didn't understand what a sacrifice he asked his wife to make."

"I think so too," was the reply. "But he begins to see it now, I can tell you. He says nothing but –"

There was a tap at the door, and a hurried tremulous voice begged the landlady to go upstairs.

"What is it, sir?" she asked.

"I'm afraid she's worse," said Christopherson, turning his haggard face to me with startled recognition.

"Do come up at once, please."

Without a word to me he disappeared with the landlady. I could not go away; for some ten minutes I fidgeted about the little room, listening to every sound in the house. Then came a footfall on the stairs, and the landlady rejoined me.

"It's nothing," she said. "I almost think she might drop off to sleep, if she's left quiet. He worries her, poor man, sitting there and asking her every two minutes how she feels. I've persuaded him to go to his room, and I think it might do him good if you went and had a bit o' talk with him."

I mounted at once to the second-floor sitting-room, and found Christopherson sunk upon a chair, his head falling forwards, the image of despairing misery. As I approached he staggered to his feet. He took my hand in a shrinking, shamefaced way, and could not raise his eyes. I uttered a few words of encouragement, but they had the opposite effect to that designed.

"Don't tell me that," he moaned, half resentfully. "She 's dying – she 's dying – say what they will, I know it."

"Have you a good doctor?"

"I think so – but it's too late – it's too late."

As he dropped to his chair again I sat down by him. The silence of a minute or two was broken by a thunderous rat-tat at the house-door. Christopherson leapt to his feet, rushed from the room; I, half fearing that be had gone mad, followed to the head of the stairs.

In a moment he came up again, limp and wretched as before.

"It was the postman," he muttered. "I am expecting a letter."

Conversation seeming impossible, I shaped a preliminary to withdrawal; but Christopherson would not let me go.

"I should like to tell you," he began, looking at me like a dog under punishment, "that I have done all I could. As soon as my wife fell ill, and when I saw – I had only begun to think of it in that way – how she felt the disappointment, I went at once to Mrs. Ketting's house to tell her that I would sell the books. But she was out of town. I wrote to her – I said I regretted my folly – I entreated her to forgive me and to renew her kind offer. There has been plenty of time for a reply, but she doesn't answer."

He had in his hand what I saw was a bookseller's catalogue, just delivered by the postman. Mechanically he tore off the wrapper and oven glanced over the first page. Then, as if conscience stabbed him, he flung the thing violently away.

"The chance has gone!" he exclaimed, taking a hurried step or two along the little strip of floor left free by the mountain of books. "Of course she said she would rather stay in London! Of course she said what she knew would please me! When – when did she ever say anything else! And I was cruel enough – base enough – to let her make the sacrifice!" He waved his arms frantically. "Didn't I know what it cost her? Couldn't I see in her face how her heart leapt at the hope of going to live in the country! I knew what she was suffering; I knew it, I tell you! And, like a selfish coward, I let her suffer – I let her drop down and die – die!"

"Any hour," I said, "may bring you the reply from Mrs. Keeting. Of course it will be favourable, and the good news –"

"Too late, I have killed her! That woman won't write. She's one of the vulgar rich, and we offended her pride; and such as she never forgive."

He sat down for a moment, but started up again in an agony of mental suffering.

"She is dying – and there, there, that's what has killed her!" He gesticulated wildly towards the books. "I have sold her life for these. Oh! Oh!"

With this cry he seized half a dozen volumes, and, before I could understand what he was about, he had flung up the window-sash, and cast the books into the street. Another batch followed; I heard the thud upon the pavement. Then I caught him by the arm, held him fast, begged him to control himself.

"They shall go!" he cried. "I loathe the sight of them. They have killed my dear wife!"

He said it sobbing, and at the last words tears streamed from his eyes. I had no difficulty now in restraining him. He met my look with a gaze of infinite pathos, and talked on while he wept.

"If you knew what she has been to me! When she married me I was a ruined man twenty years older."

"I have given her nothing but toil and care. You shall know everything – for years and years I have lived on the earnings of her labour. Worse than that, I have starved and stinted her to buy books. Oh, the shame of it! The wickedness of it! It was my vice – the vice that enslaved me just as if it had been drinking or gambling. I couldn't resist the temptation – though every day I cried shame upon myself and swore to over- come it. She never blamed me; never a word – nay, not a look – of a reproach. I lived in idleness. I never tried to save her that daily toil at the shop. Do you know that she worked in a shop? – She, with her knowledge and her refinement leading such a life as that! Think that I have passed the shop a thousand times, coming home with a book in ray hands! I had the heart to pass, and to think of her there! Oh! Oh!"

Some one was knocking at the door. I went to open, and saw the landlady, her face set in astonishment, and her arms full of books.

"It's all right," I whispered. "Put them down on the floor there; don't bring them in. An accident."

Christopherson stood behind me his look asked what he durst not speak. I said it was nothing, and by degrees brought him into a calmer state. Luckily, the doctor came before I went away, and he was able to report a slight improvement. The patient had slept a little and seemed likely to sleep again. Christopherson asked me to come again before long – there was no one else, he said, who cared anything about him – and I promised to call the next day.

I did so, early in the afternoon. Christopherson must have watched for my coming; before I could raise the knocker the door flew open, and his face gleamed such a greeting as astonished me. He grasped my hand in both his.

"The letter has come! We are to have the house."

"And how is Mrs. Christopherson?"

"Better, much better. Heaven be thanked! She slept almost from the time when you loft yesterday afternoon till early this morning. The letter came by the first post, and I told her – not the whole truth," he added, under his breath. "She thinks I am to be allowed to take the books with me; and if you could have seen her smile of contentment. But they will all be sold and carried away before she knows about it; and when she sees that I don't care a snap of the fingers –"

He had turned into the sitting-room on the ground floor. Walking about excitedly, Christopherson gloried in the sacrifice he had made. Already a letter was dispatched to a bookseller, who would buy the whole library as it stood. But would he not keep a few volumes? I asked. Surely there could be no objection to a few shelves of books; and how would he live without them? At first he declared vehemently that not a volume should be kept – he never wished to see a book again as long as he lived. But Mrs. Christopherson? I urged. Would she not be glad of something to read now and then? At this he grew pensive. We discussed the matter, and it was arranged that a box should be packed with select volumes and taken down into Norfolk together with the rest of their luggage. Not even Mrs. Keeting could object to this, and I strongly advised him to take her permission for granted.

And so it was done. By discreet management the piled volumes were stowed in bags, carried downstairs, emptied into a cart, and conveyed away, so quietly that the sick woman was aware of nothing. In telling me about it, Christopherson crowed as I had never heard him; but methought his eye avoided that part of the floor which had formerly been hidden, and in the course of our conversation he now and then became absent, with head bowed. Of the joy he felt in his wife's recovery there could, however, be no doubt. The crisis through which he had passed had made him, in appearance, a yet older man; when he declared his happiness tears came into his eyes, and his head shook with a senile tremor.

Before they left London, I saw Mrs. Christopherson – a pale, thin, slightly made woman, who had never been what is called good-looking, but her face, if ever face did so, declared a brave and loyal spirit. She was not joyous, she was not sad; but in her eyes, as I looked at them again and again, I read the profound thankfulness of one to whom fate has granted her soul's desire.

Little is known about May Wentworth (1830? - 1899). She was one of the few female writers in San Francisco during the city's notorious early history.

Joshua Norton (1819 - 1880), the self-proclaimed "Emperor of the United States", has appeared frequently in literature, including books by Mark Twain and Robert Louis Stevenson. Perhaps Emperor Norton's best-known modern appearance is in Neil Gaiman's Sandman. Gaiman portrays him as a heart-breaking figure, protected (or cursed) to live in a dream.

Wentworth, living in San Francisco and writing in the man's own lifetime, paints a very different picture of Emperor Norton. Unlike Gaiman's charming mooncalf, Wentworth's Norton – demeaningly called "Dumpy" – is a fortune-hunter with more ambition than sense. While Gaiman depicts Norton as an inspirational figure, Wentworth uses him to demonstrate the price of hubris.

EMPEROR NORTON

MAY WENTWORTH

Once upon a time there lived near a small village on the shore of the Atlantic, an honest farmer named Norton, who had three sons.

The two elder were smart, active lads, but the youngest was quiet, and so much given to dreaming that his brothers ridiculed and often slighted him.

"He is so stupid," they would say, "he will be a disgrace to the family," but what annoyed him most, they gave him the unpleasant sobriquet of Dumpy, on account of his fat, rosy cheeks.

As the boys grew up, the eldest took the farm, and was to take care of the father and mother, the second became clerk to a merchant in a neighboring city, but poor Dumpy, in the indolence of his disposition, did nothing. He was always hoping some impossible thing would "turn up," but he had no rich relations, indeed no one seemed to take much interest in him but the mother, who would always say, "Poor Dumpy, he is a good-hearted boy," then she would sigh heavily, as though there was nothing more to be said.

At last the father became quite out of patience, and calling the boy to him one day, he said: "You are now twenty years old, and never have earned so much as your salt, and it is quite time for you to do something for yourself. Your brother, who has taken the farm, complains that he is obliged to support you in idleness, which certainly is not right."

"For the farm, he will take care of your mother and me, but you and your other brother must look out for yourselves."

"Give me," answered Dumpy, "what money you can spare, I ask nothing more, I will go and seek my fortune, and you shall hear of me when I become a rich man."

Fairy Tales from Gold Lands. San Francisco: A. Roman: 1868.

The father gave him what money he could, and he went away, no one at home knew whither, leaving only the mother to weep for him.

When Dumpy left the farm-house he walked on to the village, feeling that he was going into the great world full of promise, but he never dreamed of disappointment.

When he arrived at the village inn the stage was standing at the door. "I will go," he said, "where fortune leads me." So he took his seat in. the stage, and paid his fare to the end of the route, which happened to be the great city of New York.

All day long he was very happy looking out of the windows upon the changing landscape, and indulging in daydreams. Sometimes he would come to a pretty village nestling among the hills. "I would like," he would think, "of all things to stop here, 'tis so very pleasant, but I have paid my money, and I must go on."

It was night when the stage entered the city, its heavy wheels rumbling over the paved streets, and crowding along past carts, omnibuses, and carriages, till poor Dumpy, who had never been in the city before, began to feel very much bewildered and confused.

"Where shall I go," said Dumpy to the driver, when the stage stopped. "'Tis so noisy I can't hear myself think. Oh, dear! I don't know what to do," and he looked so pitiably helpless that the driver was sorry for him, though he could not help laughing. "Come with me, my boy," he said, so he went with the driver to the cheap lodging-house, where he stopped when in town.

To enumerate all poor Dumpy's adventures while in New Yorkwould be impossible. Enough to say it was not long before his money was gone, and he shipped before the mast in a merchant vessel for California.

Poor Dumpy! Now came woeful experiences, for a time he was wretchedly sea-sick, and he soon found that to go before the mast was no joke, but in his way he was quite a philosopher, and after a few weeks became a very good sailor.

As he was pleasant and obliging he became a favorite with all on board, but he loved most of all when off duty, to sit by himself in the soft starlit evenings as the good ship sailed over the tropic seas, and dream of the land of gold to which he was going.

He possessed a vivid imagination, and his visions of the wealth of the new El Dorado were most glowing.

I would be great as well as rich.

He would picture to himself how, like a prince, he would luxuriate in riches, how great and generous he would be, even to the brothers who had despised him. It is a happiness to be able to revel in dreams as he did, for the pleasures of anticipation are but too often greater than the reality.

He loved his mother, she at least had always been kind and gentle to him.

"My dear mother," he would say to himself, with a bright tear in his eye, "she shall yet live in a palace. God bless her, dear mother."

Then he would sigh till a bright thought drove away the sad one. "Oh, 'tis so delightful to be rich," he would say.

Then he would rub his hands as complacently as though the wealth of the Indies lay at his feet.

"I shall give the father every thing he wishes of course," he would continue, "and I will make the brothers rich men, for to be generous and forgive is the attribute of true greatness, and for myself I will marry the prettiest woman in the world, and I will give her every thing she can possibly desire."

Often the sharp quick bell, for change of watch, would call him to duty, and scatter his gorgeous dreams, leaving only the dull, hard present in his mind and heart.

At length the good ship arrived in San Francisco, and there again Dumpy found all the wild bustle and confusion of the early days.

Gold was plenty in dust and bars.

When a man bought anything he would take out of his bag of gold dust as much dust as he was to pay for the article, and he would be off.

The highest price was paid for labor, and Dumpy soon engaged to drive a cart for two hundred and fifty dollars per month, but he determined to make this arrangement only for a short time, till he could get money enough to go out prospecting in the mining districts.

This he soon accomplished, but he found a life in the mines even harder than before the mast, but the golden future was before him, and he persevered.

He and another young adventurer built a cabin together by a little spring of clear, bubbling water.

They worked early and late, with the wearisome pick and shovel for the precious gold that was to pave the pathway of their lives with happiness, but often night found them disappointed and weary, and they would return to their lonely cabins, cook and eat their coarse supper, and lie down upon the hard floor, wrap their blankets around them, with heavy and hopeless hearts. But thank God, sunshine and the fresh morning brings renewed life and hope to young hearts.

One morning when Dumpy awoke he found his companion had risen and gone out before him, so he went out alone, thinking, "who knows what will turn up before night, I may become a millionaire. I'll try my luck alone today". So he did not go to the ledge they had been prospecting the day before, but started off in a new direction.

All day long he worked diligently, but the sunset found him as poor as the dawning, and quite worn out, he threw himself down upon the ledge to rest a little before going home. "Ah, me!" thought he, sadly. "How long the poor mother will have to wait for her palace."

As the sunset deepened into twilight, he rose, and shouldering his pick and shovel, started for the cabin. "I can not call it home," he said to himself, "there is no mother there."

He had not gone far, before a little shrill voice arrested him, and looking down, he saw a little old man, sitting among the loose stones, rubbing his foot and ankle, and groaning piteously.

He was very quaintly dressed, in a little red jacket, and wore a Spanish hat with little gold bells around it, and his long gray beard swept the ground, as he sat dismally among the rocks.

"Oh, dear! I cannot move," said the little man. "I have sprained my foot, will not you help me home? Oh dear! Oh dear!" He moaned so piteously that Dumpy, who was kind-hearted, was very sorry for him; so he took the old man up in his arms as tenderly as if he had been an infant.

The old man pointed out the way, and Dumpy trudged wearily on, for though he was no bigger than a child of eight years old, he seemed quite heavy to Dumpy. After working all day with the pick and shovel, and finding nothing, his heart was heavy with hope deferred. "If I had found gold today," thought he, "a light heart would have made a light burden; but thank God I am well, and this poor man suffers fearfully."

Poor Dumpy! He went on, down the canyon, then up the mountain, it seemed to him for miles; at last the little man pointed to a crevice in the rock, through which

Dumpy managed with some difficulty to creep; but as he went on it widened, and suddenly opened into a large cavern.

"Go on," said the old man, sharply, as Dumpy stopped and gazed around with astonishment. So he went on till they came to a large hall sparkling with crystal, and glowing with precious stones.

A large chandelier hung from the roof, and cast a flood of softened light through the whole cavern, and Dumpy could see in the stone floor large masses of pure yellow gold.

He saw in the huge irregular pillars that rose to the dome of the cavern, great veins of the precious ore, and everywhere it was scattered about with the most lavish profusion.

Curious golden figures, carved with strange devices, stood in the niches, and there were couches with golden frames, and tables of gold, so that the light, reflected from the clear crystal dome, glittering with shining pendants, by the softening yellow tinge, was mellow and pleasant.

Poor Dumpy had been so long in the twilight and darkness, that he was dazzled by the brilliant scene, and for a few moments was obliged to close his eyes, and when he opened them, he saw that he was surrounded by a large crowd of the little people, who were fall of anxious fears about the old man he held in his arms, but he assured them he was suffering only from a sprain, which, though very painful, was not dangerous. They gathered anxiously around the little man as he laid him upon a couch.

He soon discovered that the man he had assisted was king over the little people who guard the mountain treasures, covering the rich places with unpromising stones and earth, and often misleading the honest miner by scattering grains of the precious metal in waste places; thus it is we hear so often of disappointed hopes, and abandoned mines.

After they had in some measure relieved the suffering of their chief, they turned to Dumpy, who stood in the most profound astonishment, drinking in all he saw or heard.

"You have done me a great kindness," said the chief, "and, though it is our business to mislead miners, we can be grateful, and you may now claim any reward you desire."

"I have saved your ruler," said Dumpy, looking at the crowd of little people, and trying to think of something great to ask as a reward.

"Our chief! Our king!" cried all the little people, together. "Ask what you will and it shall be granted."

"I would be great as well as rich," thought Dumpy, so he said aloud: "Make me emperor of all the mines, and let all the miners pay tribute to me."

"It shall be so," said the king. Then he called one of his servants to bring the golden crown and scepter, and bidding Dumpy kneel before him, he placed the scepter in his hand and the crown upon his head, and striking him a sharp blow upon his shoulder, he said, "Arise, Emperor Norton."

"As long as you preserve this crown and scepter from moth or rust, dew or fog, you shall be the true emperor of all the mines in California and Nevada, and all the miners shall pay you yearly tribute, but if you lose either crown or scepter, or moth, rust, midnight dews and damps fall upon them, they will fade away, and you will be emperor in name only, and the miners shall pay you no yearly tribute."

"So let it be," said the newly-made emperor; and they all sat down to a table spread with every delicacy, and feasted till the noon of the following day.

When the emperor bade the knights of the mountain adieu, the little gray king said: "Beware of the dews and damps of the night," and he started for his cabin.

"I will first visit my old comrade," he said, "though he is now one of my subjects, I will not be proud and haughty."

One of the little men ran before him, and led the way out of the cave into the sunlight, which was so bright that the emperor shaded his eyes with his hand, and when he had removed it the little man had disappeared.

The emperor looked around, but could see no trace of him; even the crevice through which he had passed, was nowhere to be seen.

"It is a wonderful dream," said he; but – no! – there was the golden crown upon his head, and the scepter in his hand.

"I will find that cave," thought he, so he began to look for it very eagerly, till the lengthening shadows told of the coming of evening, and he thought of the gray king's warning: "Beware of the dews and damps of night."

"Oh dear! If I should lose the tribute money," he said, in great distress, "I should be emperor but could build no palace for the mother, nor could I marry the prettiest woman in the world, and supply her innumerable wants," so he started in great haste for the camp, always keeping fast hold of the crown and scepter.

On he rushed till the shades of twilight filled the deep canyon, through which he was obliged to pass, then he broke into a run, crying, "Oh me! If I should be too late! Too late! Now that my hopes are crowned with success. Too late! Too late!"

"Haste makes waste," and so the emperor found it. He lost the path and became entangled in brush and rocks, until he became almost wild with despair.

The night came on with a heavy mist that near morning deepened into rain.

With the gray twilight of the dawning, weary and worn, he reached his cabin door, but the golden crown and scepter had passed away into the mists of night.

The poor emperor told of his wanderings to his comrades, and mourned over the night in which his crown and scepter had departed from him, but they only laughed, saying, "You have been dreaming again. Emperor Norton!"

He never took the pick and shovel again. "Shall an emperor work," he would say, "while thousands of his subjects roll in luxury?"

An emperor, he thought, should reside in the chief city of his realm, so he left the mines and came to San Francisco.

Here for years he has lived, always wearing a well-worn suit of blue, with epaulettes upon the shoulders, which, perhaps, might have been an unmentioned gift of the gray king of the mountains.

At the table of all restaurants and hotels he is a free and welcome guest, and all places of amusement are open to him; in fact, where ever you go in San Francisco, you are almost sure to meet the Emperor Norton.

"This world is full of weak or foolish people. So is the next. You need not mix with them, any more than you do in this world. One chooses one's companions."
— Sir Arthur Conan Doyle, The New Revelation (1918)

In "The Secret of Goresthorpe Grange", Argentine D'Odd takes this advice to the extreme, and tries to bring a companion from the next world to join him in this one. The weak and foolish D'Odd aspires to be a modern Medieval baron with the glamour of a ghost to call his own. But he eventually learns that he cannot buy the magic of fiction.

The story, with its deliberately demystifying ending, stands in stark contrast to Sir Arthur Conan Doyle's own relationship with the "world beyond the veil". The creator of Sherlock Holmes and Professor Challenger began his career as a doctor and "convinced materialist", a skepticism reflected in "The Secret of Goresthorpe Grange". Yet, twenty years after the story's publication, Sir Arthur (1859 - 1930) had become the spiritualist movement's most vocal champion.

Like Argentine D'Odd, Sir Arthur sought answers in the occult. But while D'Odd slinks back to his banal suburban reality at the end of his story, Sir Arthur clung to his dreams for the rest of his life. While his character existed in a land of groceries and chemistry, Sir Arthur himself lived in a world of fairies and spirits. Sir Arthur knew his beliefs provoked "ridicule and worldly disadvantage", but it is difficult not to envy him his certainty of a better world.

THE SECRET OF GORESTHORPE GRANGE

SIR ARTHUR CONAN DOYLE

I am sure that Nature never intended me to be a self-made man. There are times when I can hardly bring myself to realize that twenty years of my life were spent behind the counter of a grocer's shop in the East End of London, and that it was through such an avenue that I reached a wealthy independence and the possession of Goresthorpe Grange. My habits are Conservative, and my tastes refined and aristocratic. I have a soul which spurns the vulgar herd. Our family, the D'Odds, date back to a prehistoric era, as is to be inferred from the fact that their advent into British history is not commented on by any trustworthy historian. Some instinct tells me that the blood of a Crusader runs in my veins. Even now, after the lapse of so many years, such exclamations as "By'r Lady!" rise naturally to my lips, and I feel that, should circumstances require it, I am capable of rising in my stirrups and dealing an infidel a blow – say with a mace – which would considerably astonish him.

Goresthorpe Grange is a feudal mansion – or so it was termed in the advertisement which originally brought it under my notice. Its right to this adjective had a most remarkable effect upon its price, and the advantages gained may possibly be more sentimental than real. Still, it is soothing to me to know that I have slits in my staircase through which I can discharge arrows: and there is a sense of power in the fact of possessing a complicated apparatus by means of which I am enabled to pour molten lead upon the head of the casual visitor. These things chime in with my peculiar humour, and I do not grudge to pay for them. I am proud of my battlements and of the circular uncovered sewer which girds me round. I am proud of my portcullis and donjon and keep. There is but one thing wanting to round off the medievalism of my abode, and to render it symmetrically and completely antique. Goresthorpe Grange is not provided with a ghost.

Any man with old-fashioned tastes and ideas as to how such establishments should be conducted would have been disappointed at the omission. In my case it was particularly unfortunate. From my childhood I had been an earnest student of the supernatural, and a firm believer in it. I have revelled in ghostly literature until there is hardly a tale bearing upon the subject which I have not perused. I learned the German language for the sole purpose of mastering a book upon demonology. When an infant I have secreted myself in dark rooms in the hope of seeing some of those bogies with which my nurse used to threaten me; and the same feeling is as strong in me now as then. It was a proud moment when I felt that a ghost was one of the luxuries which my money might command.

It is true that there was no mention of an apparition in the advertisement. On reviewing the mildewed walls, however, and the shadowy corridors, I had taken it for granted that there was such a thing on the premises. As the presence of a kennel pre-supposes that of a dog, so I imagined that it was impossible that such desirable quarters should be untenanted by one or more restless shades. Good heavens, what can the noble family from whom I purchased it have been doing during these hundreds of years! Was there no member of it spirited enough to make away with his sweetheart, or take some other steps calculated to establish a hereditary spectre? Even now I can hardly write with patience upon the subject.

For a long time I hoped against hope. Never did a rat squeak behind the wainscot, or rain drip upon the attic-floor, without a wild thrill shooting through me as I thought that at last I had come upon traces of some unquiet soul. I felt no touch of fear upon these occasions. If it occurred in the night-time, I would send Mrs. D'Odd – who is a strong-minded woman – to investigate the matter while I covered up my head with the bed-clothes and indulged in an ecstasy of expectation. Alas, the result was always the same! The suspicious sound would be traced to some cause so absurdly natural and commonplace that the most fervid imagination could not clothe it with any of the glamour of romance.

I might have reconciled myself to this state of things had it not been for Jorrocks of Havistock Farm. Jorrocks is a coarse, burly, matter-of-fact fellow whom I only happen to know through the accidental circumstance of his fields adjoining my demesne. Yet this man, though utterly devoid of all appreciation of archeological unities, is in possession of a well-authenticated and undeniable spectre. Its existence only dates back, I believe, to the reign of the Second George, when a young lady cut her throat upon hearing of the death of her lover at the battle of Dettingen. Still, even that gives the house an air of respectability, especially when coupled with bloodstains upon the floor. Jorrocks is densely unconscious of his good fortune; and his language when he reverts to the apparition is painful to listen to. He little dreams how I covet every one of those moans and nocturnal wails which he describes with unnecessary objurgation. Things are indeed coming to a pretty pass when democratic spectres are allowed to desert the landed proprietors and annul every social distinction by taking refuge in the houses of the great unrecognized.

I have a large amount of perseverance. Nothing else could have raised me into my rightful sphere, considering the uncongenial atmosphere in which I spent the earlier part of my life. I felt now that a ghost must be secured, but how to set about securing one was more than either Mrs. D'Odd or myself was able to determine. My reading taught me that such phenomena are usually the outcome of crime. What crime was to be done, then, and who was to do it? A wild idea entered my mind that Watkins, the house-steward, might be prevailed upon – for a consideration – to immolate himself or someone else in the interests of the establishment. I put the matter to him in a half jesting manner; but it did not seem to strike him in a favourable light. The other servants sympathized with him in his opinion – at least, I cannot account in any other way for their having left the house in a body the same afternoon.

"My dear," Mrs. D'Odd remarked to me one day after dinner as I sat moodily sipping a cup of sack – I love the good old names – "my dear, that odious ghost of Jorrocks' has been gibbering again."

"Let it gibber!" I answered recklessly.

Mrs. D'Odd struck a few chords on her virginal and looked thoughtfully into the fire.

"I'll tell you what it is, Argentine," she said at last, using the pet name which we usually substituted for Silas, "we must have a ghost sent down from London."

"How can you be so idiotic, Matilda?" I remarked severely. "Who could get us such a thing?"

"My cousin, Jack Brocket, could," she answered confidently.

Now, this cousin of Matilda's was rather a sore subject between us. He was a rakish clever young fellow, who had tried his hand at many things, but wanted perseverance to succeed at any. He was, at that time, in chambers in London, professing to be a general agent, and really living, to a great extent, upon his wits. Matilda managed so that most of our business should pass through his hands, which certainly saved me a great deal of trouble, but I found that Jack's commission was generally considerably larger than all the other items of the bill put together. It was this fact which made me feel inclined to rebel against any further negotiations with the young gentleman.

"O yes, he could," insisted Mrs. D., seeing the look of disapprobation upon my face. "You remember how well he managed that business about the crest?"

"It was only a resuscitation of the old family coat-of-arms, my dear," I protested.

Matilda smiled in an irritating manner. "There was a resuscitation of the family portraits, too, dear," she remarked. "You must allow that Jack selected them very judiciously."

I thought of the long line of faces which adorned the walls of my banqueting-hall, from the burly Norman robber, through every gradation of casque, plume, and ruff, to the sombre Chesterfieldian individual who appears to have staggered against a pillar in his agony at the return of a maiden MS. which he grips convulsively in his right hand. I was fain to confess that in that instance he had done his work well, and that it was only fair to give him an order – with the usual commission – for a family spectre, should such a thing be attainable.

It is one of my maxims to act promptly when once my mind is made up. Noon of the next day found me ascending the spiral stone staircase which leads to Mr. Brocket's chambers, and admiring the succession of arrows and fingers upon the whitewashed wall, all indicating the direction of that gentleman's sanctum. As it happened, artificial aids of the sort were entirely unnecessary, as an animated flap-dance overhead could proceed from no other quarter, though it was replaced by a deathly silence as I groped my way up the stair. The door was opened by a youth evidently astounded at the appearance of a client, and I was ushered into the presence of my young friend, who was writing furiously in a large ledger – upside down, as I afterwards discovered.

After the first greetings, I plunged into business at once.

"Look here, Jack," I said, "I want you to get me a spirit, if you can."

"Spirits you mean!" shouted my wife's cousin, plunging his hand into the waste-paper basket and producing a bottle with the celerity of a conjuring trick. "Let's have a drink!"

I held up my hand as a mute appeal against such a proceeding so early in the day; but on lowering it again I found that I had almost involuntarily closed my fingers round the tumbler which my adviser had pressed upon me. I drank the contents hastily off, lest anyone should come in upon us and set me down as a toper. After all there was something very amusing about the young fellow's eccentricities.

"Not spirits," I explained smilingly; "an apparition – a ghost. If such a thing is to be had, I should be very willing to negotiate."

"A ghost for Goresthorpe Grange?" inquired Mr. Brocket, with as much coolness as if I had asked for a drawing-room suite.

"Quite so," I answered.

"Easiest thing in the world," said my companion, filling up my glass again in spite of my remonstrance. "Let us see!" Here he took down a large red notebook, with all the letters of the alphabet in a fringe down the edge. "A ghost you said, didn't you? That's G. G – gems – gimlets – gaspipes – gauntlets – guns – galleys. Ah, here we are. Ghosts. Volume nine, section six, page forty-one. Excuse me!" And Jack ran up a ladder and began rummaging among a pile of ledgers on a high shelf. I felt half inclined to empty my glass into the spittoon when his back was turned; but on second thoughts I disposed of it in a legitimate way.

"Here it is!" cried my London agent, jumping off the ladder with a crash, and depositing an enormous volume of manuscript upon the table. "I have all these things tabulated, so that I may lay my hands upon them in a moment. It's all right – it's quite weak" (here he filled our glasses again). "What were we looking up, again?"

"Ghosts," I suggested.

"Of course; page 41. Here we are. 'J. H. Fowler & Son, Dunkel Street, suppliers of mediums to the nobility and gentry; charms sold – love-philtres – mummies – horoscopes cast.' Nothing in your line there, I suppose?"

I shook my head despondingly.

"Frederick Tabb," continued my wife's cousin, "solo channel of communication between the living and dead. Proprietor of the spirits of Byron, Kirke White, Grimaldi, Tom Cribb, and Inigo Jones. That's about the figure!"

"Nothing romantic enough there," I objected. "Good heavens! Fancy a ghost with a black eye and a handkerchief tied round its waist, or turning summersaults, and saying, 'How are you to-morrow?'" The very idea made me so warm that I emptied my glass and filled it again.

"Here is another," said my companion, "Christopher McCarthy; bi-weekly séances – attended by all the eminent spirits of ancient and modern times. Nativities – charms – abracadabras, messages from the dead. He might be able to help us. However, I shall have a hunt round myself to-morrow, and see some of these fellows. I know their haunts, and it's odd if I can't pick up something cheap. So there's an end of business," he concluded, hurling the ledger into the corner, "and now we'll have something to drink."

We had several things to drink – so many that my inventive faculties were dulled next morning, and I had some little difficulty in explaining to Mrs. D'Odd why it was that I hung my boots and spectacles upon a peg along with my other garments before retiring to rest. The new hopes excited by the confident manner in which my agent had undertaken the commission caused me to rise superior to alcoholic reaction, and I paced about the rambling corridors and old-fashioned rooms, picturing to myself the appearance of my expected acquisition, and deciding what part of the building would harmonize best with its presence. After much consideration, I pitched upon the banqueting-hall as being, on the whole, most suitable for its reception. It was a long low room, hung round with valuable tapestry and interesting relics of the old family to whom it had belonged. Coats of mail and implements of war glimmered fitfully as the light of the fire played over them, and the wind crept under the door, moving the hangings to and fro with a ghastly rustling. At one end there was the raised dais, on which in ancient times the host and his guests used to spread their table, while a descent of a couple of steps led to the lower part of the hall, where the vassals and retainers held wassail. The floor was uncovered by any sort of carpet, but a layer of rushes had been scattered over it by my direction. In the whole room there was nothing to remind one of the nineteenth century; except, indeed, my own solid silver plate, stamped with the resuscitated family arms, which was laid out upon an oak table in the centre. This, I determined, should be the haunted room, supposing my wife's cousin to succeed in his negotiation with the spirit mongers. There was nothing for it now but to wait patiently until I heard some news of the result of his inquiries.

A letter came in the course of a few days, which, if it was short, was at least encouraging. It was scribbled in pencil on the back of a playbill, and sealed apparently with a tobacco-stopper. "Am on the track," it said. "Nothing of the sort to be had from any professional spiritualist, but picked up a fellow in a pub yesterday who says he can manage it for you. Will send him down unless you wire to the contrary. Abrahams is his name, and he has done one or two of these jobs before." The letter wound up with some incoherent allusions to a cheque, and was signed by my affectionate cousin, John Brocket.

I need hardly say that I did not wire, but awaited the arrival of Mr. Abrahams with all impatience. In spite of my belief in the supernatural, I could scarcely credit the fact that any mortal could have such a command over the spirit-world as to deal in them and barter them against mere earthly gold. Still, I had Jack's word for it that such a trade existed; and here was a gentleman with a Judaical name ready to demonstrate it by proof positive. How vulgar and commonplace Jorrock's eighteenth-century ghost would appear should I succeed in securing a real medieval apparition! I almost thought that one had been sent down in advance, for, as I walked down the moat that night before retiring to rest, I came upon a dark figure engaged in surveying the machinery of my portcullis and drawbridge. His start of surprise, however, and the manner in which he hurried off into the darkness, speedily convinced me of his earthly origin, and I put him down as some admirer of one of my female retainers mourning over the muddy Hellespont which divided him from his love. Whoever he may have been, he disappeared and did not return, though I loitered about for some time in the hope of catching a glimpse of him and exercising my feudal rights upon his person.

Jack Brocket was as good as his word. The shades of another evening were beginning to darken round Goresthorpe Grange, when a peal at the outer bell, and the sound of a fly pulling up, announced the arrival of Mr. Abrahams. I hurried down to meet him, half expecting to see a choice assortment of ghosts crowding in at his rear. Instead, however, of being the sallow-faced, melancholy-eyed man that I had pictured to myself, the ghost-dealer was a sturdy little podgy fellow, with a pair of wonderfully keen sparkling eyes and a mouth which was constantly stretched in a good-humoured, if somewhat artificial, grin. His sole stock-in-trade seemed to consist of a small leather bag jealously locked and strapped, which emitted a metallic chink upon being placed on the stone flags of the hall.

"And 'ow are you, sir?" he asked, wringing my hand with the utmost effusion. "And the missis, 'ow is she? And all the others – 'ow's all their 'ealth?"

I intimated that we were all as well as could reasonably be expected; but Mr. Abrahams happened to catch a glimpse of Mrs. D'Odd in the distance, and at once plunged at her with another string of inquiries as to her health, delivered so volubly and with such an intense earnestness that I half expected to see him terminate his cross-examination by feeling her pulse and demanding a sight of her tongue. All this time his little eyes rolled round and round, shifting perpetually from the floor to the ceiling, and from the ceiling to the walls, taking in apparently every article of furniture in a single comprehensive glance.

Having satisfied himself that neither of us was in a pathological condition, Mr. Abrahams suffered me to lead him upstairs, where a repast had been laid out for him to which he did ample justice. The mysterious little bag he carried along with him, and deposited it under his chair during the meal. It was not until the table had been cleared and we were left together that he broached the matter on which he had come down.

"I hunderstand," he remarked, puffing at a trichinopoly, "that you want my 'elp in fitting up this 'ere 'ouse with a happarition."

I acknowledged the correctness of his surmise, while mentally wondering at those restless eyes of his, which still danced about the room as if he were making an inventory of the contents.

"And you won't find a better man for the job, though I says it as shouldn't," continued my companion. "Wot did I say to the young gent wot spoke to me in the bar of the Lame Dog? 'Can you do it?' says he. 'Try me,' says I, 'me and my bag. Just try me.' I couldn't say fairer than that."

My respect for Jack Brocket's business capacities began to go up very considerably. He certainly seemed to have managed the matter wonderfully well. "You don't mean to say that you carry ghosts about in bags?" I remarked, with diffidence.

Mr. Abrahams smiled a smile of superior knowledge. "You wait," he said; "give me the right place and the right hour, with a little of the essence of Lucoptolycus" – here he produced a small bottle from his waistcoat-pocket – "and you won't find no ghost that I ain't up to. You'll see them yourself, and pick your own, and I can't say fairer than that."

As all Mr. Abraham's protestations of fairness were accompanied by a cunning leer and a wink from one or other of his wicked little eyes, the impression of candour was somewhat weakened.

"When are you going to do it?" I asked reverentially.

"Ten minutes to one in the morning," said Mr. Abrahams, with decision. "Some says midnight, but I says ten to one, when there ain't such a crowd, and you can pick your own ghost. And now," he continued, rising to his feet, "suppose you trot me round the premises, and let me see where you wants it; for there's some places as attracts 'em, and some as they won't hear of – not if there was no other place in the world."

Mr. Abrahams inspected our corridors and chambers with a most critical and observant eye, fingering the old tapestry with the air of a connoisseur, and remarking in an undertone that it would "match uncommon nice." It was not until he reached the banqueting-hall, however, which I had myself picked out, that his admiration reached the pitch of enthusiasm. "'Ere's the place!" he shouted, dancing, bag in hand, round the table on which my plate was lying, and looking not unlike some quaint little goblin himself. "'Ere's the place; we won't get nothin' to beat this! A fine room – noble, solid, none of your electro-plate trash! That's the way as things ought to be done, sir. Plenty of room for 'em to glide here. Send up some brandy and the box of weeds; I'll sit here by the fire and do the preliminaries, which is more trouble than you think; for them ghosts carries on hawful at times, before they finds out who they've got to deal with. If you was in the room they'd tear you to pieces as like as not. You leave me alone to tackle them, and at half-past twelve come in, and I'll lay they'll be quiet enough by then."

Mr. Abraham's request struck me as a reasonable one, so I left him with his feet upon the mantelpiece, and his chair in front of the fire, fortifying himself with stimulants against his refractory visitors. From the room beneath, in which I sat with Mrs. D'Odd, I could hear that after sitting for some time he rose up, and paced about the hall with quick impatient steps. We then heard him try the lock of the door, and afterwards drag some heavy article of furniture in the direction of the window, on which, apparently, he mounted, for I heard the creaking of the rusty hinges as the diamond-paned casement folded backwards, and I knew it to be situated several feet above the little man's reach. Mrs. D'Odd says that she could distinguish his voice speaking in low and rapid whispers after this, but that may have been her imagination. I confess that I began to feel more impressed than I had deemed it possible to be. There was something awesome in the thought of the solitary mortal standing by the open window and summoning in from the gloom outside the spirits of the nether world. It was with a trepidation which I could hardly disguise from Matilda that I observed that the clock was pointing to half-past twelve, and that the time had come for me to share the vigil of my visitor.

He was sitting in his old position when I entered, and there were no signs of the mysterious movements which I had overheard, though his chubby face was flushed as with recent exertion.

"Are you succeeding all right?" I asked as I came in, putting on as careless an air as possible, but glancing involuntarily round the room to see if we were alone.

"Only your help is needed to complete the matter," said Mr. Abrahams, in a solemn voice. "You shall sit by me and partake of the essence of Lucoptolycus, which removes the scales from our earthly eyes. Whatever you may chance to see, speak not and make no movement, lest you break the spell." His manner was subdued, and his usual cockney vulgarity had entirely disappeared. I took the chair which he indicated, and awaited the result.

My companion cleared the rushes from the floor in our neighbourhood, and going down upon his hands and knees, described a half circle with chalk, which enclosed the fireplace and ourselves. Round the edge of this half circle he drew several hieroglyphics, not unlike the signs of the zodiac. He then stood up and uttered a long invocation, delivered so rapidly that it sounded like a single gigantic word in some uncouth guttural language. Having finished this prayer, if prayer it was, he pulled out the small bottle which he had produced before, and poured a couple of teaspoonfuls of clear transparent fluid into a phial, which he handed to me with an intimation that I should drink it.

The liquid had a faintly sweet odour, not unlike the aroma of certain sorts of apples. I hesitated a moment before applying it to my lips, but an impatient gesture from my companion overcame my scruples, and I tossed it off. The taste was not unpleasant; and, as it gave rise to no immediate effects, I leaned back in my chair and composed myself for what was to come. Mr. Abrahams seated himself beside me, and I felt that he was watching my face from time to time while repeating some more of the invocations in which he had indulged before.

A sense of delicious warmth and languor began gradually to steal over me, partly, perhaps, from the heat of the fire, and partly from some unexplained cause. An uncontrollable impulse to sleep weighed down my eyelids, while, at the same time, my brain worked actively, and a hundred beautiful and pleasing ideas flitted through it. So utterly lethargic did I feel that, though I was aware that my companion put his hand over the region of my heart, as if to feel how it were beating, I did not attempt to prevent him, nor did I even ask him for the reason of his action. Everything in the room appeared to be reeling slowly round in a drowsy dance, of which I was the centre. The great elk's head at the far end wagged solemnly backward and forward, while the massive salvers on the tables performed cotillions with the claret cooler and the epergne. My head fell upon my breast from sheer heaviness, and I should have become unconscious had I not been recalled to myself by the opening of the door at the other end of the hall.

This door led on to the raised dais, which, as I have mentioned, the heads of the house used to reserve for their own use. As it swung slowly back upon its hinges, I sat up in my chair, clutching at the arms, and staring with a horrified glare at the dark passage outside. Something was coming down it – something unformed and intangible, but still a something. Dim and shadowy, I saw it flit across the threshold, while a blast of ice-cold air swept down the room, which seemed to blow through me, chilling my very heart. I was aware of the mysterious presence, and then I heard it speak in a voice like the sighing of an east wind among pine-trees on the banks of a desolate sea.

It said: "I am the invisible nonentity. I have affinities and am subtle. I am electric, magnetic, and spiritualistic. I am the great ethereal sigh-heaver. I kill dogs. Mortal, wilt thou choose me?"

I was about to speak, but the words seemed to be choked in my throat; and, before I could get them out, the shadow flitted across the hall and vanished in the darkness at the other side, while a long-drawn melancholy sigh quivered through the apartment.

I turned my eyes toward the door once more, and beheld, to my astonishment, a very small old woman, who hobbled along the corridor and into the hall. She passed backward and forward several times, and then, crouching down at the very edge of the circle upon the floor, she disclosed a face the horrible malignity of which shall never be banished from my recollection. Every foul passion appeared to have left its mark upon that hideous countenance.

"Ha! ha!" she screamed, holding out her wizened hands like the talons of an unclean bird. "You see what I am. I am the fiendish old woman. I wear snuff-coloured silks. My curse descends on people. Sir Walter was partial to me. Shall I be thine, mortal?"

I endeavoured to shake my head in horror; on which she aimed a blow at me with her crutch, and vanished with an eldritch scream.

By this time my eyes turned naturally toward the open door, and I was hardly surprised to see a man walk in of tall and noble stature. His face was deadly pale, but was surmounted by a fringe of dark hair which fell in ringlets down his back. A short pointed beard covered his chin. He was dressed in loose-fitting clothes, made apparently of yellow satin, and a large white ruff surrounded his neck. He paced across the room with slow and majestic strides. Then turning, he addressed me in a sweet, exquisitely-modulated voice.

"I am the cavalier," he remarked. "I pierce and am pierced. Here is my rapier. I clink steel. This is a blood-stain over my heart. I can emit hollow groans. I am patronized by many old Conservative families. I am the original manor-house apparition. I work alone, or in company with shrieking damsels."

I am the plaintive and sentimental, the beautiful and ill-used.

He bent his head courteously, as though awaiting my reply, but the same choking sensation prevented me from speaking; and, with a deep bow, he disappeared.

He had hardly gone before a feeling of intense horror stole over me, and I was aware of the presence of a ghastly creature in the room of dim outlines and uncertain proportions. One moment it seemed to pervade the entire apartment, while at another it would become invisible, but always leaving behind it a distinct consciousness of its presence. Its voice, when it spoke, was quavering and gusty. It said, "I am the leaver of footsteps and the spiller of gouts of blood. I tramp upon corridors. Charles Dickens has alluded to me. I make strange and disagreeable noises. I snatch letters and place invisible hands on people's wrists. I am cheerful. I burst into peals of hideous laughter. Shall I do one now?" I raised my hand in a deprecating way, but too late to prevent one discordant outbreak which echoed through the room. Before I could lower it the apparition was gone.

I turned my head toward the door in time to see a man come hastily and stealthily into the chamber. He was a sunburned powerfully-built fellow, with earrings in his ears and a Barcelona handkerchief tied loosely round his neck. His head was bent upon his chest, and his whole aspect was that of one afflicted by intolerable remorse. He paced rapidly backward and forward like a caged tiger, and I observed that a drawn knife glittered in one of his hands, while he grasped what appeared to be a piece of parchment in the other. His voice, when he spoke, was deep and sonorous. He said, "I am a murderer. I am a ruffian. I crouch when I walk. I step noiselessly. I know something of the Spanish Main. I can do the lost treasure business. I have charts. Am able-bodied and a good walker. Capable of haunting a large park." He looked toward me beseechingly, but before I could make a sign I was paralyzed by the horrible sight which appeared at the door.

It was a very tall man, if, indeed, it might be called a man, for the gaunt bones were protruding through the corroding flesh, and the features of a leaden hue. A winding sheet was wrapped round the figure, and formed a hood over the head, from under the shadow of which two fiendish eyes, deep-set in their grisly sockets, blazed and sparkled like red-hot coals. The lower jaw had fallen upon the breast, disclosing a withered, shrivelled tongue and two lines of black and jagged fangs. I shuddered and drew back as this fearful apparition advanced to the edge of the circle.

"I am the American blood-curdler," it said, in a voice which seemed to come in a hollow murmur from the earth beneath it. "None other is genuine. I am the embodiment of Edgar Allan Poe. I am circumstantial and horrible. I am a low-caste spirit-subduing spectre. Observe my blood and my bones. I am grisly and nauseous. No depending on artificial aid. Work with grave-clothes, a coffin-lid, and a galvanic battery. Turn hair white in a night." The creature stretched out its fleshless arms to me as if in entreaty, but I shook my head; and it vanished, leaving a low sickening repulsive odour behind it. I sank back in my chair, so overcome by terror and disgust that I would have very willingly resigned myself to dispensing with a ghost altogether, could I have been sure that this was the last of the hideous procession.

A faint sound of trailing garments warned me that it was not so. I looked up, and beheld a white figure emerging from the corridor into the right. As it stepped across the threshold I saw that it was that of a young and beautiful woman dressed in the fashion of a bygone day. Her hands were clasped in front of her, and her pale proud face bore traces of passion and of suffering. She crossed the hall with a gentle sound, like the rustling of autumn leaves, and then, turning her lovely and unutterably sad eyes upon me, she said,

"I am the plaintive and sentimental, the beautiful and ill-used. I have been forsaken and betrayed. I shriek in the night-time and glide down passages. My antecedents are highly respectable and generally aristocratic. My tastes are aesthetic. Old oak furniture like this would do, with a few more coats of mail and plenty of tapestry. Will you not take me?"

Her voice died away in a beautiful cadence as she concluded, and she held out her hands as in supplication. I am always sensitive to female influences. Besides, what would Jorrocks' ghost be to this? Could anything be in better taste? Would I not be exposing myself to the chance of injuring my nervous system by interviews with such creatures as my last visitor, unless I decided at once? She gave me a seraphic smile, as if she knew what was passing in my mind. That smile settled the matter. "She will do!" I cried; "I choose this one;" and as, in my enthusiasm, I took a step toward her, I passed over the magic circle which had girdled me round.

"Argentine, we have been robbed!"

I had an indistinct consciousness of these words being spoken, or rather screamed, in my ear a great number of times without my being able to grasp their meaning. A violent throbbing in my head seemed to adapt itself to their rhythm, and I closed my eyes to the lullaby of "Robbed, robbed, robbed." A vigorous shake caused me to open them again, however, and the sight of Mrs. D'Odd in the scantiest of costumes and most furious of tempers was sufficiently impressive to recall all my scattered thoughts, and make me realize that I was lying on my back on the floor, with my head among the ashes which had fallen from last night's fire, and a small glass phial in my hand.

I staggered to my feet, but felt so weak and giddy that I was compelled to fall back into a chair. As my brain became clearer, stimulated by the exclamations of Matilda, I began gradually to recollect the events of the night. There was the door through which my supernatural visitors had filed. There was the circle of chalk with the hieroglyphics round the edge. There was the cigar-box and brandy bottle which had been honoured by the attentions of Mr. Abrahams. But the seer himself – where was he? And what was this open window with a rope running out of it? And where, O where, was the pride of Goresthorpe Grange, the glorious plate which was to have been the delectation of generations of D'Odds? And why was Mrs. D. standing in the gray light of dawn, wringing her hands and repeating her monotonous refrain? It was only very gradually that my misty brain took these things in, and grasped the connection between them.

Reader, I have never seen Mr. Abrahams since; I have never seen the plate stamped with the resuscitated family crest; hardest of all, I have never caught a glimpse of the melancholy spectre with the trailing garments, nor do I expect that I ever shall. In fact my night's experiences have cured me of my mania for the supernatural, and quite reconciled me to inhabiting the humdrum nineteenth century edifice on the outskirts of London which Mrs. D. has long had in her mind's eye.

As to the explanation of all that occurred – that is a matter which is open to several surmises. That Mr. Abrahams, the ghost-hunter, was identical with Jemmy Wilson, alias the Nottingham crackster, is considered more than probable at Scotland Yard, and certainly the description of that remarkable burglar tallied very well with the appearance of my visitor. The small bag which I have described was picked up in a neighbouring field next day, and found to contain a choice assortment of jimmies and centrebits. Footmarks deeply imprinted in the mud on either side of the moat showed that an accomplice from below had received the sack of precious metals which had been let down through the open window. No doubt the pair of scoundrels, while looking round for a job, had overheard Jack Brocket's indiscreet inquiries, and had promptly availed themselves of the tempting opening.

And now as to my less substantial visitors, and the curious grotesque vision which I had enjoyed – am I to lay it down to any real power over occult matters possessed by my Nottingham friend? For a long time I was doubtful upon the point, and eventually endeavoured to solve it by consulting a well-known analyst and medical man, sending him the few drops of the so-called essence of Lucoptolycus which remained in my phial. I append the letter which I received from him, only too happy to have the opportunity of winding up my little narrative by the weighty words of a man of learning.

Arundel Street.

Dear Sir,

> Your very singular case has interested me extremely. The bottle which you sent contained a strong solution of chloral, and the quantity which you describe yourself as having swallowed must have amounted to at least eighty grains of the pure hydrate. This would of course have reduced you to a partial state of insensibility, gradually going on to complete coma. In this semi-unconscious state of chloralism it is not unusual for circumstantial and bizarre visions to present themselves – more especially to individuals unaccustomed to the use of the drug. You tell me in your note that your mind was saturated with ghostly literature, and that you had long taken a morbid interest in classifying and recalling the various forms in which apparitions have been said to appear. You must also remember that you were expecting to see something of that very nature, and that your nervous system was worked up to an unnatural state of tension.

Under the circumstances, I think that, far from the sequel being an astonishing one, it would have been very surprising indeed to anyone versed in narcotics had you not experienced some such effects.

I remain, dear sir, sincerely yours,

T.E. Stube, M.D.

Argentine D'Odd, Esq.,
The Elms, Brixton.

WAR

Archer Latrobe Carroll (1894 - 1996) was born in Washington DC and served in the U.S. Army Corps of Engineers before becoming a writer. The exceptionally long-lived Carroll was the author of over twenty books for children, illustrated by his wife, Ruth.

"A Butterfly in the Fog" is the story of Graham and Phebe, a couple separated by the outbreak of World War I. It was written while Carroll was a student at Harvard. As with several of the other stories in this collection, it depicts the end of an age of innocence. Graham struggles with questions of duty and sacrifice, but, from Phebe's perspective, he appears extraordinarily callous. Ultimately, the reader is left to determine if Phebe's own actions are selfish or not.

A BUTTERFLY
IN THE FOG

LATROBE CARROLL

I

Phebe was slight, and so blonde that cream and gold seemed the chief ingredients of her. She had alert, very sparkling blue eyes, and she laughed with the effortlessness of a brook tinkling over rooks.

Graham Stanford saw her first in Murren. She was spending the summer there with her mother, as she had spent numerous summers in Bar Harbor and Brighton and Dieppe. He had gone to the Bernese Oberland to climb, and stayed on because of Phebe. They would pass each other in the village street, and he would think her delicately attractive, and she would admire his air of distinction and a certain sureness in the way he held himself. At last, after a tentative acquaintanceship of glances which said: "I should like to know you," they succeeded in being introduced.

The highly charged days preceding the war brought them down to Interlaken. Graham spent most of his time in the streets, where there were the latest bulletins and people conversing with the bonne camaraderie of those shipwrecked on a desert island. When he wasn't in the streets he was with Phebe. Her mother gave no trouble; she was a semi-invalid who allowed her daughter to have her own way because, when she didn't, Phebe wept. So, by a tacit compact, the mother paid all bills and asked no questions; in return, Phebe saw that her mother's eggs were cooked to the proper gradation between soft and hard.

The Best College Short Stories. Henry T. Schnittkind, ed. Boston: Stratford Company, 1919.

Graham had interested Phebe at first because she liked Englishmen, and he seemed a very nice one. Together they had taken drives in Phebe's roadster, made long tramps, and stood on mountain tops, isolated in surrounding immensity. A certain massiveness about him gave her a feeling of security. By degrees his personality wove itself into the texture of her nature: became a strand that could not easily be wrenched away.

After a month of good times together came the war. It permeated the Oberland like an invisible, blighting exhalation. The holiday mood vanished. No one spoke of scenery now. No one spoke of Switzerland. Most of the tourists scattered to remote lands; few were left in the mournful sunshine and unheeded magnificence of the Alps. Through this new gloom Phebe flitted, puzzled, unhappy and a little chilled. She was nineteen and unable to comprehend her environment of depression. Worst of all Graham grew serious. She could have borne anything but this.

II

On the day that England declared war Phebe and Graham walked up the path that leads to the top of the Harder. He climbed with restless strides and Phebe kept up with him, only panting a little. Now and again he thrust his walking stick fiercely into the pine needles on the path. At length, he brought it down upon a rock with such force that it split.

"Oh, what a pity, Graham," she said. "You've broken your nicest cane."

"It was a nice cane," he said, absently. "Filthy mess. That's what it's going to be. A filthy mess. And that England should be drawn into it…"

"It all seems nonsense to me, somehow," said Phebe.

Viciously he cut at the branches overhead with his stick.

"Don't do that, Graham," she remonstrated. "Look, you just snipped off those pretty little baby leaves."

"Oh, damn the leaves!"

She said nothing. Two facile tears sparkled in her eyes.

They stepped into a little clearing and the Jungfrau appeared, amazingly. Its whiteness was as fresh as the bloom of a flower.

"Funny old fat, cottony Jungfrau," said Graham. "I shall hate to leave it. I can't have a crack at climbing it after all." He spoke of his departure as though she had foreseen it.

The color ebbed from her face. "Graham, you're not going!"

"Of course. They'll need me. You see, I've had training with the volunteers. I couldn't stay messing about in Switzerland."

She flushed vividly. "Graham, you're not! It's such nonsense – its going to be over so soon –"

"It may last," he said. "It might last – even a year. In a war like this –"

"Please don't talk about the war," she interrupted. "Let's –," she smiled, "let's talk about our climb tomorrow. I do hope it's a day like this."

"Oh, I haven't told you," he said. I'm going back to England tomorrow."

"Tomorrow?" She turned the word into a little cry. A listener would have imagined he had struck her.

He nodded. "My train leaves at five in the afternoon."

"Oh," she said faintly,

"Come on, let's tramp," he cried, bounding up.

Never had they walked as on that day. They walked desperately, unheedingly, stumbling over roots, hardly noticing which paths they chose. They didn't speak at all. An old woman, burdened with twigs, gazed after them in amazement. Why was this fragile girl, out of breath, almost running up the mountain beside the tall grim man with a split cane.

They were a little surprised, at last, to find themselves again in the hotel. Phebe was white. Stones had gashed the delicate leather of her shoes.

"Are you feeling better?" she asked sympathetically.

He started as her words pierced his abstraction.

"Yes" he said. "But you poor girl! I was mad to set that pace."

"My blouse is wringing, and I'm almost dead."

There in the hallway, before the elevator, they faced each other silently.

"I'm an idiot," he accused himself.

"No, you're not; but can you come with me for a last drive tomorrow?"

Then an absurd thing happened. It must have been the tired droop of her head, or the word "last", or perhaps it was the way she spoke; but tears rose to his eyes. It was most embarrassing, he reflected, to be snivelling in a hotel hallway.

He achieved a smile.

"Good. We'll have that last drive."

Then the elevator lifted her from his view.

III

Phebe slept little that night. She thought constantly of Oraham and the five o'clock train to Geneva. By early morning she had decided that there was no necessity for his going, and that it would be better for him if he stayed on for a few days with her. She would try and persuade him. But if he persisted – how could she keep him?

She tossed until the bedclothes rolled themselves into a ball and she got up to unwind them. As she was tucking the comer of a sheet under the mattress she had an inspiration which made her feel a little as though ahe were dropping in an express eleyator. Graham must miss his train.

She opened her Baedeker and spent a long time adding up distances on the road from Interlaken to Brienz and dividing these by the number of miles the roadster would travel on one gallon of gasoline. It worried her terribly; she had never been good at arithmetic.

IV

In spite of her sleepless night Phebe was in a gay mood the next day. They took the road toward Brienz that skirts the lake, with its overtopping rim of mountains. It was one of those days of unappreciated sunshine which passed in cloudless succession during that tragic August. Phebe drove superbly. On her head she wore a limp vermilion cap which enveloped her hair like a nonchalant flame. With cushioned speed the car drove through the rich meadow air and again plunged into cool forests.

"Isn't it a glorious day!" Phebe said. "And there'll be lots more like it, and you're not really going away this afternoon, are you, Graham?"

He smiled. "I'm afraid I am," he said. "But I've today with you and – Jove, I've never seen the sky so blue!"

"I wish I had a dress just that color," she laughed. "Don't you think it would be becoming?"

But he was reviving old memories. "When you were a child," he said reminiscently, "did you ever think that the most delicious life one could possibly lead would be to live on one of those big, rumpled clouds? Your feet would sink into it a little like walking on feather pillows and every once in a while you'd come to a torn place where the blue shines through. And those would be lakes, and you'd fish."

Phebe had been listening intently, her face alight.

"How funny," she said. "Because I used to think exactly that thing. And you'd bask all day on its back, wouldn't you, in a sort of sweet dozy dream."

"And you'd never see the black under side when it rains," said Graham.

A bird, flying low, passed over their heads and darted along the road in front of the car.

"Oh, look!" Phebe shouted. "Let's race it!"

Magnificently the roadster gathered speed under her hand. A blast of wind ruffed Graham's hair and tugged at her vermilion cap.

"Almost up with him," Graham shouted. "Just a bit faster!"

But the bird swerved off the road into the forest. They laughed as their eyes met.

"The beggar didn't play fair!" cried Graham. "I say, you can drive!"

"Can't I," thought Phebe.

Neither spoke for a time. Then he gave a little groan.

"What is it?" Phebe asked, startled.

"Something amazing happened then," he said. "I'd forgotten – I'd forgotten about the war."

"Oh, that" said Phebe. "When we were having such a good time, why bring in the war?" She paused, with pouting lips. "Everybody's been horrid for the last few days," she continued. "Everybody except mother, and she never knows what's going on. We sit in the dining-room of the hotel and in that big room hardly anyone says a word. And when I laugh it sounds like a cannon and everybody turns around and stares at me. I never saw anything so gloomy in my whole life. And now you begin again." She sounded the horn in a series of discontented little bursts.

"I can't help it," he answered. "I try to, but I can't. Why, do you know, today I've only had one moment when I wasn't feeling as if I –" Instead of ending the sentence he sighed. "It was when we raced the bird, and I forgot."

Phebe turned to him. "Just don't worry about it," she advised. "I haven't worried a bit. Except about your going. And do you know what I think about that?"

"What?"

"I think you'd be a perfect goose to go."

He smiled. "Then what on earth am I to do?"

"Wait."

"But don't you see – all my friends will be in it? I'd be thought an absolute rotter if I didn't go."

"But you don't have to fight," she asserted.

"Oh, don't I though, just."

"But why? Why not come to America?"

"Oh, don't talk rot," he said.

She tilted her chin defiantly. "I'm not talking rot," she protested, "and I never talk rot, and I don't think you should use that word about me anyway."

"Sorry." he said with a smile. There was a silence tempered by the humming of the wind.

Through a gap in the trees a steamer, far out on the lake, came into view. In its wake hung a low, level stratum of soiled air. High above it towered the broken ranges that cluster round the Faulhom. A glade opened before them, rich in ferns and bespattered with sunshine. Then the trees closed in again. The landscape had done its best to pour itself into their thoughts, but neither of them had given it a moment's attention.

"Graham." said Phebe.

"Yes?"

"Won't you stay!"

"See here, Phebe," he answered impatiently, "I can't stay. The thing's impossible. There are certain things, you know, that one can't do."

Viciously the car leaped forward. Trees and pastures swept by them in a rush of greenery.

"See here," Graham shouted above the wind, "if you aren't careful we'll hit something, you know."

The roadster slackened its pace. Phebe turned blazing eyes on him. "I wish we did," she said vehemently. "I'd just like to hit something!"

He smiled. "It wouldn't be a bad death," he said. "There are worse ways," he added in a voice touched with grimness.

"Listen," she said decisively, "if you talk about the war again I'll put on full speed and this car can go eighty miles an hour and we'll probably kill a child."

He laughed. "To save a child," he said, "I won't."

But he broke his promise at once.

"Do you know," he remarked, "It's odd, but all this gives me a queer sort of intoxicated sensation. I've been feeling a bit drunk all day."

"Drunk on war?" she smiled. "Why, what a funny idea!"

"Yes, isn't it?" he asked. You never heard of it affecting anyone like that, did you?"

"No."

"Hm," he commented. "I must be a rum sort of chap."

"Rum is good," she remarked.

He stared.

"I said rum was good. Silly, it's only a joke."

"Oh," he replied vaguely, and lapsed into silence.

"What are you thinking about?" she demanded, after a time.

"Thinking? Oh, I'm – one might say – re-adjusting myself."

"Please don't re-adjust yourself with me. You're awfully dull when you do it."

"Yes, I dare say I am," he admitted frankly.

"You've been dull all day."

"You see, I haven't much tried to be interesting."

"Most of the time," she said as their glances brushed for an instant, "you are without trying."

He laughed and put his arm about her.

"You are an amusing girl," he said.

For some time she had been hoping he would do just this. She leaned back against his arm with a smile. She appeared to have been constructed for such situations: every particle of her was delicately responsive to moments like this.

"Now you're being interesting for the first time today," she said.

They slipped on through the thick radiance of the summer afternoon. A moth, oddly striped, settled on her arm and clung there as the wind lifted its wings.

"What kind of a queer insect is that?" she asked.

"The worst thing about this war –" he began.

"Oh heavens," she burst out, "if you only knew how I hate to hear you talk about the war. It's too senseless to last – I've heard people in the hotel say it will be over in a month. You'd be too silly to leave, Graham. So, why go to England and arrive, and find it all over?"

"You don't realize," he said, "what England has to face."

"Oh, stop talking about it," she begged. "There wouldn't be any war if people hadn't talked and talked and brought it on."

She reflected, stroking the curve of her chin with a pliant forefinger.

"Oh, Graham," she said, at length. "I brought you out to ask you something, and I intended to say it later, but I might as well say it now. You know what it is. I want you to stay on – for me. I'll take you on the longest rides and well make all the stunning climbs we planned –"

He interrupted her. "I can't," he said simply.

She was silent. Then:

"What will I do when you're gone?" she asked. "I might as well die – there won't be anything else to do."

He drew a deep, painful breath and let it escape in a sigh.

"Oh, Phebe," he said, "it's hard enough for you, but it's not so very hard because you can go back to America and leave it all. But the thing I've been thinking is – I have two younger brothers who will have to go. And there's an end to all the dreams I've had for those youngsters. So you see –" His voice thickened and died.

"Oh, please don't take it so seriously," she said. "Nothing would hurt if you didn't take anything seriously."

He startled her by laughing. "Jove," he said, "I can't deny that!"

"But it's true, isn't it?" she asked.

"Yes," he said. "And you don't know how much good that laugh did. I rather thought I was never going to again, you know."

She turned off the highway into a narrow road. Branches met above their heads; vivid tatters of the sky blazed through. She had taken off her cap. Her bobbed hair hung in a rich layer from which the intermittent sunbeams struck golden sparkles. Never before had he thought her so daintily luminous. He leaned dose and patted her cheek as though she were a child. But Phebe was unresponsive. She listened for a break in the throb of the engine and grew cold. Then in last appeal, an uprush of words overwhelmed her:

"Please stay, Graham! Oh please! You can stay just a few days longer and I'll be so nice to you – nicer than I ever have been. Graham, please don't leave on the five o'clock train!"

"You don't know how I'm feeling, Phebe," he said gravely. His head drooped forward for an instant as though his neck muscles had grown too weak to hold it erect. "If you knew how I feel, you'd only be rather sorry for me."

Phebe listened with trepidation to the pulse of the engine. Presently the car slackened its pace, moved more and more slowly, then came to a standstill.

"Hello!" he cried. "That's odd. It's never broken down before."

Phebe's voice fluttered as she said: "It didn't break down. It stopped because I didn't put in enough gasoline."

He faced her squarely.

"You don't mean you planned to have it stop?"

She nodded in silent assent, trembling a little.

He gazed at her in amazement. "But you couldn't do a thing like that."

"Yes, I could," she said faintly. She bit at the corner of her handkerchief. "Oh, please don't be mad at me, Graham. It was killing me to have you go today and now you can't. You see – I had just enough gasoline put in to bring us here. I've been here before and we're miles from anywhere."

His face set in grim lines.

"Are you ragging me," he demanded, "or is this true?"

"You can look in the gasoline tank if you want to."

"To think," he said in a voice of detached wonder, "that a girl so sweet could do a thing so stupidly devilish."

He stepped to the road.

"What are you going to do, Graham?" Her question was a cry.

"I'm going," he said coldly.

"But you can't catch your train."

"I'll catch that train," he said, "if I have to run every step of the way. But I may be picked up when I get to the main road."

Phebe looked as though all her blood had turned watery, gray and cold.

"Graham, you're leaving – you're leaving me."

He took out his cigarette case and stared at it vacantly. Then he found his watch, glanced at it, and began to run up the road.

"Graham," she cried, "come back – if you love me."

He halted for a moment, without turning.

"Graham, give me – give me something – your cigarette case – something solid to hold and keep."

"When I get down to the road," he called back, "I'll send some one up for you."

He disappeared in a grove of pines. Birds chirruped in the distance and a breeze hissed through the branches overhead.

Phebe wept silently, a slender figure drooped over the steering wheel.

Phebe was still in Interlaken when a letter and a package came. They were sent from a hospital in France. The letter was short; it said:

It is with deep regret that I inform you that Private Graham Stanford died of his wounds this morning at three-thirty. He directed me to send you the accompanying cigarette case. He wished me to say he did not realize you had asked for it until he was in the train for Geneva. He wished me to say he was sorry.

Yours sincerely,
D. L. Roberts
Army Hospital Corps.

When Phebe read this, an odd trembling passed over her; she felt ill.

She dropped the letter in her lap and gazed about the room. Everything in it seemed strange. Even the dress she wore seemed strange. She opened her eyes wide: an inhabitant of a world she did not understand.

"Unfortunately, as a general thing, people of the upper classes – savants, scholars, artists, writers, judges, priests, physicians, etc. – maintain a discreet reserve, as though afraid to speak out. They are less free, have their own interests to protect, and are silent while others talk. Such faint-heartedness, such cowardice, is absolutely despicable. What is there to fear? It is excusable to deny facts through ignorance. But not to dare admit things seen – a sad state of affairs!"

  – Camille Flammarion, Death and Its Mystery (1922)
  (Latrobe Caroll, trans.)

"This magnificent butterfly finds a little heap of dirt and sits still on it; but man will never on his heap of mud keep still. He wants to be a saint, and he wants to be a devil – and every time he shuts his eyes he sees himself as a very fine fellow – so fine as he can never be."

  – Joseph Conrad, Lord Jim (1900)

H.P. Lovecraft, in a 1927 letter to Clark Ashton Smith, referred to Robert W. Chambers as a "Fallen Titan – equipped with the right brains and education but wholly out of the habit of using them".

Lovecraft's derision proved prophetic, and, if Robert Chambers (1865 - 1933) is remembered at all today, it is as a failed author of "Weird" fiction. But although Lovecraft paints a compellingly tragic picture of genius wasted, it is neither accurate nor just.

Chambers wrote almost a hundred books. These were primarily romantic or historical fiction, but he also dabbled in children's books, fishing guides, essays and contemporary "issue-based" literary novels, the latter probing such sensitive topics as adultery, alcoholism and divorce. While only a few of his novels contained elements of the supernatural, nearly all of them were best-sellers: during his lifetime, Chambers was a literary sensation.

The King in Yellow (1895) demonstrated that Chambers could portray the unknowable Weird if he so wished – the collection remains one of the defining works of American horror. But Chambers consciously chose to devote the bulk of his effort to writing the knowable and the relevant instead of the weird and uncanny. Although much of his output was shamelessly commercial, to label him a literary failure is to impose Lovecraft's own values on Chambers' decisions. Whatever Lovecraft thought of his writing, Chambers was phenomenally successfully and lived a life of ease and comfort.

A survey of Chambers' non-Weird fiction also turns up a number of gems, not the least of which is "Marooned". This story was first published in Barbarians (1917). Unlike his later war-related novels, Chambers eschews the epic for the personal in this collection. Each of the book's interlinked stories focuses on an individual triumph or tragedy rather than the great sweep of conflict.

"Marooned" captures a uniquely unsettling atmosphere. It also portrays Chambers' traditionally square-jawed protagonists in an unusual light, depicting their slow degeneration into madness. Upon its publication, The New York Times called "Marooned" the "queerest and grimmest" of all the tales in Barbarians, and slated the author for writing something so "obviously improbable".

MAROONED

ROBERT W. CHAMBERS

I

"Will they do anything for us?" repeated Carfax.

The staff officer thought it very doubtful. He stood in the snow switching his wet puttees and looking out across a world of tumbled mountains. Over on his right lay Germany; on his left, France; Switzerland towered in ice behind him against an arctic blue sky.

It grew warm on the Falcon Peak, almost hot in the sun. Snow was melting on black heaps of rocks; a black salamander, swollen, horrible, stirred from its stiff lethargy and crawled away blindly across the snow.

"Our case is this," continued Carfax; "somebody's made a mistake. We've been forgotten. And if they don't relieve us rather soon some of us will go off our bally nuts. Do you get me, Major?"

"I beg your pardon –"

"Do you understand what I've been saying?"

"Oh, yes; quite so."

"Then ask yourself, Major, how long can four men stand it, cooped up here on this peak? A month, two months, three, five? But it's going on ten months – ten months of solitude – silence – not a sound, except when the snowslides go bellowing off into Alsace down there below our feet." His bronzed lip quivered. "I'll get aboard one if this keeps on."

He kicked a lump of ice off into space; the staff officer glanced at him and looked away hurriedly.

Barbarians. New York: D. Appleton, 1917.

"Listen," said Carfax with an effort; "we're not regulars – not like the others. The Canadian division is different. Its discipline is different – in spite of Salisbury Plain and K. of K. In my regiment there are half-breeds, pelt-hunters, Nome miners, Yankees of all degrees, British, Canadians, gentlemen adventurers from Cosmopolis. They're good soldiers, but do you think they'd stay here? It is so in the Athabasca Battalion; it is the same in every battalion. They wouldn't stay here ten months. They couldn't. We are free people; we can't stand indefinite caging; we've got to have walking room once every few months."

The staff officer murmured something.

"I know; but good God, man! Four of us have been on this peak for nearly ten months. We've never seen a Boche, never heard a shot. Seasons come and go, rain falls, snow falls, the winds blow from the Alps, but nothing else comes to us except a half-frozen bird or two."

The staff officer looked about him with an involuntary shiver. There was nothing to see except the sun on the wet, black rocks and the whitewashed observation station of solid stone from which wires sagged into the valley on the French side.

"Well – good luck," he said hastily, looking as embarrassed as he felt. "I'll be toddling along."

"Will you say a word to the General, like a good chap? Tell him how it is with us – four of us all alone up here since the beginning. There's Gary, Captain in the Athabasca Battalion, a Yankee if the truth were known; there's Flint, a cockney lieutenant in a Calgary battery; there's young Gray, a lieutenant and a Prince Edward Islander; and here's me, a major in the Yukon Battalion – four of us on the top of a cursed French mountain – ten months of each other, of solitude, silence – and the whole world rocking with battles – and not a sound up here – not a whisper! I tell you we're four sick men! We've got a grip on ourselves yet, but it's slipping. We're still fairly civil to each other, but the strain is killing. Sullen silences smother irritability, but –" he added in a peculiarly pleasant voice, "I expect we are likely to start killing each other if somebody doesn't get us out of here very damn quick."

The staff captain's lips formed the words, "Awfully sorry! Good luck!" but his articulation was indistinct, and he went off hurriedly, still murmuring.

Carfax stood in the snow, watching him clamber down among the rocks, where an alpinist orderly joined them.

If I could only sleep. It's the silence, or the voices — I don't know which.

Gary presently appeared at the door of the observation station. "Has he gone?" he inquired, without interest.

"Yes," said Carfax.

"Is he going to do anything for us?"

"I don't know... No!"

Gary lingered, kicked at a salamander, then turned and went indoors. Carfax sat down on a rock and sucked at his empty pipe.

Later the three officers in the observation station came out to the door again and looked at him, but turned back into the doorway without saying anything. And after a while Carfax, feeling slightly feverish, went indoors, too.

In the square, whitewashed room Gray and Flint were playing cut-throat poker; Gary was at the telephone, but the messages received or transmitted appeared to be of no importance. There had never been any message of importance from the Falcon Peak or to it. There was likely to be none.

Ennui, inertia, dry rot – and four men, sometimes silently, sometimes violently cursing their isolation, but always cursing it – afraid in their souls lest they fall to cursing one another aloud as they had begun to curse in their hearts.

Months ago rain had fallen; now snow fell, and vast winds roared around them from the Alps. But nothing else ever came to the Falcon Peak, except a fierce, red-eyed Lèmmergeyer sheering above the peak on enormous pinions, or a few little migrating birds fluttering down, half frozen, from the high air lanes. Now and then, also, came to them a staff officer from below, British sometimes, sometimes French, who lingered no longer than necessary and then went back again, down into friendly deeps where were trees and fields and familiar things and human companionship, leaving them to their hell of silence, of solitude, and of each other.

The tide of war had never washed the base of their granite cliffs; the highest battle wave had thundered against the Vosges beyond earshot; not even a deadened echo of war penetrated those silent heights; not a Taube floated in the zenith.

In the squatty, whitewashed ruin which once had been the eyrie of some petty predatory despot, and which now served as an observatory for two idle divisions below in the valley, stood three telescopes. Otherwise the furniture consisted of valises, trunks, a table and chairs, a few books, several newspapers, and some tennis balls lying on the floor.

Carfax seated himself at one of the telescopes, not looking through it, his heavy eyes partly closed, his burnt-out pipe between his teeth.

Gary rose from the telephone and joined the card players. They shuffled and dealt listlessly, seldom speaking save in monosyllables.

After a while Carfax went over to the card table and the young lieutenant cashed in and took his place at the telescope.

Below in the Alsatian valley spring had already started the fruit buds, and a delicate green edged the lower snow line.

The lieutenant spoke of it wistfully; nobody paid any attention; he rose presently and went outdoors to the edge of the precipice – not too near,for fear he might be tempted to jump out through the sunshine, down into that inviting world of promise below.

Far underneath him – very far down in the valley – a cuckoo called. Out of the depths floated the elfin halloo, the gaily malicious challenge of spring herself, shouted up melodiously from the plains of Alsace – *Cuckoo! Cuckoo! Cuckoo!* – You poor, sullen, frozen foreigner up there on the snowy rocks! – *Cuckoo! Cuckoo! Cuckoo!*

The lieutenant of Yukon infantry, whose name was Gray, came back into the room.

"There's a bird of sorts yelling like hell below," he said to the card players.

Carfax ran over his cards, rejected three, and nodded. "Well, let him yell," he said.

"What is it, a Boche dicky-bird insulting you?" asked Gary, in his Yankee drawl.

Flint, declining to draw cards, got up and went out into the sunshine.

When he returned to the table, he said: "It's a cuckoo... I wish to God I were out of this," he added.

They continued to play for a while without apparent interest. Each man had won his comrades' money too many times to care when Carfax added up debit and credit and wrote down each man's score. In nine months, alternately beggaring one another, they had now, it appeared, broken about even.

Gary, an American in British uniform, twitched a newspaper toward himself, slouched in his chair, and continued to read for a while. The paper was French and two weeks old; he jerked it about irritably.

Gray, resting his elbows on his knees, sat gazing vacantly out of the narrow window. For a smart officer he had grown slovenly.

"If there was any trout fishing to be had," he began; but Flint laughed scornfully.

"What are you laughing at? There must be trout in the valley down there where that bird is," insisted Gray, reddening.

"Yes, and there are cows and chickens and houses and women. What of it?"

Gary, in his faded service uniform of a captain, scowled over his newspaper. "It's bad enough to be here," he said heavily; "so don't let's talk about it. Quit disputing."

Flint ignored the order.

"If there was anything sportin' to do –"

"Oh, shut up," muttered Carfax. "Do you expect sport on a hog-back?"

Gray picked up a tennis ball and began to play it against the whitewashed stone wall, using the palm of his hand. Flint joined him presently; Gary went over to the telephone, set the receiver to his ear and spoke to some officer in the distant valley on the French side, continuing a spiritless conversation while watching the handball play. After a while he rose, shambled out and down among the rocks to the spring where snow lay, trodden and filthy, and the big, black salamanders crawled half stupefied in the sun. All his loathing and fear of them kindled again as it always did at sight of them. "Dirty beasts," he muttered, stumping and stumbling among the stunted fir trees; "some day they'll bite some of these damn fools who say they can't bite. And that'll end 'em."

Flint and Gray continued to play handball in a perfunctory way while Carfax looked on from the telephone without interest. Gary came back, his shoes and puttees all over wet snow.

"Unless," he said in a monotonous voice, "something happens within the next few days I'll begin to feel queer in my head; and if I feel it coming on, I'll blow my bally nut off. Or somebody's." And he touched his service automatic in its holster and yawned.

After a dead silence:

"Buck up," remarked Carfax; "think how our men must feel in Belfort, never letting off their guns. Ross rifles, too – not a shot at a Boche since the damn war began!"

"God!" said Flint, smiting the ball with the palm of his hand, "to think of those Ross rifles rusting down there and to think of the pink-skinned pigs they could paunch so cleanly. Did you ever paunch a deer? What a mess of intestines all over the shop!"

Gary, still standing, began to kick the snow from his shoes. Gray said to him: "For a dollar of your Yankee money I'd give you a shot at me with your automatic – you're that slack at practice."

"If it goes on much longer like this I'll not have to pay for a shot at anybody," returned Gary, with a short laugh.

Gray laughed too, disagreeably, stretching his facial muscles, but no sound issued.

"We're all going crazy together up here; that's my idea," he said. "I don't know which I can stand most comfortably, your voices or your silence. Both make me sick."

"Some day a salamander will nip you; then you'll go loco," observed Gary, balancing another tennis ball in his right hand. "Give me a shot at you?" he added. "I feel as though I could throw it clean through you. You look soft as a pudding to me."

Far, clear, from infinite depths, the elf-like hail of the cuckoo came floating up to the window.

To Flint, English born, the call meant more than it did to Canadian or Yankee.

"In Devon," he said in an altered voice, "they'll be calling just now. There's a world of primroses in Devon... And the thorn is as white as the damned snow is up here."

Gary growled his impatience and his profile of a Greek fighter showed in clean silhouette against the window.

"Aw, hell," he said, "did I come out here for this? Nine months of it?" He hurled the tennis ball at the wall. "Can the home talk, if you don't mind."

The cuckoo was still calling.

"Did you ever play cuckoo," asked Carfax, "at ten shillings a throw? It's not a bad game – if you're put to it for amusement."

Nobody replied; Gray's sunken, boyish face betrayed no interest; he continued to toss a tennis ball against the wall and catch it on the rebound.

Toward sundown the usual Alpine chill set in; a mist hung over the snow-edged cliffs; the rocks breathed steam under a foggy and battered moon.

II

Carfax, on duty, sat hunched up over the telephone, reporting to the fortress.

Gray came in, closed the wooden shutters, hung blankets over them, lighted an oil stove and then a candle. Flint took up the cards, looked at Gary, then flung them aside, muttering.

Nobody attempted to read; nobody touched the cards again. An orderly came in with soup. The meal was brief and perfectly silent.

Flint said casually, after the table had been cleared: "I haven't slept for a month. If I don't get some sleep I'll go queer. I warn you; that's all. I'm sorry to say it, but it's so."

"They're dirty beasts to keep us here like this," muttered Gary – "nine months of it, and not a shot."

"There'll be a few shots if things don't change," remarked Flint in a colourless voice. "I'm getting wrong in my head. I can feel it."

Carfax turned from the switchboard with a forced laugh: "Thinking of shooting up the camp?"

"That or myself," replied Flint in a quiet voice; "ever since that cuckoo called I've felt queer."

Gary, brooding in his soiled tunic collar, began to mutter presently: "I once knew a man in a lighthouse down in Florida who couldn't stand it after a bit and jumped off."

"Oh, we've heard that twenty times," interrupted Carfax wearily.

Gray said: "What a jump! I mean down into Alsace below –"

"You're all going dotty!" snapped Carfax. "Shut up or you'll be doing it – some of you."

"I can't sleep. That's where I'm getting queer," insisted Flint. "If I could get a few hours' sleep now –"

"I wish to God the Boches could reach you with a big gun. That would put you to sleep, all right!" said Gray.

"This war is likely to end before any of us see a Fritz," said Carfax. "I could stand it, too, except being up here with such" – his voice dwindled to a mutter, but it sounded to Gary as though he had used the word "rotters."

Flint's face had a white, strained expression; he began to walk about, saying aloud to himself: "If I could only sleep. That's the idea – sleep it off, and wake up somewhere else. It's the silence, or the voices – I don't know which. You dollar-crazy Yankees and ignorant Provincials don't realize what a cuckoo is. You've no traditions, anyway – no past, nothing to care for –"

"Listen to 'Arry!" retorted Gary. "'Arry and his cuckoo!"

Carfax stirred heavily. "Shut up!" he said, with an effort. "The thing is to keep doing something – something – anything – except quarrelling."

He picked up a tennis ball. "Come on, you funking brutes! I'll teach you how to play cuckoo. Every man takes three tennis balls and stands in a corner of the room. I stand in the middle. Then you blow out the candle. Then I call 'cuckoo!' in the dark and you try to hit me, aiming by the sound of my voice. Every time I'm hit I pay ten shillings to the pool, take my place in a corner, and have a shot at the next man, chosen by lot. And if you throw three balls apiece and nobody hits me, then you each pay ten shillings to me and I'm cuckoo for another round."

"We aim at random?" inquired Gray, mildly interested.

"Certainly. It must be played in pitch darkness. When I call out cuckoo, you take a shot at where you think I am. If you all miss, you all pay. If I'm hit, I pay."

Gary chose three tennis balls and retired to a corner of the room; Gray and Flint, urged into action, took three each, unwillingly.

"Blow out the candle," said Carfax, who had walked into the middle of the room. Gary blew it out and the place was in darkness.

They thought they heard Carfax moving cautiously, and presently he called, "Cuckoo!" A storm of tennis balls rebounded from the walls; "Cuckoo!" shouted Carfax, and the tennis balls rained all around him.

Once more he called; not a ball hit him; and he struck a match where he was seated upon the floor.

There was some perfunctory laughter of a feverish sort; the candle was relighted, tennis balls redistributed, and Carfax wrote down his winnings.

The next time, however, Gray, throwing low, caught him. Again the candle was lighted, scores jotted down, a coin tossed, and Flint went in as cuckoo.

It seemed almost impossible to miss a man so near, even in total darkness, but Flint lasted three rounds and was hit, finally, a stinging smack on the ear. And then Gary went in.

It was hot work, but they kept at it feverishly, grimly, as though their very sanity depended upon the violence of their diversion. They threw the balls hard, viciously hard. A sort of silent ferocity seemed to seize them. A chance hit cut the skin over Flint's cheekbone, and when the candle was lighted, one side of his face was bright with blood.

Early in the proceedings somebody had disinterred brandy and Schnapps from under a bunk. The room had become close; they all were sweating.

Carfax emptied his iced glass, still breathing hard, tossed a shilling and sent in Gary as cuckoo.

Flint, who never could stand spirits, started unsteadily for the candle, but could not seem to blow it out. He stood swaying and balancing on his heels, puffing out his smooth, boyish cheeks and blowing at hazard.

"You're drunk," said Gray, thickly; but he was as flushed as the boy he addressed, only steadier of leg.

"What's that?" retorted Flint, jerking his shoulders around and gazing at Gray out of glassy eyes.

"Blow out that candle," said Gary heavily, "or I'll shoot it out! Do you get that?"

"Shoot!" repeated Flint, staring vaguely into Gary's bloodshot eyes; "you shoot, you old slacker —"

"Shut up and play the game!" cut in Carfax, a menacing roar rising in his voice. "You're all slackers — and rotters, too. Play the game! Keep playing — hard! — or you'll go clean off your fool nuts!"

Gary walked heavily over and knocked the tennis balls out of Flint's hands.

"There's a better game than that," he said, his articulation very thick; "but it takes nerve — if you've got it, you spindle-legged little cockney!"

Flint struck at him aimlessly. "I've got nerve," he muttered, "plenty of nerve, old top! What d'you want? I'm your man; I'll go you — eh, what?"

"Go on with the game, I tell you!" bawled Carfax.

Gary swung around: "Wait till I explain –"

"No, don't wait! Keep going! Keep playing! Keep doing something, for God's sake!"

"Will you wait!" shouted Gary. "I want to tell you –"

Carfax made a hopeless gesture: "It's talk that will do the trick for us all –"

"I want to tell you –"

Carfax shrugged, emptied his full glass with a gesture of finality.

"Then talk, damn you! And we'll all be at each other's throats before morning."

Gary got Gray by the elbow: "Reggie, it's this way. We flip up for cuckoo. Whoever gets stuck takes a shot apiece from our automatics in the legs – eh, what?"

"It's perfectly agreeable to me," assented Gray, in the mincing, elaborate voice characteristic of him when drunk.

Flint wagged his head. "It's a sportin' game. I'm in," he said.

Gary looked at Carfax. "A shot in the dark at a man's legs. And if he gets his – it will be Blighty in exchange for hell."

Carfax, sullen with liquor, shoved his big hand into his pocket, produced a shilling, and tossed it.

A brighter flush stained the faces which ringed him; the risky hazard of the affair cleared their sick minds to comprehension.

Tails turned uppermost; Flint and Gary were eliminated. It lay between Carfax and Gray, and the older man won.

"Mind you fire low," said the young fellow, with an excited laugh, and walked into the middle of the room.

Gary blew out the candle. Presently from somewhere in the intense darkness Gray called "Cuckoo!" and instantly a slanting red flash lashed out through the gloom. And, when the deafening echo had nearly ceased: "Cuckoo!"

Another pistol crashed. And after a swimming interval they heard him moving. "Cuckoo!" he called; a level flame stabbed the dark; something fell, thudding through the staccato uproar of the explosion. At the same moment the outer door opened on the crack and Carfax's orderly peeped in.

Carfax struck a match with shaky fingers; the candle guttered, sank, flared on Flint, who was laughing without a sound. "Got the beggar, by God!" he whispered

– "through the head! Look at him. Look at Reggie Gray! Tried for his head and got him –"

He reeled back, chuckling foolishly, and levelled at Carfax. "Now I'll get you!" he simpered, and shot him through the face.

As Carfax pitched forward, Gary fired.

"Missed me, by God!" laughed Flint. "Shoot? Hell, yes. I'll show you how to shoot –"

He struck the lighted candle with his left hand and laughed again in the thick darkness.

"Shoot? I'll show you how to shoot, you old slacker –"

Gary fired.

After a silence Flint giggled in the choking darkness as the door opened cautiously again, and shot at the terrified orderly.

"I'm a cockney, am I? And you don't think much of the Devon cuckoos, do you? Now I'll show you that I understand all kinds of cuckoos –"

Both flashes split the obscurity at the same moment. Flint fell back against the wall and slid down to the floor. The outer door began to open again cautiously.

But the orderly, half dressed, remained knee-deep in the snow by the doorway.

After a long interval Gary struck a match, then went over and lit the candle. And, as he turned, Flint fired from where he lay on the floor and Gary swung heavily on one heel, took two uncertain steps. Then his pistol fell clattering; he sank to his knees and collapsed face downward on the stones.

Flint, still lying where he had fallen, partly upright, against the wall, began to laugh, and died a few moments later, the wind from the slowly opening door stirring his fair hair and extinguishing the candle.

And at last, through the opened door crept Carfax's orderly; peered into the darkness within, shivering in his unbuttoned tunic, his boots wet with snow.

Dawn already whitened the east; and up out of the ghastly fog edging the German Empire, silhouetted, monstrous, against the daybreak, soared a Lèmmergeyer, beating the livid void with enormous, unclean wings.

The orderly heard its scream, shrank, cowering, against the door frame as the huge bird's ferocious red and yellow eyes blazed level with his.

Suddenly, above the clamor of the Lèmmergeyer, the shrill bell of the telephone began to ring.

The terrible racket of the Lèmmergeyer filled the sky; the orderly stumbled into the room, slipped in a puddle of something wet, sent an empty bottle rolling and clinking away into the darkness; stumbled twice over prostrate bodies; reached the telephone, half fainting; whispered for help.

After a long, long while, the horror still thickly clogging vein and brain, he scratched a match, hesitated, then holding it high, reeled toward the door with face averted.

Outside the sun was already above the horizon, flashing over Haut Alsace at his feet.

The Lèmmergeyer was a speck in the sky, poised over France.

Up out of the infinite and sunlit chasm came a mocking, joyous hail – up through the sheer, misty gulf out of vernal depths: *Cuckoo! Cuckoo! Cuckoo!*

III

And that was the way Carfax ended – a tiny tragedy of incompetence compared to the mountainous official fiasco at Gallipoli. Here, a few perished among the filthy salamanders in the snow; there, thousands died in the burning Turkish gorse…

But that's history; and its makers are already officially damned.

Anne Douglas Sedgwick (1873 – 1935) was born in Englewood, New Jersey, but moved to Britain as a child. She married the writer Basil de Sélincourt in 1908. "Hepaticas" was first published in 1918, and draws upon Sedgwick's own experience as a volunteer in hospitals during World War I.

When collected into Atlantic Narratives (1918), editor Charles Swain Thomas wrote that the reader's "sustained sympathy rests with the mother", and that the mother's "supreme merit lies in her willing acceptance of the burdening problem". Contemporary readers may disagree. The character's sacrifices can also be read as thinly-veiled self-interest, masking a stifling elitism and chillingly medieval convictions.

Although the Great War itself features very little in this story — indeed the mother prefers not to think of it at all — its disruptive influence is felt throughout.

HEPATICAS

ANNE DOUGLAS SEDGWICK

I

Other people's sons were coming home for the three or four days' leave. The first gigantic struggle "furious onslaught and grim resistance" was over. Paris, pale, and slightly shuddering still, stood safe. Calais was not taken, and, dug into their trenches, it was evident that the opposing armies would lie face to face, with no decisive encounter possible until the spring.

There was, with all their beauty and terror, an element of the facetious in these unexpected holidays, of the matter-of-factness, the freedom from strain or sentiment that was the English oddity and the English strength. Men who had known the horrors of the retreat from Mons or the carnage of Ypres, who had not taken off their clothes for ten days at a stretch or slept for four nights, came home from trenches knee-deep in mud, from battlefields heaped with unburied dead, and appeared immaculate and cheerful at breakfast; a little sober and preoccupied, perhaps; touched, perhaps, with strangeness; but ready for the valorous family jest, and alluding to the war as if, while something too solemn for adequate comment, it were yet something that lent itself to laughter. One did such funny things, and saw them; of the other things one did not speak; and there was the huge standing joke of an enemy who actually hated one. These grave and cheerful young men hated nobody; but they were very eager to go back again; and they were all ready, not only to die but to die good-humoredly. From the demeanor of mothers and wives and sisters it was evident that nothing would be said or done to make this readiness difficult; but Mrs. Bradley, who showed serenity

Atlantic Narratives: Modern Short Stories. Charles Swain Thomas, ed. Boston: Atlantic Monthly Press, 1918.

to the world and did not, even when alone, allow herself to cry, suspected that the others, beneath their smiles, carried hearts as heavy with dread as their own.

It had been heavy, with hope now as well as with dread, for the past week. It was a week since she had last heard from Jack. Mrs. Crawley, over the hill, had had her wire, and her husband was now with her; and Lady Wrexham expected her boy to-morrow. There was no certainty at all as regarded herself; yet at any moment she might have a wire; and feeling to-day the stress of waiting too great to be borne in passivity, she left her books and letters, and put on her gardening shoes and gloves, and went out to her borders.

For weeks now the incessant rain had made the relief and solace of gardening almost an impossibility; but to-day was mild and clear. There was no radiance in the air; curtains of pearly mist shut out the sky; yet here and there a soft opening in the white showed a pale, far blue, gentle and remote as the gaze of a wandering goddess, and the hills seemed to smile quietly up at the unseen sun. Mrs. Bradley, as she went along the river-path, could look across at the hills; the river-path and the hills were the great feature of Dorrington, the placid, comely red brick house to which she and Jack had come fifteen years ago, after the death of her husband in India. Enclosed by woods, and almost catching sight of the road – from its upper windows and over its old brick wall, the house could have seemed to her too commonplace and almost suburban, in spite of the indubitably old oak-paneling of the drawing-room, had it not been for the river and the hills. Stepping out on to the lawn from the windows of the drawing-room, she and Jack, on that April day, had found themselves confronting both – the limpid, rapid little stream, spanned near the house by its mossy bridge, and the hills, beyond the meadows, streaked with purple woodlands and rising, above the woods, to slopes russet, fawn, and azure. Jack, holding her by the hand, had pointed at once with an eager "Isn't it pretty, mummy" – even at eight he had cared almost as much as she, and extraordinarily in the same way, for the sights of the country; and if the hills had not settled the question, it was settled, quite finally, ten minutes later, by the white hepaticas.

They had come upon them suddenly, after their tour of the walled kitchen garden and their survey of the lawn with its ugly shrubberies, now long forgotten, penetrating a thicket of hazels and finding themselves in an opening under trees where neighboring woods looked at them over an old stone wall, and where, from an old stone bench, one could see the river. The ground was soft with the fallen leaves of many an autumn; a narrow path ran, half obliterated, down to the river; and among the faded brown, everywhere, rose the thick clusters, the dark leaves, and the snowy flowers, poignant, amazing in their beauty.

She and Jack had stopped short to gaze. She had never seen such white hepaticas, or so many, or so placed. And Jack, presently, lifting his dear nut-brown head and nut-brown eyes, had said, gazing up at her as he had gazed at the flowers, "They are just like you, mummy."

She had felt at once that they were like her; more like than the little boy's instinct could grasp. He had thought of the darkness and whiteness; her widow's weeds and pale face had suggested that; but he could not know the sorrow, the longing, the earthly sense of irreparable loss, the heavenly sense of a possession unalterably hers, that the dark, melancholy leaves and celestial whiteness of the flowers expressed to her. Tears had risen to her eyes and she had stooped and kissed her child, how like her husband's that little face! and had said, after a moment, "We must never leave them, Jack."

They had never left them. Dorrington had been their home for fifteen years, and the hepaticas the heart of it, it had always seemed to them both; the loveliest ritual of the year that early spring one when, in the hazel copse, they would find the white hepaticas again in flower. And of all the autumnal labors none were sweeter than those which cherished and divided and protected the beloved flowers.

Mrs. Bradley, today, worked in her long border, weeding, troweling, placing belated labels. She was dressed in black, her straw hat bound beneath her chin by a ribbon and her soft gardening gloves rolling back from her firm, white wrists. Her gestures expressed a calm energy, an accurate grace. She was tall, and when she raised herself to look over the meadows at the hills, she showed small, decisive features, all marked, in the pallor of her face, as if with the delicate, neutral emphasis of an etching: the gray, scrutinizing eyes, the charming yet ugly nose, the tranquil mouth which had, at the corners, a little drop, half sweet, half bitter, as if with tears repressed or a summoned smile. Squared at brow and chin, it would, but for the mildness of the gaze, have been an imperious face; and her head, its whitened hair drawn back and looped in wide braids behind, had an air at once majestic and unworldly.

She had worked for over an hour and the last label was set beside a precious clump of iris. The hazel copse lay near by; and gathering up her tools, drawing off her wet gloves, she followed the path under the leafless branches and among the hepaticas to the stone bench, where, sinking down, she knew that she was very tired. She could see, below the bank, the dark, quick stream; a pale, diffused light in the sky showed where the sun was dropping toward the hills.

Where was Jack at this moment, this quiet moment of a monotonous English winter day? – so like the days of all the other years that it was impossible to think of what was happening a few hours journey away across the Channel. Impossible to think of it; yet the thick throb of her heart spoke to the full of its significance. She had told herself from the beginning, – passionate, rebellious creature as, at bottom, she knew herself to be, always in need of discipline and only in these later years schooled to a control and submission that, in her youth, she would have believed impossible to her, she had told herself, when he had gone from her, that, as a soldier's widow, she must see her soldier son go to death. She must give him to that; be ready for it; and if he came back to her it would be as if he were born again, a gift, a grace, unexpected and unclaimed. She must feel, for herself as well as for her country, that these days of dread were also days of a splendor and beauty unmatched by any in England's history, and that a soldier's widow must ask for no more glorious fate for her son than death in such a cause. She had told herself all this many times; yet, as she sat there, her hands folded on her lap, her eyes on the stream below, she felt that she was now merely motherhood, tense, huddled, throbbing and longing, longing for its child.

Then, suddenly, she heard Jack's footsteps. They came, quick and light, along the garden path; they entered the wood; they were near, but softened by the fallen leaves.

And, half rising, afraid of her own joy, she hardly knew that she saw him before she was in his arms; and it was better to meet thus, in the blindness and darkness of their embrace, her cheek pressed against his hair, his head buried close between her neck and shoulder.

"Jack! Jack!" she heard herself say.

He said nothing, holding her tightly to him, with quick breaths; and even after she had opened her eyes and could look down at him, – her own, her dear, beautiful Jack, could see the nut-brown head, the smooth brown cheek, the firm brown hand which grasped her, he did not for a long time raise his head and look at her. When, at last, he did look up, she could not tell, through her tears, whether, like herself, he was trying to smile.

They sat down together on the bench. She did not ask him why he had not wired. That question pressed too sharply on her heart; to ask might seem to reproach.

"Darling, you are so thin – so much older, but you look strong and well."

"We're all of us extraordinarily fit, mummy. It's wholesome, living in mud."

"And wholesome living among bursting shells? I had your last letter telling of that miraculous escape."

"There have been a lot more since then. Every day seems a miracle that one's alive at the end of it."

"But you get used to it?"

"All except the noise. That always seems to daze me still. Some of our fellows are deaf from it. You heard of Toppie, mother?" Jack asked.

Toppie was Alan Thorpe, Jack's nearest friend. He had been killed ten days ago.

"I heard it, Jack. Were you with him?"

"Yes. It was in a bayonet charge. He didn't suffer. A bullet went right through him. He just gave a little cry and fell." Jack's voice had the mildness of a sorrow which has passed beyond the capacity for emotion. "We found him afterwards. He is buried out there."

"You must tell Frances about it, Jack. I went to her at once." Frances was Toppie's sister. "She is bearing it so bravely."

"I must write to her. She would be sure to be plucky,"

He answered all her questions, sitting closely against her, his arm around her; looking down, while he spoke, and twisting, as had always been his boyish way, a button on her coat. He was at that enchanting moment of young manhood when the child is still apparent in the man. His glance was shy, yet candid; his small, firm lips had a child's gravity. With his splendid shoulders, long legs, and noble little head, he was yet as endearing as he was impressive.

His mother's heart ached with love and pride and fear as she gazed at him.

And a question came, near the sharp one, yet hoping to evade it:

"Jack, dearest, how long will you be with me? How long is the leave?"

He raised his eyes then and looked at her; a curious look.

Something in it blurred her mind with a sense of some other sort of fear.

"Only till to-night," he said.

It seemed confusion rather than pain that she felt. "Only till to-night, Jack? But Richard Crawley has been back for three days already. I thought they gave you longer?"

"I know, mummy." His eyes were dropped again and his hand at the button – did it tremble? – twisted and untwisted. "I've been back for three days already. I've been in London."

"In London?" Her breath failed her. The sense of alien fear became a fog, horrible, suffocating. "But Jack why?"

"I didn't wire, mummy, because I knew I'd have to be there for most of my time. I felt that I couldn't wire and tell you. I felt that I had to see you when I told you. Mother, I'm married. I came back to get married. I was married this morning. Oh mother, can you ever forgive me?"

His shaking hands held her and his eyes could not meet hers.

She felt the blood rush, as if her heart had been divided with a sword, to her throat, to her eyes, choking her, burning her; and as if from far away she heard her own voice saying, after a little time had passed, "There's nothing I couldn't forgive you, Jack. Tell me. Don't be afraid of hurting me."

He held her tightly, still looking down as he said, "She is a dancer, mother, a little dancer. It was in London, last summer. A lot of us came up from Aldershot together. She was in the chorus of one of those musical comedies. Mother, you can never understand. But it wasn't just low and vulgar. She was so lovely, so very young, with the most wonderful golden hair and the sweetest eyes.

I don't know. I simply went off my head when I saw her. We all had supper together afterwards. Toppie knew one of the other girls, and Dollie was there. That's her name – Dollie Vaughan – her stage name. Her real name was Byles. Her people, I think, were little tradespeople, and she'd lost her father and mother, and an aunt had been very unkind. She told me all about it that night. Mother, please believe just this: it wasn't only the obvious thing. I know I can't explain. But you remember, when we read *War and Peace*," his broken voice groped for the analogy, "You remember Natacha, when she falls in love with Anatole, and nothing that was real before seems

236

real, and she is ready for anything. It was like that. It was all fairyland, like that. No one thought it wrong. It didn't seem wrong. Everything went together."

She had gathered his hand closely in hers and she sat there, quiet, looking at her hopes lying slain before her.

Her Jack. The wife who was, perhaps, to have been his. The children that she, perhaps, should have seen. All dead. The future blotted out. Only this wraith-like present; only this moment of decision; Jack and his desperate need the only real things left.

And after a moment, for his laboring breath had failed, she said, "Yes, dear?" and smiled at him.

He covered his face with his hands. "Mother, I've ruined your life."

He had, of course, in ruining his own; yet even at that moment of wreckage she was able to remember, if not to feel, that life could mend from terrible wounds, could marvelously grow from compromises and defeats. "No, dearest, no," she said. "While I have you, nothing is ruined. We shall see what can be done. Go on. Tell me the rest."

He put out his hand to hers again and sat now a little turned away from her, speaking on in his deadened, bitter voice.

"There wasn't any glamour after that first time. I only saw her once or twice again. I was awfully sorry and ashamed over the whole thing. Her company left London, on tour, and then the war came, and I simply forgot all about her. And the other day, over there, I had a letter from her. She was in terrible trouble. She was ill and had no money, and no work. And she was going to have a child, my child; and she begged me to send her a little money to help her through, or she didn't know what would become of her."

The fog, the horrible confusion, even the despair, had passed now. The sense of ruin, of wreckage almost irreparable, was there; yet with it, too, was the strangest sense of gladness. He was her own Jack, completely hers, for she saw now why he had done it; she could be glad that he had done it; she could be glad that he had done it. "Good, dear," she said. 'I understand; I understand perfectly."

"Oh mother, bless you!" He put her hand to his lips, bowing his head upon it for a moment. "I was afraid you couldn't. I was afraid you couldn't forgive me. But I had to do it. I thought it all over out there. Everything had become so different after what one had been through. One saw everything differently. Some things didn't matter at all, and other things mattered tremendously. This was one of them. I knew I couldn't just send her money. I knew I couldn't bear to have the poor child born without a name and with only that foolish little mother to take care of it. And when I found I could get this leave, I knew I must marry her. That was why I didn't wire. I thought I might not have time to come to you at all."

"Where is she, Jack?" Her voice, her eyes, her smile at him, showed him that, indeed, she understood perfectly.

"In lodgings that I found for her; nice and quiet, with a kind landlady. She was in such an awful place in Ealing. She is so changed, poor little thing. I should hardly have known her. Mother, darling, I wonder, could you just go and see her once or twice? She's frightfully lonely; and so very young. If you could... if you would just help things along a little till the baby comes, I should be so grateful. And, then, if I don't come back, will you, for my sake, see that they are safe?"

"But, Jack," she said, smiling at him, "she is coming here, of course. I shall go and get her tomorrow."

He stared at her and his color rose. "Get her? Bring her here, to stay?"

"Of course, darling. And if you don't come back, I will take care of them, always."

"But, mother," said Jack, and there were tears in his eyes, "you don't know, you don't realize. I mean, she's a dear little thing, but you couldn't be happy with her. She'd get most frightfully on your nerves. She's just... just a silly little dancer who has got into trouble."

Jack was clear-sighted. Every vestige of fairyland had vanished. And she was deeply thankful that they should see alike, while she answered, "It's not exactly a time for considering one's nerves, is it, Jack? I hope I won't get on hers. I must just try and make her as happy as I can."

She made it all seem natural and almost sweet. The tears were in his eyes, yet he had to smile back at her when she said, "You know that I am good at managing people. I'll manage her. And perhaps when you come back, my darling, she won't be a silly little dancer."

They sat now for a little while in silence. While they had talked, a golden sunset, slowly, had illuminated the western sky. The river below them was golden, and the wintry woodlands bathed in light. Jack held her hands and gazed at her. Love could say no more than his eyes, in their trust and sorrow, said to her; she could never more completely possess her son. Sitting there with him, hand in hand, while the light slowly ebbed and twilight fell about them, she felt it to be, in its accepted sorrow, the culminating and transfiguring moment of her maternity.

When they at last rose to go it was the hour for Jack's departure, and it had become almost dark. Far away, through the trees, they could see the lighted windows of the house which waited for them, but to which she must return alone.

With his arms around her shoulders, Jack paused a moment, looking about him. "Do you remember that day – when we first came here, mummy?" he asked.

She felt in him suddenly a sadness deeper than any he had yet shown her. The burden of the past she had lifted from him; but he must bear now the burden of what he had done to her, to their life, to all the future. And, protesting against his pain, her mother's heart strove still to shelter him while she answered, as if she did not feel his sadness, "Yes, dear, and do you remember the hepaticas on that day"

"Like you," said Jack in a gentle voice. "I can hardly see the plants. Are they all right?"

"They are doing beautifully."

"I wish the flowers were out," said Jack. "I wish it were the time for the flowers to be out, so that I could have seen you and them together, like that first day." And then, putting his head down on her shoulder, he murmured, "It will never be the same again. I've spoiled everything for you."

But he was not to go from her uncomforted. She found the firmest voice in which to answer him, stroking his hair and pressing him to her with the full reassurance of her resolution. "Nothing is spoiled, Jack, nothing. You have never been so near me – so how can anything be spoiled?

And when you come back, darling, you'll find your son, perhaps, and the hepaticas may be in flower, waiting for you."

II

Mrs. Bradley and her daughter-in-law sat together in the drawing-room. They sat opposite each other on the two chintz chesterfields placed at right angles to the pleasantly blazing fire, the chintz curtains drawn against a rainy evening. It was a long, low room, with paneled walls; and, like Mrs. Bradley's head, it had an air at once majestic, decorated, and old-fashioned. It was a rather crowded room, with many deep chairs and large couches, many tables with lamps and books and photographs upon them, many porcelains, prints, and pots of growing flowers. Mrs. Bradley, her tea-table before her, was in her evening black silk; lace ruffles rose about her throat; she wore her accustomed necklace of old enamel, blue, black, and white, set with small diamonds, and the enamel locket which had within it Jack's face on one side and his father's on the other; her white hands, moving gently among the teacups, showed an ancient cluster of diamonds above the slender wedding-ring.

From time to time she lifted her eyes and smiled quietly over at her daughter-in-law. It was the first time that she had really seen Dollie, that is, in any sense that meant contemplative observation. Dollie had spent her first week at Dorrington in bed, sodden with fatigue rather than ill. "What you need," Mrs. Bradley had said, "is to go to sleep for a fortnight"; and Dollie had almost literally carried out the prescription.

Stealing carefully into the darkened room, with its flowers and opened windows and steadily glowing fire, Mrs. Bradley had stood and looked for long moments at all that she could see of her daughter-in-law – a flushed, almost babyish face lying on the pillow between thick golden braids, sleeping so deeply, so unconsciously – her sleep making her mother-in-law think of a little boat gliding slowly yet steadily on and on, between new shores; so that, when she was to awake and look about her, it would be as if, with no bewilderment or readjustment, she found herself transformed, a denizen of an altered world. That was what Mrs. Bradley wanted, that Dollie should become an inmate of Dorrington with as little effort or consciousness for any of them as possible; and the drowsy days and nights of infantine slumbers seemed indeed to have brought her very near.

She and Pickering, the admirable woman who filled so skillfully the combined positions of lady's maid and parlor-maid in her little establishment, had braided Dollie's thick tresses, one on either side, Mrs. Bradley laughing a little and both older women touched, almost happy in their sense of something so young and helpless to take care of. Pickering understood, nearly as well as Jack's mother, that Master Jack, as he had remained to her, had married very much beneath him; but at this time of tragic issues and primitive values, she, nearly as much as Jack's mother, felt only the claim, the pathos of youth and helplessness. It was as if they had a singularly appealing case of a refugee to take care of: social and even moral appraisals were inapplicable to such a case, and Mrs. Bradley felt that she had never so admired Pickering as when seeing that for her, too, they were in abeyance. It was a comfort to feel so fond of Pickering at a time when one was in need of any comfort one could get; and to feel that, creature of codes and discriminations as she was, to a degree that had made her mistress sometimes think of her as a sort of Samurai of service, a function rather than a person, she was even more fundamentally a kind and Christian woman. Between them, cook intelligently sustaining them from below and the housemaids helpful in their degree, they fed and tended and nursed Dollie, and by that eighth day she was more than ready to get up and go down and investigate her new surroundings.

She sat there now, in the pretty tea-gown her mother-in-law had bought for her, leaning back against her cushions, one arm lying along the back of the couch and one foot in its patent-leather shoe, with its sparkling buckle and alarming heel, thrusting forward a carefully arched instep. The attitude made one realize, however completely tenderer preoccupations held the foreground of one's consciousness, how often and successfully she must have sat to theatrical photographers. Her way of smiling, too, very softly, yet with the effect of a calculated and dazzling display of pearly teeth, was impersonal, and directed, as it were, to the public via the camera rather than to any individual interlocutor. Mrs. Bradley even imagined, unversed as she was in the methods of Dollie's world, that of allurement in its conscious and determined sense, she was almost innocent. She placed herself, she adjusted her arm and her foot, and she smiled gently; intention hardly went further than that wish to look her best.

Pink and white and gold as she was, and draped there on the chesterfield in a profusion of youth and a frivolity that was yet all passivity, she made her mother-in-law think, and with a certain sinking of the heart, of a Dorothy Perkins rose, a flower she had never cared for; and Dollie carried on the analogy in the sense she gave that there were such myriads more just like her. On almost every page of every illustrated weekly paper, one saw the ingenuous, limpid eyes, the display of eyelash, the lips, their outline emphasized by just that touch of rouge, those copious waves of hair. Like the Dorothy Perkins roses on their pergolas, so these pretty faces seemed

– looped, draped, festooned – to climb over all the available spaces of the modern press.

But this, Mrs. Bradley told herself, was to see Dollie with a dry, hard eye, was to see her superficially, from the social rather than from the human point of view. Under the photographic creature must lie the young, young girl – so young, so harmless that it would be very possible to mould her, with all discretion, all tenderness, into some suitability as Jack's wife. Dollie, from the moment that she had found her, a sodden, battered rose indeed, in the London lodging-house, had shown herself grateful, even humble, and endlessly acquiescent. She had not shown herself at all abashed or apologetic, and that had been a relief; had counted for her, indeed, in her mother-in-law's eyes, as a sort of innocence, a sort of dignity. But if Dollie were contented with her new mother, and very grateful to her, she was also contented with herself; Mrs. Bradley had been aware of this at once; and she knew now that, if she were being carefully and commendingly watched while she poured out the tea, this concentration did not imply unqualified approval. Dollie was the type of young woman to whom she herself stood as the type of the "perfect lady"; but with the appreciation went the proviso of the sharp little London mind, versed in the whole ritual of smartness as it displayed itself at theatre or restaurant, that she was a rather dowdy one. She was a lady, perfect but not smart, while, at the same time, the quality of her defect was, she imagined, a little bewildering and therefore a little impressive. Actually to awe Dollie and to make her shy, it would be necessary to be smart; but it was far more pleasant and perhaps as efficacious merely to impress her, and it was as well that Dollie should be impressed; for anything in the nature of an advantage that she could recognize would make it easier to direct, protect, and mould her.

She asked her a good many leisurely and unstressed questions on this first evening, and drew Dollie to ask others in return; and she saw herself stooping thoughtfully over a flourishing young plant which yet needed transplanting, softly moving the soil about its roots, softly finding out if there were any very deep tap-root that would have to be dealt with. But Dollie, so far as tastes and ideas went, hardly seemed to have any roots at all; so few that it was a question if any change of soil could affect a creature so shallow. She smiled, she was at ease; she showed her complete assurance that a young lady so lavishly endowed with all the most significant gifts, need not occupy herself with mental adornments.

"You're a great one for books, I see," she commented, looking about the room. "I suppose you do a great deal of reading down here to keep from feeling too dull"; and she added that she herself, if there was "nothing doing", liked a good novel, especially if she had a box of sweets to eat while she read it.

"You shall have a box of sweets to-morrow," Mrs. Bradley told her, "with or without the novel, as you like."

And Dollie thanked her, watching her cut the cake, and, as the rain lashed against the windows, remarking on the bad weather and cheerfully hoping that "poor old Jack" wasn't in those horrid trenches. "I think war's a wicked thing, don't you, Mrs. Bradley?" she added.

When Dollie talked in this conventionally solicitous tone of Jack, her mother-in-law could but wish her upstairs again, merely young, merely the tired and battered refugee. She had not much tenderness for Jack, that was evident, nor much imaginativeness in regard to the feelings of Jack's mother. But she soon passed from the theme of Jack and his danger. Her tea was finished and she got up and went to the piano, remarking that there was one thing she could do. "Poor mother used to always say I was made of music. From the time I was a mere tot I could pick out anything on the piano." And placing herself, pressing down the patent-leather shoe on the loud pedal, she surged into a waltz as foolish and as conventionally alluring as her own eyes. Her inaccuracy was equaled only by her facility. Smiling, swaying over the keys with alternate speed and languor, she addressed her audience with altogether the easy mastery of a music-hall artiste: "It's a lovely thing – one of my favorites. I'll often play, Mrs. Bradley, and cheer us up. There is nothing like music for that, is there? It speaks so to the heart." And, whole-heartedly indeed, she accompanied the melody by a passionate humming.

The piano was Jack's and it was poor Jack who was made of music. How was he to bear it, his mother asked herself, as she sat listening. Dollie, after that initiation, spent many hours at the piano every day – so many and such noisy hours, that her mother-in-law, unnoticed, could shut herself in the little morning-room that overlooked the brick wall at the front of the house and had the morning sun.

It was difficult to devise other occupations for Dollie.

She earnestly disclaimed any wish to have proper music lessons; and when her mother-in-law, patiently persistent, arranged for a skillful mistress to come down twice a week from London, Dollie showed such apathy and dullness that any hope of developing such musical ability as she possessed had to be abandoned. She did not like walking, and the sober pageant of the winter days was a blank book to her. Sewing, she said, had always given her frightful fidgets; and it was with the strangest sense of a privilege, a joy unhoped-for and now thrust upon her, that Mrs. Bradley sat alone working at the little garments which meant all her future and all Jack's. The baby seemed already more hers than Dollie's.

Sometimes, on a warm afternoon, Dollie, wrapped in her fur cloak, would emerge for a little while and watch her mother-in-law at work in her borders. The sight amused and surprised, but hardly interested her, and she soon went tottering back to the house on the preposterous heels which

Mrs. Bradley had, as yet, found no means of tactfully banishing. And sometimes, when the piano again resounded, Mrs. Bradley would leave her borders and retreat to the hazel copse, where, as she sat on the stone bench, she could hear, through the soft sound of the running water, hardly more than the distant beat and hum of Dollie's waltzes; and where, with more and more the sense of escape and safety, she could find a refuge from the sight and sound and scent of Dollie – the thick, sweet, penetrating scent which was always to be indelibly associated in her mother-in-law's mind with this winter of foreboding, of hope, and of growing hopelessness.

In her letters to Jack, she found herself, involuntarily at first, and then deliberately, altering, suppressing, even falsifying. While Dollie had been in bed, when so much hope had been possible of a creature so unrevealed, she had written very tenderly, and she continued, now, to write tenderly, and it was not false to do that; she could feel no hardness or antagonism against poor Dollie. But she continued to write hopefully, as, every day, hope grew less.

Jack, himself, did not say much of Dollie, though there was always the affectionate message and the affectionate inquiry. But what was difficult to deal with were the hints of his anxiety and fear that stole among the terse, cheerful descriptions of his precarious days. What was she doing with herself? How were she and Dollie getting on? Did Dollie care about any of the things she cared about?

She told him that they got on excellently well, that Dollie spent a good deal of time at the piano, and that when they went out to tea people were perfectly nice and understanding. She knew, indeed, that she could depend on her friends to be that. They accepted Dollie on the terms she asked for her. From friends so near as Mrs. Crawley and Lady Wrexham she had not concealed the fact that Dollie was a misfortune; but if others thought so, they were not to show it. She still hoped, by degrees, to make Dollie a figure easier to deal with at such neighborly gatherings. She had abandoned any hope that Dollie would grow: anything so feeble and so foolish could not grow; there was no other girl under the little dancer; she was simply no more and no less than she showed herself to be; but, at this later stage of their relationship, Mrs. Bradley essayed, now and then, a deliberate if kindly severity – as to heels, as to scents, as to touches of rouge.

"Oh, but I'm as careful, just as careful, Mrs. Bradley!"

Dollie protested. "I can't walk in lower heels. They hurt my instep. I've a very high instep and it needs support."

She was genuinely amazed that any one could dislike her scent and that any one could think the rouge unbecoming.

She seemed to acquiesce, but the acquiescence was followed by moods of mournfulness and even by tears. There was no capacity in her for temper or rebellion, and she was all unconscious of giving a warning as she sobbed, "It's nothing – really nothing, Mrs. Bradley. I'm sure you mean to be kind. Only, it's rather quiet and lonely here. I've always been used to so many people, to having everything so bright and jolly."

She was not rapacious; she was not dissolute; she could be kept respectable and even contented if she were not made too aware of the contrast between her past existence and her present lot. With an air only of pensive pride she would sometimes point out to Mrs. Bradley, in the pages of those same illustrated weeklies with which her mother-in-law associated her, the face of some former companion.

One of these young ladies had recently married the son of a peer. "She is in luck, Floss," said Dollie. "We always thought it would come to that. He's been gone on her for ages, but his people were horrid."

Mrs. Bradley felt that, at all events, Dollie had no ground for thinking her "horrid"; yet she imagined that there lay drowsing at the back of her mind a plaintive little sense of being caught and imprisoned. Floss had stepped, triumphant, from the footlights to the registrar's office, and apparently had succeeded in uniting the radiance of her past and present status. No, Dollie could be kept respectable and contented only if the pressure were of the lightest. She could not change, she could only shift; and although Mrs. Bradley felt that for herself, her life behind her, her story told, she could manage to put up with a merely shifted Dollie, she could not see how Jack was to manage it. What was Jack to do with her? Was the thought that pressed with a growing weight on her mother's heart. She could never be of Jack's life; yet here she was, in it, planted there by his own generous yet inevitable act, and by hers – in its very centre, and not to be evaded or forgotten.

And the contrast between what Jack's life might have been and what it now must be was made more poignantly apparent to her when Frances Thorpe came down to stay from a Saturday to Monday: Frances in her black, tired and thin from Red Cross work in London; bereaved in more, her old friend knew, than dear Toppie's death; yet with her leisurely, unstressed cheerfulness almost unaltered, the lightness that went with so much tenderness, the drollery that went with so much depth. Dearest, most charming of girls, but for Jack's wretched stumble into "fairyland" last summer, destined obviously to be his wife. Could any presence have shown more disastrously, in its contrast with poor Dollie, how Jack had done for himself?

She watched the two together that evening, Frances with her thick, crinkled hair and clearly curved brow and her merry, steady eyes, leaning, elbow on knee, to talk and listen to Dollie; and Dollie, poor Dollie, flushed, touched with an unbecoming sulkiness, aware, swiftly and unerringly, of a rival type. Frances was of the type that young men married when they did not "do for themselves". There was now no gulf of age or habit to veil from Dollie her disadvantage. She answered shortly, with now and then a dry, ironic little laugh; and, getting up at last, she went to the piano and loudly played.

"He couldn't have done differently. It was the only thing he could do," Frances said that night before her bedroom fire. She did not hide her recognition of Jack's plight, but she was staunch.

"I wouldn't have had him do differently. But it will ruin his life," said the mother. "If he comes back, it will ruin his life."

"No, no," said Frances, looking at the flames. "Why should it? A man doesn't depend on his marriage like that. He has his career."

"Yes. He has his career. A career isn't a life."

"Isn't it?" The girl gazed down. "But it's what so many people have to put up with. And so many haven't even a career." Something came into her voice and she turned from it quickly. "He's crippled, in a sense, of course. But you are here. He will have you to come back to always."

"I shall soon be old, dear, and she will always be here. That's inevitable. Some day I shall have to leave her to Jack to bear with alone."

"She may become more of a companion."

"No; no, she won't."

The bitterness of the mother's heart expressed itself in the dry, light utterance. It was a comfort to express bitterness, for once, to somebody.

"She is a harmless little thing," Frances offered after a moment.

"Harmless?" Mrs. Bradley turned it over dryly and lightly. "I can't feel her that. I feel her blameless if you like. And it will be easy to keep her contented. That is really the best that one can say of poor Dollie. And then, there will be the child. I am pinning all my hopes to the child, Frances."

Frances understood that.

Dollie, as the winter wore on, kept remarkably well. She had felt it the proper thing to allude to Jack and his danger; and so, now, she more and more frequently felt it the proper thing to allude, humorously, if with a touch of melancholy, to "baby". Her main interest in baby, Mrs. Bradley felt, was an alarmed one. She was a good deal frightened, poor little soul, and in need of constant reassurances; and it was when one need only pet and pity Dollie that she was easier to deal with. Mrs. Bradley tried to interest her in plans for the baby; what it should be named, and how its hair should be done if it were a little girl – for only on this assumption could Dollie's interest be at all vividly roused; and Mrs. Bradley hoped more than ever for a boy when she found Dollie's idle yet stubborn thoughts fixed on the name of Gloria.

She was able to evade discussion of this point, and when the baby came, fortunately and robustly, into the world on a fine March morning, she could feel it as a minor but very real cause for thanksgiving that Dollie need now never know what she thought of Gloria as a name. The baby was a boy, and now that he was here, Dollie seemed as well pleased that he should be a commonplace Jack, and that there should be no question of tying his hair with cockades of ribbon over each ear. Smiling and rosy and languid, she lay in her charming room, not at all more maternal, though she showed a bland satisfaction in her child and noted that his eyes were just like Jack's, yet subtly more wifely. Baby, she no doubt felt, with the dim instinct that did duty for thought with her, placed and rooted her and gave her final rights. She referred now to Jack with the pensive but open affection of their shared complacency, and made her mother-in-law think, as she lay there, of a soft and sleepy and tenacious creeper, fixing tentacle after tentacle in the walls of Jack's house of life.

If only one could feel that she had furnished it with a treasure. Gravely, with a sad fondness, the grandmother studied the little face, so unfamiliar, for signs of Jack. She was a helplessly clear-sighted woman, and remembrance was poignantly vivid in her of Jack's face at a week old.

Already she loved the baby since its eyes, indubitably, were his; but she could find no other trace of him. It was not a Bradley baby; and in the dreamy, foreboding flickers of individuality that pass uncannily across an infant's features, her melancholy and steady discernment could see only the Byles ancestry.

She was to do all she could for the baby: to save him, so far as might be, from his Byles ancestry, and to keep him, so far as might be, Jack's and hers. That was to be her task. But with all the moulding that could, mercifully, be applied from the very beginning, she could not bring herself to believe that this was ever to be a very significant humanbeing.

She sent Jack his wire: "A son. Dollie doing splendidly." And she had his answer: "Best thanks. Love to Dollie." It was curious, indeed, this strange new fact they had now, always, to deal with; this light little "Dollie" that must be passed between them. The baby might have made Jack happy, but it had not solved the problem of his future.

III

A week later the telegram was brought to her telling her that he had been killed in action.

It was a beautiful spring day, just such a day as that on which she and Jack had first seen Dorrington, and she had been working in the garden. When she had read, she turned and walked down the path that led to the hazel copse. She hardly knew what had happened to her; there was only an instinct for flight, concealment, secrecy;

but, as she walked, there rose in her, without sound, as if in a nightmare, the terrible cry of her loneliness. The dark wet earth that covered him seemed heaped upon her heart.

The hazel copse was tasseled thickly with golden green, and as she entered it she saw that the hepaticas were in flower. They seemed to shine with their own celestial whiteness, set in their melancholy green among the fallen leaves. She had never seen them look so beautiful.

She followed the path, looking down at them, and she seemed to feel Jack's little hand in hers and to see, at her side, his nut-brown head. It had been on just such a morning. She came to the stone bench; but the impulse that had led her here was altered. She did not sink down and cover her face, but stood looking around her at the flowers, the telegram still open in her hand; and slowly, with stealing calm, the sense of sanctuary fell about her.

She had lost him, and with him went all her life. He was dead, his youth and strength and beauty. Yet what was this strange up-welling of relief, deep, deep relief, for Jack; this gladness, poignant and celestial, like that of the hepaticas? He was dead and the dark earth covered him; yet he was here, with her, safe in his youth and strength and beauty forever. He had died the glorious death, and no future, tangled, perplexed, fretful with its foolish burden, lay before him. There was no loss for Jack – no fading, no waste. The burden was for her, and he was free.

Later, when pain should have dissolved thought, her agony would come to her unalleviated; but this hour was hers, and his. She heard the river and the soft whisperings of spring. A bird dropped lightly, unafraid, from branch to branch of a tree near by. From the woods came the rapid, insistent tapping of a woodpecker; and, as in so many springs, she seemed to hear Jack say, "Hark, mummy," and his little hand was always held in hers. And, everywhere, telling of irreparable loss, of a possession unalterable, the tragic, the celestial hepaticas.

She sat down on the stone bench now and closed her eyes

for a little while, so holding them more closely – Jack and the hepaticas – together.

"Natasha heard nothing, saw nothing, understood nothing of what was going on before her; she felt that she was irrevocably drawn again into that strange, mad world, so far removed £rom the past world, where it was impossible to know what was right and what was wrong, what was reasonable and what was foolish. Behind her sat Anatol, and she was conscious of his nearness."
    – Leo Tolstoy, War and Peace (1889 edition)

John N. Reynolds (? - 1895) was an inmate of the federal prison outside Leavenworth, Kansas for sixteen months.

The circumstances of his imprisonment, according to Reynolds, were this: he first came to Kansas with his family, having been recommended the "South" for the health of his wife. Upon arriving in Atchinson, Reynolds founded a newspaper and promptly uncovered "one of the worst and most corrupt political rings on the face of the earth". Reynolds concluded that his imprisonment, on trumped up charges, was the work of his shadowy enemies.

The truth of the matter was something else entirely.

Reynolds began as a teacher in Nebraska, but seduced and impregnated one of his pupils. He quit teaching to become an evangelist and, even according to his detractors, he was "one of the best in the land". Nonetheless, the authorities caught up with him. After spending two years in jail, he moved to Kansas for a fresh start. Once there, Reynolds committed insurance fraud, bilking wealthy locals of their fortunes. When that scheme was halted, he founded his newspaper and methodically abused his earlier dupes. When he was caught committing fraud a second time, he was sent to Leavenworth.

As Reynolds himself wrote, however, "the big wheel of life keeps on revolving". He railed against authority, even from prison, culminating in a surprisingly successful run for the State Senate. Reynolds placed second, and found the results such a vindication of his character that he sent them to President Cleveland in the hopes of a pardon. (Cleveland never answered, much to Reynolds' disappointment.)

Upon his release from Leavenworth, Reynolds found employment as a speaker, regaling crowds with cautionary tales of his time in prison. He claimed to have learned shorthand in prison and to have secretly taken notes of his experiences. A Kansas Hell, his first book, was published in 1889. Following a visit to a Missouri penitentiary (this time as a guest), Reynolds extended his work to The Twin Hells. Reynolds toured the country for years, giving lectures while dressed in his prison garb. After a collapse on stage in Texas, Reynolds was declared insane and committed to an asylum in 1894. He remained there until his death.

Reynolds' prose tended towards the self-aggrandizing, melodramatic and, as noted above, occasionally fabricated. His writing demonstrated more enthusiasm than skill, but despite its shortcomings, his books successfully communicated a vision of pure terror: the horrors of the prison coal mines, unrepentant sinners and cruel miscarriages of justice.

This selection has been adapted by native Midwesterner Osgood Vance, who has generously spared the reader some of Reynolds' more grandiose turns of phrase.

THE PRISONERS

JOHN REYNOLDS

Thinking that it may be of interest to some of my readers, I will now give, in as brief a form as possible, the histories of some of the most noted inmates of the penitentiary. Let their fates be warning both as to the wages of sin and the steep price of thoughtless "justice" when meted out on circumstantial evidence.

Bovine Trouble

Woodward R. Lopeman was came to Leavenworth for murder in the first degree. Under his sentence he was to be hanged at the close of the first year. However, this part of the sentence is never carried out in Kansas, so he was condemned to spend the remainder of his days behind walls instead.

Lopeman was a well-to-do farmer residing in Neosho County, and never had any difficulties with the law before this fatal incident. He was an old soldier and had served his country faithfully and bravely for four years.

Lopeman and one of his neighbors had suffered a little difficulty over some trivial cause, but it was thought nothing would ever come of it. Each of them had been advised by their friends to bury their animosity before it should lead to graver results.

Lopeman seemed willing to do this, but his irate neighbor refused to meet him halfway. One day, a calf of Lopeman's – worth but a few dollars – got through the fence and over into the neighbor's pasture. The irate neighbor sent word that if Lopeman would come over and pay for the trouble of penning the calf up then he could have his property back. Lopeman was greatly displeased by both the statement and the tone of its delivery. With his revolver in his pocket and his grown son for company, Lopeman

---

went to the neighbor's propertly and stolled directly to the lot where the calf was shut in. He had begun to lay down the bars to let it out when the neighbor came from the house with *his* son, and the two ordered Lopeman to leave the pen alone.

The neighbor, who was a strong, muscular man, proceeded to chastise Lopeman; the two sons also squared off, ready for an encounter. Lopeman, being by far the smaller man of the two, backed away slowly. His enemy continued to advanced upon him, all the while brandishing a club. When he was almost near enough to Lopeman to strike him, Lopeman, in self-defense, as he claims, drew his revolver and shot him down. The neighbor's son, reserving the better part of valor, dashed back into the house.

Lopeman and his son calmly liberated the worthless calf and took it back home. Lopeman then went on to the county seat and gave himself up to the authorities. As soon as the news spread over the neighborhood, excitement ran high. The neighbor, despite his irascibility, had been a popular man, and there was talk of lynching. Better judgment prevailed and, after six months, the Lopeman was tried, convicted and sentenced to prison.

This man was my cell mate.

My first evening, he told me of all his troubles. I learned from his own lips that I was to room with a murderer. Never had home seemed so far away, as I sat there, locked in that small cell with a man whose hands were dyed with the blood of his neighbor. As the sun set on my first night in Leavenworth, my unease grew – only to subside when the old man, as solemnly as the Apostle Paul, took down the Bible, read a few verses, and then knelt down and prayed. I sat there, mute with astonishment. How was it possible for a man who was guilty of such a grave crime to be devout?

For six months I shared that room with the murderous old man, a cell so small that, when the sleeping bunks were down, we could scarcely move.

Lopeman often told me that he had no consciousness whatever of guilt, nor the fear and dread of a murderer. Yet, when I asked him if, when he dreamed, he could see the face of his victim – with a shrug of the shoulders, he admitted that he could. Still – a kinder-hearted man I never met. Whenever he received any little delicacies from home he would always divide them with me, and in such a cheerful spirit that I soon came to think a good deal of the old man. If we had both been on the outside world I would not have desired a kinder neighbor.

Later on, his son was convicted as an accomplice, and sent up for two years. The son's wife, Lopeman's daughter-in-law, has been left in care of their several children. They have the sympathy of all their neighbors in their affliction.

Oh, Righteous Judge!

The story of Gus Arndt demonstrates the dangerous combination of whiskey and Dutchmen. Gus came to this country a number of years ago, and went to work for his uncle in Wabaunsee County. Not being able to speak English, Gus' uncle took advantage of him, paying the hard-working immigrant only only ten dollars a month for his services as a farm hand during the summer season, and nothing but his board during the winter. Gus remained with his uncle for some time, but after three or four years of suffering at these wages, he had learned to understand a little English.

One day as Gus was pitching grain in the field, an Irishman came by – a farmer who owned land a few miles distant. Needing a hand and noticing that Arndt handled himself in a satisfactory manner, the Irishman offered him twenty dollars per month to go and work for him. Arndt accepted his proposition and agreed to report the following Monday.

That night, Ardnt settled up with his disappointed uncle and received the balance of his wages, some $75. He had been in America long enough to reach that point in our civilization that, after working awhile, and getting a balance ahead, he must take a rest and go on a "spree".

For a couple of days Gus fared sumptuously. At length, his continuous drinking reached a point below zero. Half crazed by the whiskey, Gus staggered out of the saloon and over to the fence across the way, where the farmers – in town for their Saturday shopping – had hitched their teams. Untying a horse, Gus thought he might take a ride. He lumbered into the buggy, and, as only a drunken man can, he drove down the main street of the town in broad daylight and out into the country.

In an hour or so, the buggy's owner returned. Making numerous inquiries about his missing transport and getting nothing satisfactory in response, the farmer placed the matter in the hands of the sheriff.

The lawman soon overtook the noted horse-thief. Gus was sitting in the buggy sound asleep; the lines were hanging down over the dashboard, and the old horse was marching along at a snail's pace. He was approximately two miles from town, and, no doubt, had travelled at this furious gait all the way. Gus was faced about, and, assisted by the sheriff, drove back to town. He was then placed under arrest and sent to jail – for this little drive, he was sent to the penitentiary for five years. I have never heard a more unjust sentence.

Gus served his time out and there never was a better-behaved person behind the walls. When he regained his liberty, instead of returning to his uncle's house, he found his way to Marysville, Kansas. Here resided a number of prosperous German farmers, and the ex-convict soon got work. Somehow, when he presented himself, Gus neglected to tell his new employer that he had just finished up a contract for the State of Kansas. An understandable oversight.

Gus worked industriously for some months, accumulating a neat little sum of money, and beginning to feel happy once more. At this time a man passed through Marysville that was acquainted with Arndt's antecedents, and being a dirty dog, he felt it was his duty to inform the farmer that his hired man was an ex-convict, horse-thief and a desperado of the very worst type. Some men are extremely anxious to do their duty when it is in their power to injure a fellow-man. Gus immediately got the "bounce". He was informed by his employer that he did not want to make his home a harbor for horse-thieves and other such bandits.

Gus could not bear the idea of being discharged and again applied to the bottle for consolation. He went on another spree. When crazed with liquor he acted just as he did before: Gus went to a hitching post and untied a buggy and its team of horses. One of the horses had had its leg broken at some former time, while the other one was very old – both were almost completely without value. Gus seemed to select the very worst team he could find. Perhaps it was the buggy he was after – or maybe he was tired and looking for an easy place to rest. It was in the afternoon and the streets were full of people, but Gus went unchallenged as he crawled into the buggy and started off down the road.

Again, Gus was retrieved by the local sheriff. In his two hours of flight, Gus had made it about half a mile from town. When the sheriff found him, the elderly horses were quietly standing at one side of the road and the Dutchman was lying in the buggy – sound asleep, soaked in the contents of his uncorked bottle of whiskey. Gus was taken to jail, and the news soon spread that he was an ex-convict and horse-thief.

He was tried on a charge of stealing horses, and was returned to the penitentiary for another two years. Seven years' service for two drunks!

After Gus had completed his narration to me he wound up by saying, "Ven I shall oudt git this time, I let von visky alones." Wiser words were never spoken.

Skilled Labor

William Hurst is a man of rough personal appearance. He is of Irish descent, and his age is now about fifty-five. He came to Kansas as an early day, settling in Doniphan County, where he courted and married one of the pretty girls in the state.

Time went along, as time does, and in a few years, several little cherubs had blessed the household of Hurst. But, as sometimes happens, the husband turned to drink. Love grew colder, the necessities of the family grew greater and poverty in all its hideousness came to curse their once-happy home. Hurst's poor, distracted wife did all she could by taking in washing and ironing to prevent the starvation of her little ones.

The husband, through bleary eyes, imagined he could see that other men were all too friendly to his wife. He charged her with unfaithfulness; she denied the charge. Incensed, Hurst beat and mistreat her out of all reason. For her own protection and that of her children, she had him arrested, intending to bind him over to keep the peace. On the advice of officers, who are so very full of useful advice, Hurst's wife withdrew the charge and he was set at liberty.

For a few days Hust kept quiet, but soon the red liquor poured down his throat, and like a mountain devil, it stirred all the dark passions of his lost and ruined nature. Overcome by whiskey, he attempted to debauch his own daughter, and was only prevented by the physical force of the ever-watchful mother. The father (great God! is such a human being entitled to the endearing term?) turned upon her, and, as had happened before, abused, kicked and mistreated her in a most shameful manner. Battered and shamed, but again thinking only of her children, she bravely had him arrested a second time.

The lawmen of Doniphan County again proved their worth. While in their charge, Hurst convinced an officer that he must see his wife. Hurst and his escort met Hurst's wife at the outskirts of the little village. Before the officer could prevent it, Hurst sprang upon his wife – the mother of his child – and cut her throat from ear to ear. He leapt away and made escaped into the woods. The officer, meanwhile, deemed it more important to stay with the stricken woman, not realising that the wound was fatal. Eventually, others were called who took charge of the body, and the officer struck out in hot pursuit of the murderer.

Hurst was followed through the woods until a few miles from White Cloud, where the officer finally overtook him. The depraved man was overpowered, and conducted to the county seat. There, he was tried and convicted of murder in the first degree, sentenced to be hanged and sent to the penitentiary to await the final execution, which, in our State, never comes. Hurst remained in Leavenworth for about twenty months when he was declared insane, and sent to the state asylum. He was there about three and a half years, at which time he was pronounced "cured" and returned to the penitentiary.

Now comes the queerest part of this narrative.

You have all in your younger days read the story of the maniac that paced his cell, repeating "once one is two". Hurst seems anxious to talk to every one that calls, and especially eager to shake hands; but if you say anything to him, or ask any question, his only answer is "skilled labor," and he keeps on repeating these words as he walks up and down his place of confinement.

Has the infinite God destroyed Hurst's reason to prevent the power of darkness over this poor, unfortunate being? Or is it the demands of justice, met in the terrible conscience, which have staggered and shattered that which originally was in the image of God?

The Female Convicts

In the Kansas penitentiary, just outside the high stone wall, but surrounded by a fence some fifteen feet high, stands a second stone structure – the female prison. In this lonely place, shut out from society, there are thirteen female prisoners. Many of these women are here for murder: when a woman falls, she generally descends to the lowest plane.

During the week these women spend their time in domestic labor, sewing, patching and washing. Their keepers are a couple of noble Christian ladies, who endeavor to surround them with all the sunshine possible, given their grim surroundings. For these inmates it is wash, patch and sew from one year's end to the other. The only pause in their routine is the Sabbath, which is spent in reading and religious exercises. On Sunday afternoons, the chaplain visits them and preaches a discourse.

A few days before I was discharged, there came to the prison a little old grandmother, at least seventy years of age. She had lived with her husband for fifty-two years, was the mother of ten children and had fifteen grand-children. She and her had husband owned a very beautiful farm and were in good circumstances, probably worth $50,000.

Her husband had passed away very suddenly. After the funeral, the widow went over into Missouri to make her home with one of her married daughters. She had only been there a short time when her eldest son secured a requisition and had his aged mother dragged back to Kansas and tried for murder. She was convicted. The sentence imposed was one year in the penitentiary, at the end of which time she was to be hanged by the neck until dead. In Kansas, this is equivalent to a life sentence.

The old woman will do well if she lives out a single year in prison. She claims that her eldest son desires her property and that was the motive which induced him to swear her life away. During her long life of three score and ten years, this was the only charge against her character for anything whatsoever. She always bore a good name and was highly esteemed in the neighborhood in which she lived.

Another notable female prisoner is Mary J. Scales. She is sixty-five years of age, and is called "Aunt Mary" in the prison. Aunt Mary is a murderess. She took the life of her husband and was sentenced to be hanged on April 16, 1871. Her sentence, is always the fashion, was commuted to a life imprisonment. For eighteen years this old woman has been an inmate of the Kansas penitentiary. She is very popular inside the prison, and all the officers and their families are very fond of Aunt Mary. But it seems that she has but few, if any, friends on the outside. Several old men have been pardoned of far fouler crimes, but Aunt Mary still bides her time behind the prison walls.

Mrs. Henrietta Cook

Henrietta Cook was a mere twenty-five years of age when she came to the Kansas penitentiary to serve out a life's sentence. She was sentenced for having poisoned her husband. For years she remained in close confinement. Fifteen years of imprisonment are sufficient to bring wrinkles to the face, and change the color of the hair to gray. When Mrs. Cook entered the prison she was young and beautiful, but when she left she was old and broken-down.

Henrietta made the mistake of her life in getting married. She, a young woman, married an old man of seventy. She was poor and lovely; he was rich and elderly. After they had been married but a short time, she awoke one morning to find her aged husband a corpse at her side. The town's gossips soon reported that she had poisoned her elderly husband to obtain his wealth and clear the way so that she might spend the rest of her days with a younger and handsomer man. Spurred by the tongue of scandal, the authorities exhumed the husband's body from its grave and examined. The corpse's stomach showed the presence of arsenic, and in sufficient quantity to kill. The Cook home was searched and a package of the deadly poison found. Mrs. Cook was tried, and the prosecution produced sufficient circumstantial evidence to secure her conviction.

A short time before this sad event happened, a young clerk departed from the town where the Cook family resided and took up his abode in California. After fifteen years of absence he returned. Learning of the Cook murder, he went before the board of pardons and swore out an affidavit that the old gentleman was in the habit of using arsenic, and that, while a clerk in the drug store, he had sold him the identical package found in the house.

Other evidence was produced supporting this testimony, and the board of pardons decided that the husband had died from an overdose of arsenic taken by himself and of his own accord.

Henrietta Cook was immediately pardoned, but how will she ever to obtain satisfaction for her fifteen years of intense suffering? The State of Kansas should pension this poor woman, who now is scarcely able to work; and juries in the future should not be so hasty in sending people to the penitentiary on flimsy, circumstantial evidence.

In the Mines

In the coal mines, the convicts are permitted to converse while they work. I used this opportunity to acquire the histories of the five hundred criminals with whom I labored in the dark, eight hundred feet below the surface.

As a rule, convicts deny their crimes to those who are not, like themselves, criminals. But my readers should also know that a convict will also tell a fellow prisoner every detail of his crime. It is not difficult for one prisoner to get the confidence of his fellow. In fact, criminals so love to unburden their minds – and at such length – that it becomes tiresome.

Nearly all the life men are in the mines, which means there are many murderers there. Some of them speak of their crimes with a bravado that's simply astonishing, reveling in their utter depravity. Others, admitting their guilt, are more withdrawn, and will give but little in the way of details.

The following story will give the reader a sample of the sort of tale that greeted my ears every day for a year, and led me to conclude that the coal mines of the penitentiary are not inhabited exclusively by Sunday school scholars.

This particular wretch murdered an old man and his wife. The old people lived on a farm adjoining the one where the criminal, who was then a hired man, worked. It was the talk of the neighborhood that the couple had money, so one day, this human fiend took it upon himself to secure their "loose change," as he so deemed it.

He procured a shotgun and an axe, and, in the dead of night, slunk into their house. Forcing open the kitchen door, he made his way inside. He quietly stole through their home and into their bedroom, where they slept, innocent and unaware. He had brought with him a lantern, but the fiend found that he had had no need for it – the moonlight shone through the window opposite and fell upon the faces of the unconscious victims.

Setting his gun down by the side of the bed, so it would be handy for use, he took the axe and struck each of his victims a blow on the head. He bragged, with a demonic chuckle, that it was more difficult to kill the woman – she required two swings from the axe, while one was sufficient for her husband. The hard work done, he ransacked the house. Underneath the straw-bed – now soaked in their life's blood – he found a small bag, which contained some gold, silver and paper money, amounting to over one thousand dollars. In a cold-blooded manner he further detailed (and as I pen his words my blood nearly freezes in my veins) that, in order to search the bed, it became necessary for him to move the bodies. He lifted them up one at a time, and placed them upon the floor. Face downward, he noted, for their eyes bulged out and seemed to stare at him.

Leaving the bodies, he crept back to the farm at which he worked. He slept in the barn, as is very often the case with farm laborers during the summer season. Procuring an old bucket, he placed the money in it, covered the top with a piece of board, and buried it in the earth east of the barn. He also buried the axe near the bucket. He said there were clots of blood and hair on the axe, so he thought it best to remove it from sight. He then returned to the barn, and, strange to say, slept sweetly until morning.

The murderer reported to work the next day as usual. As he performed his labor about the farm, his mind was taken up by pleasant thoughts of what a good time he would have spending that money. He shed no tears over the terrible crime he had committed, reasoning that the money would do the old people no good, and that he could use it to better advantage.

The murder was discovered the next day about noon. The alarm was given, and the whole country was aroused over such a hideous crime – two helpless and highly-respected elders, savagely murdered for their money. A couple of tramps had passed through the neighborhood the day before, and were immediately the suspects of local suspicion.

The tramps were captured a day's walk from town and brought back to the scene of the murder. They both stoutly denied any knowledge of the crime. They were separated, and each was told that the other had confessed. Still, they continued to affirm their innocence. The tramps were then taken to the woods near by and each hanged, almost until death, yet they denied committing the crime.

Local "justice" exhausted, the tramps were at length taken to the county seat, not far distant, and were bound over to appear at the next term of the District Court.

The majority of the people believed that the perpetrators of this crime had been arrested. The excitement soon passed away, and very little was said about it.

"It was at this time," said my informant, "that I made the mistake of my life. I had worked hard on the farm for several months, and deserved a break. I made up my mind to have a time, and treated myself to drink and the company of a woman. A large reward had been offered for the murderer of those old people. I must have got to talking, and the harlot obtained my secret while I was drunk. She went to the marshal and made an arrangement that, for half of the reward offered, she would show him the man who had committed the crime.

While I was drinking and having a good time with my woman, three deputies were on the road to the farm where I had been working. They dug up the old bucket and found the axe. I was arrested and bound over to the District Court. The officers had to keep me secreted before my trial, as there was talk of lynching.."

I asked him if he had any hope of pardon.

"Oh yes, of course," bragged he, "in the course of eight or ten years I will be out once more."

"What became of the tramps that suffered on your behalf?"

"They were released as soon as I was arrested. A snug little sum of money was raised for them and they even got new clothes. They're undoubtedly congratulating themselves on their good fortune."

As we sat together in a secluded place in the mines, with the faint light of my miner's lamp falling on his hideous face, the cool, deliberate manner in which he related his atrocious doings, the fiendish spirit he displayed, led me to regard him as one among the most debased and hardened criminals I had met in the mines – a human being utterly devoid of moral nature – *a very devil in the form of man!*

Yellow Back Literature

A boy was brought into the hospital one day while I was there. This youth had become suddenly ill in the mines, and had to be assisted from his place of work to the ward for the sick. The opportunity presenting itself, I got into conversation with him while he convalesced, and he told me the history of his crime. His tale is worth relating, as it shows the fatal effects of bad literature upon the human mind.

The boy was an orphan. Following the death of both his parents in the East he had come to Kansas to make his home with an uncle. This relative was very kind, and after a time adopted the boy. The lad had a pleasant home, and his prospects for the future were bright. How often the case that the bright sky of the future turns overcast...

This boy was a constantly reader of the life of Jesse James, and other literature of that ilk. Steeped in their vile influence, he decided to go on the "war path" and follow in the footsteps of his literary idol. With this plan firmly in mind, he provided himself with two large revolvers. One night, after all the household had retired, he crept stealthily into the bed-room of one of the hired men and stole seventy dollars. He went to the barn, took one of his uncle's horses and started for the Indian Territory.

The uncle woke up an hour and discovered that one of his best horses was gone – and also that his nephew was nowhere to be found. He gathered together several of his neighbors and started in pursuit. The next day, about noon, the youth was overtaken and surrounded. The uncle rode up to him and questioned the boy as to his strange conduct. The boy drew one of his revolvers, and, pointing it at his uncle, shot him dead.

The youth had been determined to play Jesse James to the last, but when he saw his uncle fall dead, he realized what he had done. The bravado spirit forsook him and he shook in fear. The neighbors closed in upon him and took his firearms from his trembling hands. In due time he had his trial and was sent to the penitentiary for life.

Bad books are our worst companions. I have narrated the history of this young murderer, and now urge my own boy readers to let yellow back literature alone. It wrecked the future of this youth, and what it did for one it may do for another.

A Youthful Murderer

Inside the prison, Willie Sells is called the "baby convict". When he came to the penitentiary in 1886, he was but sixteen years of age, and, truthfully, in appearance he seemed much younger. He is charged with one of the most sickening murders committed in Kansas.

Willie's home was in Neosho County. His father, a prosperous farmer, lived happily with his wife and three children, of which Willie was the oldest. Early one morning, he rushed from his home and made his way to the nearest neighbor, about half a mile distant. With his face and hands covered with blood, the child conveyed the startling news that his entire family had been murdered, and he only had escaped.

Soon an excited crowd gathered at the home of the victims, and the sight that they saw has but few parallels in the fatal and fearful histories of crime. The victims had been murdered while asleep. In one room lay the father and mother, on their bed of death. Their heads had been split open with an axe that lay nearby, and the blood of one mingled with that of the other. In an adjoining bedroom were found the little brother and sister, covered with their own life's blood. They had been foully murdered with the same edged instrument that had caused the death of their parents.

Where was the monster that had committed this terrible and atrocious act?

A search of the premises disclosed the fact that robbery was not the motive. No property was missing. Willie, the sole survivor, was questioned again and again. He said that a burly-looking tramp had entered into the house through a window during the night; that he being awake at the moment, and becoming alarmed, Willie hid himself, and, unperceived, beheld his father and mother, his brother and sister, thus foully murdered. A thorough and extensive search was made, but the tramp was never found.

The surviving child was then taken into custody. It was claimed that his statements of the circumstances varied, and in several instances he had contradicted himself. The evidence introduced at his trial was purely circumstantial, but after much deliberation and hesitancy, the jury decided on a verdict of guilty: the child was sentenced to imprisonment for life.

Willie conducts himself well in the prison. On account of his extreme youth he is given a great deal of liberty. It is with great reluctance that he talks about his crime, and it is obvious that he greatly longs for freedom.

Is this boy guilty? This question has never been satisfactorily answered. I am informed there was a grave doubt in the mind of the judge who tried the case and imposed sentence upon the child. A chill of horror creeps over me as I think of the members of this family weltering in each other's blood. But, should Willie Sells be innocent, it would be awful for the boy to remain in the Kansas Hell for a lifetime.

❦FOUND❦

The deranged logic of the fairy tale is on full display in "The Devil's Age", as the impoverished Peli is caught up in situations beyond his comprehension.

This story was first published in a collection of Basque folklore, carefully transcribed by Reverend Wentworth Webster in 1879. As dictated by Franchun Beltzarri, it is a bizarre tale, and one that's all too brief.

David Bryher's interpretation keeps the delightful irrationality and the sense of moral ambiguity of the original, but builds it into a complete story with unique personality.

THE DEVIL'S AGE

FRANCHUN BELTZARRI & DAVID BRYHER

Many years ago, somewhere far away but quite like this, there lived a penniless man called Peli and his wife, Irune. While Irune cooked and cleaned and got things done, Peli would spend his days taking indulgent, melancholic walks – walks that usually ended with a long mope at a crossroads a few miles from his home. One day, his mope was interrupted by footsteps crunching up the road behind him. He turned and there was a gentleman in a grey suit.

Now, Peli was a bad liar. All the town knew it. His face was as easy to read as your lover's handwriting, so he wasn't all that surprised to hear the gentleman ask, without any preamble, "Why are you so sad?"

Peli's chest heaved with a big sigh, like a rolling ocean wave. "Because my wife and I don't have enough money to live."

The gentleman's eyebrow twitched. "I will give you as much money as you like." Peli was about to say something but the gentleman raised his hand to stop him. "As much as you like – if, before you die, you can learn the age of the Devil."

Peli felt a smile crackle across his face. The gentleman nodded curtly, turned on his heel and walked away from the crossroads. Peli dashed off in the other direction, back towards home, happy as you like.

For the rest of their lives, Peli and Irune wanted for nothing. They lived a merry life, full of fine food and sumptuous silks, and they lived it at a great rate. The days flew by until, one day, Peli woke and knew his time was near. He swung his legs out of bed and the hundred little aches and pains he'd collected over the years suddenly joined their voices to sing an elegy.

And he thought: Oh but the Devil's age. I had forgotten all about it!

© David Bryher 2012. Inspired by "The Devil's Age" by Franchun Beltazarri. *Basque Legends*. Wentworth Webster, ed. London: Griffin and Farran, 1879.

He came down to a breakfast of eggs and tomatoes and peppers and onions (Irune still insisted on cooking, despite their forty servants). He slumped into a high-backed, velvet-padded chair at the dining table. He lowered his hand on to the linen tablecloth, feeling the crisp, white fabric against the soft skin of his palm. The only table we once had, he thought, was wobbly and enjoyed more by woodlice than by us. A sigh rolled across his chest.

"What's the matter with you, then?" asked Irune. "You're not happy? Look around you! We want for nothing! How can you be sad?"

And so, Peli told Irune how their riches were bought. Her eyes turned to ice as he lowered his own in shame. Bargains at crossroads, he knew, always had a cost. Peli hadn't asked the gentleman what the price would be if he didn't learn the Devil's age, but he knew it would be more than all the money they had spent since the bargain was made.

Irune took a breath and blinked and it was like storm clouds clearing. "If you have no worries but that," she said, "then you have nothing at all. Now, Peli, you must do exactly as I say."

And she took him to the cellar of their house, where Peli saw many things he tried to ignore, for he loved his wife and did not want to be frightened of her. "Get into this barrel of honey," she said, and he did. "Now, get into this barrel of feathers," she said, and he did. "Now, go back to the crossroads and wait there for the Devil. When he arrives, drop to all fours, walk backwards and forwards and all around him and through his legs."

Peli blinked a sticky feather from his eye and Irune caught his look. "If you want to know the Devil's age, Peli, if you want to settle your bargain at the crossroads, then do as I say."

It had been many years since Peli had walked to the crossroads, but it hadn't changed much at all. For a moment, he longed for the simpler days of his indulgent walks and his moping, but then he thought of his riches and remembered that nostalgia is a terrible liar. After a few minutes of swatting away wasps, he heard footsteps crunching up the road behind him. He turned and there was the Devil.

The two men stared at each other for a moment. Peli's treacherous face was hidden by honeyed feathers, so the Devil could not read the terror written there. The

Devil, for his part, looked a little stunned. So stunned was the Devil, in fact, that he took a step backwards.

Peli's breath caught in his throat, but he knew he had to do what his wife had told him. He fell to his hands and knees. Then, he walked backwards and forwards and all around the Devil and through his legs. For good measure, once all that was done, he scrabbled in the dirt around the Devil's feet. All the while, the Devil's stare followed him, his eyes growing ever wider.

"Well, I do declare," said the Devil, "I have never seen such a frightful animal in all my life. And I am so many years old!"

Except he didn't say "so many" but you don't really think I'd tell you the Devil's age, do you?

Peli had heard enough. Still on his hands and knees, he bolted home at full speed, crashing through the door and past a number of startled servants, and told his wife what he had done.

"We will never want for another thing," he said, smiling, plucking feathers from his forehead. "I did everything you told me to, to the letter. And the Devil? Pah, I am no longer afraid of him!"

And Peli and Irune lived rich and happily. And if they lived well, they died well too.

Amelia B. Edwards (1831 - 1892) was an author, journalist and prominent Egyptologist. Although her early novels were best-sellers, it was her travelogue, A Thousand Miles Up the Nile (1876), that made her an international sensation. Based on her first-hand experiences, A Thousand Miles Up the Nile captured the thriving trade in Egyptian antiquities and deplored the haphazard plundering of ancient monuments.

Edwards co-founded the Egypt Exploration Fund (now the Egypt Exploration Society) and spent the latter years of her life campaigning for responsible, scientific research. She was also a prominent activist for women's suffrage.

"The Four-Fifteen Express" is a classic ghost story. Remarkably, it contains one of the bureaucratic manifestations of the undead ever written: the central spirit is obsessed not with avenging its untimely death, but with with completing a legal transaction.

THE FOUR-FIFTEEN EXPRESS

AMELIA B. EDWARDS

The events which I am about to relate took place between nine and ten years ago. Sebastopol had fallen in the early spring, the peace of Paris had been concluded since March, our commercial relations with the Russian Empire were but recently renewed; and I, returning home after my first northward journey since the war, was well pleased with the prospect of spending the month of December under the hospitable and thoroughly English roof of my excellent friend, Jonathan Jelf, Esq., of Dumbleton Manor, Clayborough, East Anglia. Traveling in the interests of the well-known firm in which it is my lot to be a junior partner, I had been called upon to visit not only the capitals of Russia and Poland, but had found it also necessary to pass some weeks among the trading ports of the Baltic; whence it came that the year was already far spent before I again set foot on English soil, and that, instead of shooting pheasants with him, as I had hoped, in October, I came to be my friend's guest during the more genial Christmas-tide.

My voyage over, and a few days given up to business in Liverpool and London, I hastened down to Clayborough with all the delight of a schoolboy whose holidays are at hand. My way lay by the Great East Anglian line as far as Clayborough station, where I was to be met by one of the Dumbleton carriages and conveyed across the remaining nine miles of country. It was a foggy afternoon, singularly warm for the 4th of December, and I had arranged to leave London by the 4:15 express. The early darkness of winter had already closed in; the lamps were lighted in the carriages; a clinging damp dimmed the windows, adhered to the door-handles, and pervaded

Mixed Sweets from Routledge's Annual, 1867.

all the atmosphere; while the gas-jets at the neighbouring book-stand diffused a luminous haze that only served to make the gloom of the terminus more visible. Having arrived some seven minutes before the starting of the train, and, by the connivance of the guard, taken sole possession of an empty compartment, I lighted my traveling-lamp, made myself particularly snug, and settled down to the undisturbed enjoyment of a book and a cigar. Great, therefore, was my disappointment when at the last moment, a gentleman came hurrying along the platform, glanced into my carriage, opened the locked door with a private key, and stepped in.

It struck me at the first glance that I had seen him before – a tall, spare man, thin-lipped, light-eyed, with an un-graceful stoop in the shoulders, and scant gray hair worn somewhat long upon the collar. He carried a light waterproof coat, an umbrella, and a large brown japanned deed-box, which last he placed under the seat. This done, he felt carefully in his breast-pocket, as if to make certain of the safety of his purse or pocketbook, laid his umbrella in the netting overhead, spread the waterproof across his knees, and exchanged his hat for a traveling-cap of some Scotch material. By this time the train was moving out of the station and into the faint gray of the wintry twilight beyond.

I now recognized my companion. I recognized him from the moment when he removed his hat and uncovered the lofty, furrowed, and somewhat narrow brow beneath. I had met him, as I distinctly remembered, some three years before, at the very house for which, in all probability, he was now bound, like myself. His name was Dwerrihouse; he was a lawyer by profession, and, if I was not greatly mistaken, was first cousin to the wife of my host. I knew also that he was a man eminently "well-to-do", both as regarded his professional and private means. The Jelfs entertained him with that sort of observant courtesy which falls to the lot of the rich relation, the children made much of him, and the old butler, albeit somewhat surly "to the general", treated him with deference. I thought, observing him by the vague mixture of lamplight and twilight, that Mrs. Jelf's cousin looked all the worse for the three years' wear and tear which had gone over his head since our last meeting. He was Wf paJt, and had a restless light in his eye that I did not remember to have observed before. The anxious lines, too ^ about his mouth were deepened, and there was a cavernous, hollow look about his cheeks and temples which seemed to speak of sickness or sorrow. He had glanced at me as he came in, but without any gleam of recognition in his face. Now he glanced again, as I fancied, somewhat doubtfully.

When he did so for the third or fourth time I ventured to address him.

"Mr. John Dwerrihouse, I think?"

"That is my name," he replied.

"I had the pleasure of meeting you at Dumbleton about three years ago."

Mr. Dwerrihouse bowed.

"I thought I knew your face," he said; "but your name, I regret to say–"

"Langford – William Langford. I have known Jonathan Jelf since we were boys together at Merchant Taylor's, and I generally spend a few weeks at Dumbleton in the shooting season. I suppose we are bound for the same destination?"

"Not if you are on your way to the manor," he replied. "I am traveling upon business – rather troublesome business too. While you, doubtless, have only pleasure in view."

"Just so. I am in the habit of looking forward to this visit as to the brightest three weeks in all the year."

"It is a pleasant house," said Mr. Dwerrihouse.

"The pleasantest I know."

"And Jelf is thoroughly hospitable."

"The best and kindest fellow in the world!"

"They have invited me to spend Christmas week with them," pursued Mr. Dwerrihouse, after a moment's pause.

"And you are coming?"

"I can not tell. It must depend on the issue of this business which I have in hand. You have heard perhaps that we are about to construct a branch line from Blackwater to Stockbridge."

I explained that I had been for some months away from England, and had therefore heard nothing of the contemplated improvement.

Mr. Dwerrihouse smiled complacently.

"It will be an improvement," he said, "a great improvement. Stockbridge is a flourishing town, and needs but a more direct railway communication with the metropolis to become an important centre of commerce. This branch was my own idea. I brought the project before the board, and have myself superintended the execution of it up to the present time."

"You are an East Anglian director, I presume?"

"My interest in the company," replied Mr. Dwerrihouse, "is threefold. I am a director, I am a considerable shareholder, and, as head of the firm of Dwerrihouse, Dwerrihouse & Craik, I am the company's principal solicitor."

Loquacious, self-important, full of his pet project, and apparently unable to talk on any other subject, Mr. Dwerrihouse then went on to tell of the opposition he had encountered and the obstacles he had overcome in the cause of the Stockbridge branch. I was entertained with a multitude of local details and local grievances. The rapacity of one squire, the impracticability of another, the indignation of the rector whose glebe was threatened, the culpable indifference of the Stockbridge townspeople, who could not be brought to see that their most vital interests hinged upon a junction with the Great East Anglian line; the spite of the local newspaper, and the unheard-of difficulties attending the Common question, were each and all laid before me with a circumstantiality that possessed the deepest interest for my excellent fellow-traveller, but none whatever for myself. From these, to my despair, he went on to more intricate matters: to the approximate expenses of construction per mile; to the estimates sent in by different contractors; to the probable traffic returns of the new line; to the provisional clauses of the new act as enumerated in Schedule D of the company's last half-yearly report; and so on and on and on, till my head ached and my attention flagged and my eyes kept closing in spite of every effort that I made to keep them open. At length I was roused by these words:

"Seventy-five thousand pounds, cash down."

"Seventy-five thousand pounds, cash down," I repeated in the heartiest tone I could assume. "That is a heavy sum."

"A heavy sum to carry here," replied Mr. Dwerrihouse, pointing significantly to his breast-pocket; "but a mere fraction of what we shall ultimately have to pay."

"You do not mean to say that you have seventy-five thousand pounds at this moment upon your person?" I exclaimed.

"My good sir, have I not been telling you so for the last half-hour?" said Mr. Dwerrihouse, testily. "That money has to be paid over at half-past eight o'clock this evening, at the office of Sir Thomas's solicitors, on completion of the deed of sale."

"But how will you get across by night from Blackwater to Stockbridge with seventy-five thousand pounds in your pocket?"

"To Stockbridge," echoed the lawyer. "I find I have made myself very imperfectly understood. I thought I had explained how this sum only carries us as far as Mailingford – the first stage, as it were, of our journey – and how our route from Blackwater to Mailingford lies entirely through Sir Thomas Liddell's property."

"I beg your pardon," I stammered. "I fear my thoughts were wandering. So you only go as far as Mailingford tonight?"

"Precisely. I shall get a conveyance from the Blackwater Arms. And you?"

"Oh, Jelf sends a trap to meet me at Clayborough. Can I be the bearer of any message from you?"

"You may say, if you please, Mr. Langford, that I wished I could have been your companion all the way, and that I will come over, if possible, before Christmas."

"Nothing more?"

Mr. Dwerrihouse smiled grimly. "Well," he said, "You may tell my cousin that she need not burn the hall down in my honour this time, and that I shall be obliged if she will order the blue-room chimney to be swept before I arrive."

"That sounds tragic. Had you a conflagration on the occasion of your last visit to Dumbleton?"

"Something like it. There had been no fire lighted in my bedroom since the spring, and the flue was foul, and the rooks had built in it; so when I went up to dress for dinner I found the room full of smoke and the chimney on fire. Are we already at Blackwater."

The train had gradually come to a pause while Mr. Dwerrihouse was speaking, and, on putting my head out of the window, I could see the station some few hundred yards ahead. There was another train before us blocking the way, and the guard was making use of the delay to collect the Blackwater tickets. I had scarcely ascertained our position when the ruddy-faced official appeared at our carriage door.

"Tickets, sir," said he.

"I am for Clayborough," I replied, holding out the tiny pink card.

He took it, glanced at it by the light of his little lantern, gave it back, looked, as I fancied, somewhat sharply at my fellow-traveller, and disappeared.

"He did not ask for yours," I said, with some surprise.

"They never do," replied Mr. Dwerrihouse, "they all know me, and of course I travel free."

"Blackwater! Blackwater!" cried the porter, running along the platform beside us as we glided into the station.

Mr. Dwerrihouse pulled out his deed-box, put his travelling-cap in his pocket, resumed his hat, took down his umbrella, and prepared to be gone.

"Many thanks, Mr. Langford, for your society," he said, with old-fashioned courtesy. "I wish you a good-evening."

"Good-evening," I replied, putting out my hand.

But he either did not see it or did not choose to see it, and, slightly lifting his hat, stepped out upon the platform.

Having done this, he moved slowly away and mingled with the departing crowd.

Leaning forward to watch him out of sight, I trod upon something which proved to be a cigar-case. It had fallen, no doubt, from the pocket of his waterproof coat, and was made of dark morocco leather, with a silver monogram upon the side. I sprang out of the carriage just as the guard came up to lock me in.

"Is there one minute to spare?" I asked, eagerly. "The gentleman who travelled down with me from town has dropped his cigar-case; he is not yet ont of the station."

"Just a minute and a half, sir," replied the guard. "Best be quick."

I dashed along the platform as fast as my feet could carry me. It was a large station, and Mr. Dwerrihouse had by this time got more than half-way to the farther end.

I, however, saw him distantly, moving slowly with the stream. Then, as I drew nearer, I saw that he had met some friend, that they were talking as they walked, that they presently fell back somewhat from the crowd and stood aside in earnest conversation. I made straight for the spot where they were waiting. There was a vivid gas-jet just above their heads, and the light fell full upon their faces. I saw both distinctly – the face of Mr. Dwerrihouse and the face of his companion. Running, breathless, eager as I was, getting in the way of porters and passengers, and fearful every instant lest I should see the train going on without me, I yet observed that the new-comer was considerably younger and shorter than the director, that he was sandy-haired, moustachioed, small-featured, and dressed in a close-cut suit of Scotch tweed. I was now within a few yards of them. I ran against a stout gentleman, I was nearly knocked down by a luggage-truck, I stumbled over a carpet-bag; I gained the spot just as the driver's whistle warned me to return.

To my utter stupefaction, they were no longer there. I had seen them but two seconds before – and they were gone! I stood still; I looked to right and left; I saw no sign of them in any direction. It was as if the platform had gaped and swallowed them.

"There were two gentlemen standing here a moment ago," I said to a porter at my elbow. "Which way can they have gone?"

"I saw no gentlemen, sir," replied the man.

The whistle shrilled out again. The guard, far up the platform, held up his arm, and shouted to me to come on.

"If you're going on by this train, sir," said the porter, "you must run for it."

I did run for it, just gained the carriage as the train began to move, was shoved in by the guard, and left, breathless and bewildered, with Mr. Dwerrihouse's cigar-case still in my hand.

It was the strangest disappearance in the world; it was like a transformation trick in a pantomime. They were there one moment palpably there, talking, with the gaslight full upon their faces – and the next moment they were gone. There was no door near, no window, no staircase; it was a mere slip of barren platform, tapestried with big advertisements. Could anything be more mysterious?

It was not worth thinking about, and yet, for my life, I could not help pondering upon it – pondering, wondering, conjecturing, turning it over and over in my mind, and beating my brains for a solution of the enigma. I thought of it all the way from Blackwater to Clayborough. I thought of it all the way from Clayborough to Dumbleton, as I rattled along the smooth highway in a trim dog-cart, drawn by a splendid black mare and driven by the silentest and dapperest of East Anglian grooms.

We did the nine miles in something less than an hour, and pulled up before the lodge gates just as the church clock was striking half-past seven. A couple of minutes more, and the warm glow of the lighted hall was flooding out upon the gravel, a hearty grasp was on my hand, and a clear jovial voice was bidding me "Welcome to Dumbleton".

"And now, my dear fellow," said my host, when the first greeting was over, "you have no time to spare. We dine at eight, and there are people coming to meet you, so you must just get the dressing business over as quickly as may be. By the way, you will meet some acquaintances; the Biddulph's are coming, and Prendergast (Prendergast of the Skirmishers) is staying in the house. Adieu! Mrs. Jelf will be expecting you in the drawing-room."

I was ushered to my room – not the blue room, of which Mr. Dwerrihouse had his disagreeable experience, but a pretty little bachelor's chamber, hung with a delicate chintz and made cheerful by a blazing fire. I unlocked my portmanteau. I tried to be expeditious, but the memory of my railway adventure haunted me. I could not get free of it; I could not shake it off. It impeded me, it worried me, it tripped me up, it caused me to mislay my studs, to mistie my cravat, to wrench the buttons off my gloves. Worst of all, it made me so late that the party had all assembled before I reached the drawing-room. I had scarcely paid my respects to Mrs. Jelf when dinner was announced, and we paired off, some eight or ten couples strong, into the dining-room.

I am not going to describe either the guests or the dinner. All provincial parties bear the strictest family resemblance, and I am not aware that an East Anglian banquet offers any exception to the rule. There was the usual country baronet and his wife; there were the usual country parsons and their wives; there was the sempiternal turkey and haunch of venison. *Vanitas vanitatum*. There is nothing new under the sun.

I was placed about midway down the table. I had taken one rector's wife down to dinner, and I had another at my left hand. They talked across me, and their talk was about babies; it was dreadfully dull. At length there came a pause. The entrées had just been removed, and the turkey had come upon the scene. The conversation had all along been of the languidest, but at this moment it happened to have stagnated altogether. Jelf was carving the turkey; Mrs. Jelf looked as if she was trying to think of something to say; everybody else was silent. Moved by an unlucky impulse, I thought I would relate my adventure.

"By the way, Jelf," I began, "I came down part of the way today with a friend of yours."

"Indeed!" said the master of the feast, slicing scientifically into the breast of the turkey. "With whom, pray?"

"With one who bade me tell you that he should, if possible, pay you a visit before Christmas."

"I can not think who that could be," said my friend, smiling.

"It must be Major Thorp," suggested Mrs. Jelf. I shook my head.

"It was not Major Thorp." I replied, "It was a neat relation of your own, Mrs. Jelf."

"Then I am more puzzled than ever," replied my hostess. "Pray tell me who it was."

"It was no less a person than your cousin, Mr. John Dwerrihouse."

Jonathan Jelf laid down his knife and fork. Mrs. Jelf looked at me in a strange startled way, and said never a word.

"And he desired me to tell you, my dear madam, that you need not take the trouble to burn the hall down in his honour this time, but only to have the chimney of the blue room swept before his arrival."

Before I had reached the end of my sentence I became aware of something ominous in the faces of the guests. I felt I had said something which I had better have left un-said, and that for some unexplained reason my words had evoked a general consternation. I sat confounded, not daring to utter another syllable, and for at least two whole minutes there was dead silence round the table. Then Captain Prendergast came to the rescue.

"You have been abroad for some months, have you not, Mr. Langford?" he said, with the desperation of one who flings himself into the breach. "I heard you had been to Russia. Surely you have something to tell us of the state and temper of the country after the war?"

I was heartily grateful to the gallant Skirmisher for this diversion in my favour. I answered him, I fear, somewhat lamely; but he kept the conversation up, and presently one or two others joined in, and so the difficulty, whatever it might have been, was bridged over – bridged over, but not repaired. A something, an awkwardness, a visible constraint remained. The guests hitherto had been simply dull, but now they were evidently uncomfortable and embarrassed.

The dessert had scarcely been placed upon the table when the ladies left the room. I seized the opportunity to select a vacant chair next Captain Prendergast.

"In Heaven's name!" I whispered, "What was the matter just now? What had I said?"

"You mentioned the name of John Dwerrihouse."

"What of that? I had seen him not two hours before."

"It is a most astounding circumstance that you should have seen him" said Captain Prendergast. "Are you sure it was him?"

"As sure as of my own identity. We were talking all the way between London and Blackwater. But why does that surprise you?"

"Because," replied Captain Prendergast, dropping his voice to the lowest whisper, "– because John Dwerrihouse absconded three months ago with seventy-five thousand pounds of the company's money and has never been heard of since."

John Dwerrihouse had absconded three months ago – and I had seen him only a few hours back! John Dwerrihouse had embezzled seventy-five thousand pounds of the company's money, yet told me that he carried that sum upon his person! Were ever facts so strangely incongruous, so difficult to reconcile? How should he have ventured again into the light of day? How dared he show himself along the line? Above all, what had he been doing throughout those mysterious three months of disappearance?"

Perplexing questions these – questions which at once suggested themselves to the minds of all concerned, but which admitted of no easy solution. I could find no reply to them. Captain Prendergast had not even a suggestion to offer. Jonathan Jelf, who seized the first opportunity of drawing me aside and learning all that I had to tell, was more amazed and bewildered than either of us. He came to my room that night, when all the guests were gone, and we talked the thing over from every point of view; without, it must be confessed, arriving at any kind of conclusion.

"I do not ask you," he said, "whether you can have mistaken your man. That is impossible."

"As impossible as that I should mistake some stranger for yourself."

"It is not a question of looks or voice, but of facts. That he should have alluded to the fire in the blue room is proof enough of John Dwerrihouse's identity. How did he look?"

"Older, I thought; considerably older, paler, and more anxious."

"He has had enough to make him look anxious anyhow," said my friend, gloomily, "be he innocent or guilty."

"I am inclined to believe that he is innocent," I replied. "He showed no embarrassment when I addressed him, and no uneasiness when the guard came round. His conversation was open to a fault. I might almost say that he talked too freely of the business which he had in hand."

"That again is strange, for I know no one more reticent on such subjects. He actually told you that he had the seventy-five thousand pounds in his pocket?"

"He did."

"Humph. My wife has an idea about it, and she may be right."

"What idea?"

"Well, she fancies — women are so clever, you know, at putting themselves inside people's motives — she fancies that he was tempted, that he did actually take the money, and that he has been concealing himself these three months in some wild part of the country, struggling possibly with his conscience all the time and daring neither to abscond with his booty nor to come back and restore it."

"But now that he has come back?"

"That is the point She conceives that he has probably thrown himself upon the company's mercy, made restitution of the money, and, being forgiven, is permitted to carry the business through as if nothing whatever had happened."

"The last," I replied, "is an impossible case. Mrs. Jelf thinks like a generous and delicate-minded woman, but not in the least like a board of railway directors. They would never carry forgiveness so far."

"I fear not; and yet it is the only conjecture that bears a semblance of likelihood. However, we can run over to Clayborough tomorrow and see if anything is to be learned. By the way, Prendergast tells me you picked up his cigar-case."

"I did so, and here it is."

Jelf took the cigar-case, examined it by the light of the lamp, and said at once that it was beyond doubt Mr. Dwerrihouse's property, and that he remembered to have seen him use it.

"Here, too, is his monogram on the side," he added. "A big J transfixing a capital D. He used to carry the same on his note-paper."

"It offers, at all events, a proof that I was not dreaming."

"Ay, but it is time you were asleep and dreaming now. I am ashamed to have kept you up so long. Good-night."

"Good-night, and remember that I am more than ready to go with you to Clayborough, or Blackwater, or London, or anywhere, if I can be of the least service."

"Thanks! I know you mean it, old friend, and it may be that I shall put you to the test. Once more, good night."

So we parted for that night, and met again in the breakfast room at half past eight next morning. It was a hurried, silent, uncomfortable meal; none of us had slept well, and all were thinking of the same subject. Mrs. Jelf had evidently been crying, Jelf was impatient to be off, and both Captain Prendergast and myself felt ourselves to be in the painful position of outsiders who are involuntarily brought into a domestic trouble. Within twenty minutes after we had left the breakfast table the dog-cart was brought round, and my friend and I were on the road to Clayborough.

"Tell you what it is, Langford," he said, as we sped along between the wintry hedges, "I do not much fancy to bring up Dwerrihouse's name at Clayborough. All the officials know that he is my wife's relation, and the subject just now is hardly a pleasant one. If you don't much mind, we will take the 11:10 to Blackwater. It's an important station, and we shall stand a far better chance of picking up information there than at Clayborough."

So we took the 11.10, which happened to be an express, and, arriving at Blackwater about a quarter before twelve, proceeded at once to prosecute our inquiry.

We began by asking for the station-master, a big, blunt, business-like person, who at once averred that he knew Mr. John Dwerrihouse perfectly well, and that there was no director on the line whom he had seen and spoken to so frequently.

"He used to be down here two or three times a week about three months ago," said he, "when the new line was first set afoot; but since then, you know, gentlemen —"

He paused significantly.

Jelf flushed scarlet.

"Yes, yes," he said, hurriedly, "we know all about that. The point now to be ascertained is whether anything has been seen or heard of him lately."

"Not to my knowledge," replied the station-master.

"He is not known to have been down the line any time yesterday, for instance?"

The station-master shook his head.

"The East Anglian, sir," said he, "is about the last place where he would dare to show himself. Why, there isn't a station-master, there isn't a guard, there isn't a porter, who doesn't know Mr. Dwerrihouse by sight as well as he knows his own face in the looking-glass, or who wouldn't telegraph for the police as soon as he had set eyes on him at any point along the line. Bless you, sir! There's been a standing order out against him ever since the 25th of September last."

"And yet," pursued my friend, "a gentleman who travelled down yesterday from London to Clayborough by the afternoon express testifies that he saw Mr. Dwerrihouse in the train, and that Mr. Dwerrihouse alighted at Blackwater Station."

"Quite impossible, sir," replied the station-master, promptly.

"Why impossible?"

"Because there is no station along the line where he is so well known or where he would run so great a risk. It would be just running his head into the lion's mouth; he would have been mad to come nigh Blackwater station; and if he had come he would have been arrested before he left the platform."

"Can you tell me who took the Blackwater tickets of that train?"

"I can, sir. It was the guard, Benjaimn Somers."

"And where can I find him?"

"You can find him, sir, by staying here if you please, till one o'clock. He will be coming through with the up express from Crampton, which stays at Blackwater for ten minutes."

We waited for the up express beguiling the time as best we could by strolling along the Blackwater road till we came almost to the outskirts of the town, from which the station was distant nearly a couple of miles. By one o'clock we were back again on the platform and waiting for the train. It came punctually, and I at once recognised the ruddy-faced guard who had gone down with my train the evening before.

"The gentlemen want to ask you something about Mr. Dwerrihouse, Somers," said the station-master, by way of introduction.

The guard flashed a keen glance from my face to Jelf's and back again to mine.

"Mr. John Dwerrihouse, the late director?" said he interrogatively.

"The same," replied my friend. "Should you know him if you saw him?"

"Anywhere, sir."

"Do you know if he was in the 4:15 express yesterday afternoon?"

"He was not, sir."

"How can you answer so positively?"

"Because I looked into every carriage and saw every face in that train, and I could take my oath that Mr. Dwerrihouse was not in it. This gentleman was," he added, turning sharply upon me. "I don't know that I ever saw him before in my life, but I remember his face perfectly. You nearly missed taking your seat in time at this station, sir, and you got out at Clayborough."

"Quite true, sir," I replied, "but do you not also remember the face of the gentleman who travelled down in the same carriage with me as far as here?"

"It was my impression, sir, that you travelled down alone," said Somers, with a look of some surprise.

"By no means. I had a fellow-traveller as far as Blackwater, and it was in trying to restore him the cigar-case which he had dropped in the carriage that I so nearly let you go on without me."

"I remember your saying something about a cigar-case, certainly," replied the guard, "but –"

"You asked for my ticket just before we entered the station."

"I did, sir."

"Then you must have seen him. He sat in the corner next the very door to which you came."

"No, indeed; I saw no one."

I looked at Jelf. I began to think the guard was in the ex-director's confidence, and paid for his silence.

"If I had seen another traveller I should have asked for his ticket," added Somers. "Did you see me ask for his ticket, sir?"

"I observed that you did not ask for it, but he explained that by saying –," I hesitated. I feared I might be telling too much, and so broke off abruptly.

The guard and the station-master exchanged glances. The former looked impatiently at his watch.

"I am obliged to go on in four minutes more, sir," he said.

"One last question, then," interposed Jelf with a sort of desperation. "If this gentleman's fellow-traveller had been Mr. John Dwerrihouse, and he had been sitting in the corner next the door by which you took the tickets, could you have failed to see and recognize him?"

"No, sir; it would have been quite impossible."

"And you are certain you did not see him?"

"As I said before, sir, I could take my oath I did not see him. And if it wasn't that I don't like to contradict a gentleman, I would say I could also take my oath that this gentleman was quite alone in the carriage the whole way from London to Clayborough. Why, sir," he added, dropping his voice so as to be inaudible to the station-master, who had been called away to speak to some person else, "you expressly asked me to give you a compartment to yourself and I did so. I locked you in, and you were so good as to give me something for myself."

"Yes, but Mr. Dwerrihouse had a key of his own."

"I never saw him, sir; I saw no one in that compartment but yourself. Beg pardon, sir, my time's up."

And with this the ruddy guard touched his cap and was gone. In another minute the heavy panting of the engine began afresh, and the train glided slowly out of the station.

We looked at each other for some moments in silence. I was the first to speak.

"Mr. Benjamin Somers knows more than he chooses to tell," I said.

"Humph! Do you think so?"

"It must be. He could not have come to the door without seeing him, it's impossible."

"There is one thing not impossible, my dear fellow."

"What is that?"

"That you may have fallen asleep and dreamed the whole thing."

"Could I dream of a branch line that I had never heard of? Could I dream of a hundred and one business details that had no kind of interest for me? Could I dream of the seventy-five thousand pounds?"

"Perhaps you might have seen or heard some vague account of the affair while you were abroad. It might have made no impression upon you at the time, and might have come back to you in your dreams, recalled perhaps by the mere names of the stations on the line."

"What about the fire in the chimney of the blue room – should I have heard of that during my journey?"

"Well, no. I admit there is a difficulty about that point."

"And what about the cigar-case?"

"Ay, by Jove! There is the cigar-case. That is a stubborn fact. Well, it is a mysterious affair, and it will need a better detective than myself, I fancy, to clear it up. I suppose we may as well go home."

A week had not gone by when I received a letter from the secretary of the East Anglian Railway Company, requesting the favour of my attendance at a special board meeting not then many days distant. No reasons were alleged and no apologies offered for this demand upon my time, but they had heard, it was clear, of my inquiries about the missing director, and had a mind to put me through some sort of official examination upon the subject. Being still a guest at Dumbleton Hall, I had to go up to London for the purpose, and Jonathan Jelf accompanied me. I found the direction of the Great East Anglian line represented by a party of some twelve or fourteen gentlemen seated in solemn conclave round a huge green baize table, in a gloomy boardroom adjoining the London terminus.

Being courteously received by the chairman (who at once began by saying that certain statements of mine respecting Mr. John Dwerrihouse had come to the knowledge of the direction, and that they in consequence desired to confer with me on those points), we were placed at the table, and the inquiry proceeded in due form.

I was first asked if I knew Mr. John Dwerrihouse, how long I had been acquainted with him, and whether I could identify him at sight. I was then asked when I had seen him last. To which I replied: "On the 4th of this present month, December, 1856." Then came the inquiry of where I had seen him on that fourth day of December; to which I replied that I met him in a first-class compartment of the 4:15 down express, that he got in just as the train was leaving the London terminus, and that he alighted at Blackwater station. The chairman then inquired whether I had held any communication with my fellow-traveller; whereupon I related, as nearly as I could remember it, the whole bulk and substance of Mr. John Dwerrihouse's diffuse information respecting the new branch line.

To all this the board listened with profound attention, while the chairman presided and the secretary took notes. I then produced the cigar-case. It was passed from hand to hand, and recognized by all. There was not a man present who did not remember that plain cigar-case with its silver monogram, or to whom it seemed anything less than entirely corroborative of my evidence. When at length I had told all that I had to tell, the chairman whispered something to his secretary. The secretary touched a silver hand-bell, and the guard, Benjamin Somers, was ushered into the room. He was then examined as carefully as myself. He declared that he knew Mr. John Dwerrihouse perfectly well, that he could not be mistaken in him, that he remembered going down with the 4:15 express on the afternoon in question, that he remembered me, and that there being one or two empty first-class compartments on that especial afternoon, he had, in compliance with my request, placed me in a carriage by myself. He was positive that I remained alone in that compartment all the way from London to Clayborough. He was ready to take his oath that Mr. Dwerrihouse was neither in that carriage with me, nor in any compartment of that train. He remembered distinctly to have examined my ticket at Blackwater; was certain that there was no one else at that time in the carriage; could not have failed to observe a second person, if there had been one; had that sighted person been Mr. John Dwerrihouse should have quietly double-locked the door of the carriage and have at once given information to the Blackwater station-master. So clear, so decisive so ready, was Somers with this testimony, that the board looked fairly puzzled.

"You hear this person's statement, Mr. Langford," said the chairman. "It contradicts yours in every particular. What have you to say in reply?"

"I can only repeat what I said before. I am quite as positive of the truth of my own assertions as Mr. Somers can be of the truth of his."

"You say that Mr. Dwerrihouse alighted at Blackwater, and that he was in possession of a private key. Are you sure that he had not alighted by means of that key before the guard came round for the tickets?"

"I am quite positive that he did not leave the carriage till the train had fairly entered the station, and the other Blackwater passengers alighted. I even saw that he was met there by a friend."

"Indeed! Did you see that person distinctly?"

"Quite distinctly."

"Could you describe his appearance?"

"I think so. He was short and very slight, sandy-haired, with a bushy moustache and beard, and he wore a closely fitting suit of gray tweed. His age I should take to be about thirty-eight or forty."

"Did Mr. Dwerrihouse leave the station in this person's company?"

"I can not tell. I saw them walking together down the platform, and then I saw them standing aside under a gas-jet, talking earnestly. After that I lost sight of them quite suddenly, and just then my train went on, and I with it."

The chairman and secretary conferred together in an undertone. The directors whispered to one another. One or two looked suspiciously at the guard. I could see that my evidence remained unshaken, and that, like myself, they suspected some complicity between the guard and the defaulter.

"How far did you conduct that 4:15 express on the day in question, Somers?" asked the chairman.

"All through, sir," replied the guard, "from London to Crampton."

"How was it that you were not relieved at Clayborough? I thought there was always a change of guards at Clayborough."

"There used to be, sir, till the new regulations came in force last midsummer, since when the guards in charge of express trains go the whole way through."

The chairman turned to the secretary.

"I think it would be as well," he said, "if we had the daybook to refer to upon this point."

Again the secretary touched the silver hand-bell, and desired the porter in attendance to summon Mr. Raikes. From a word or two dropped by another of the directors I gathered that Mr. Raikes was one of the under-secretaries.

He came, a small, slight, sandy-haired, keen-eyed man, with an eager, nervous manner, and a forest of light beard and moustache. He just showed himself at the door of the boardroom, and, being requested to bring a certain daybook from a certain shelf in a certain room, bowed and vanished.

He was there such a moment, and the surprise of seeing him was so surest and sudden, that it was not till the door had closed upon him that I found voice to speak. He was no sooner gone, however, than I sprang to my feet.

"That person," I said, "is the same who met Mr. Dwerrihouse upon the platform at Blackwater!"

There was a general movement of surprise. The chairman looked grave and somewhat agitated.

"Take care, Mr. Langford," he said, "take care what you say."

"I am as positive of his identity as of my own."

"Do you consider the consequences of your words? Do you consider that you are bringing a charge of the gravest character against one of the company's servants?"

"I am willing to be put upon my oath, if necessary. The man who came to that door a minute since is the same whom I saw talking with Mr. Dwerrihouse on the Blackwater platform. Were he twenty times the company's servant, I could say neither more nor less."

The chairman turned again to the guard.

"Did you see Mr. Raikes in the train or on the platform?" he asked.

Somers shook his head.

"I am confident Mr. Raikes was not in the train," he said, "and I certainly did not see him on the platform."

The chairman turned next to the secretary.

"Mr. Raikes is in your office, Mr. Hunter," he said. "Can you remember if he was absent on the 4th instant?"

"I do not think he was," replied the secretary, "but I am not prepared to speak positively. I have been away most afternoons myself lately, and Mr. Raikes might easily have absented himself if he had been disposed."

At this moment the under-secretary returned with the daybook under his arm.

"Be pleased to refer, Mr. Raikes," said the chairman, "to the entries of the 4th instant, and see what Benjamin Somers' duties were on that day."

Mr. Raikes threw open the cumbrous volume, and ran a practised eye and finger down some three or four successive columns of entries. Stopping suddenly at the foot of the page, he then read aloud that Benjamin Somers had on that day conducted the 4:15 express from London to Crampton."

The chairman leaned forward in his seat and looked the tinder-secretary full in the face, and said quite sharply and suddenly:

"And where were you, Mr. Raikes, on the same afternoon?"

"I, sir?"

"You, Mr. Raikes. Where were you on the afternoon and evening of the 4th of the present month?"

"Here, sir, in Mr. Hunter's office. Where else should I be?"

There was a dash of trepidation in the under-secretary's voice as he said this, but his look of surprise was natural.

"We have some reason for believing, Mr. Raikes, that you were absent that afternoon without leave. Was this the case?"

"Certainly not, sir. I have not had a day's holiday since September. Mr. Hunter will bear me out in this."

Mr. Hunter repeated what he had previously said on the subject, but added that the clerk in the adjoining office would be certain to know. Whereupon the senior clerk, a grave, middle-aged person in green glasses, was summoned and interrogated.

His testimony cleared the under-secretary at once. He declared that Mr. Raikes had, in no instance to his knowledge, been absent during office hours since his return from his annual holiday in September.

I was confounded. The chairman turned to me with a smile, in which a shade of covert annoyance was scarcely apparent.

"You hear, Mr. Langford?" he said.

"I hear, sir; but my conviction remains unshaken."

"I fear, Mr. Langford, that your convictions are very insufficiently based," replied the chairman, with a doubtful cough. "I fear that you dream dreams, and mistake them for actual occurrences. It is a dangerous habit of mind, and might lead to dangerous results. Mr. Raikes here would have found himself in an unpleasant position had he not proved so satisfactory an alibi."

I was about to reply, but he gave me no time.

"I think, gentlemen," he went on to say, addressing the board, "that we should be wasting time to push this inquiry further. Mr. Langford's evidence would seem to be of an equal value throughout. The testimony of Benjamin Somers disproves his first statement, and the testimony of the last witness disproves his second. I think we may conclude that Mr. Langford fell asleep in the train on the occasion of his journey to Clayborough, and dreamed an unusually vivid and circumstantial dream, of which, however, we have now heard quite enough."

There are few things more annoying than to find one's positive convictions met with incredulity. I could not help feeling impatience at the turn that affairs had taken. I was not proof against the civil sarcasm of the chairman's manner. Most intolerable of all, however, was the quiet smile lurking about the corners of Benjamin Somers's mouth, and the half-triumphant, half-malicious gleam in the eyes of the under- secretary. The man was evidently puzzled and somewhat alarmed. His looks seemed furtively to interrogate me. Who was I? What did I want? Why had I come there to do him an ill turn with his employers? What was it to me whether or no he was absent without leave?

Seeing all this, and perhaps more irritated by it than the thing deserved, I begged leave to detain the attention of the board for a moment longer. Jelf plucked me impatiently by the sleeve.

"Better let the thing drop," he whispered. "The chairman's right enough; you dreamed it, and the less said now the better."

I was not to be silenced, however, in this fashion. I had yet something to say, and I would say it. It was to this effect: that dreams were not usually productive of tangible results, and that I requested to know in what way the chairman conceived I had evolved from my dream so substantial and well-made a delusion as the cigar-case which I had had the honour to place before him at the commencement of our interview.

"The cigar-case, I admit, Mr. Langford," the chairman replied, "is a very strong point in your evidence. It is your only strong point, however, and there is just a possibility that we may all be misled by a mere accidental resemblance. Will you permit me to see the case again?"

"It is unlikely," I said, as I handed it to him, "that any other should bear precisely this monogram, and yet be in all other particulars exactly similar."

The chairman examined it for a moment in silence, and then passed it to Mr. Hunter. Mr. Hunter turned it over and over, and shook his head.

"This is no mere resemblance," he said. "It is John Dwerrihouse's cigar-case to a certainty. I remember it perfectly; I have seen it a hundred times."

"I believe I may say the same," added the chairman; "yet how account for the way in which Mr. Langford asserts that it came into his possession?"

"I can only repeat," I replied, "that I found it on the floor of the carriage after Mr. Dwerrihouse had alighted. It was in leaning out to look after him that I trod upon it, and it was in running after him for the purpose of restoring it that I saw, or believed I saw, Mr. Raikes standing aside with him in earnest conversation."

Again I felt Jonathan Jelf plucking at my sleeve.

"Look at Raikes," he whispered, "look at Raikes!"

I turned to where the under-secretary had been standing a moment before, and saw him, white as death, with lips trembling and livid, stealing toward the door.

To conceive a sudden, strange, and indefinite suspicion, to fling myself in his way, to take him by the shoulders as if he were a child, and turn his craven face, perforce, toward the board, were with me the work of an instant.

"Look at him!" I exclaimed. "Look at his face! I ask no better witness to the truth of my words."

The chairman's brow darkened.

"Mr. Raikes," he said, sternly, "if you know anything you had better speak."

Vainly trying to wrench himself from my grasp, the under-secretary stammered out an incoherent denial.

"Let me go," he said. "I know nothing – you have no right to detain me – let me go!"

"Did you, or did you not, meet Mr. John Dwerrihouse at Blackwater station? The charge brought against you is either true or false. If true, you will do well to throw yourself upon the mercy of the board and make full confession of all that you know."

The under-secretary wrung his hands in an agony of helpless terror.

"I was away!" he cried. "I was two hundred miles away at the time! I know nothing about it – I have nothing to confess – I am innocent – I call God to witness I am innocent!"

"Two hundred miles away!" echoed the chairman. "What do you mean?"

"I was in Devonshire. I had three weeks' leave of absence – I appeal to Mr. Hunter – Mr. Hunter knows I had three weeks' leave of absence! I was in Devonshire all the time; I can prove I was in Devonshire!"

Seeing him so abject, so incoherent, so wild with apprehension, the directors began to whisper gravely among themselves, while one got quietly up and called the porter to guard the door.

"What has your being in Devonshire to do with the matter?" said the chairman. "When were you in Devonshire?"

"Mr. Raikes took his leave in September," said the secretary, "about the time when Mr. Dwerrihouse disappeared."

"I never even heard that he had disappeared till I came back!"

"That must remain to be proved," said the chairman. "I shall at once put this matter in the hands of the police. In the meanwhile, Mr. Raikes, being myself a magistrate and used to deal with these cases, I advise you to offer no resistance, but to confess while confession may yet do you service. As for your accomplice –"

The frightened wretch fell upon his knees.

"I had no accomplice!" he cried. "Only have mercy upon me – only spare my life, and I will confess all! I didn't mean to harm him! I didn't mean to hurt a hair of his head! Only have mercy upon me, and let me go!"

The chairman rose in his place, pale and agitated. "Good heavens," he exclaimed, "what horrible mystery is this? What does it mean?"

"As sure as there is a God in heaven," said Jonathan Jelf, "it means that murder has been done."

"No! No! No!" shrieked Raikes, still upon his knees and cowering like a beaten hound. "Not murder! No jury that ever sat could bring it in murder. I thought I had only stunned him – I never meant to do more than stun him! Manslaughter – manslaughter – not murder!"

Overcome by the horror of this unexpected revelation, the chairman covered his face with his hand and for a moment or two remained silent.

"Miserable man," he said at length, "you have betrayed yourself."

"You bade me confess! You urged me to throw myself upon the mercy of the board!"

"You have confessed to a crime which no one suspected you of having committed," replied the chairman, "and which this board has no power either to punish or forgive. All that I can do for you is to advise you to submit to the law, to plead guilty, and to conceal nothing. When did you do this deed?"

The guilty man rose to his feet, and leaned heavily against the table. His answer came reluctantly, like the speech of one dreaming.

"On the 2nd of September."

On the 2nd of September! I looked in Jonathan Jelf's face, and he in mine. I felt my own paling with a strange sense of wonder and dread. I saw his blanch suddenly, even to the lips.

"Merciful heaven!" he whispered. "What was it then, that you saw in the train?"

What was it that I saw in the train? That question remains unanswered to this day. I have never been able to reply to it. I only know that it bore the living likeness of the murdered man, whose body had then been lying some ten weeks under a rough pile of branches and brambles and rotting leaves, at the bottom of a deserted chalk-pile about halfway between Blackwater and Mailingford. I know that it spoke and moved and looked as that man spoke and moved and looked in life; that I heard, or seemed to hear, things related which I could never otherwise have learned; that I was guided, as it were ⌃ by that vision on the platform to the identification of the murderer; and that, a passive instrument myself, I was destined, by means of these mysterious teachings, to bring about thee ends of justice. For these tidings I have never been able to account.

As for that matter of the cigar-case, it proved, on inquiry, that thee carriage in which I travelled down that afternoon to Clayborough had not been in use for several weeks, and was, in point of fact, the same in which poor John Dwerrihouse had performed his last journey. The case had doubtless been dropped, by him, and had lain unnoticed till I found it.

Upon the details of the murder I have no need to dwell. Those who desire more ample particulars may find them, and the written confession of Augustus Raikes; in the files of the *Times* for 1856. Enough that the under-secretary, knowing the history of the new line, and following the negotiation step by step through all its stages, determined to waylay Mr. Dwerrihouse, rob him of the seventy-five thousand pounds, and escape to America with his booty.

In order to effect these ends he obtained leave of absence a few days before the time appointed for the payment of the money, secured his passage across the Atlantic in a steamer advertised to start on the 23d, provided himself with a heavily loaded life-preserver, and went down to Blackwater to await the arrival of his victim.

How he met him on the platform with a pretended message from the board, how he offered to conduct him by a short cut across the fields to Mailingford, how, having brought him to a lonely place, he struck him down with the life-preserver, and so killed him, and how, finding what he had done, he dragged the body to the verge of an out-of-the-way chalk-pit and there flung it in and piled it over with branches and brambles, are facts still fresh in the memories of those who, like the connoisseurs in De Quincey's famous essay, regard murder as a fine art. Strangely enough, the murderer, having done his work, was afraid to leave the country. He declared that he had not intended to take the director's life, but only to stun and rob him; and that, finding the blow had killed, he dared not fly for fear of drawing down suspicion upon his own head. As a mere robber he would have been safe in the States, but as a murderer he would inevitably have been pursued and given up to justice. So he forfeited his passage, returned to the office as usual at the end of his leave, and locked up his ill-gotten thousands till a more convenient opportunity. In the meanwhile he had the satisfaction of finding that Mr. Dwerrihouse was universally believed to have absconded with the money, no one knew how or whither.

Whether he meant murder or not, however, Mr. Augustus Raikes paid the full penalty of his crime, and was hanged at the Old Bailey in the second week in January, 1857. Those who desire to make his further acquaintance may see him any day (admirably done in wax) in the Chamber of Horrors at Madame Tussaud's exhibition, in Baker Street. He is there to be found in the midst of a select society of ladies and gentlemen of atrocious memory, dressed in the close-cut tweed suit which he wore on the evening of the murder, and holding in his hand the identical life-preserver with which he committed it.

"The Parrot" discovers a lost soul in the unlikeliest of places. Martha is a lonely woman with only her pet for company. The daughter of a minister and a devout churchgoer, Martha spends much of her time worrying whether or not her beloved parrot has a soul.

As the story unfolds, it becomes clear that, soul or not, the parrot – "screaming and laughing" – possesses the spirit that the inhibited Martha lacks..

THE PARROT

MARY WILKINS FREEMAN

The parrot was a superb bird: a vociferous symmetry of green and gold and ruby red, with eyes like jewels, with their identical irresponsibility of fire, with a cling, not of loving dependence, but of ruthless insistence, to his mistress's hand, or the wires of his cage, and a beak of such a fine curve of cruelty as was never excelled.

The parrot's mistress was a New England woman, with the influence of a stern training strong upon her, and yet with a rampant force of individuality constantly at war with it. She lived alone, except for the parrot, in a sharply angled village house, looking upon the world with a clean repellent glare of windows, and white broadside of wall, in a yard whose grass seemed as if combed always by one wind, so evenly slanted was it. There was a decorously trimmed rose-bush on either side of the front door, and one elm-tree at the gate which leaned decidedly to the south with all its green sweep of branches, and always in consequence gave the woman a vague and unreasoning sense of immorality.

Inside, the house showed stiff parallelograms of white curtains, and dull carpets threadbare with cleanliness, and little pools of reflected light from the polished surfaces of old tables and desks, and one glass-doored bookcase filled with works on divinity bound uniformly in rusty black.

The woman's father had been a Congregational clergyman, and this was his old library. She had read every book over and over with a painful concentration, and afterwards admitted her crime of light-mindedness and prayed to be forgiven, and have her soul so wrought upon by grace that she might truthfully enjoy these goodly publications. She had never read a novel; she looked upon cards as wiles of the devil; once and once only had she been to a concert of strictly secular music in the

---

Understudies. New York: Harper and Brothers, 1901.

town-hall, and had felt thereby contaminated for days, having a temperament which was strangely wrought upon by music, and yet with a total ignorance of it. She felt guilty under the influence of all harmonies which did not, through being linked to spiritual words, turn her soul to thoughts of heaven; and yet sometimes, to her sore bewilderment, the tunes which she heard in church did not so sway her wayward fancy; and then she accused herself of being perverted in her comprehension of good through the influence of that worldly concert.

This woman went nowhere except to church, to prayer-meeting, to the village store, and once a month to the missionary sewing circle, and the supper and sociable in the evening. She dressed always in black, her hair was delicately spare, her lips were a compressed line of red, and yet she was pretty, with a prettiness almost of youth, from that undiminished fire of the spirit which dwelt within her, as securely caged by her training and narrowness of life as was the parrot by the strong wires of his house.

The parrot was the one bright thing in the woman's life; he was the link with that which was outside her, and yet with that which was of her truest inwardness of self. This tropical thing, screaming and laughing, and shrieking out dissonant words, and oftentimes speeches, with a seemingly diabolical comprehension of the situation, was the one note of utter freedom and irresponsibility in her life. She adored him, but always with a sense of guilt upon her. Often she said to herself that some judgment would come upon her for so loving such a bird, for there was in truth about him as much utter gracelessness as can be conceived of in one of the lower creation. He swore such oaths that his mistress would fairly fly out of the door with hands to her ears. Always, when she saw a caller coming, she would remove his cage to a distant room and shut all the doors between. She felt that if any one heard him sending forth those profane shrieks, possibly to his spiritual contamination, she might be driven by her sense of duty to have the bird put to death. She knew, as she believed, that she risked her own soul by listening and yet loving, but that she had no courage to forego.

As for the parrot, he loved his mistress if he loved anything. He would extend an ingratiating but deceitful claw toward her between his cage wires whenever she approached. If ever she had a torn finger in consequence, she made light of it, like any wound of love. He would take morsels of food from between her thin lips.

When she talked to him with that language of love which every soul knows by instinct, and which is intelligible to all who are not too deadened and deafened with self, he would cock his glittering head and look at her with that inscrutable jewel-eye of his, and thrust out a claw toward her with that insistence which was ruthless, and yet not more ruthless than the insistence of love, and often say something which confounded her with its apparent wisdom of sequence, and then the doubt and the conviction which at once tormented and enraptured her would seize upon her.

She tried to conceal it from herself, she held it as the rankest atheism, she thought vaguely of the idols of wood and stone in the hymn-book, of Baal, and the golden calf, and the witch of Endor, and every forbidden thing which is the antithesis of holiness, and yet she could not be sure that her parrot had not a soul. Sometimes she wondered if she ought to speak of her state of mind to the minister and ask his advice, but she shrank from doing that, both because of her natural reserve and because he was unmarried, and she knew that people had coupled his name with hers. He was of suitable age, and it was argued that a match for him with the solitary daughter of the former minister would be eminently appropriate.

The woman had never considered the possibility of such a thing, although she had heard of the plan of the parish from many a female friend. She had had her stifled dreams in her early youth, but she had not been one to attract lovers, being perchance bound as to her true graces somewhat too much after the fashion of her father's old divinity books. No man in her whole life had ever looked at her with a look of love, and she had never heard the involuntary break of it in his voice. Sometimes on summer evenings, she, sitting by her open window, saw village lovers going past with covert arms of affection around slim girlish waists. One night she saw, half shrinking from the sight, a fond pair standing in the shadow of the elm-tree at her gate, and clasped in each other's arms, and saw the girl's face raised to the young man's for his eager kisses, the while a murmur of love, like a song in an unknown tongue, came to her ears.

It was a warm night, and the parrot's cage was slung for coolness on a peg over the window, and he shrieked out, with his seemingly unholy apprehension of things: "What is that? what is that? Do you know what that is, Martha?" Then ended his query with such a wild clamor of laughter that the lovers at the gate fled, and his mistress, Martha, rose and took in the bird.

She set him on the sitting-room table along with the Bible and the Concordance, and a neat little pile of religious papers, while she lighted a lamp. Then she looked half affrightedly, half with loving admiration, at the gorgeous thing, swinging himself frantically on the ring in his cage.

Then, swifter than lightning, down on his perch he dropped, cast a knowing eye like a golden spark at the solitary woman, and shrieked out again:

"What was that, what was that, Martha? Martha, Martha, Martha, Martha. Polly don't want a cracker; Polly don't want a cracker; Polly will be damned if she eats a cracker. You don't want a cracker, do you, Martha? Martha, Martha, Martha want a cracker? What was that, Martha? Martha want a cracker? Martha will be damned if she eats a cracker. Martha, Martha, Martha!"

Then the bird was off in such another explosion of laughs, thrusting a claw through his wires at his mistress, that the house rang with them. Martha took the extended claw tenderly; she put her pretty, delicate, faded face to that treacherous beak; she murmured fond words. Then ceased suddenly as she heard a step on the walk, and the parrot cried out, with a cry of sharpest and most sardonic exultation,

"He's coming, he's coming, Martha!"

Then, to Martha's utter horror, before she had time to remove the bird, a knock came on her front door, which stood open, and there was the minister.

He had called upon her before, in accordance with his pastoral duty, but seldom, and always with his mother, who kept his house with him. This time he was alone, and there was something new in his manner.

He was a handsome man, no younger than she, but looking younger, with a dash of manner which many considered not ministerial. He would not allow Martha to remove the parrot, though she strove tremblingly to do so, and laughed with a loud peal like a boy, when the parrot shrieked, to his mistress's sore discomfiture:

"He's come, Martha, damned if he ain't. Martha, Martha, where in hell is that old cracker?"

Martha felt as if her hour of retribution had come, and she was vaguely and guiltily pleased and relieved when the minister not only did not seem shocked with the free speaking of her bird, but rather seemed amused.

She watched him touch the parrot caressingly, and heard him talk persuasively, coaxing him to further speech, and for the first time in her life a complete sense of human comradeship came to her.

After a while the parrot resolved himself into a gorgeous plumy ball of slumber on his perch, then his mistress sat an hour in the moonlight with the minister.

She had put out the lamp at his request, timidly, and yet with a conviction that such a course must be strictly proper, since it was proposed by the minister.

The two sat near each other at the open window, and the soft sweetness of the summer night came in, and the influence of the moonlight was over them both. The lovers continued to stroll past the gate, and a rule of sequence holds good in all things. Presently, for the first time in her life, this solitary woman felt a man's hand clasping her own little slender one in her black cashmere lap. The minister made no declaration of love in words, but the tones of his voice were enough.

When he spoke of exchanging with a neighboring clergyman in two weeks, the speech was set to the melody of a love-song, and there was no cheating ears which were attuned to it, no matter if it had been long in coming.

When the minister took his leave, and Martha lighted her lamp again, the parrot stirred and woke, and brought that round golden eye of his to bear upon her face flushed like a girl's, and cried out:

"Why, Martha! why, Martha! what is the matter?"

Then Martha dropped on her knees beside the cage, and touched the bird's head with a finger of tenderest caressing.

"Oh, you darling, you darling, you precious!" she murmured, and began to weep. And the parrot did not laugh, but continued to eye her.

"He has come, hasn't he, Martha?" said he.

Then Martha was more than ever inclined to think that the bird had a soul; still she doubted, because of the unorthodoxy of it, and the remembrance of man and man alone being made in God's own image.

Still, through having no friend in whom to confide her new hope and happiness, the parrot became doubly dear to her. Curiously enough, in the succeeding weeks he was not so boisterous, he did not swear so much, but would sit watching his mistress as she sat dreaming, and now and then he said something which seemed inconceivable to her simple mind, unless he had a full understanding of the situation.

The minister came oftener and oftener, staid longer. He came home on Sunday nights with her after meeting. He kissed her at the door. He always held her little hand, which yielded to his with an indescribably gentle and innocent maidenliness, while he talked about the mission work in foreign lands, and always his lightest speech was set to that love-melody.

Martha began to expect to marry him. She overlooked her supply of linen. Visions of a new silk for a wedding dress, brown instead of black, flashed before her eyes. She talked more than usual to the parrot in those days, using the words and tone which she might have used toward the minister, had not the restraints of her New England birth and training enclosed her like the wires of a cage, and the parrot eyed her with wise attentiveness which grew upon him, only now and then uttering one of his favorite oaths.

Then suddenly the disillusion of the poor soul as to her first gospel of love came. She went to the sewing circle one Wednesday in early spring, after the minister had been to see her for nearly a year, and she wore her best black silk, thinking he would be there, and she had crimped her hair, and looked as radiant as a girl when she entered the low vestry filled with the discordant gabble of sewing women.

Then she heard the news. It was told her with some protest and friendly preparation, for everybody had thought that the match between herself and the minister was as good as made. There was a whispered discussion among groups of women, with sly eyes upon her face; then one, who was a leader among them, a woman of affectionate glibness, approached her, after Martha had heard a feminine voice lingering in the outskirts of a sudden hush say,

"And she's got on her best silk too, poor thing."

Martha now looked up, and her radiant face paled slowly as the woman began to talk to her. The news seemed to smite her like some hammer of fate, her brain reeled, and her ears rang with it.

The minister was engaged, and had in fact gone to be married. He would bring his bride home the next week; another minister was to occupy his pulpit the next Sunday. He was to marry a woman to whom he had been attached for years, but the marriage had been delayed.

Martha listened, then suddenly the color flashed back into her white cheeks – she had stanch blood in her.

"Well, I am glad to hear it," she said, and lied with no compunction for the first time in her life, and never repented it. "I have always thought it was much better for a minister to be married," she said. "I have always thought that his usefulness would be much enhanced. Father used to say so." Then she took out her needle and thread and went to work with the others.

The women eyed her furtively, but she made no sign of noticing it. When one said to her that she had kind of thought that maybe the minister was shining up to her, she only laughed, and said gently that they were very good friends, but there had never been a word of anything else between them.

She overheard one woman whisper to another that "if Martha wasn't cut up, she would deceive the very elect," and the other reply "that maybe he had told Martha all about the woman he was going to marry."

Martha staid as usual to the supper and the entertainment. A young couple sat on a settee in front of her while some singing was going on, and at a tender passage she saw the boy furtively press the girl's hand, and she set her lips hard.

But at last she was free to go home, and when she had unlocked the door and entered her lonely house, down upon the floor in her sitting-room she flung herself, with all the floodgates of her New England nature open at last. She wept and wailed her grief and anger aloud like a Southern woman.

Then in the midst of it all came a wild wailing cry from the parrot, a cry of uncanny sympathy and pain and tenderness outside the pale of humanity.

"Why, Martha! why, Martha! what's the matter?"

Then the woman rose and went to the cage, her delicate face and lips so swollen with grief that she was appalling; she had even trailed her best black silk in the mud on her way home. She was past the bounds of decency in her frenzy of misery. She opened the cage door, and the parrot flew out and to her slender shoulder, and she sobbed out her grief to him amid his protesting cries.

"Poor Martha, why, poor Martha," he said, and she felt almost certain that he had a soul, and she no longer felt so shocked by her leaning toward that belief, but was comforted.

But all of a sudden the parrot on her shoulder gave a tweak at her hair, and shrieked out:

"That was a damned cracker, Martha," and her belief wavered.

She put him back in his cage, and locked up her house for the night and put out her lamp, and went to bed, but she could not go to sleep, for the loss of her old dream of love gave the whole world and all life such a hollowness and emptiness that it was like thunder in her ears, and forced its waking realization upon her.

All during the next week, if it had not been for the parrot, she felt that she would have gone mad. She went out in her small daily tracks to the village store, and the prayer-meetings, and on Sunday to church, her agony of concern being that no one should know that she was fretting over the minister's desertion of her.

She talked about the engagement and marriage with her gentle stateliness of manner, which never failed her, but when she got home to her parrot, and the healing solitariness of her own house, she felt like one who had a cooling lotion applied to a burn.

And she wondered more and more if the parrot had not verily a soul, and could not approach her with a sympathy which was better than any human sympathy, since it was so beyond all human laws, but she was not fully convinced of it until the minister brought his new wife to call upon her a few weeks after his marriage.

She had wondered vaguely if he would do it, if he could do it, but he came in with all his dashing grace of manner, and his bride was smiling at his side, in her wedding silks, and Martha greeted them with no disturbance of her New England calm and stiffness, but inwardly her very soul stormed and protested, and as they were sitting in the parlor there came of a sudden from the next room, where he had been at large, the parrot, like a very whirlwind of feathered rage, and with a wild shriek he dashed upon the bridal bonnet, plucking furiously at roses and plumes.

Then there was a frightened and flurried exit, with confusion, and apologies, and screams of baffled wrath, and rueful smoothing of torn finery.

And after the minister and his bride had gone, Martha looked at her parrot, and his golden eyes met hers, and she recognized in the fierce bird a comradeship and an equality, for he had given vent to an emotion of her own nature, and she knew forevermore that the parrot had a soul.

"A volume of short stories from the pen of Mary E. Wilkins is sure to awaken pleasant expectations in the minds of readers, and in the case of Understudies, her latest production of this kind, the expectations will not be disappointed. It would be idle to say that these little sketches are works of large literary importance. Of course, there are those who believe that no short stories can be, but they are mistaken. One has has only to recall the short stories of Poe or Robert Louis Stevenson to remember that a short story may rise to an importance far above that of many pretentious novels. Miss Wilkin's sketches are not of this kind, but they have decided merits none the less, and are worth reading."

– The New York Times (27 April, 1901)

The life of William Sydney Porter (1862 - 1910) is as dramatic as any of his stories. Initially a bank-teller in Austin, Texas, Porter was found guilty of embezzlement and dismissed from his position. He fled to Honduras to avoid imprisonment, but later returned to the United States when his wife became fatally ill.

After surrendering himself to the authorities, Porter spent three years in prison – publishing fourteen short stories while he served his sentence. It was there he began to use the pen name "O. Henry". After his release, Porter moved to New York. There, he engaged in a whirlwind relationship with his childhood sweetheart (who left him in under two years), published a short story every week and eventually drank himself to death.

"A Double-Dyed Deceiver" features the Llano Kid, a Texas gunslinger who, like the author, decides to flee the country after committing a crime. In a nameless South American country, "The Kid" finds not only a new life but also an unexpected chance at redemption.

A DOUBLE-DYED DECEIVER

O. HENRY

I

The trouble began in Laredo. It was the Llano Kid's fault, for he should have confined his habit of manslaughter to Mexicans. But the Kid was past twenty; and to have only Mexicans to one's credit at twenty is to blush unseen on the Rio Grande border.

It happened in old Justo Valdos's gambling house. There was a poker game at which sat players who were not all friends, as happens often where men ride in from afar to shoot Folly as she gallops. There was a row over so small a matter as a pair of queens; and when the smoke had cleared away it was found that the Kid had committed an indiscretion, and his adversary had been guilty of a blunder. For, the unfortunate combatant, instead of being a Greaser, was a high-blooded youth from the cow ranches, of about the Kid's own age and possessed of friends and champions. His blunder in missing the Kid's right ear only a sixteenth of an inch when he pulled his gun did not lessen the indiscretion of the better marksman.

The Kid, not being equipped with a retinue, nor bountifully supplied with personal admirers and supporters – on account of a rather umbrageous reputation, even for the border – considered it not incompatible with his indisputable gameness to perform that judicious tractional act known as "pulling his freight".

Quickly the avengers gathered and sought him. Three of them overtook him within a rod of the station. The Kid turned and showed his teeth in that brilliant but

Roads of Destiny. New York: Doubleday, Page and Company, 1909.

mirthless smile that usually preceded his deeds of insolence and violence, and his pursuers fell back without making it necessary for him even to reach for his weapon.

But in this affair the Kid had not felt the grim thirst for encounter that usually urged him on to battle. It had been a purely chance row, born of the cards and certain epithets impossible for a gentleman to brook that had passed between the two. The Kid had rather liked the slim, haughty, brown-faced young chap whom his bullet had cut off in the first pride of manhood. And now he wanted no more blood. He wanted to get away and have a good long sleep somewhere in the sun on the mesquite grass with his handkerchief over his face. Even a Mexican might have crossed his path in safety while he was in this mood.

The Kid openly boarded the north-bound passenger train that departed five minutes later. But at Webb, a few miles out, where it was flagged to take on a traveller, he abandoned that manner of escape. There were telegraph stations ahead; and the Kid looked askance at electricity and steam. Saddle and spur were his rocks of safety.

The man whom he had shot was a stranger to him. But the Kid knew that he was of the Coralitos outfit from Hidalgo; and that the punchers from that ranch were more relentless and vengeful than Kentucky feudists when wrong or harm was done to one of them. So, with the wisdom that has characterized many great fighters, the Kid decided to pile up as many leagues as possible of chaparral and pear between himself and the retaliation of the Coralitos bunch.

Near the station was a store; and near the store, scattered among the mesquites and elms, stood the saddled horses of the customers. Most of them waited, half asleep, with sagging limbs and drooping heads. But one, a long-legged roan with a curved neck, snorted and pawed the turf. Him the Kid mounted, gripped with his knees, and slapped gently with the owner's own quirt.

If the slaying of the temerarious card-player had cast a cloud over the Kid's standing as a good and true citizen, this last act of his veiled his figure in the darkest shadows of disrepute. On the Rio Grande border if you take a man's life you sometimes take trash; but if you take his horse, you take a thing the loss of which renders him poor, indeed, and which enriches you not – if you are caught. For the Kid there was no turning back now.

With the springing roan under him he felt little care or uneasiness. After a five-mile gallop he drew in to the plainsman's jogging trot, and rode northeastward

The devil may have sent me on this trail instead of God,
but I'll travel it to the end.

toward the Nueces River bottoms. He knew the country well – its most tortuous and obscure trails through the great wilderness of brush and pear, and its camps and lonesome ranches where one might find safe entertainment. Always he bore to the east; for the Kid had never seen the ocean, and he had a fancy to lay his hand upon the mane of the great Gulf, the gamesome colt of the greater waters.

So after three days he stood on the shore at Corpus Christi, and looked out across the gentle ripples of a quiet sea.

Captain Boone, of the schooner *Flyaway*, stood near his skiff, which one of his crew was guarding in the surf. When ready to sail he had discovered that one of the necessaries of life, in the parallelogrammatic shape of plug tobacco, had been forgotten. A sailor had been dispatched for the missing cargo. Meanwhile the captain paced the sands, chewing profanely at his pocket store.

A slim, wiry youth in high-heeled boots came down to the water's edge. His face was boyish, but with a premature severity that hinted at a man's experience. His complexion was naturally dark; and the sun and wind of an outdoor life had burned it to a coffee brown. His hair was as black and straight as an Indian's; his face had not yet been upturned to the humiliation of a razor; his eyes were a cold and steady blue. He carried his left arm somewhat away from his body, for pearl-handled .45s are frowned upon by town marshals, and are a little bulky when placed in the left armhole of one's vest. He looked beyond Captain Boone at the gulf with the impersonal and expressionless dignity of a Chinese emperor.

"Thinkin' of buyin' that'ar gulf, buddy?" asked the captain, made sarcastic by his narrow escape from a tobaccoless voyage.

"Why, no," said the Kid gently, "I reckon not. I never saw it before. I was just looking at it. Not thinking of selling it, are you?"

"Not this trip," said the captain. "I'll send it to you C.O.D. when I get back to Buenas Tierras. Here comes that capstanfooted lubber with the chewin'. I ought to've weighed anchor an hour ago."

"Is that your ship out there?" asked the Kid.

"Why, yes," answered the captain, "if you want to call a schooner a ship, and I don't mind lyin'. But you better say Miller and Gonzales, owners, and ordinary plain, Billy-be-damned old Samuel K. Boone, skipper."

"Where are you going to?" asked the refugee.

"Buenas Tierras, coast of South America – I forgot what they called the country the last time I was there. Cargo – lumber, corrugated iron, and machetes."

"What kind of a country is it?" asked the Kid – "hot or cold?"

"Warmish, buddy," said the captain. "But a regular Paradise Lost for elegance of scenery and be-yooty of geography. Ye're wakened every morning by the sweet singin' of red birds with seven purple tails, and the sighin' of breezes in the posies and roses. And the inhabitants never work, for they can reach out and pick steamer baskets of the choicest hothouse fruit without gettin' out of bed. And there's no Sunday and no ice and no rent and no troubles and no use and no nothin'. It's a great country for a man to go to sleep with, and wait for somethin' to turn up. The bananys and oranges and hurricanes and pineapples that ye eat comes from there."

"That sounds to me!" said the Kid, at last betraying interest. "What'll the expressage be to take me out there with you?"

"Twenty-four dollars," said Captain Boone; "grub and transportation. Second cabin. I haven't got a first cabin."

"You've got my company," said the Kid, pulling out a buckskin bag.

With three hundred dollars he had gone to Laredo for his regular "blowout". The duel in Valdos's had cut short his season of hilarity, but it had left him with nearly $200 for aid in the flight that it had made necessary.

"All right, buddy," said the captain. "I hope your ma won't blame me for this little childish escapade of yours." He beckoned to one of the boat's crew. "Let Sanchez lift you out to the skiff so you won't get your feet wet."

II

Thacker, the United States consul at Buenas Tierras, was not yet drunk. It was only eleven o'clock; and he never arrived at his desired state of beatitude – a state wherein he sang ancient maudlin vaudeville songs and pelted his screaming parrot with banana peels – until the middle of the afternoon. So, when he looked up from his hammock at the sound of a slight cough, and saw the Kid standing in the door of the consulate, he was still in a condition to extend the hospitality and courtesy due from the representative of a great nation. "Don't disturb yourself," said the Kid, easily. "I just dropped in. They told me it was customary to light at your camp before starting in to round up the town. I just came in on a ship from Texas."

"Glad to see you, Mr.—" said the consul.

The Kid laughed.

"Sprague Dalton," he said. "It sounds funny to me to hear it. I'm called the Llano Kid in the Rio Grande country."

"I'm Thacker," said the consul. "Take that cane-bottom chair. Now if you've come to invest, you want somebody to advise you. These dingies will cheat you out of the gold in your teeth if you don't understand their ways. Try a cigar?"

"Much obliged," said the Kid, "but if it wasn't for my corn shucks and the little bag in my back pocket I couldn't live a minute." He took out his "makings," and rolled a cigarette.

"They speak Spanish here," said the consul. "You'll need an interpreter. If there's anything I can do, why, I'd be delighted. If you're buying fruit lands or looking for a concession of any sort, you'll want somebody who knows the ropes to look out for you."

"I speak Spanish," said the Kid, "about nine times better than I do English. Everybody speaks it on the range where I come from. And I'm not in the market for anything."

"You speak Spanish?" said Thacker thoughtfully. He regarded the kid absorbedly.

"You look like a Spaniard, too," he continued. "And you're from Texas. And you can't be more than twenty or twenty-one. I wonder if you've got any nerve."

"You got a deal of some kind to put through?" asked the Texan, with unexpected shrewdness.

"Are you open to a proposition?" said Thacker.

"What's the use to deny it?" said the Kid. "I got into a little gun frolic down in Laredo and plugged a white man. There wasn't any Mexican handy. And I come down to your parrot-and-monkey range just for to smell the morning-glories and marigolds. Now, do you *sabe?*"

Thacker got up and closed the door.

"Let me see your hand," he said.

He took the Kid's left hand, and examined the back of it closely.

"I can do it," he said excitedly. "Your flesh is as hard as wood and as healthy as a baby's. It will heal in a week."

"If it's a fist fight you want to back me for," said the Kid, "don't put your money up yet. Make it gun work, and I'll keep you company. But no barehanded scrapping, like ladies at a tea-party, for me."

"It's easier than that," said Thacker. "Just step here, will you?"

Through the window he pointed to a two-story white-stuccoed house with wide galleries rising amid the deep-green tropical foliage on a wooded hill that sloped gently from the sea.

"In that house," said Thacker, "a fine old Castilian gentleman and his wife are yearning to gather you into their arms and fill your pockets with money. Old Santos Urique lives there. He owns half the gold-mines in the country."

"You haven't been eating loco weed, have you?" asked the Kid.

"Sit down again," said Thacker, "and I'll tell you. Twelve years ago they lost a kid. No, he didn't die – although most of 'em here do from drinking the surface water. He was a wild little devil, even if he wasn't but eight years old. Everybody knows about it. Some Americans who were through here prospecting for gold had letters to Señor Urique, and the boy was a favorite with them. They filled his head with big stories about the States; and about a month after they left, the kid disappeared, too. He was supposed to have stowed himself away among the banana bunches on a fruit steamer, and gone to New Orleans. He was seen once afterward in Texas, it was thought, but they never heard anything more of him. Old Urique has spent thousands of dollars having him looked for. The madam was broken up worst of all. The kid was her life. She wears mourning yet. But they say she believes he'll come back to her some day, and never gives up hope. On the back of the boy's left hand was tattooed a flying eagle carrying a spear in his claws. That's old Urique's coat of arms or something that he inherited in Spain."

The Kid raised his left hand slowly and gazed at it curiously.

"That's it," said Thacker, reaching behind the official desk for his bottle of smuggled brandy. "You're not so slow. I can do it. What was I consul at Sandakan for? I never knew till now. In a week I'll have the eagle bird with the frog-sticker blended in so you'd think you were born with it. I brought a set of the needles and ink just because I was sure you'd drop in some day, Mr. Dalton."

"Oh, hell," said the Kid. "I thought I told you my name!"

"All right, 'Kid,' then. It won't be that long. How does Señorito Urique sound, for a change?"

"I never played son any that I remember of," said the Kid. "If I had any parents to mention they went over the divide about the time I gave my first bleat. What is the plan of your round-up?"

Thacker leaned back against the wall and held his glass up to the light.

"We've come now," said he, "to the question of how far you're willing to go in a little matter of the sort."

"I told you why I came down here," said the Kid simply.

"A good answer," said the consul. "But you won't have to go that far. Here's the scheme. After I get the trademark tattooed on your hand I'll notify old Urique. In the meantime I'll furnish you with all of the family history I can find out, so you can be studying up points to talk about. You've got the looks, you speak the Spanish, you know the facts, you can tell about Texas, you've got the tattoo mark. When I notify them that the rightful heir has returned and is waiting to know whether he will be received and pardoned, what will happen? They'll simply rush down here and fall on your neck, and the curtain goes down for refreshments and a stroll in the lobby."

"I'm waiting," said the Kid. "I haven't had my saddle off in your camp long, pardner, and I never met you before; but if you intend to let it go at a parental blessing, why, I'm mistaken in my man, that's all."

"Thanks," said the consul. "I haven't met anybody in a long time that keeps up with an argument as well as you do. The rest of it is simple. If they take you in only for a while it's long enough. Don't give 'em time to hunt up the strawberry mark on your left shoulder. Old Urique keeps anywhere from $50,000 to $100,000 in his house all the time in a little safe that you could open with a shoe buttoner. Get it. My skill as a tattooer is worth half the boddle. We go halves and catch a tramp steamer for Rio Janeiro. Let the United States go to pieces if it can't get along without my services. *Que dice, señor?*"

"It sounds to me!" said the Kid, nodding his head. "I'm out for the dust."

"All right, then," said Thacker. "You'll have to keep close until we get the bird on you. You can live in the back room here. I do my own cooking, and I'll make you as comfortable as a parsimonious Government will allow me."

Thacker had set the time at a week, but it was two weeks before the design that he patiently tattooed upon the Kid's hand was to his notion. And then Thacker called a *muchacho*, and dispatched this note to the intended victim:

El Señor Don Santos Urique
La Casa Blanca

My Dear Sir,

I beg permission to inform you that there is in my house as a temporary guest a young man who arrived in Buenas Tierras from the United States some days ago. Without wishing to excite any hopes that may not be realized, I think there is a possibility of his being your long-absent son. It might be well for you to call and see him. If he is, it is my opinion that his intention was to return to his home, but upon arriving here, his courage failed him from doubts as to how he would be received.

Your true servant,
Thompson Thacker

Half an hour afterward – quick time for Buenas Tierras – Señor Urique's ancient landau drove to the consul's door, with the barefooted coachman beating and shouting at the team of fat, awkward horses.

A tall man with a white moustache alighted, and assisted to the ground a lady who was dressed and veiled in unrelieved black.

The two hastened inside, and were met by Thacker with his best diplomatic bow. By his desk stood a slender young man with clear-cut, sun-browned features and smoothly brushed black hair.

Señora Urique threw back her black veil with a quick gesture. She was past middle age, and her hair was beginning to silver, but her full, proud figure and clear olive skin retained traces of the beauty peculiar to the Basque province. But, once you had seen her eyes, and comprehended the great sadness that was revealed in their deep shadows and hopeless expression, you saw that the woman lived only in some memory.

She bent upon the young man a long look of the most agonized questioning. Then her great black eyes turned, and her gaze rested upon his left hand. And then with a sob, not loud, but seeming to shake the room, she cried "*Hijo mio!*" and caught the Llano Kid to her heart.

A month afterward the Kid came to the consulate in response to a message sent by Thacker.

He looked the young Spanish *caballero*. His clothes were imported, and the wiles of the jewellers had not been spent upon him in vain. A more than respectable diamond shone on his finger as he rolled a shuck cigarette.

"What's doing?" asked Thacker.

"Nothing much," said the Kid calmly. "I eat my first iguana steak to-day. They're them big lizards, you sabe? I reckon, though, that frijoles and side bacon would do me about as well. Do you care for iguanas, Thacker?"

"No, nor for some other kinds of reptiles," said Thacker.

It was three in the afternoon, and in another hour he would be in his state of beatitude.

"It's time you were making good, sonny," he went on, with an ugly look on his reddened face. "You're not playing up to me square. You've been the prodigal son for four weeks now, and you could have had veal for every meal on a gold dish if you'd wanted it. Now, Mr. Kid, do you think it's right to leave me out so long on a husk diet? What's the trouble? Don't you get your filial eyes on anything that looks like cash in the Casa Blanca? Don't tell me you don't. Everybody knows where old Urique keeps his stuff. It's U.S. currency, too; he don't accept anything else. What's doing? Don't say 'nothing' this time."

"Why, sure," said the Kid, admiring his diamond, "there's plenty of money up there. I'm no judge of collateral in bunches, but I will undertake for to say that I've seen the rise of $50,000 at a time in that tin grub box that my adopted father calls his safe. And he lets me carry the key sometimes just to show me that he knows I'm the real little Francisco that strayed from the herd a long time ago."

"Well, what are you waiting for?" asked Thacker, angrily. "Don't you forget that I can upset your apple-cart any day I want to. If old Urique knew you were an imposter, what sort of things would happen to you? Oh, you don't know this country, Mr. Texas Kid. The laws here have got mustard spread between 'em. These people here'd stretch you out like a frog that had been stepped on, and give you about fifty sticks at every corner of the plaza. And they'd wear every stick out, too. What was left of you they'd feed to alligators."

"I might just as well tell you now, pardner," said the Kid, sliding down low on his steamer chair, "that things are going to stay just as they are. They're about right now."

"What do you mean?" asked Thacker, rattling the bottom of his glass on his desk.

"The scheme's off," said the Kid. "And whenever you have the pleasure of speaking to me address me as Don Francisco Urique. I'll guarantee I'll answer to it. We'll let Colonel Urique keep his money. His little tin safe is as good as the time-locker in the First National Bank of Laredo as far as you and me are concerned."

"You're going to throw me down, then, are you?" said the consul.

"Sure," said the Kid cheerfully. "Throw you down. That's it. And now I'll tell you why. The first night I was up at the colonel's house they introduced me to a bedroom. No blankets on the floor – a real room, with a bed and things in it. And before I was asleep, in comes this artificial mother of mine and tucks in the covers. 'Panchito,' she says, 'my little lost one, God has brought you back to me. I bless His name forever.' It was that, or some truck like that, she said. And down comes a drop or two of rain and hits me on the nose. And all that stuck by me, Mr. Thacker. And it's been that way ever since. And it's got to stay that way. Don't you think that it's for what's in it for me, either, that I say so. If you have any such ideas, keep 'em to yourself. I haven't had much truck with women in my life, and no mothers to speak of, but here's a lady that we've got to keep fooled. Once she stood it; twice she won't. I'm a low-down wolf, and the devil may have sent me on this trail instead of God, but I'll travel it to the end. And now, don't forget that I'm Don Francisco Urique whenever you happen to mention my name."

"I'll expose you today, you – *you double-dyed traitor*," stammered Thacker.

The Kid arose and, without violence, took Thacker by the throat with a hand of steel, and shoved him slowly into a corner. Then he drew from under his left arm his pearl-handled .45 and poked the cold muzzle of it against the consul's mouth.

"I told you why I come here," he said, with his old freezing smile. "If I leave here, you'll be the reason. Never forget it, pardner. Now, what is my name?"

"Er – Don Francisco Urique," gasped Thacker.

From outside came a sound of wheels, and the shouting of some one, and the sharp thwacks of a wooden whipstock upon the backs of fat horses.

The Kid put up his gun, and walked toward the door. But he turned again and came back to the trembling Thacker, and held up his left hand with its back toward the consul.

"There's one more reason," he said slowly, "why things have got to stand as they are. The fellow I killed in Laredo had one of them same pictures on his left hand."

Outside, the ancient landau of Don Santos Urique rattled to the door. The coachman ceased his bellowing. Señora Urique, in a voluminous gay gown of white lace and flying ribbons, leaned forward with a happy look in her great soft eyes.

"Are you within, dear son?" she called, in the rippling Castilian.

"*Madre mia, yo vengo*," answered the young Don Francisco Urique.

"Not very long ago some one invented the assertion that there were only 'Four Hundred' people in New York City who were really worth noticing. But a wiser man has arisen – the census taker – and his larger estimate of human interest has been preferred in marking out the field of these little stories of the Four Million."
– O. Henry, *The Four Million* (1906)

CONTRIBUTORS

VINCENT SAMMY is a South African artist and graphic designer. His work has appeared in *Something Wicked*, *Black Static*, comics and commercial design.

DAVID BRYHER has written short stories, magazine features, kids' books, and scripts. The most recent was for the PlayStation game *Doctor Who: The Eternity Clock*.

OSGOOD VANCE lives in New Orleans with his prize-winning collection of stuffed nutria. His short fiction appears in anthologies by by Jurassic London and Kazka Press.

ANNE C. PERRY hails from California and lives in London. She reviews monster movies for the geek culture blog *Pornokitsch* and edits books for a living.

JARED SHURIN also writes for *Pornokitsch*. He is a trained BBQ judge.

ACKNOWLEDGEMENTS

The editors would like to thank Joe Vaz, Lauren Beukes and David Bailey for their support in bringing this peculiar volume to life, as well as our long-suffering families and overburdened postman.

www.ingramcontent.com/pod-product-compliance
Lightning Source LLC
Chambersburg PA
CBHW061931170626
46813CB00006B/2356